# Dancing
# with
# Panthers

## Patrick C. Notchtree

When you're queer, what's the point of having dreams?

1

www.notchtree.com

X (Twitter) handle: @pcnotchtree

24/8

# Contents

4

# Foreword

This is a work of fiction. If any names used for the fictional characters in this book coincide with real people, there is no connection between the two.

Oscar Wilde should need no introduction but I suppose there's now a new generation to whom the name is just that, a name. The Irish playwright was the darling of Victorian society in London in the late nineteenth century. His best known play is perhaps the witty *The Importance of Being Earnest*. His best known novel is the Faustian *The Picture of Dorian Gray*. He was a married man with children but he was also homosexual. The term itself was fairly new then because before that people weren't classified so much by who they happened to have sex with. Indeed, throughout history, people have had sex with those to whom they felt attracted and that could be both sexes if the chemistry were right. There are many reasons why this idea of defining someone by their sexual activity became common but there's not room here for that. The reader is welcome to do their own research. Back to chemistry because when Wilde met Lord Alfred Douglas, known to all as Bosie after his mother's pet name for him, in 1891 he became besotted with this young poet. Bosie was then twenty-one. The two embarked on a rash affair also holding sex orgies with other young men. Such activity by that time was highly illegal in England but they revelled in the notoriety and the risk that it entailed. Inevitably they were found out and to cut a long story short, Wilde was convicted and sentenced to two years imprisonment with hard labour.

The imprisonment broke Wilde and he died young, aged 46 in exile just two years after his release. Bosie lived on, later married and fathered a child, dying in 1945 aged 74.

On his release Wilde in 1897 wrote to Bosie, In his letter he wrote:

It was like feasting with panthers. The danger was half the excitement.

In the days before the decriminalization of homosexual activity in England in 1967, many gay men would identify with that, risking all for the thrill of the chase and its culmination in the pleasure of the sex act whether oral or anal. Even after decriminalization there were strict limits on homosexual relationships, there was no recognition in law and there was still social ostracism. So gay men tended to form safe, closed social circles apart from the rest of their lives.

I was going to title this book "Feasting with Panthers" but there are already several books with that title. We follow Mark as he meets his 'panthers' but how much he dances or is even devoured depends on your viewpoint.

This novel is set in the early 1960s when despite the recommendations of the 1957 Wolfenden Report in the UK, decriminalization still seemed never likely to happen.

There are one or two instances of racially stereotypical terms. These were terms often used at that time in relation to business people from ethnic minorities and does not imply racism on the part of the speakers, and certainly not on the part of the author.

The language used to write is British English. American readers may see one or two unfamiliar spellings and words.

A style note: Direct speech is indicated by double quotes (") and silent private thoughts by a character are indicated by single quotes (').

In the UK, an apartment is usually referred to as a flat, presumably because it is normally all on one level. Chips in the UK are what Americans call fries, except that they are usually much thicker and have more potato than French Fries. What Americans call chips are called crisps in the UK. A nappy in the UK is a diaper in the US. In the UK, a back yard is usually an enclosed area at the rear of a property which is hard surfaced with paving or concrete and is utilitarian in nature. . If it has grass and flowers etc. it's a back garden.

A note about floors in buildings. In the UK, the floor at ground level is called the ground floor. Up one level is the first floor and so on. In the USA, the floor at ground level is often referred to as the first floor.

A shilling was a small unit of the old sterling currency, twenty shillings made a pound. £5 in 1961 is the equivalent in 2024 of £114! (US$ 150).

You can view larger images of those in the book at http://www.dancingwithpanthers.com/

# PART ONE 1961

## Chapter 1 Summer 1961

Mark Martin was not a happy child. The product of a broken home after his parents divorced he was now living in a strange new city, taken, aged fourteen from his friends, his school and life as he had known it, he was desperately unhappy. From the reasonably spacious house in his birth city he was now in a cramped top floor two bedroom flat with his mother and sister. He missed home, he missed his school and he missed his friends, especially Tony, his closest friend. Tony was an only child and had always wanted a brother. Mark had his older sister but he too always wanted a brother. In each other they had found the brother they had wanted. All the more so because they had chosen each other. After all there is no reason why genetic brothers should get on and often don't. In rare cases they are the same age but inevitably there is an age gap, sometimes quite large. Mark and Tony were born within a month of each other and grew up together. They had no secrets from each other and after primary school both passed the eleven-plus and went on to the same secondary school, a grammar school. They were in the same class and sat together. Both had fair hair and blue eyes but Mark was taller than Tony, tall for his age. Some others thought they really were brothers until their different surnames became evident. They worked together doing their homework and played together. In sleepovers, they slept together. It was all perfectly innocent.

As puberty arrived it seemed perfectly natural to them to share this joint experience, taking advantage of whatever privacy they could find to make the inevitable anatomical comparison as each was already familiar with the other's body. As puberty progressed comparison moved to mutual masturbation. Kissing followed and eventually experimenting with penetration. Mark was never happy

1

taking the active part and Tony soon took that role every time. Given sufficient Vaseline, Mark enjoyed that and found the penetration exciting and arousing. He was unaware of the prostate gland but well aware of its erotic potential. Mark knew that he loved Tony and he thought Tony felt the same but neither dare articulate that to the other. Despite their physical intimacy and frequent union, that would seem to cross an invisible line somehow; from experimentation and boyish fooling around into the territory of a 'relationship'.

Mark missed Tony more and more as the weeks since his move passed. He wrote to him but his replies were always late. At first he told Mark what was going on with the people they both knew but it all seemed so distant to Mark now and irrelevant. Gradually the letters stopped. His mother had taken him to his new school two bus rides from the Northside flat, complaining that it was so far away (it was the nearest grammar school) instead of the secondary modern school up the road. At school Mark was regarded as an oddity so while his schoolwork was good, socially he was isolated. Nobody from his school seemed to live close by and it seemed there were no kids his age in Calvert House. All were either grown up or much younger. Mark had no friends. He wasn't disliked at school and on a surface level got on with other boys but that's as far as it went. He missed Tony more and more.

He was often alone in the flat while his mother was late back from one of her cash-in-hand cleaning jobs and his older sister was out a lot. He would spend the time in his room, becoming addicted to the release he got from masturbation and once that was done, sitting alone watching the rented television. He hated his life, he hated the flat, he hated this city, he hated his school, he hated his mother. He hated himself.

There were frequent rows, often about money, more often about his sister's late night return or even failure to come home at all. It came to a head one evening.

"Where were you all night?" demanded Mam when his sister appeared the next day.

"Just out," was the usual petulant reply.

"Well don't dare ever come back here and say you're expecting," said Mam. "If you let some lad fuck you and end up pregnant, don't come crying to me."

"I know what I'm doing, Mam. Stop nagging me."

"I'll stop nagging when you stop being a slut."

"Well it's not me who was shagging around with that berk from your work!"

"How dare you fucking question me! If you don't like it here, sod off back to your father!"

"Gladly! I hate this fucking place anyway."

. . .

The next day she was gone.

"Mam, why'd you let her go?"

"I wasn't going to stop her, if that's what she wanted. Anyway Mark, it's just you and me now, eh love?"

"I suppose so," said Mark, grumpily.

"And at least now I'll have my bedroom to myself," said Mam.

So life settled into a new routine. Mark was still alone and unhappy. He would often take the trolley bus into Bilthaven city centre in the evening, just to walk around, away from the cramped flat. He preferred the trolley bus. It was smooth and quiet and didn't churn out black filth from the exhaust like the diesel buses. In fact, Mark realized, they didn't have an exhaust because they were all electric. And there was always the added excitement when one of the two collectors came off the overhead wires with a thump, causing the bus to come to an abrupt halt. The conductor had to get out, and with a long bamboo pole, push it back onto the wire so the bus could continue.

For a large city, the central area of Bilthaven was fairly compact and he could walk across it in less than twenty minutes. Mostly that's all he did, walk around for a couple of hours, exploring and finding his way around. Sometimes he would buy a drink in a café. He rarely spoke to anybody and rarely was he spoken to. As the darker evenings approached he continued this routine for that's what it had become.

"Are you going out again?" asked Mam.

"Yes. Can I have some money for bus fare, please?"

"Why don't you get yourself a Saturday job instead of asking me for money all the time?" replied Mam tartly.

"I'm only fourteen still. Can you get a job aged fourteen?"

"You'll never know if you don't ask. Anyway, if they ask, tell them you're older. Most just give a few shillings out of pocket anyway."

Mark thought about this. "Mam, I'll think about it. But can I have some bus fare now?"

"You won't get a job just thinking about it," said Mam, opening her purse. "Here you are, and don't be late because I want to bolt the door when it's dark."

"That means my key wouldn't work," complained Mark. "Can you not just drop the latch so I can get in?"

"I have to go to bed so I can get up for work. I feel safer."

"You'll be fine," said Mark.

"One of these days, I'll lock you out and then you'll learn."

But she left the bolt off.

# Chapter 2 Autumn 1961

On one such city evening stroll, he realised he was being followed. This had happened before and it unnerved him. It was always a man and Mark wondered what he wanted. He usually went into a shop and then straight out again which made them give up. Sometimes he did a quick about turn and noticed the man would stop and pretend to be looking into a shop window. They then usually didn't follow after that. He sometimes turned round to see what the man was doing, often just staring after him. Mark wondered what they were thinking.

This time the man seemed more persistent. Mark changed direction, so did the man. He went into a shop and then straight out again. So did the man. He started walking faster. So did the man. Taking a shortcut through a narrow alley but under a street light, Mark suddenly turned to see the man's reaction. He looked about thirty years old, well dressed and seemed surprised by Mark's sudden turn. He was holding a five pound note.

"Is that for me?" asked Mark, thinking of that large amount of money.

"If you want it," said the man. "Are you trade?"

Mark looked blank.

"Do you do rent?"

"What do you mean?" asked Mark, thinking about the rented flat.

"Doing things for money?"

"Things? What things?"

"I think you know what I mean. Sex. Have sex for money."

"No," said Mark. "Well, I haven't done."

"Have you ever had sex with another man or boy?"

"Yes, I had a boyfriend," Mark offered warily.

"That's OK then, come with me." The man smiled and pushed the five pound note into Mark's jacket pocket. "So you can trust me," he said. "My name's Gordon, what's yours?"

"Mark."

"Come on then, Mark." He led the way back into the busier streets with better street lights. Mark could see now he seemed quite young, with brown hair under his hat and blue eyes above a nice smile. Mark thought he was quite good looking and he seemed kind. He had already given Mark the money so he could have just run off with it. It was doubtful if Gordon would complain to the police because Mark could then tell them why he had been approached. Something within stopped Mark from doing that. Mark started to feel his pulse race and arousal beginning. He was led to a pub called The Vault which Mark had not seen before in a close off a city centre lane. It was quite busy and many were smoking. Mark noticed that all the customers were men although in those days that was not unusual.

"Hey, Gordy!" A man in a group of about six round a table called out to them. "Struck lucky, mate?"

Gordon led Mark over to the table and they squeezed on to the leather bench on one side.

"Mark, what do you like to drink?" asked Gordon.

"No alcohol for this handsome lad," said one of the group, laughing.

"Coke please." Gordon went to the bar.

"Not seen you around before," said the man on Mark's right, who placed his hand on Mark's thigh, gently squeezing. Mark's arousal level went up a notch. This man was older than Gordon by some years, as were most of this group.

"No, I've not been here before."

The man's hand moved up Mark's thigh and gently gripped Mark's now hard penis through his trousers. "Very nice," he said. The others laughed. One said, "Careful Fred, he's too young for you."

At that point Gordon returned holding a glass of coke and his own pint glass. He sat to Mark's left. "Off, Fred," he said. "Paid in advance so you'll have to wait your turn. And

6

I've got the key." Fred withdrew his hand smiling and didn't seem to mind Gordon's command.

As the men talked, Mark was the centre of attention. He was aware that they were eyeing him up, taking in his fair hair and skin, blue eyes and tall, slim body; no doubt assessing his sexual attraction. He rather enjoyed that. Mark knew that some people said he was good looking so he liked that.

Gordon finished his drink. "Drink up, Mark," he said. "Time to earn your money," he added with a smile.

He stood up and led Mark through the bar, through a door marked 'Residents Only' and up some stairs at the back of the pub. The passage and stairs were well lit, carpeted and the doors had numbers on them.

"Is this a hotel?" asked Mark.

"Just bed and breakfast," replied Gordon.

On the second floor they came to a door marked 'Private'. Gordon led Mark though but now the stairs and the passage were bare linoleum. The lighting was dimmer with a bare bulb.

On the third floor, Gordon took a key from his pocket and unlocked a door. Mark was now feeling both excited and nervous. They went into a small room. It was sparsely furnished and the predominant colour was brown. There was a double bed with a mattress and a lamp on a small table next to it. There was a washbasin in the corner near the window. A worn, mainly brown carpet covered the floor. The room was warm from a brown painted radiator by the window which was covered with brown patterned curtains. Mark wanted to back out but he had taken the money. Gordon locked the door and took what seemed to be a clean sheet from a drawer and spread it on the mattress. Mark stood inside the door watching. Gordon came up to Mark. His eyes looked kind, he thought, which helped Mark relax a bit. Gordon put his arms round Mark and kissed him on the mouth, while his hand ran down Mark's back and stroked and squeezed his bum. Mark felt all resistance ebb out of him. Unsure he put his hands round Gordon and placed them

7

on Gordon's bum. He felt Gordon's hand move round and pressure Mark's cock then started undoing Mark's belt.

"Lie on the bed, Mark," whispered Gordon. Mark did as he was told. Slowly and sensually Gordon stripped Mark naked. "Lovely," said Gordon, and he then quickly undressed. His body was slim and athletic and there was chest hair and more in a line from his navel down to his now stiff penis. They lay on the bed and kissed and stroked.

"What do you want?" asked Mark after a while.

"For that much, all the way," said Gordon. He reached over to the little table and out of a small drawer produced a jar of Vaseline. Then Mark knew what was coming. Gordon applied some to his penis. "Turn over, Mark."

Mark lay on his front and felt Gordon's finger probing inside him, spreading more Vaseline. Then he felt Gordon's weight on him and the entry which was slow and gentle. It took Mark straight back to his past friend Tony with whom he had experimented. Gordon kissed the back of Mark's neck as he started to move. Instinctively and involuntarily, Mark started to respond.

"You're a horny young lad, aren't you?" whispered Gordon. Mark reached round and pulled Gordon down, deeper. The pace increased and then with a sigh, Gordon reached his climax and Mark felt him start to soften.

"Stay there," said Mark, as emotions swept over him. Both elation and fear at what he had done.

"You're a sweet lad," said Gordon, eventually withdrawing. He then quickly brought Mark to climax. While Mark got dressed, Gordon cleaned himself with some tissues, and put the bed sheet in a box in the corner before dressing himself. Mark noticed two light bulbs above the door, one was red, the other blue.

They left the room and Gordon locked the door. On the landing he gave Mark a hug and a kiss.

"Thank you, Mark. That was lovely."

Mark followed Gordon back down the stairs.

# Chapter 3 An education

Back in the bar with the same drinks again, they rejoined the same group.

"Is he a good un?" one asked Gordon, eyeing Mark.

"He's lovely," said Gordon. "Worth every penny."

"Not his first time then?" asked the older man called Fred.

"Said he used to have a boyfriend; that right, Mark?" said Gordon.

"Yes. He was called Tony," replied Mark.

"Was he older than you or younger?" asked Fred.

"Older but only by a few days. We were basically the same age," said Mark, sipping his coke.

"I wish I'd had that when I was a lad," said another well dressed, younger man. "I'm Philip, by the way, but I get called Pip," said Pip, reaching out to shake hands with Mark.

"We call him that because he has great expectations," joked Gordon.

Mark was puzzled by that but one or two of the men chuckled, so he guessed it was some kind of in-joke.

"Not often fulfilled though," said Pip. "So did you and Tony take turns on each other?"

"No, if I think I know what you mean. He was always like the male."

"So he was a top. Do you like being bottom?"

"I certainly got that impression," said Gordon. "You seemed to be enjoying it, didn't you, Mark?"

Mark flushed but just nodded. It was true, he had enjoyed it. He had liked the idea of being under the control of another man, of being used even. And he had five pounds in his pocket!

Mark looked round the group. "Are you all," and here Mark hesitated, "sort of, queer?"

That drew some smiles. Gordon replied, "Yes Mark, we are all good friends of Dorothy here."

"Who's Dorothy," asked Mark, puzzled.

"If a man says he's a friend of Dorothy," said Gordon, "it means he's queer, homosexual."

"So is she here?" asked Mark.

"No, Mark," said Pip. "It comes from the film, *The Wizard of Oz*. Judy Garland plays the part of Dorothy."

"I didn't know that's where it's from," said Fred.

"I've seen that," said Mark, still confused.

"I hope Gordy paid you well," said Fred. "It's hard enough to get him to buy his round."

"Five pounds," said Mark.

"And he said you were worth it," said Pip. "So is that your standard charge?"

"It was his first time, for rent anyway," said Gordon.

On an impulse, Mark said, "Yes, it is. For all the way."

"Oooh," said most of the group.

"Sharp lad, aren't you?" said another man that they had called Tom. "A quick learner."

Pip produced a five pound note. "Would you come upstairs with me?"

"Give the lad a break," said Gordon. "He's only just had it."

"I'm all right," said Mark, sizing up the opportunity for earning money that beat a Saturday job for just one pound if he were lucky. Mark reached across and took the five pound note.

Pip laughed and stood up. "Come on then, you beauty," he said. Pip went to the bar and gave the barman some money and received a key in return.

Mark followed Pip back up the stairs to the brown room. Pip unlocked the door and turned on the light, closed the door and locked it again.

"Gordy must have put the sheet away. I hope there's still some clean ones left." Pip got a folded sheet from the same drawer as earlier and spread it on the mattress while Mark watched. Pip then turned on the small lamp and coming over to where Mark was standing, turned out the centre light. He took Mark's hand and led him to the bed.

10

"Lie with me," said Pip.

"Don't you want to get undressed?" asked Mark, surprised.

"What's the rush?" said Pip. "We've got the room for an hour. Gordy might have been in a rush but I like to take my time, especially with a handsome lad like you."

So Mark lay on the bed next to Pip. He thought Pip was attractive and found himself wanting him. When Pip took him in his arms and kissed him, Mark felt fresh arousal and mounting desire. A part of him also knew he was being well paid and so needed to please Pip. Gordon had said he was good so now he felt that praise to live up to.

He started to become more proactive, responding more to Pip's kiss, running his hand down Pip's body and feeling through his trousers where his stiff cock was evident. He felt for the belt buckle and loosened it then slid his hand inside Pip's pants and took hold of Pip's hard cock.

"You're a sexy kid," muttered Pip, feeling Mark's cock and undoing his jeans, pushing his hand down and taking hold of Mark's balls. Mark shuddered with desire and felt himself getting too close. He made to push Pip's trousers down over his hips and onto his thighs but couldn't because of Pip's weight on them.

"Can't wait for it, can you?" smiled Pip. "Come on then." They lay undressing each other, rolling in a sensuous tangle as each moved to allow the other access to remove clothes.

They lay briefly after the activity, pressing their naked bodies against each other. Like he used to do with Tony. Mark found Pip's body exciting. He was fit and had an obvious six pack without being like a bodybuilder. A fit young man and good looking too.

"Let me massage you," said Pip. "Lie on your front."

Obediently Mark rolled on to his front, wondering what would happen next. Pip sat astride him on his thighs and Mark felt his hands on his neck, his thumbs rubbing the top of his spine. His fingers came round the sides, massaging his neck as they went, meeting by Mark's Adam's apple.

11

Slowly his grip tightened, fingers pressing in on Mark's throat. Mark found that extremely erotic. A sense of total surrender. But then Pip's hands withdrew and he was kneading Mark's shoulders.

"You liked that, didn't you?" Pip said quietly.

Mark whispered, "Yes."

"Did you think I was going to kill you?"

"Sort of, but not really," replied Mark.

"Why not really?" asked Pip, running his hands down Mark's spine.

"Because everybody would know it's you and they'd hang you."

"But you like me taking charge?"

Mark simply nodded. Then Pip slapped Mark hard on his bum. Mark jumped, partly from the surprise, partly from the sting. Then another slap.

"Did you like that?" asked Pip.

Mark nodded, feeling compliant. After all, he did find it oddly stimulating and there was the five pounds to think about. So Pip spanked him again. He pushed his hand between Mark's legs and felt his hard cock.

"You're more than ready," he said,

On his front still, Mark saw Pip reach into the bedside drawer.

"Good," said Pip, as he found the same Vaseline jar. Pip's entry was easy. As Pip started to thrust, Mark lifted toward him.

"Deeper," he sighed and Pip obliged. Mark was getting more aroused when Pip withdrew.

"Turn over, on your back," commanded Pip.

Mark did so and Pip lifted Mark's legs onto his shoulders and leaning forward kissed Mark as he entered again. Mark reached up and pulled Pip down, kissing again. Then with his right hand he grasped his own cock and started masturbating as Pip continued to fuck him, their eyes locked to each other.

"Don't come before me," said Pip.

Mark slackened his own pace. Pip got faster reaching a crescendo gripping Mark tightly as the final thrust went deeper.

"That was so good," said Pip, as he withdrew.

Then to Mark's surprise, Pip knelt on the bed and, taking hold of Mark's cock, licked it, caressed it with his tongue then took it in his mouth working up and down, sometimes looking up to see Mark's reaction. Mark couldn't help thrusting upwards into Pip's throat and then his climax came as he unloaded into Pip's mouth.

"Sorry," gasped Mark. "It just came so quickly I couldn't warn you."

"What do you mean?" said Pip. "I wanted you to come."

"Oh," was all Mark could say. This was something he and Tony had never even thought of doing. The evening was certainly being an education for Mark.

# Chapter 4 Job opportunity

When they went back down to the bar Mark saw that one or two of the group had left. Gordon was still there though and greeted Pip and Mark with a knowing grin.

"Good, isn't he?" he said to Pip.

"Oh yes, beats Peter for my money," said Pip. "Likes a bit of spanking too. I'd like to do that again."

"I notice you used the whole hour," said Gordon.

"I believe in getting value for money," was Pip's response.

"I wish I could afford him," said the older Fred, eying Mark. "Five pounds is almost half of what I get a week."

"Don't listen to his sob story, Mark," said Gordon. "He's just trying to get you to lower your price."

"Who's Peter?" asked Mark.

"Another lad who calls in from time to time," answered Gordon.

"I think it's time for me to go home," said Mark. "I'll miss my bus."

"You know where to find us," said Pip. "Come again."

They all laughed at the innuendo but Mark didn't understand.

As his bus hummed its way towards his Northside home, Mark sat thinking about his extraordinary evening. He had ten pounds in his pocket, more than some men earned in a week and he had got that in less than three hours. And after his initial nervousness he had enjoyed it. He thought about the unknown Peter. It had not occurred to him that the group might know other boys but then on reflection, it was obvious.

He went up to the flat door and put his key in the lock hoping the bolt wasn't on the inside, even though it was not yet the time Mam usually went to bed. The door opened to Mark's relief. Mam was sitting in front of the television. A western was showing. Every other TV show seemed to be a western these days, thought Mark, not a type he was fond of.

He liked informative programmes. *Zoo Quest* a favourite. He also thought David Attenborough was rather good looking.

"Is there anything to eat?" asked Mark.

"There's some bread left. I've no money for shopping."

Mark looked at the clock. "Is that the right time?"

"I expect so, it's a fucking clock," was the terse reply.

"The late chippy should still be open. Fancy some fish and chips?" asked Mark.

"Yes," said Mam. "I fancy a nice steak dinner too and a bottle of fucking champagne! The chippy doesn't give tick, stupid!"

"I'll treat us," said Mark, unthinking.

"Using what? Robbed a bank or something?"

Mark got out one of his five pound notes. "I found this on the bus," he lied.

"A fiver on a bus? That's probably half some poor bastard's wage packet," said Mam. "I'll have mushy peas with mine. Off you go then."

Mark went down stairs and along the high street to Northside's fish and chip shop, 'Frank's Fish'n'Chips'. Still open mercifully.

"Hello, Mark," said Frank from behind the glass top counter with its few fish and a pile of fresh chips just being thrown in. "What will it be tonight, then, Sixpennorth of chips?"

"Fish and chips twice please. And mushy peas."

Frank laughed. "Payday is it? Not often you ask for the lot, never mind twice."

"Sort of," said Mark. Then quickly correcting himself, "Found a note on the bus."

"You should hand that in," said Frank. "Someone might need that to get by."

"Finders keepers," said Mark. "And right now Mam's skint so we need it."

Frank shook his head while he wrapped up the fish and chips, first in plain paper and then more old newspaper around it for insulation. A scoop of mushy peas into a little lidded cardboard cup, also wrapped in newspapers.

"With your mushy peas, that's three and six to you," said Frank.

Mark didn't have three shillings and sixpence in change so he handed over the five pound note and received his change in pound notes and coins. He was glad to have some smaller currency because the fiver attracted attention in his area. Maybe not in posh places but Mark made no pretence to be posh.

Mark noticed a sign at the end of the counter. 'Saturday help wanted, Apply within.'

"How much does that pay?" asked Mark, indicating the notice. He thought if he had a Saturday job it would please Mam and he could use it as cover to explain having money if he went back to The Vault.

"It's in the upstairs room, getting the chips ready for the evening trade. Always need a lot more on a Saturday. Start at ten, work until you finish the bags."

"Doing what?" asked Mark.

"Open the sacks of potatoes, wash them, peel them, cut them up into chips. Then soak them in whitener to stop them browning before the evening."

"How many sacks?"

"Four, maybe five."

Mark had in his mind the sacks he had seen in the greengrocer that Mam sometimes bought. Easy, he thought.

"So how much is the pay?" asked Mark again.

"Ten shillings, in your hand," said Frank.

"That's not much," said Mark.

"How old are you now?" asked Frank with a frown.

"Fourteen," replied Mark.

"Then you get a boy's wage, not a man's," retorted Frank.

"That's not fair," objected Mark. "It's the same work whoever does it. You should pay for the work done, not for who the worker is."

"A right little communist, aren't you?"

16

"Thirty shillings," said Mark.

"I take it back! A real capitalist. No way son. Fifteen shillings maybe."

Mark picked up his wrapped bundle of fish and chips. "No good. Won't do it for less than a pound." He made towards the door.

"You win! A pound. But you'd better not let me down. And it's only because I know you since you moved here and you are obviously a bright lad."

Mark turned back to the counter and held out his hand. "It's a deal," he said as Frank shook hands with him. He had big hands, Mark noted. But he was a big, well built man.

Back in the flat, Mam had set the small table in the lounge with a cloth and knives and forks.

"Why've you done that?" asked Mark, who had been expecting to eat it off their laps.

"Not often my son treats me to a feast," said Mam. And she gave him a hug. Mark felt a pang of guilt at his deception. But the treat of the good meal went some way to reconcile that in his mind.

"Got some more news for you as well," said Mark as Mam unwrapped the food and put it onto plates she had been warming in front of the gas fire. "I've got a Saturday job like you said."

"Where? Doing what?"

"At the chippy, peeling spuds and making chips. Going to pay me a pound for just four or five of those sacks."

Mam started laughing. She couldn't stop.

"What's so funny?" asked Mark, sitting down and bashing the base of the ketchup bottle to get some out.

"You are," said Mam, almost in tears with her laughter. "Not those little sacks you idiot. The chippy gets them delivered in hundredweight sacks, almost as big as you. That's a quarter of a ton of tatties to peel!" And then she started laughing again.

"Stop it," said Mark, annoyed at his naivety and at her laughing at him. "Of course I knew that," he lied to preserve his 'face'.

"If you say so," said Mam, but in a tone that made it clear she didn't believe him. But she reached out and squeezed his hand. "You'll have to keep your eyes peeled on the bus more and then we can have fish and chips more often."

"Just luck," said Mark shoving battered fish into his mouth.

"I'll put the kettle on for a cuppa," said Mam. "Wash all this down."

Mark now felt the need to visit the toilet. He had sometimes felt this after sex with Tony but this seemed more urgent. But he reasoned he had taken on two loads and from men so there was bound to be more.

"Just nipping to the loo," he said, getting up. Mam made no comment but carried on eating.

In the bathroom Mark saw tell tale traces on his underpants so once finished he went to his bedroom and changed. He felt a bit sore but assumed, based on his past experience, that it would be short lived and gone by the morning.

"All right if I have a bath?" he asked.

"Tonight?" Mam asked. "I'm not sure if there's enough hot water. I'll turn the immersion heater on for you if you can wait a short time. I don't want to discourage my boy from being clean."

Mark lay in the bath which soothed him and thought about the day. He had eaten well, got a Saturday job, had found a possibly very lucrative source of income and still had almost ten pounds in his pocket. Not a bad day, he thought. School on Monday, what would he say? Nothing obviously. Oh fuck! Not done my homework. He stood up suddenly, water cascading off his body and splashing on to the bathroom floor. He dried himself quickly and in his dressing gown went to his bedroom. He had a small table in his room he used as a desk. He put his books on the bed and his exercise book on the table. I need a proper desk, he thought. Got GCE exams next year. He smiled to himself as he thought he could probably buy a desk. He buried himself in his geometry.

# Chapter 5 Graft

At school Mark found it hard to concentrate. He kept thinking back to his extraordinary evening. He looked round his classmates and wondered what they would say if they knew. In fact he knew very well what they would say. He would face ostracism, insults and possibly violent attack. He tried to behave as normally as he could but when some of his school friends were bragging about their sexual conquests, most of which Mark was sure were fantasy and bravado, he just had to smile to himself. Not only was he getting sex in plenty but getting well paid for it as well. But he knew it must remain a closely guarded secret. He got through the day and on the bus going home he wondered whether he should go back into the city centre again, visit The Vault and see what happened from there. But he also had a lot of homework to get through and Mark wanted to do well at school. Not that he had any idea what job or career he wanted to follow eventually but he knew he had a good brain and it seemed a waste not to use it to the full.

In the end he decided to give The Vault a miss. Let them wait for me, he mused.

"You out again tonight?" asked Mam.

"Too much homework," said Mark. He also thought going out again so soon might raise questions.

"Right little bookworm, aren't you?" said Mam, whose reading didn't extend much beyond the *Daily Mirror* and *People's Friend* magazine. But while Mark knew she didn't understand his need he knew that she was at heart proud of him. He dreaded to think what she would think of his time in The Vault.

On Saturday morning, Mark went round to the chippy just after nine to start his day's work. The metal shutters were down so he knocked on them making them rattle loudly and shake. He waited and then heard Frank's voice from inside.

"We open at four o'clock!"

"It's me, Mark," he shouted through the shutter.

"Come round the back," was the reply.

Mark walked along the row of shops and turned left into the next street and then left again down the back lane that ran along behind the row. He wasn't sure which back featureless gate, as high as the wall in which it was set, belonged to the chippy so he guessed by distance and stopped.

Facing his chosen gate and the brick wall with 'Tommy is a homo' scrawled on it, he shouted "Hello!"

He wondered who Tommy was. Maybe he should get to know Tommy.

The gate one along from where he was standing opened and Frank stuck his head out.

"Come on, lad," he said. "No time to waste."

As Mark walked the few yards towards Frank he asked, "Who's Tommy?"

"Tommy? Kid that lives above the butcher's shop. Why?"

"His name's been put on the wall here."

Frank emerged from his gate and looked at the graffiti. "Bloody hell, it's on my wall instead of theirs. That's your first job then, lad. Cleaning that off."

"I thought I was here to make the chips," said Mark.

"And so you will but I'm paying you for your time and how I choose to use that time is up to me. An early lesson in the world of work."

Frank gave Mark a bucket of hot soapy water and a scrubbing brush. The bucket was heavy which made Mark struggle a bit.

"How are you going to manage the tatey sacks if you can't handle a bucket of water?" said Frank, disappearing back through his gate.

Mark set to scrubbing at the letters. Part of the letter m in homo was a bit higher so Mark scrubbed the rest of the m out. It was hard and he could see that it would take some time to clean it all off. He stepped back and reviewed his progress. It now read 'Tommy is a hoho' or near enough, anyway. Mark wondered whether to leave it and if the mysterious Tommy would appreciate it. He thought he would rather be described as a hoho than a homo but, being realistic, he thought Frank would not appreciate it. Also, the clean brick showed where the wall had been scrubbed so the original message was still obvious. Mark sighed and carried on. When he got as far as all that remained was 'Tommy is a', Frank appeared again.

"Haven't you finished that yet?" he demanded.

"It's hard," replied Mark. "It must have been there a while." He carried on scrubbing, more vigorously while Frank was watching in order to give the impression this was the usual scrubbing rate. Frank shook his head and disappeared. Mark slowed down the scrubbing rate to get his breath back.

A short, dumpy woman was coming towards him along the back lane carrying a shopping bag in each hand. She swayed from side to side as she walked, making Mark wonder that if she expended as much energy on forward motion as she did on side to side she would get to her destination much more quickly. As she got close to Mark, both the rolling and forward motions stopped and she put the two bags on the cobbles either side of her and looked at Mark who stopped scrubbing and stood, dripping scrubbing brush in hand.

"I'm sure these bags get heavier," she said to Mark. "You're doing a good job there. Who's Tommy and what is he?"

Mark looked at his efforts so far. 'Tommy is'.

"I think he's some kid who lives above the butcher's shop. It was just some insulting stuff but Frank at the chip shop asked me to clean it off because this bit of the wall is the back of the chip shop."

"Oh, the butcher's boy," said the woman. "I think I know who you mean. Didn't know they called him Tommy though."

"I don't know him," said Mark. "How old is he?" he asked, wondering about a possible kindred spirit, and close by, too.

"Dunno. Probably about your age. Haven't seen you around before. You're not Frank's lad, are you?"

"Only on a Saturday," replied Mark with a smile. "I've just started a Saturday job at the chip shop. I live in the flats round the corner, Calvert House, but we've not been there long. Just me and Mam now."

"That's a shame, love," she said. "Lost your Da then?"

"No, but they split up."

"Well, you seem like a nice lad. I won't keep you from your scrubbing. You're a good little scrubber," she finished with a laugh and, picking up her shopping, continued her waddle walk along the back lane, turning right at the end, going out of sight.

Mark continued his cleaning, her use of the word "scrubber" on his mind. He knew it was a slang term for a woman of a certain type, what Dad would call "common" and most likely a prostitute or at least, promiscuous. He felt a pang of guilt because, he reasoned, a prostitute lets blokes fuck her for money, and wasn't that exactly what he had done? He was unnerved and then started to wonder if she knew more about him than she had let on. After her affair with the man he and his sister always referred to as "the berk from work", was Mam a scrubber? Raised anxiety made Mark scrub harder and soon the wall was clear with a clean patch where the graffiti had been. Could a male be a scrubber? Admiring his clean wall, Mark persuaded himself that the bag woman had just enjoyed the play on words.

"Don't just bloody stand there!" Frank was peering out of the gate. "Those sacks won't empty themselves." Frank then advanced into the lane and looked at the wall. "Good job there, son. Well done. Come on then." Mark followed Frank back through the gate, clutching the scrubbing brush.

"Where's the bucket, idiot?"

"Oh," said Mark, and retrieved the bucket from the back lane. He emptied the water down a drain in the back yard and went into the back of the shop.

"Right, lad, upstairs with me," said Frank.

Mark felt a moment of panic and was back climbing the stairs at The Vault. Was Frank going to fuck him? He entered a room above the shop. At one side were large sacks of potatoes, like Mam had said, much bigger than the little sacks they bought at the shop.

"How do those big sacks get up here?" asked Mark.

"They grow wings and fly up," answered Frank tartly. "How d'you bloody think? I carry them." Mark felt stupid for asking.

In the middle were three large tin baths like Nana had hanging in her back yard and in which she said she used to have a bath in front of the parlour fire when she was little. Mark realized he was missing Nana. Along the other side of the room was a bench with some kind of machinery and at the end near the grubby window overlooking the main road was a white pot sink with two taps above it and a short hose attached. There was no bed and Mark exhaled a breath in relief.

"Stairs too much for you, lad?" asked Frank on hearing that.

"No, it's fine," said Mark.

"Right, first job is to fill the tin tubs with water using that hose. Keep your eye on that so the tub doesn't overflow before filling the next one and try not to flood the shop downstairs."

"I'll try not to," said Mark.

"You'd better not," replied Frank, annoyed at first and then realizing Mark was having a little joke, relaxed and smiled. Frank then showed Mark the peeling machine which had to be connected with the hose once the bathtubs were full. This electric machine was basically an uneven turntable at the base of a drum that would make the potatoes rub against the turntable and the sides of the drum which was very rough to the touch as water flowed through. The scrapings were then flushed into the sink. Frank warned Mark not to let the plughole get blocked and to make sure the tiny peelings drained away on the water that was flushing through the machine. Mark was happy there was a machine because he had feared he would be standing all day peeling each potato with a knife. He was glad the whole process seemed to be mechanized.

By this time the first bath was almost full so Mark was then instructed to switch the hose to the next bath without wetting the linoleum floor.

"You can do it if you're quick enough," said Frank, "but if you're not sure, turn the tap off. Then you have to put the whitener in otherwise by tonight the chips will have gone brown."

"Even under water?" asked Mark.

"Yes, there's oxygen in the water and that's what makes 'em brown."

"So does the whitener powder de-oxygenate the water then?" asked Mark.

Frank frowned. "I don't bloody know, sharp shit," he answered. "It just bloody works, that's all I know."

"I just wondered about the chemistry of it," said Mark, unwisely. He reasoned that if the oxygen were removed from water it would release hydrogen and there'd be no water left.

"For fucks sake, stop being a clever clogs. You're here to make chips, not be a fucking Einstein."

Next Mark was shown the chipping machine. This was not electric and each peeled potato had to be inserted and then pushed through the grill by bringing down a lever. Any large eyes left in the potato had to be dug out first. So not as mechanized as his first hopes had been.

"Right lad, off you go. I've got a load of fish to gut and get ready," said Frank, disappearing down the stairs.

Soon Mark developed a rhythm of peeling, taking eyes out and chipping. The peeling machine took a few potatoes at a time, maybe about the same as a large casserole dish might hold, and once peeled, were chipped while the next lot peeled.

Slowly the first sack got emptier and the first bath started to look fuller. When the peeling machine was stopped between loads, Mark could hear Frank moving around downstairs. His arm was aching from the effort of pulling down the lever on the chipper.

# Chapter 6 Saturday Boy

Load, peel, drain, chip, bath. Load, peel, drain, chip, bath. Load, peel, drain, chip, bath. On it went, Mark slipping into automatic mode as his mind wandered to other things.

He was stirring the whitener into the next bath when over the hum and rumbling of the tumbling potatoes from the peeling machine he heard a strange crackle. He turned and to his horror he saw sparks and flames rising from the power plug of the machine where it was plunged in to the wall socket above the machine.

"Fire!" he shouted and going to the top of the staircase, shouted again, "Fire! There's a fire up here!" But Frank did not appear. Mark looked back into the room and the flames seemed bigger to him, going up the wall. He looked around for a fire extinguisher but could not see one.

"Can't throw water on an electrical fire," said Mark to himself. In desperation he ran downstairs to find Frank. He wasn't there. The shutters were still down and Mark didn't know how to raise them. Mark ran out into the small back yard, no sign of Frank. He wasn't in the shop at all. He tried the back gate, it was locked and there was no key in the lock. Frank must have gone out of the back and locked the gate, taking the key with him. Mark feared if the whole shop went up, even in the small yard he would be in great danger. Mark was trapped in the shop that was on fire!

He ran back into the shop and his eyes fell on the telephone. The shop had a telephone! Mark remembered that you could phone up and order in advance. Some other places were copying the idea. Frank wanted to do deliveries as well so the phone was an investment. The trouble was, so many of his likely customers didn't have a telephone and by the time they'd gone to the phone box they might as well have just gone to the chippy. All these thoughts raced through Mark's mind as he picked up the phone and dialled 999. As the dial rotated back each time from the 9 it seemed an age to Mark.

"Emergency. Which service do you require?" came the voice of the operator.

"Fire, quick please, I'm trapped in."

After a moment another operator answered. Quickly Mark gave the address and said he was trapped inside the shop.

"How many people are with you?"

"Nobody, I'm on my own."

"How old are you?"

"Fourteen," said Mark. "Am I still worth rescuing?"

"Of course. A fish and chip shop. Is it a fat fire?"

"No, electrical socket," said Mark. "But hurry up, all these questions."

"They're already on their way, son. Don't worry. Is there much smoke?"

"Not down here, I've not been upstairs where the fire is for a few minutes now. I'll go and check."

Mark put the receiver down and failed to hear the operator telling him not to go near the fire. Climbing the stairs there was indeed smoke now. He could see the flames were larger now. But then on the half landing he saw the fuse box for the electrics. Grabbing a stool that was luckily nearby he stood on it and threw the main switch. The light went out. Mark now reasoned that as there was now no power, it would be safe to use water to douse the flames. He crouched low and went back into the room. The smoke was choking him. The big baths were too heavy to lift but there was the bucket intended to be used to empty the baths. Coughing, he picked it up and immersed one side in one of the baths that didn't have too many chips in it. He flung the water at the flames. There was a hissing and a lot of steam. He flung another bucket as he heard heavy footsteps on the stairs. Mark could see the fire was out as a fireman came into the room.

"Are you OK, son," asked the fireman.

"Yes, I think so," coughed Mark.

"Come with me," said the fireman as two more entered the room carrying extinguishers. One started hacking at the wall with an axe.

"It's OK," said Mark. "I put it out."

"You did brilliant," said the fireman, "but we have to be sure that there's no smouldering left in the wall cavity."

Mark had to accept that as he was ushered downstairs. One of the shutters was up. Mark could see it had been forced. Then he saw Frank running towards him along the High Street. In the pub where he had gone for a lunchtime drink his attention had been drawn to the fire engines and wisps of smoke coming from the upstairs of his shop.

By this time the police were there and an ambulance.

"What's happened?" asked Frank breathlessly of a fireman.

"It's OK, sir," said the fireman. "Keep back please."

"It's my shop!" said Frank and then, seeing Mark with the fireman, called out, "Mark! Are you all right, son? What happened?"

"Is that your son, sir?" asked another, obviously more senior fire officer.

"No, he works for me, Saturday boy," said Frank.

"Come with me, sir. The fire is out, thanks to your Saturday boy. Clever lad, that one."

Mark was coughing and sitting in the back of the ambulance when Frank came up to him. "I think I might have spilled some water upstairs which might have gone downstairs, but in my defence it was to put out the fire."

"Don't worry about that now, Mark. As long as you're not hurt."

"He's breathed in some smoke," said an ambulance man.

Then an official looking man holding a notebook started asking Mark questions.

"What's your name, son?" he asked.

"Mark."

"Your surname?"

"Martin."

"Sorry, is it Mark or Martin?"

"No, my name is Mark Martin."

He continued to ply Mark with questions while the fire officer and Frank listened while Mark explained how the fire had started and how he had found himself locked in but had turned off the electrics before using water to quell the flames.

"Why did you lock the lad in?" the fire officer demanded of Frank.

Frank looked flustered. "Well, I usually nip out for a pint at lunchtime in The Bull and I lock up. I knew Mark was working upstairs at the front and thought if scallywags came in through the back gate he wouldn't hear them so I locked up. I'm sorry, Mark. I really am."

"You should have let the lad see you out and he could have locked up so when he went back upstairs he would have had the key," said the fire officer.

"But then how would I get back in?" asked Frank but in a tone that expected no reply.

"Who are you, sir?" asked the officer of the notebook man.

"Terry Perkins, *Bilthaven Chronicle and Star*,"

"Press!" said the officer, evidently annoyed. "I must ask you to leave."

"Certainly," said Perkins. "I've got all I need, thank you." Perkins then stepped back.

"We're taking you to the hospital," said the ambulance man.

"I've got another sack to do," said Mark.

"With no electricity, going to do them all by hand, are you?" said Frank. "Stop being an idiot and go t    o    the hospital and get checked out."

"That socket just caught fire," said Mark as he was ushered further into the ambulance. "I want danger money," he shouted as the doors closed.

He just heard Frank's retort. "Cheeky little sod." But it was said in a friendly tone.

"Where's the bells?" asked Mark as the ambulance set off steadily towards the hospital. "Aren't I an emergency?"

"Something of a hero if I hear right," said the ambulance man. "But an emergency? Not now."

At the hospital the doctors listened to Mark's lungs, checked his heart and all vital signs.

"Is your mother with you?" asked the doctor.

"Oh, no," said Mark. Mam! He hadn't thought about it. "She doesn't even know about this. She was still in bed when I went out. She'll be thinking I'm at work in the chippy."

"Have you a telephone at home?"

Mark shook his head.

"We'll keep you here for a while anyway," said the doctor. He took some details from Mark who was then left to sit in the side room, idly flicking the pages of magazines that all seemed months out of date. *Women's Weekly* and *People's Friend* figured largely among those available. Mark thought Mam would be happy there. Every so often a nurse would come in and check his pulse. Once or twice the doctor came back and listened to his heart and lungs.

# Chapter 7 Press

The nurse came in closely followed by Mam.

"Mark, I'm glad you're OK. What happened?" she asked, giving him an embarrassing hug.

"I'm alright, Mam," he said. "There was a fire at the chippy but as you can see I'm fine. Breathed in a bit of smoke and they're all panicking about it."

"So where was that Frank? He should have been looking after you. You're only fourteen for fuck's sake. It's a good job the fire brigade turned up or you could have been burnt alive."

"He'd nipped out to the pub for his pint. And I called the fire brigade. There's a phone in the shop."

"And left you alone? And is it right he locked you in? Wait till I get my hands round his fat neck!"

"Mam, just leave it. How did you find out anyway?"

"The cops came round and told me. Looks great having the police at my door."

"Just doing their job, Mam."

At that moment, mercifully, the doctor came in. "Ah, are you Mark's mother?"

"I am. How is he?"

"Well. Mrs Martin, I just want to check him over again, but after that I think he'll be good to go."

The doctor examined Mark again and then announced that Mark could go home, especially as his mother was there to care for him.

"I can discharge him into your care, Mrs Martin."

"Thank you very much, doctor. Come on, Mark. Let's go."

At the hospital entrance they were confronted by the reporter Perkins along with a photographer.

"Mrs Martin, what's it like to have a hero for a son?"

"He's always been my hero," said Mam, quickly putting her arm around Mark and smiling for the camera. "Of course, I'm very proud of him. Smile, Mark."

32

Mark tried to smile as the flashbulb went off again.

"Mrs Martin, we understand that Mark was alone in the shop when the fire started caused by an electrical fault. What do you say about that? Do you think the police should take action?"

Mark feared what indiscreet things Mam might say so he butted in quickly. "The fact that I was alone in the shop didn't affect the timing of when the fire started. The power socket caught fire and luckily I was in the room at the time. As for the police, that's up to them what they want to do."

Mark started to pull Mam away. "Come on, Mam. Let's go."

He dragged Mam away from her enjoyment of being the centre of attention. "I just want to get home, Mam," he said. Mark suddenly felt very tired and in need of a lie down.

It was two buses to get home from the hospital and Mark couldn't face that - he felt so stressed. He walked over to the taxi rank. "Come on, Mam."

But she hung back. "I've got no money for a taxi, Mark. What are you playing at?"

"Allow me to pay for your taxi," said Perkins, who had followed them.

"Yes, thank you," said Mam, before Mark could decline. She got into the taxi, giving the driver the address of the flat. Mark got in, followed by Perkins. Mark sighed; this was not what he wanted. But Mam revelled in it, chatting to Perkins all the way, telling him all about Mark, his school, what a clever boy he was and so on. How he had started to learn Spanish on a family holiday to Majorca a couple of years ago. But that led to questions about Mark's father and sister. She skirted around questions about Mark's father and the reasons for the separation. She gave the implication that it was the father who was at fault. Mark was angry but just kept quiet.

The taxi dropped them outside Calvert House.

"Are you hungry, love?" asked Mam as they climbed the stairs rather than wait for the lift. The block was only four storeys.

Mark wondered why he wasn't hungry. "No Mam. Just going for a lie down."

He went into his bedroom and slid the bolt on the door. He was feeling stressed and he knew that a wank would go a long way to relieving that. He slid his jeans and pants to his thighs and lay back. He found himself thinking about Gordon but more about Pip, the slaps on his bum. He came with such force it hit his jumper although he had lifted that well out of the way. Fuck it, he thought. He cleaned up, and threw the jumper into the corner. He would put it in the launderette bag later.

Feeling somewhat calmer he crossed into the lounge. Mam was smoking and watching television. More cowboys.

"Feeling any better, love?" she asked.

"Yes," said Mark. "I think I'll wander round to the chippy and see what's going on."

"He won't be open tonight," said Mam in a tone of the obvious. "He's got no fucking chips." She laughed. "That new Chinese might be open," said Mam. "Mine's sweet and sour chicken." She laughed again.

Mark just grabbed his jacket from the peg in the small hallway and walked round to the chippy. The damaged shutter was padlocked down again. There was a notice on the shutter. 'Open at 7pm. No chips because of fire damage. Fish etc. available'

Trust Frank not to miss a trick, thought Mark. He walked round the back down the back lane. The back gate was unlocked so he went in.

"Hello, Mark," said Frank, surprised. "Come to finish making the chips?"

"Is the machine fixed?" asked Mark, incredulous.

"Don't be daft, lad, I'm joking with you, Hoping to get the electrics upstairs fixed on Monday. Got some people coming tomorrow to clean and decorate over the smoke damage upstairs. So with a bit of luck, open normally on Monday night. Can you come in on Monday to make the chips?"

"I'll be at school," replied Mark.

"Of course," said Frank.

"Do I get paid for today?" asked Mark.

Frank frowned and looked at Mark. "You get paid for making chips, three baths full. You didn't do three baths and the ones you did do were spoiled. So I'm not paying good money for spoiled chips." Frank turned away and opened the till while Mark stood speechless. He felt angry.

Frank turned back. "But for saving my shop, my business and my livelihood, I'll gladly pay you for that," he said and thrust a ten pound note at Mark, whose jaw literally dropped at that. He could not remember the last time he saw a tenner.

"Thank you," he said, taking the note and looking at it.

"See you on Saturday, then?" said Frank.

Mark nodded. "Yes. Thanks again," he said. He walked out into the back lane and out onto High Street.

He decided to go the Chinese to surprise Mam, and he was hungry now.

"You going to set the table and put the kettle on again?" he called as he hung his jacket up.

"Don't tell me he was open!" called Mam from the lounge.

"No, but the new Chinkies was," said Mark, carrying the bag of food containers through to the kitchen.

"What you got?" said Mam, stubbing out her cigarette and following him.

"What you asked for, and more," said Mark. "He gave me extra for saving his livelihood."

"How much?"

"Five pounds," lied Mark. He knew Mam would ask for some so he wanted to play down his acquired wealth.

"Come on then, clever son, let's eat like royalty," smiled Mam.

"Chinese royalty, though," said Mark. "I'll be the Emperor and you the Dowager Empress."

"What the fuck are you on about?" laughed Mam. "China's communist, doesn't have an emperor or even a king. Just Mao thingy."

"China had an emperor until about fifty years ago or so," said Mark.

"Fuck off, smart arse," said Mam. "Eat your food."

Mark smiled because he knew that Mam secretly liked that he knew things, read quite widely and did well at school, which she never had. He had passed his eleven plus but she had gone to an elementary school and left to get work as soon as she could.

. . .

Mark slept in most of Sunday and on Monday was off to school. He said nothing to the other boys except to mention he had a Saturday job. Again this was to cover himself in case for some reason he spent more money than expected.

Mark came out of school in a group and walking along to get his bus, Ethan stopped, looking at the newsstand where copies of the *Chronicle and Star* were piled up. "Mark Martin, that's you!" he exclaimed.

All the boys turned to look. There on the front page was a large photograph of Mark, smiling uneasily with Mam's arm round him and a big grin on her face.

'Saturday Boy Saves the Day' was the headline, and underneath in slightly smaller type. 'Boy's bravery and quick thinking saves business from inferno', Terry Perkins, City Correspondent.

# Chapter 8 Accusations

Immediately all the boys crowded round Mark, asking what happened.

"What did you do?"

"Was anybody hurt?"

"Were you hurt?"

"Did you rescue people from the fire?"

"How did the fire start?"

"Did you start the fire to get famous?"

"What did you say?" demanded Mark, after that last question.

"It's just a joke," was the weak reply as Mark's anger became threatening.

"Calm down, Mark," said Ethan. "He's just an idiot. We know you wouldn't start it, but what did?"

"An electrical fault. And it was hardly an inferno. Just in the one room."

"Did you put the fire out?" asked Danny.

"Yes," said Mark impatiently.

"What about the fire brigade?" queried Eddie.

"They arrived after that."

"I'll buy a copy of that," offered Steve.

He bought the paper and then held the front page photo up next to Mark.

The news seller noticed. "Hey, is that the lad?" he called.

"Yes, our friend here is the fire fighting hero!" replied Steve.

"Come here, son. Let me shake your hand," said the news seller.

Mark went over to the newsstand and reached over and shook the man's hand. He was now feeling acutely self-conscious and embarrassed by the attention. The news seller insisted on Mark taking a free copy of the *Chronicle and Star*. He was glad when his bus came. His group all cheered him on to the bus. He moved along and sat down.

The conductor had seen this. "You seem a popular lad," he said as he gave Mark his ticket. He then looked again at Mark. "You look like that boy on the front of the paper. That's you, isn't it?"

Mark felt it was useless to deny it so he just said, "Yes, but it wasn't like that. There was no inferno."

Other passengers had heard this, one said, "No, it says, if you read on, that he prevented it from turning into an inferno."

Then the passengers started clapping. Rather than just sit still, Mark stood up and gave a theatrical bow. "All I did was chuck some water on it."

"It says here it was an electrical fire. You can't chuck water on an electrical fire," said someone.

"Well I did, but after I turned the power off."

"Well done, Mark Martin!" said another passenger.

"How do you know my name?" asked Mark, stupidly realizing as he asked what a dumb question that was. Everybody laughed and one person held up a copy of the paper.

"You're famous now, Mark Martin," said the passenger.

Mark sat down again waiting for his stop to get his second Northside bus. He hoped that he would not be recognized on that bus. He managed to avoid attention; after all, he was not cheered on this time by his school friends. He thought school the next day would be horrendous.

As he walked towards Calvert House he heard a shout, "Here he is, he's coming now!" His heart sank as he saw practically everybody from the building either at their window or out on the balcony which some larger flats had. All he could do was keep walking. They started clapping so he waved and as he stood in front of the entrance he stopped and repeated his theatrical bow to cheers from the residents. He went into the building and ran up the stairs to the top floor and along to his flat.

Mam was sitting in the lounge as usual. "What's going on out there?" she asked. "What's all the noise about?"

Mark stopped. "Mam, are you the only person on Planet Earth who doesn't know?"

"Know what? What's up?"

Mark took the paper he had been given and dropped the front page onto her lap.

Mam looked at it. "Fuck me! I'm on the front page of the *Chron*," she said.

Mark sighed. "Yes, Mam. You're on the front page."

"So are you, Mark."

"I had noticed," said Mark sarcastically, which seemed to go over Mam's head.

" I thought I heard someone knocking earlier, but I didn't answer because I thought it was a Caller," she said, referring to the men who came round to collect payments for loans.

"A Caller?" said Mark. "The Provy again? How much? No wonder there's hardly any food in the cupboard."

"Just four pounds, twelve and six now."

"Bloody hell," said Mark. He took out his remaining five pound note he had earned at The Vault and gave it to her. "Pay it off. Please!"

"Mark, that's your fiver for saving the shop what Frank gave you. I can't take that."

Fuck, she would think that of course. "Well you have to. Put it under the clock and when he comes back, get it paid."

"I will, Mark, I promise. And I'll pay you back when I can. I am looking for a better job, you know."

"So here's the paper, there's job adverts in the back. Proper jobs. Start looking."

"It's got to be the right job. I don't want to get a crap one and lose me social," said Mam. "I could end up worse off."

"So don't apply for crap jobs, then," said Mark with teenage logic.

"Just watch your lip, Mark," said Mam angrily. "At least I won't set the fucking place on fire."

"I didn't, and you know it!" shouted Mark, turning round and storming out of the room. He slammed the door of his bedroom and threw himself on the bed, wishing he'd never taken the job at Frank's shop. It was only to provide a cover for his more lucrative earnings. His hand went down to his cock for his usual stress relief but then he thought, 'Fuck it, I'll go into town and make some money having fun.' He quickly changed out of his school uniform and put on casual clothes. He went out of his room and, grabbing his jacket, called out, "I'm going out."

"What about your tea?" was Mam's answer.

"Not hungry," he called back, closing the flat door behind him. He hurried down the stairs hoping not to meet anybody and suffer more embarrassment. He waited anxiously for the bus in case he was trapped there by being recognized. At last the bus came and as it hummed its way into the city centre he realized it was probably too early to meet the men in The Vault. He also realized that he was hungry after all. But he had money in his pocket, so he could afford to buy a meal. He found a café and ordered egg and chips and a coke. There were a few other people in and to his horror he saw that some of them were reading the *Chron* as they ate. He tried to appear inconspicuous as he sat at an empty table waiting for his meal. He saw a woman looking at him closely and whispering something to her female companion who then looked at Mark and down at the paper and back again. He felt like just getting up running and out but at that moment the waitress brought his egg and chips and his coke.

He heard the woman say quietly, "I'm sure it's him." She beckoned the waitress and pointed to the paper, nodding towards Mark. 'Not again!' thought Mark, dreading the attention. He reached for the ketchup bottle and started to eat his egg and chips. But the waitress came over to him.

"Are you this Mark Martin?" she asked.

"No," said Mark, shaking his head.

"He looks just like you."

Mark sighed again. "Yes, OK. That's me. But I just want to eat my food."

The waitress turned round and called across to the table where the two women were sitting, "Yes, it's him." That had the effect of alerting everybody else in the café. He became the centre of attention and wanted to leave but it wasn't opening time yet for The Vault and even then he couldn't go in himself unless he knew that at least one of the others was there. And they might not turn up at all. His plan now seemed stupid. 'I bet they only come on a Friday or Saturday' he thought. So he waited in the café sipping his coke. One advantage though was that he wasn't given a bill and when he asked for it as the cafe was closing at seven o'clock, he was told his meal was on the house. Fame had its advantages, it seemed.

He made his way through the now darker city to the alley where The Vault was. Now he felt stupid, standing there looking up at the building. Above the pub entrance was Victorian stonework with pillars up to the roof. He noticed stone letters along the portico with the words 'Martins Bank'. 'How appropriate' thought Mark. So the building had once been a bank, he thought, which explained the name. What was he going to do? Stand there all night in case one of the group happened by?

He decided he'd felt stupid long enough and turned to walk out of the close.

"Hello, Mark." It was Pip, walking briskly toward Mark and The Vault. "Were you waiting for me?" he added with a smile. Mark liked his smile.

"No. Well, yes. Someone, anyway," replied Mark, summoning as much self-confidence as he could.

"Have you been in?" asked Pip.

"No, I don't think I can on my own," said Mark.

"Nothing to stop you sticking your head round the door of the saloon bar to see who's there," advised Pip. "Come on, let's do just that."

Mark followed Pip into the pub and to the saloon bar. He could see nobody he recognized but Pip went straight up to a man sitting with a pint in front of him that looked as though he had so far taken only a sip.

"Evening, Gerry," he said by way of greeting this man.

"Hello, Pip," responded Gerry with a nice smile. Mark guessed his age at about thirty. "Fresh meat?" he added in an enquiring tone.

"Gerry, this is Mark. He's already met some of our little group, myself and Gordy, upstairs, if you get my meaning."

"He looks familiar," said Gerry. "Have we met before, son?" he asked of Mark.

"No," said Mark.

At that moment the door of the saloon bar opened and Gordon came in. He looked surprised to see Mark there. "Well, if it's not the famous and heroic Mark Martin!" he said with a broad grin on his face. "Well done, Mark. I knew you were a bright boy."

"What's he done?" asked a puzzled Pip.

"Not seen the paper yet?" replied Gordon, pulling a folded copy from his coat pocket. He opened it out and laid it on the table. Pip and Gerry read it, and kept looking at Mark. Mark was annoyed again because of course now they knew his surname and even where he lived, although it just said Calvert House, Northside, without the flat number. But especially now, everybody in Calvert House knew him.

"Come and sit next to me," said Pip. "Coke again, is it?"

"Yes please," said Mark. Pip came back with his pint and Mark's coke.

"Go on then, tell us all about it," urged Pip. Mark recounted the events of Saturday while Pip, Gerry and Gordy listened. There were congratulations all round.

"This deserves a celebration," said Pip. "You want another fiver, Mark?" he asked, placing his hand on Mark's thigh. Mark started to feel very horny and he wanted Pip again, as well as the five pounds.

"I was going to ask that," said Gordon.

"I beat you to it," said Pip, getting up and going to the bar. A quiet word, some cash handed over and Pip returned with the key.

"Why don't I come up as well?" said Gordon.

"Only for another fiver," said Mark quickly. He wasn't going to be fucked at half price.

"I remember Tom saying he's a quick learner," said Gordon, laughing.

"What about me?" said Gerry.

"You come as well, if you've a fiver," said Mark rashly, but thinking of fifteen pounds, a fortune by his standards.

The deal was done and the four trooped upstairs to the brown room. Pip went over to the window and closed the curtain before putting on the table lamp.

"I like to undress Mark," announced Pip. He came over to Mark who was standing by the bed and putting his arms around him, kissed him while feeling for his belt. Mark's arousal heightened as he felt his jeans and underpants being pushed down.

Mark heard Gerry say, "He's lovely" from close by and then a hand that was not Pip's was caressing his bum. Mark was gently eased onto the bed and his clothes were removed. He saw that Gordon and Gerry had already done that and their desire was obvious. Pip quickly undressed and all four squeezed onto the double bed. Mark found all three of them attractive, Pip most of all, followed by Gerry and then Gordon, but it was close. Mark felt he couldn't get any harder and several hands caressed his body. On his back, looking at them, with his knees up, he felt Pip move between his legs, felt his hard cock against his body and just wanted it. Mark lifted his head and reached down for Pip's cock pulling it towards him.

"Vaseline," whispered Pip and the tub appeared. Mark felt himself being lubricated and the slow entry. He forced himself not to come because he knew the others wanted their turn as well. As Pip came, Gordon took hold of Mark's cock and started to wank him.

43

"Not yet," said Mark. "After all three."

So Gordon took Pip's place and once more Mark felt him inside, a feeling that gave Mark extreme satisfaction, not just physically but psychologically as well; as though this was what he was meant for. Gerry was standing close to the bed and Mark reached out and took hold of his cock. He felt it was not as big as the others which he thought would be better by that time.

Pip was washing his cock at the washbasin when Mark felt Gordon come.

"I've waited for this," said Gerry. "Lie on your front, Mark."

Mark obliged and felt the weight of Gerry on him, Gerry's knees pushing Mark's legs further apart. Gerry slowly fucked him and reaching round, put his fingers into Mark's mouth which he thought was to stress Gerry's dominance and Mark's submission so he liked that.

After that, all four lay on the bed, Mark between Gerry and Pip who both kept stroking him. Once more Pip leaned and turned and took Mark's cock in his mouth. Mark was so aroused he came quickly, not worried this time about unloading.

"We'll be getting the red soon," said Gordon.

"What's that mean?" asked Mark.

"When the red light comes on it means our time in the room is up," explained Gordon.

"What does the blue one mean?" asked Mark.

"It means the cops are downstairs," said Pip.

Mark felt a sudden panic. "What do we do if that happens?"

"We get enough time to get sorted. Don't worry," said Pip.

As they made to leave the room, Mark said, "What about my money?"

"No problem, Mark," said Pip, who was rapidly becoming Mark's favourite of the group. They each gave him five pounds, Pip a five pound note, the others in one pound notes.

A good night's work, thought Mark. He stayed with them for another coke and then got his bus home feeling satisfied in more ways than one.

# Chapter 9 Adulation

It was with a certain degree of trepidation that Mark set off for school the next day. He knew that by this time everybody would have seen Monday night's *Chronicle and Star*. His hopes of a relatively normal day were dashed as he walked from the bus stop to the school gate. One or two of his classmates joined him.

"How's the hero today?"

"I'm not a hero. All I did was turn the power off and chuck some water at the flames."

"But it says you went back in to where the fire was to put it out and got smoke in your lungs and had to go to hospital. That sounds like a hero to me."

"I just did it automatically."

"It says the fire was already out by the time the fire brigade arrived and by that time the whole shop would have been on fire."

At this point some kids from other classes and year groups were looking at Mark. "That's him, isn't it? The one who put the fire out."

"Yes, that's him, Not been here long, but it's him," affirmed another.

Mark just kept walking but once inside the school gate he was surrounded and the crowd attracted more to come and see what was happening. Word spread and soon Mark was totally surrounded by a large crowd. This attracted the attention of the duty teacher, Mr Davison. Usually such a gathering was because there was a fight so as he pushed through to the centre of the crowd he was surprised to find nothing. It took him a moment to realize that Mark was the centre of attention and the cause of the melee.

"Come on," ordered Mr Davison. "Let Martin get into school unmolested."

Mark started a bit at the use of that word. He knew very well that what The Vault group did to him would be described as molestation by those in authority, even though he was a willing participant and well paid for it. As Mark

46

followed Mr Davison the crowd thinned out with just a couple from his own class, Ethan and Steve, staying with him. Mark liked them both but he found Ethan, with his fair, floppy hair and engaging smile, very attractive. Of course he said nothing.

"Come in the main entrance with me, Martin," said Mr Davison. "You two, off you go."

Pupils weren't normally allowed the use of the front entrance, it was for staff and visitors. Prefects could use it. Mr Davison led Mark into the large entrance lobby on one side of which was the Headteacher's office and the school secretary's office, on the other was that of the Deputy Head, Miss Charlton and a store cupboard. There was a sixth form prefect sitting on a chair, reading a book, his status defined by the white edging round his school black blazer and a badge. He looked up as Mark entered. Mark thought he saw an expression of recognition on the prefect's face but then he just went back to his book. Standing in the lobby Mark wondered if he were in trouble of some sort or if this was still something to do with the fire. Mr Davison knocked on the Head's door and heard Mr Harris call, "Come in."

Mr Davison went in and the door was left ajar. Mark could not hear everything that was said but he heard his name and he thought he heard talk of fire. His fears of more fuss confirmed.

He clearly heard Mr Harris's booming reply, "Yes, I read about it. I wasn't sure if he was one of our boys at the time. I don't know the boy myself. Recently moved up here I believe?"

Mr Davison replied again but more indistinctly, and then appeared at the door. "Martin, Mr Harris would like a word with you."

Mark entered the sacred sanctum of the Head's office. One wall was covered with a bookcase containing not just books but a lot of box files. A sliding window hatch into the secretary's office. There was a large desk that Mark thought looked rather untidy and by the window was a coffee table with soft chairs round it. As Mark followed Mr Davison in,

Mr Harris got up from his seat and came round the desk, holding out his hand to Mark. Automatically Mark shook hands with Mr Harris.

"Yes," said Mr Harris. "I recognize you from the newspaper now. I'm sorry that I haven't had the chance to get to know you since you came here; remiss of me. I think Miss Charlton met you and your mother when you enrolled. But we can make up for that now. Sit down," he finished indicating one of the soft chairs. Mark had only seen Mr Harris from a distance before and had been naturally wary of the Headteacher. Mark now thought he seemed very friendly. He sat down as indicated and Mr Harris sat in another chair at the coffee table. It had a newspaper on it but it was the *Times Educational Supplement* to Mark's relief.

"Thank you, Mr Davison," said Mr Harris. "Leave the door open, please."

Mr Davison left, leaving the door open as requested; or maybe ordered, thought Mark.

"How are you settling in here?" asked Mr Harris.

"Very well, thank you, sir," answered Mark.

"Who is your form tutor?" queried Mr Harris.

"Mr Farnsworth, sir."

"Ah yes, of course." Mr Harris got up and peered out of the door. "Foster, nip along to Mr Farnsworth's class and tell him that I have Mark Martin here and to mark him present."

From where he was sitting Mark saw the prefect once he stood up.

"Yes, sir," said the prefect who turned and put his book down and left.

Coming back in, Mr Harris smiled at Mark. "I always have a duty prefect each day for such purposes. Foster's turn today. He's a good lad. Talking of good lads, you seem to fit that category, Martin. The fact that we've not met before since you came means that you've not been in trouble which is good. And now we have a fire fighting hero!"

"Everybody keeps going on about it, sir. It was just a faulty power socket so I turned the power off and then doused the flames."

"I think you are being too modest, Martin," said Mr Harris. He reached into a briefcase and pulled out a copy of the *Chronicle and Star*. Mark's heart skipped a beat and sank. "It says here that you were very brave and that but for your swift actions the shop could have been burnt to the ground and quite possibly neighbouring businesses as well. I remember a chip shop fire a few years ago. With all that fat, it was an inferno and took the whole row of shops out. So well done."

"Thank you, sir," said Mark, wondering when he would rejoin his class.

"I'm not sure if this has happened since you came but when we have pupils who perform in some exemplary way we like to acknowledge that in assembly before the whole school. It's usually sporting achievements and the like but I think you are well worthy of the accolade."

Mark had seen this once when a boy was chosen as an apprentice by the local football club which was in the first division. "Really, sir, it was nothing," said Mark, hoping to avoid this fate.

"Nonsense, Martin," said the Head. "You are far too self deprecatory."

Mark wasn't sure what that meant but could guess. At that moment the school bells sounded which Mark knew was the signal for assembly in the school hall.

"I'd better get along, sir," said Mark, reaching for his bag.

"No, Martin, you're with me for this. Leave your coat and bag here until after assembly. Better tuck your shirt in though." Mark realized that one side of his school shirt was hanging out. He shoved it back into his trousers. He could hear the hubbub as all the school from aged eleven up to eighteen trooped into the hall, shepherded by their class tutors.

"Foster, did you inform Mr Farnsworth?" asked Mr Harris loudly.

Foster appeared at the door. "Yes, sir."

"Good. Now make sure there's a chair on the stage for Martin here, please. He's Laudatum today."

"The fire, sir?" asked Foster, looking at Mark.

"Exactly, Foster," said Mr Harris.

"I thought I recognized him," said Foster as he left.

Mark's butterflies were now golden eagles. Mr Harris noticed. "Don't worry, Martin. I'll ask you to say a few words..."

"I don't know what to say," said Mark, suddenly aware he had interrupted the Head Teacher who didn't seem to mind.

"You'll be fine. I'll lead you with a question or two." Mr Harris went over to a cupboard and took out a small item which he slipped into his pocket with a smile at Mark.

Mark noticed the hubbub had died down and Foster re-appeared. "School is ready, sir," Foster reported. Foster, Mr Harris and Mark Martin left the office. Mark felt terrified, far more so than when climbing the stairs at The Vault.

# Chapter 10 Stagefright

Standing in the lobby with the doors of the school hall in front of him, Mark remembered the previous laudatum event. There was an ovation and music as the head had entered, followed by the pupil to be honoured. Now he was to be the focus of all this attention. Mark wished Mam could be there to witness this; she would be so proud he knew, but he also knew she would be a fish out of water in such surroundings and could well say things that, however well-meaning, would embarrass Mark.

Foster opened the hall door. Mark could see the central aisle with the whole school either side, now standing in front of their chairs, most turning to look.

"Come on then, Martin," said Mr Harris. "This is your day!" As Foster stepped through the doors to lead Mr Harris followed by Mark down the aisle to the stage at the far end, the triumphal music of William Walton's *Crown Imperial* started playing and the school were clapping in time as Foster, then Mr Harris and then Mark walked slowly, too slowly, towards the stage where all the teachers, now also standing in front of their chairs and clapping too, were waiting. Mark felt himself flushing with the embarrassment of being the centre of so much attention.

The procession of three turned right in front of the stage to the steps up at the side and onto the middle. In the centre was the lectern and next to it three chairs instead of the normal two. On one side a single chair for the duty prefect and two on the other. Mark then realized that his ordeal would last longer because from what he remembered, the laudatum took place at the end of the assembly, so he was stuck up there in front of everybody for much longer than he had wanted. Mr Harris announced the hymn for the day and after a moment of panic Mark found a hymn book on his seat. He now had to stand and sing on the stage in front of the whole school. Close behind him Mr Bartholomew's booming voice drowned out Mark's tentative singing of *Thine be the Glory* to its rousing tune. At the end of the hymn everybody sat down while Mr Harris stood at the lectern. He spoke briefly about faith and courage and doing one's duty in the face of danger. With a shock Mark realized that, although not by name at this point, this applied to him. He tried to sit still but instead fidgeted with his thumbs, twirling them around each other.

Mr Harris finished his little homily and announced, "Let us pray." On cue everybody put their hands together and bowed their heads while the prayer was read, finishing with the *Amen*.

"Let us say the Lord's Prayer together," said Mr Harris as he did in every assembly, starting, "Our Father..." which was followed by the whole school reciting the Lord's Prayer. By this time Mark's nerves were at breaking point.

Mr Harris turned to look at Mark and then back to address the school. This is it, thought Mark, bracing himself. Everybody was looking at him and he could feel the eyes of the teachers arraigned behind him on the back of his neck.

"I spoke a few moments ago about how our faith in God can give us the courage to do our duty even at danger to ourselves. It is something we should all aspire to, as we are all human, we so often fail. But some have that courage and so become a shining example to us all. We have one such person here today. Mark Martin has not been in this school for very long and I believe has not lived in this city for very long but in that time has shown himself to be an excellent student. But that is not why he is sitting up here today for he has earned a school laudatum medal and I believe he is one of the youngest ever to do so. I think many of you will know of this young man's heroic exploits in saving not one but probably several businesses from going up in flames and so doing saved the livelihoods no doubt of many people. I now call upon Mark Martin to tell us a little more about what happened."

Mr Harris indicated to Mark to stand up at the same time clapping which set the whole school off clapping. Mark stood uneasily next to Mr Harris looking out at the sea of eyes all turned on him.

"It was the power socket that caught fire," said Mark.

"Maybe start by telling us why you were in the fish and chip shop on Saturday morning," offered Mr Harris.

"It's a Saturday job in the chippy round the corner from where I live. It's just on the High Street. I'm supposed to use this machine to peel loads of potatoes and then cut them into chips ready for the evening. It was in a room over the shop. It was the peeling machine that was plugged in to the dodgy socket. I mean, I only knew it was a dodgy socket after, not when I started it off."

"So when did you notice the fire?"

"I was putting the last load of chips into the water. The peeling machine was quite noisy because the potatoes sort of bobbled around inside it but then I heard this strange noise and when I turned round there were sparks and flames going up the wall from the socket. I went downstairs to find Frank, he owns the shop, but he wasn't there. I went out the back but the gate was locked."

"So where was this Frank?"

Mark stopped. He knew now that Frank had been in the pub but he was quick enough to think that it was not a good look to say that, so he just said, "He'd had to nip out. He locked the gate because he'd had trouble with people thieving and that so he thought that would be safer for me."

"Could you not leave by the normal shop door?"

"No, the shutters were down. So I went into the shop and he had a telephone there so I dialled 999 and told the fire brigade what had happened. They asked about smoke so to check I went back upstairs. It was well and truly alight by then. There was quite a bit of smoke too. The daft thing was I could still hear the peeling machine rumbling away."

Mt Harris smiled at that. Mark saw that everybody was listening, one could hear a pin drop in that large hall.

"But you managed to put the fire out. Tell us about that."

"Well, sir, I knew that you mustn't throw water at an electrical fire, but like halfway up the stairs there was like a small landing where the stairs turned and I saw the fuse box up near the ceiling. I stood on something and threw the main switch and all the power went off. So then I knew I could chuck water at it. So I went back into the room and used the bucket to get water from one of the chip baths and threw it at the fire and it went out."

At this the school started clapping but Mr Harris put up a hand to silence them.

"And this was even before the fire brigade arrived?"

"Yes, sir, I was still alone then. But then a fireman came into the room and took me out to an ambulance because I was coughing with the smoke."

"What did the firemen say to you about what you had done?"

"They said I had done well and saved it from being an inferno that could have destroyed the whole row of shops. I had to go to the hospital but then I was allowed home."

"Mark Martin, I think you are a very brave and resourceful young man, a credit to your family and to this school. I am happy to present you with your Laudatum medal. Wear it with pride."

Mr Harris took out of his pocket the small item he had taken from his office. It was a gold coloured badge with some Latin words on it, one of which was laudatum. He had seen a few of these mainly on older students without knowing what they were. Mr Harris pinned it to the lapel of his uniform blazer. Then the whole school erupted with applause and cheering as everybody stood. Mark just stood there, emotional yet embarrassed that this was all for him.

Afterwards, Mr Harris said, "This badge is just for the moment until yours is engraved. The front is the same, but yours will have your name on the back."

Back in his classroom the others crowded round wanting to see the badge close up, some who had never really bothered with Mark before now seemed to want to get to know him.

# Chapter 11 Savings

Mark knew he could not keep stacking up the money in his bedroom. There was always the risk Mam would find it and that would lead to a lot of awkward questions. It was passing the Post Office on the High Street after he got off his bus that gave him the idea. He would open a savings account and then he knew his money would be safe. He had a couple of pounds with him so he went in. He emerged shortly afterwards holding his new savings book. He was impressed by the large coat of arms with the crown on top. Underneath was stamped his name and the account number. Inside it showed his account balance of one pound. He put it in his blazer pocket and walked round to Calvert House. He now had the problem of keeping the bank book safe from prying eyes but he thought the little book would be easier to conceal than the money. Also he reasoned that with having cash ready to hand, he would be more likely to spend it and Mark wanted to save up. Not for any specific purpose, yet, anyway.

Mam wasn't in so he let himself in and went to his bedroom. Holding the bank book in his hand he looked for a good place. His bookshelf; put it inside a book. A hardback book would be best, and of course one that Mam would never pick up, even out of idle curiosity. He spotted the green spine of James Joyce's *Portrait of the Artist as a Young Man*. Mark was rather taken with the character of the boy Stephen Dedalus. Mark wished he were real and could meet him. He had talked about the book to Mam and he could see she was trying to seem interested but that she wasn't really. There was always the chance though that she might just decide to pick it up if she was cleaning the room or changing his bedding and saw the book and remembered. Then he saw the perfect book, *Europe in the XIX Century* by D.G.O. Ayerst, a school history book. She would never pick that up, probably wouldn't understand the *XIX* meaning even. Opening the book at random he landed on a page entitled *Middle-Class Monarchy*. That's a bit weird, Mark thought. Surely royalty weren't middle class but posher than that? He started to read and found it was about King Louis Philippe of France from 1830 to 1848. Never mind. He put the slim bank book inside the history book and put it back on the shelf.

He then set about taking off his school clothes. Standing in his underpants and knowing he was alone in the flat, he gave way to the natural impulse so slipping those off he lay on his bed and sought the release of a wank before getting dressed in casual clothes. He gathered the tissue he had used and going to the bathroom, flushed away the evidence of his surreptitious pleasure and then washed his hands. From there to the kitchen. He just fancied a bowl of corn flakes. There was only just enough milk left. He put the used bowl on the draining board as he heard the front door.

"Mark! You home, love?"

"In the kitchen, Mam," he called back.

Mark sensed she was taking off her coat and changing her shoes.

"Put the kettle on, Mark. I could murder a cup of tea," she called from the small hallway.

Mark filled the kettle and switched it on. "There's no milk left," he said as Mam came in.

"Yes there is," she said, and then Mark could see she had spotted the used cereal bowl. "Have you had all the milk? How am I supposed to have a cuppa, you stupid idiot?"

"Sorry, Mam," said Mark. "I didn't think. I'll go and get some."

"Yes, and you can fucking pay for it."

"It's fine, Mam. I've got enough," said Mark. And then, "How much is a pint of milk?"

"Eightpence usually. If you didn't know, how'd you know you had enough, then?"

"I guessed. I'll take a shilling in case it's a couple of pence more."

"So while you're there, little rich boy, get a sliced loaf."

"I'll take two bob then," said Mark.

56

Mam was right, the pint cost eight pence. The bread was just over a shilling so Mark returned with the loaf, the milk and thrupence halfpenny change. He made the tea for himself and Mam. He went to get his blazer and brought it into the lounge.

"Look, Mam. I was given this special badge today."

"That looks posh," said Mam. "I bet it's not real gold though."

"Mam, that's not the point," said Mark. "I had to go up on the stage in front of the whole school with the head and make a speech about it."

"About what?" asked Mam.

"Mam! About the fire, of course. It's called laudatum."

"What is? The fire?"

"No, Mam. The badge. It's a Latin word about getting praise for something."

"The Romans spoke Latin," said Mam with a knowledgeable air.

"Yes, Mam. I know," said Mark. "Well, what d'you think?"

"It's very nice, love. Well done. You deserve it. Come here and let me give you a hug."

Mark let Mam hug him. He was already aware that in terms of education and probably intelligence he was already well ahead of Mam, but he knew that she was proud of him and loved him, however irritating she could be at times. He just hoped that his sideline work wouldn't be discovered.

There was a tin of baked beans in the cupboard so Mark made baked beans on toast for them both.

"You're a good lad, Mark," said Mam, looking at him across the table. Mark could see the love in her eyes which he liked but at the same time made him a little uncomfortable. He wasn't sure why, maybe he felt a little embarrassed. At least here it was just the two of them, not like when she was doting over him when others were around.

. . .

At school the next day he felt somewhat self conscious wearing his laudatum badge but he did feel proud of it and some others wanted a closer look at it but the interest soon wore off and school life settled down again. He was aware though that the whole school now defined him as the fire hero. Mark thought that was a whole lot better than homo or queer.

At home, he wondered a bit about Tommy, the butcher's boy. Maybe he was a homo, or maybe someone had daubed the wall simply to insult Tommy. That set Mark an extra problem; not just how to meet Tommy but then how to find out if the daubing were true or just a provocative insult. In his mind he built up a picture of Tommy, a strong, well built boy in contrast to his own slim body, as tall as himself, maybe even a little taller and of course ready to take on the more dominant role. A blend of imagination and the real life Tony he had left behind. He wondered whether Tony had found someone else and was happily fucking him.

He thought about going to The Vault, hoping for Pip or at least Gordon, but every teacher seemed to think they were the only one giving out homework so by the time he had finished it, all he wanted to do was watch some television and go to bed to read for a while before going to sleep. He liked a new show, *The Avengers*, which made a welcome change from westerns. Mam had got hooked on *Coronation Street*; Mark liked *Hancock* but Mam wasn't so keen, it wasn't her kind of humour.

Later in bed, he picked up his latest book, a hefty book of all the Sherlock Holmes short stories. He liked the way the stories were set up and the idea of using pure intelligence, attention to the smallest detail and logic to solve the cases. He decided that for the time being at least he liked either *The Speckled Band* or the *Red Headed League* best. Some of his friends at school said they listened to pop music in the evening from Radio Luxembourg, crackly and variable as it was. Luxembourg was now almost five hundred miles away. Mark decided that one thing he would buy with his money was a portable radio he could use in his bedroom.

This of course would create the problem of explaining to Mam that amount of money. He couldn't pretend it was on the 'never-never' because of his age. He thought he should be able to buy a decent one for about fifteen pounds.

By the Friday he felt ready to try The Vault again.

# Chapter 12 Discharge

Mark cautiously put his head round the door of the bar. He saw Fred and Gerry, but no sign of Pip, Tom or Gordy. He hesitated, wondering whether to go in or not, disappointed that Pip wasn't there. But he was seen.

"Don't be shy, Mark," called Gerry. "Come and sit down."

So Mark went in and sat down next to Gerry, who promptly ordered a coke for Mark.

"What's it like being famous, then?" asked Gerry.

"It's wearing off a bit," said Mark, toying with a beer mat that was an advertisement for Bilthaven brewery. "It's made me more friends at school and the neighbours all say hello now they know who I am."

"I wouldn't have thought you'd be short of friends, a nice lad like you," said Fred.

"It's just I live quite a distance from the school so I don't see anybody outside school. And what with schoolwork, I don't see any kids locally. And anyway, I seem to spend my free time here."

"I'm very glad you do," said Gerry, "do you want to go upstairs?"

"Actually, Gerry," interposed Fred, "I had a lucky break on the dogs on Wednesday and I thought I'd treat myself next time I saw Mark here."

They both looked at Mark. He knew what Gerry was like, but Fred, older and evidently not as well-off, was unknown. But Fred's eyes looked so pleading that Mark nodded. Also it would be an extra five pounds. He wanted sex and he also wanted to accumulate as much money as he could while this lasted. He pocketed Fred's five one pound notes.

In the upstairs brown room, Fred looked around, standing in the doorway. It occurred to Mark that Fred had not been in here before.

"Haven't you been in here before?" he asked.

Fred shook his head.

"Well, lock the door then," said Mark. He threw his coat over the chair and went over to the drawer and took out one of the folded sheets. Fred turned the key and watched as Mark spread out the sheet on the mattress.

Mark turned back to face Fred. "So, what do you want me to do?"

Fred seemed hesitant. "Undress," he said, in a questioning tone.

So Mark slowly undressed, taking off his trousers and socks, and then his shirt and jumper, while Fred watched. Mark could sense the tension in him rising and Fred starting rubbing his groin. Mark stood up, clad now in just underpants. He was notably taller than Fred.

"Aren't you going to take those off?" asked Fred.

"I thought you might enjoy doing that," suggested Mark.

Fred nodded, took the few steps to Mark and gently pulled down his pants allowing his stiff cock to spring free. Fred knelt down and wrapped his mouth around it.

As Mark felt his arousal getting more, he pushed Fred's head back. "Not yet, you haven't even got undressed yet."

Mark sat on the bed as Fred quickly undressed. He soon saw that Fred was quite fat with a beer belly. His body was very hairy. His cock was quite small, even hard as it was now. Mark felt no attraction as he had with the other, younger men. But he had taken Fred's money. He also felt some sympathy for Fred because it seemed to Mark that Fred's sexual pleasure came from being around other queer men and deriving vicarious enjoyment from their exploits in the upstairs room.

Mark took the jar out of the drawer and lubricated himself, wiping his fingers on a tissue. "How do you want to do it?" he asked, lying on the bed.

Fred became suddenly assertive. "Get off the bed, boy," he said. "Kneel down next to it and bend over the bed." Despite Fred's relative physical unattractiveness, Mark experienced a thrill of excitement at this sudden dominance.

Obediently he did as he was asked, lying with his hips at the edge of the bed and his chin on the clean sheet. A sharp slap on his bum, and then another.

"I like to fuck a nice red arse," explained Fred as he hit Mark repeatedly.

Eventually Mark had to say, "It's really hurting now, it must be red enough."

The spanking stopped and Mark felt Fred's hands round his hips lifting him slightly and his knees forcing Mark's thighs further apart. Then the entry. Fred's hands pressed down on Mark's back. Fred was grunting as he thrust. Mark just wanted him to come and finish so he squeezed and reacted to heighten Fred's pleasure. That did not please Fred.

"Just lie still and take it, boy," Fred said, almost snarling. Mark did as he was told, now feeling nervous about Fred's intentions. This was a different man from the chap who sat sipping his beer. Jekyll and Hyde. At last Fred reached his climax and immediately withdrew. He patted Mark on the back. Mark looked round and stood up, running his hands over his sore buttocks. He wiped himself with tissues and Fred followed his lead.

As they dressed, Fred spoke. "Thank you, Mark. That was the best I've had for years."

"Well, you certainly seem different up here than you do downstairs."

"I'm sorry. I hope I didn't hurt you too much. It'll wear off soon."

Back downstairs, Mark sat on the leather couch rather than a wooden chair round the table.

Pip had now arrived and greeted Mark warmly. "Been giving Fred a treat, have you?"

"He said he'd won some money at the dog track so he had the five pounds," said Mark.

"Worth every penny," said Fred. "He was a very good boy for me."

"I've got a sore arse now, he must have slapped me about thirty times. He said he likes it red."

Gerry intervened. "I trust that's not spoiled it for me, Fred. Remember it was only because I let you go first."

"I'm not sure I want more tonight," said Mark.

"It's up to you, Mark, but I did ask you first," said Gerry.

Mark thought of Gerry, more attractive to Mark and not likely to beat him; and it was another fiver. Also he was still feeling horny again because he had not come with Fred. "Very well, then."

Gerry was gentle with Mark, commented on the redness ("That'll be gone by morning.") and Mark was able to relax more and enjoy it.

On the bus home, Mark decided he wouldn't have Fred again but thought of the ten pounds in his pocket.

Mam greeted him. "Are you OK, son? Where've you been?"

"Just into town, mooching around as usual."

"I don't know what you see in that, just walking round. You must know the town off by heart now. Put the kettle on, we'll have a cuppa."

. . .

On Saturday morning Mark went round early to the chippy. Frank was happy to see him. Upstairs the room was freshly painted - an unpleasant shade of green - and despite the smell of fresh paint, there was the lingering smell of burning.

"Does the machine still work?" asked Mark, looking at the peeling machine.

"Sorry lad," said Frank, "I'm afraid each tatey will have to be peeled by hand." He handed Mark a potato peeler.

"You can't expect me to peel all those with this," said Mark, aghast and waving the peeler at Frank. "And then take the eyes out and chip them. I'll be here all weekend!"

"Take the eyes out when you peel, so that'll save some time, and they've all got to be done by 4 o'clock."

Mark's face fell. He considered quitting there and then but what would he say to Mam about his money. It was hard enough as it was because if she thought about it, his one pound didn't even cover what she knew he spent. Just as he was about to speak, Frank roared with laughter.

"You should see your face, you daft lad. Of course I don't expect you to do that." Frank walked to the wall where the new power socket was and switched it down. The peeler hummed into life, quiet because it was empty. Mark let out a sigh of relief. "You had me going there," he said. "Literally - I was about to quit."

"Can't do that," said Frank. "Heroes don't quit."

"I'd better get on then," said Mark, starting to fill the first bath with water.

Mark was soon back into the routine and slowly the baths filled with chipped potatoes. It was late morning when Mark heard voices downstairs and then Frank calling him down. Mark went down into the shop. One of the shutters was up and Terry Perkins was there with a photographer. 'Oh no,' thought Mark. 'What now?'

"The young hero is back at work," smiled Terry.

"It's my Saturday job," answered Mark, sullenly.

"Now, Mark," chided Frank. "It's all good publicity for the shop, so be a good lad and go along with it."

Mark forced a smile. The photographer took a picture of Mark and Frank in the shop.

"Could we see where the fire was?" asked Terry of Frank.

"Of course, this way."

On the half landing, Terry noticed the fuse box. "Is that where you turned off the power, Mark?"

Mark nodded. "I stood on the chair."

So Mark had re-enact the switching off of the electricity, posing for the photographer with his hand on the switch but implausibly looking at the camera. Up a few more steps into the room where Mark was working. The peeler was still rumbling away. Mark went over to check it.

"They're ready," he said.

"Show us what you do," said Terry.

So Mark emptied the drum into the bowl, and took more potatoes from the sack, loaded the machine and switched it back on.

"Is that where the fire started?" asked Terry. So Mark had to pose, pointing to the now replaced switch and doing his best to smile at the camera.

Then he inspected the potatoes in the bowl for 'eyes' and, because Frank was watching, was more conscientious than normal removing them. He then chipped the potatoes and put them in the bath. By this time the potatoes in the peeler were ready so Mark started to repeat the process.

"I can see you're a hard worker; it's non-stop," said Terry.

"Pretty much," said Mark.

Terry then asked Mark about what had happened since the fire. Mark described his school-friends' reaction and his award of Laudatum. Terry asked Mark to spell that. That made Mark smile to himself.

"When will this be in the paper," asked Frank, thinking about his business.

"Too late for today, so probably Monday," said Terry. He and the photographer then left. Mark returned to routine. Perhaps because of the time, almost an hour, taken out of the day by the press, he was later than usual finishing and the shop had opened for business at 4 o'clock. Mark was given his pound and to avoid the customers who would no doubt delay him further, he slipped out of the back gate into the darkening back lane. A boy was coming out of the butcher's premises next door, wheeling a bicycle.

"Are you the one who put the fire out?" he asked.

"Yes," said Mark, looking at him, about his own age, not as tall and thin build, wearing spectacles.

"I thought so," said the boy. "You look like the picture in the paper."

"Well, that's not a surprise because it is me," said Mark, with a smile. At that the boy laughed, leaning his bike against the wall. "Are you Tommy?" asked Mark.

"Yes," said Tommy. "How did you know?"

"I had to clean some words off the wall about you, and you came out of the butcher's door."

Even in the dimming dusk, Mark could see Tommy's discomfort. "Don't worry, Tommy. I don't think it'd been there long because it came off without too much scrubbing," lied Mark to comfort Tommy.

"I hate them," said Tommy bitterly. "That lot, they're always going on about it."

"So are you a homo?" asked Mark, wondering if this was going to lead anywhere. Tommy didn't reply but looked at Mark. He then started to turn away back to his bicycle. Mark quickly thought; 'Tommy isn't at my school so there's no risk there and people here think he's queer anyway,' so he added, "If it helps, I am."

Tommy turned back. "You are what? A queer?"

Mark was now committed. Maybe he should have said nothing but now he carried on. "Yes. Before we moved here I had a boyfriend. But I don't normally tell people, obviously, otherwise my name would be all over walls, and not for putting out fires."

At that Tommy smiled and came closer to Mark. "Where do you live? Near here?"

"Calvert House, top floor. Come round sometime."

"What about your Mam and Dad?"

"It's just me and my Mam. And why shouldn't I have a friend round?"

"So are we friends now?" asked Tommy.

"Yes, if you want," said Mark.

"I want," said Tommy, and leaning up, kissed Mark on the cheek. Mark was surprised, but he felt himself becoming aroused.

But Tommy was walking away back to his bicycle. "See you, then," said Tommy. Mark could detect the happiness in Tommy's voice. "And thanks for cleaning that shite off the wall," he called as he cycled away down the back lane.

That evening and night, Mark's thoughts were all of Tommy. He imagined being naked with Tommy. Would that ever happen?

Sunday had to be spent on homework. He had a lot to catch up with so it took most of the day. He put Friday's earnings and his pound note from the chippy in the post office book hidden in the history book. He would bank most of that on Monday after school.

When he went to the bathroom before going to bed he noticed a thick, yellow liquid oozing from his cock. He had to pee but it hurt.

"Oh fuck," he said to himself. "VD I guess. What the fuck can I do about that?"

# Chapter 13 Disclosure

When Mark woke up on Monday morning his pyjama trousers were more stained. He also found pain in his balls. Mark stood in his bedroom, indecisive. His brain was frozen with the fear and uncertainty of his situation. But he had to go to school. He had to appear normal for Mam. In the bathroom he gritted his teeth as he peed. He tried to rinse his pyjama bottoms in the washbasin so that Mam would not question the staining. Mark was starting to panic and then it occurred to him he would have to put the wet bottoms on to get back to his bedroom in case Mam, whom he could hear in the kitchen, chose that moment to come into the hallway.

As he left the bathroom Mam stepped out of the kitchen. "Hurry up, Mark. You'll miss your bus at this rate."

Unthinking, Mark turned to face her. "I'm all right. Mam, I'll be ready soon."

"Mark! Have you pissed yourself? Have you wet the fucking bed?"

Mark flushed, realizing his mistake in turning round to speak. "No, Mam," he said, thinking quickly. "I splashed myself by accident when I was washing in the bathroom."

"Well hurry up, then. I've got a job to go to."

Relieved at having crossed that hurdle, Mark went into his bedroom, hung his pyjama bottoms over the back of his chair and got dressed. Mark found his toast hard to eat, he simply did not feel hungry.

He got up and picked up his bag and coat. "Bye, Mam," he said.

"Are you not going to give your Mam a hug? You're in a funny mood this morning, Mark, I must say."

Mark gave Mam a perfunctory hug. As he walked to the bus stop the discomfort in his cock and balls seemed to get worse. 'What the fuck am I going to do?' he thought. He felt himself close to tears. That would never do.

When he arrived at school, he tried to act as normally as possible, but he could not concentrate on his lessons.

"Bist du heute nicht bei uns, Martin?"

Mark was suddenly alert at hearing his name. His German teacher, Mr Hartmann, was looking at him.

"Sorry, I mean Tut mir leid, mir geht es nicht sehr gut."

"What's the matter, Martin? Are you ill?" asked Mr Hartmann, reverting to English.

"No, sir. I'll be all right." He tried to put the nagging ache in his groin to one side.

At lunchtime, Steve enquired, "What's the matter, Mark? You told Hartmann you weren't well, if I got the translation right."

"Just got a bad belly ache," offered Mark. Obviously unable to explain the real problem. But he was grateful for Steve's concern.

On the bus home. Mark tried hard to quell the mounting sense of panic. Was this God's vengeance and punishment for his sins? Mark didn't really believe in God; but then he could not really discount Him either. For him Sunday morning was for lying in, not kneeling down. He wondered which one had given him this VD. Then it occurred to him that the only people he could turn to for advice was the group in The Vault. But it was just Monday. Still, he would go to The Vault later and hope Gordon or Pip would be there.

He picked at his tea, not feeling hungry.

"What's the matter? Not hungry tonight?" demanded Mam as she chewed her beef sausage. Cheaper than pork.

"I'm OK!" snapped Mark.

"I don't know what's the matter with you lately. Moody and bad tempered. And you're only just a teenager. How many more fucking years like this have I got to put up with?"

Mark felt bad. This was not Mam's fault, after all. If anyone was to blame, it was him, for being greedy for the money and getting fucked. "I'm sorry, Mam. I'll be all right," he replied, but without much conviction.

Mam noticed this. "I know you, Mark. Something's up. Some girl is it?"

69

"Sort of," said Mark, thinking this was a good legitimate reason for his current lethargy but tinged with guilt at the deception.

"Never mind, son," said Mam, reaching out and taking hold of Mark's hand. Her eyes looked lovingly into his. Mark felt so guilty! "Plenty more fish in the sea," she concluded.

Later, Mark was on the bus heading for the city centre. He went into the bar. He saw Gerry in conversation with Tom, who was looking through the evening paper, but no Pip or Gordon. He went over and sat down.

"Oh, hello, Mark," said Tom.

Mark was smiling and laughing to himself.

"What are you so happy about?"

"When I came in I wondered who would be here, and I find Tom and Gerry. Tom and Gerry, get it?"

"Very clever," said Tom. "How would you like to chase me around a bit?"

"I need to see Pip or Gordon."

"We not good enough for you any more?" said Gerry. "You seemed to like it last time."

"Yes," said Mark. "I just want to talk to them about something. It's sort of private."

"Secrets now, have we?" said Tom.

"Leave the lad alone, Tom," said Gerry. "If he wants to talk about whatever it is, he'll tell us when he's ready."

"I suppose so," said Tom, looking at Mark with curiosity.

There was a moment's silence and then, emboldened, Mark went to the bar and ordered himself a coke. Even then there was an awkward pause. Mark's 'secret' hung in the air. The door opened and Mark looked round, hopeful, but to his dismay, it was Fred. It must have shown on his face because Fred spoke to Mark, "Well, don't look so pleased to see me!"

"Sorry," said Mark. "Got things on my mind."

"Well, I'm broke again now, so don't worry on my behalf."

Gerry spoke. "Don't pester Mark, Fred. The lad's upset about something, but he'll only talk to Gordy or Pip."

"So what will he do if they don't turn up?" challenged Fred, returning from the bar with a pint.

Mark shrugged. "Don't know," he said. The anxiety started to well up in him.

Gerry noticed as Mark seemed on the verge of tears. "What is it, Mark?" he said gently.

At that moment, Tom interrupted. "Bloody hell, he's in the paper again! Pictures and all. 'Saturday Hero returns to the Fray'," he read out.

"Oh no," said Mark. "Not again."

Tom handed the paper over to Mark. At least this time it was on the inside, not the front, but there he was with Frank, also pointing with a forced grin at the power switch. "That's stupid," said Mark. "That's the new power socket, not the one that caught fire."

At that moment, Pip came in, brandishing the newspaper and then slightly put out because his thunder had been stolen. Mark felt a sense of relief because Pip had arrived but tempered with some annoyance because the conversation was going to be about the paper article. The next few minutes were spent pouring over the article and Mark had to recount how Terry Perkins had just turned up at the shop on Saturday.

Eventually, Pip turned to Mark with a question. "So, Mark, apart from being famous all over again, what brings you down here tonight, what with Monday being a school night?"

"That's never stopped him before," said Tom. "I'm thinking he wants more money."

"No," said Mark. "Not tonight." That raised an eyebrow or two.

"It must be the scintillating conversation he enjoys here then," quipped Gerry.

Mark ignored that, and turned to Pip. "I need to speak to you," he said quietly. Now he was here and talking to Pip his anxiety resurfaced, and he felt his eyes water, try as he might to prevent that, but Pip noticed.

"What's the matter, Mark," he answered quietly.

"Not here," said Mark. "Somewhere private. That room maybe? But not for sex."

Pip pursed his lips and went to the bar. He returned without the key. "Can't go up there, someone already has the key, but we can go through to the back."

Mark followed Pip through the door, vaguely wondering who was having sex in the brown room, but instead of going up to the third floor, they went into a small stockroom off the passage marked 'Staff Only'. Pip closed the door. "Nobody can hear us here, Mark. So what is it you want to talk about? Is it Fred?"

"Fred? No, not him," said Mark, wondering why Pip would ask that, but maybe he knew of Fred's sadistic tendencies. "It's me. I think I've got VD and I don't know what to do. I've not told anybody else until now." With that release, he started to sob. "Pip, I'm frightened and I didn't know who else to turn to. I could only think of you or maybe Gordon."

Pip reached out and hugged Mark. "Don't worry, Mark. We'll get you sorted. You've done the right thing to tell me. What are the symptoms?"

"I've like this yellow stuff coming out of my cock, my balls hurt and when I go to the toilet it hurts."

"Sounds like the clap to me. Otherwise known as gonorrhoea. Do you want to show me?"

"In here?" asked Mark. "Someone might come in."

Pip pushed a chair under the door handle. Mark lowered his trousers and pants. He felt oddly shy about that but then reasoned that Pip had seen him totally naked before.

Pip peered closely for a moment and nodded. "Yes Mark, it's gonorrhoea. Luckily these days it can be easily fixed. I'm guessing you've not told your mother."

72

As Mark did his trousers and belt up, he said, "No. I've not told her about me coming here and meeting you and the others."

Pip nodded. "The next question is who you got it from. Almost certainly in the last week or two. Apart from our little group, have you had sex with anybody else?"

Mark shook his head. "No, just you lot, here."

Pip moved the chair from the door. "There's two ways of fixing this. You can go to your doctor and say you went with a girl. The doctor shouldn't say anything to your mother about it but you are under age."

"I've not been to the doctor since we moved here. I don't even know if we have a doctor. Mam probably wouldn't think of that until she had to."

"Maybe she has to now. But the other option is the pox clinic. That's supposed to be totally confidential but with your age, they might still ask questions. They will want to know how you got it so they can get treatment for that person as well."

"Would they tell my Mam?"

"Not if you give a false name, Mark."

"But I'm all over the fucking paper again," said Mark desperately, the tears flowing again. "They'll recognize me."

"You shouldn't be such a hero," smiled Pip in an attempt to cheer Mark up a bit. It didn't work. "Right, Mark. Dry your eyes. I'm not going to abandon you. We'll think of something. We need to get back to the others. It means telling them, I'm afraid, but they'll not spread it around. The news I mean, not the clap. One of them has done that already. Not me, by the way."

Mark followed Pip back to the group. Gordon was there now, along with Fred.

Mark sat down, next to Pip.

"What's going on?" asked Gordon, with concern in voice and looking from Pip to Mark.

"Our young friend here has the clap," Pip said quietly. "He says he's not been with anybody apart from here. I know

73

it's not me so which one of you has the clap and not said anything?"

# Chapter 14 Confession

There was a long pause as the group looked at each other.

"I think it might be me," said Fred eventually.

"You've got the clap and still did this kid?" demanded Gordon, angrily.

"Well I wasn't sure but I am more certain now. I'm sorry, Mark. I didn't mean it."

"If you had any doubts you shouldn't have gone near him," said Pip. "Why do you think we have our rule about a closed circle? Do you know where you picked it up?"

"There was this chap down the docks, just a quickie in a cottage," admitted Fred, now looking very shamefaced and nervous.

"A cottage by the docks?" queried Mark, visualizing a quaint little thatched roof house with roses round the door.

"Slang word for a public toilet. Men sometimes meet each other there for a quick bit of sex," explained Pip. Mark screwed up his face in an expression of disgust. Most public toilets looked bad and smelled worse in his experience.

"Probably the same one where I first met Peter," commented Tom.

"Let's not go into that now," said Pip. "Fred can look after himself, but we've got to get Mark sorted out. I don't need to spell out the consequences if this gets out; for all of us as well, I mean."

There were nods of agreement around the table.

"And in future nobody goes outside the closed circle," said Gordon, glaring at Fred.

"He should go to his doctor and say he was shagging some lass," suggested Tom.

"He doesn't have a doctor yet," said Pip. "Mark, maybe you should get your Mam to register you with a local doctor."

Mark shook his head. "I can't ask her that. She'll want to know why, and she'd probably come with me as well. And if I say it's a lass, they'll ask her name and Mam won't stop until I bring her to meet her."

"He'll have to go to the pox clinic then," said Gerry.

"I don't know where that is," said Mark, anxiously.

"I'll take you, Mark," said Pip. Mark thought that Pip was his favourite among the group and this strengthened that feeling.

"Thank you," said Mark, recognizing that was his only option but still fearful.

"I can't go in with you, Mark. That would lead to too many questions. You have to understand that."

Mark nodded. "When? I'm at school all the time so it will have to be next Saturday."

"No, Mark," said Pip. "The sooner the better. Get your jacket."

"Now?" said Mark, surprised.

"Yes, The quicker you're fixed up the better all round, and then your Mam need never know."

Pip and Mark stood and put on their coats. Pip turned and addressed Fred. "I'll talk to you later. And you should go to the clinic as well, but not now, not while Mark is there."

Fred nodded in meek acquiescence.

"I'm scared," said Mark, as they walked along to the taxi rank.

"You'll be fine," reassured Pip. "You're a clever lad and you'll cope. What name will you give?"

Mark thought for a moment. "Tony Jarvis. I'll remember that."

"Was that the boyfriend's name?" asked Pip.

Mark nodded. "What if they ask for other things like where I live, my doctor and stuff?"

"Just say you don't want to tell them. Also, I think you should say you're sixteen. At your height you could pass for that and if it was some girl you caught it with, that would save a lot of trouble."

Mark tried to take all this in. Outside the clinic door at the General Hospital, Mark stopped. "What will you do?"

"I'll wait for you, Mark. Probably in there," Pip replied, indicating a café across the road. "Don't worry, and good luck."

Mark went in. There was a mix of men and women sitting waiting, but there was a reception. Bracing himself and rehearsing what he would say, he approached the reception window. A woman he guessed was about Mam's age with a bright floral dress on that Mark thought a bit incongruous, looked up at him. "Yes, son?"

"I need to see a doctor," said Mark.

"Do you have an appointment?"

"Oh. No. I thought... I mean... No, I haven't."

"You'll have to wait then. What's your name?"

"Tony Jarvis," said Mark.

"Date of birth?"

Mark was nearly caught out but just remembered to subtract two years from his birth year so that he would be sixteen.

"Address?" asked floral dress.

"I'm not saying," said Mark. "I don't have to, do I? I was told it could be confidential and that."

Floral dress paused. She looked at Mark and frowned. Had she recognized him? "It helps us keep accurate records but as you're sixteen, you have that right," she ended disapprovingly. "Take a seat."

With relief, Mark sat down. There were some magazines lying around. Fucking *People's Friend* again! That reminded Mark of Mam and then the guilt started up again. Progress seemed painfully slow. Names were called out, people left. More came in. Mark sat, fidgeting, looking at the time. Would Pip wait this long? Over two hours passed. Mark thought about leaving, but the ache in his groin deterred.

"Anthony?" called a voice.

Another name. When would it be his turn?

"Anthony?" called the voice again. "Anthony Jarvis?"

Mark started. That was him! "I'm Tony Jarvis," he responded. "Sorry, I don't usually get Anthony."

The voice belonged to a young female nurse. "No worry," she said. "Follow me, Tony," she smiled.

Mark followed her into a corridor. Her manner reassured him but he had not expected a female nurse. This was going to be embarrassing.

She opened a door into what was evidently a consulting room. "The doctor will be here in a moment, Tony," she said. "Sit down." Mark sat down.

A young man with a stethoscope round his neck came in. A doctor. Mark wondered if all doctors had to wear a stethoscope to prove they were doctors.

The doctor sat opposite Mark and smiled. "What's the problem, young man?"

Mark launched into his prepared scenario. "Last week we were all at a party at a friend's house and I met this girl there. Maybe I drank a bit but we went upstairs and we did it together. Now I have got the clap."

"When you say you did it together, was that sexual intercourse? Your penis was inside her vagina?"

Mark was taken aback by the directness of this language. "Er, yes," he said.

"Did you ejaculate?"

Mark frowned. This detail he had not prepared for. He decided his heterosexual persona would be reinforced if he said yes. "Yes, doctor, of course."

"Were you using a sheath?"

"You mean like a Durex?" asked Mark, giving himself time to think. The doctor nodded. "No," said Mark. "And now I've this yellow stuff coming out and it hurts going to the toilet."

"Very well, Tony," said the doctor. "Lie on the couch and lower your trousers and pants."

Mark did as he was asked. It felt strange with this young man, who otherwise Mark might have rather fancied, inspecting his body but in a totally non-sexual way. He had been thinking he might get a hard-on but such was the detached way the doctor examined him that he felt no risk of that.

78

"I'm going to put a cotton bud just inside your penis. It will be uncomfortable, but won't hurt and will be quick." Mark braced himself but it was as the doctor said. The doctor felt round Mark's scrotum.

"Well, Tony," said the doctor. "We will send the sample to the lab for tests but I have no doubt you have contracted gonorrhoea, or the clap as you call it. We can give you an injection and it should clear up in a few days."

"When's that?" asked Mark.

"The antibiotic injection? I'll do that now," replied the doctor. "Lie on your side and draw your knees up."

Mark did as he was told, turning toward the doctor.

"No, Tony, facing away from me. The injection goes into your backside, your buttock. Any preference for right or left?"

Mark had expected an injection in his arm like the many inoculations he had had at school. Somewhat shaken by this development, he turned the other way. "Either side will do, I think," he replied.

Mark felt a cool rub on his skin and then the needle. He gritted his teeth but it didn't last long.

"Very well, Tony, get dressed and come and sit down."

Mark returned to the same chair and waited while the doctor made some notes in a file. The injection site was sore. He saw the name Anthony Jarvis at the top. Who had decided he was Anthony? He might have actually been named Tony. He had never heard his Tony being called Anthony. Mark watched the doctor writing while wondering what Tony would think of him being here. He missed Tony still.

"I need to take some blood," said the doctor. "Can you roll your sleeve up please?"

Mark did and winced as the needle went in. "What's that for?"

"We'll test for other infections, just in case. Press hard for a few moments," said the doctor, putting a small piece of cotton wool over the needle puncture in Mark's arm. "Can you tell me the name of the girl?"

"What for?" asked Mark, shocked.

"If you are certain that this encounter was the reason for your infection, we need to contact her to tell her to come in for treatment. Quite apart from the possibility of pregnancy. Are you certain or have there been others recently?"

Mark was confused by this. He wanted to secure his reputation as a heterosexual male by saying there were lots of girls but in the end he said, "No, just her. She was the first."

"Bad luck, young man. You need to be more careful in future and use a Durex. That would have prevented this. Do you know her name?"

"Jackie," said Mark. It was the name of girl in his class and it just came into his head.

"Do you know her surname?"

Mark shook his head.

"Please try to contact her and tell her she needs to come for treatment. It's in her own interest" he said.

"Thank you doctor."

The doctor then removed the cotton wool and put a small dressing on the site.

"Right, that's you done. And Tony, be more careful in future," advised the doctor. "Please come back in a week so we can check that your infection has cleared. It should only take about seventy-two hours. In the meantime, no sex."

"Yes, I'll come back. And I will take more care," said Mark fervently, thinking about Fred.

Breathing a sigh of relief, Mark left the clinic door. The lights in the café over the road were out. 'Pip has given up waiting,' thought Mark. 'I don't blame him.'

"That took a long time," came Pip's voice from the darkness. There he was, waiting in the cold and actually shivering.

"You waited!" Mark was happy to see Pip.

"I said I would, Mark. Mind you, I didn't think it would take that bloody long. What happened?"

Mark recounted what had happened in the clinic. "I got a prick in my arse."

Pip laughed. "I thought you liked that!"

"Not that kind, a needle," said Mark, crossly. "But it should be cured in a few days."

"There you are, I told you it'd get sorted. Now let's see if we can get you home. Your Mam will be worrying about you."

Mark's initial reaction was to think that she wouldn't care, especially as she always threatened to bolt the door, but then he thought again and knew she would worry. "I've got to come back here next week; will you come with me again?"

"Of course I will, Mark," replied Pip with a smile. "But I advise staying away from The Vault for the time being - until next Monday anyway."

They managed to get a taxi which instead of just going back to the city centre, Pip insisted on going to Calvert House. "See, the power of the press, I know where you live," said Pip with a smile.

"So does everybody else," mused Mark, wondering if the doctor had done so but just said nothing. Not that it mattered now anyway. Mark persuaded Pip to  drop him at the end of the road. Being seen getting out of a taxi at Calvert House would raise eyebrows.

He was glad that the door opened when he turned his key in the lock.

"Where've you been? What fucking time do you call this?" squawked Mam, clad in her dressing gown, was the loving welcome he got.

"Mam, I'm fine. Please don't go on. I'm tired and want to go to bed."

"Well. I wanted to ages ago. Don't think I'm getting up to get your breakfast in the morning. If you miss school, that'll be your fault." With that she went into her bedroom and closed the door with slam.

Mark sighed. In the bathroom he checked himself. The stuff was still there, but he reasoned it was silly to expect a result within an hour or so. He was glad that Pip had gone with him. At the back of his mind he wondered why, was there some hidden motive? He decided that Pip was just a kind person.

As he got into bed Mark felt overwhelmingly tired. He'd get his own breakfast in the morning.

In the end he didn't need to. Mam was there for him.

# Chapter 15 Recovery

"Why are you in the paper again?" asked Ethan at school the next morning.

"Again?" said Steve. "What's he done now, saved the world or something?"

"That reporter turned up at the chippy on Saturday and took photos," explained Mark. "I wish he hadn't."

"Why?" said Eddie. "It's good being famous, getting recognized everywhere you go."

"That's it," said Mark. "I'm sick of being recognized. I wanted it to stop."

"You're weird," said Steve. "Most people want to be famous."

"Well, I've had enough of it now," said Mark. Of course, he could not say why he was anxious to keep a low profile, but the continuing discharge and aches reminded him.

When he got home from school, one or two neighbours called out to him about his re-appearance in yesterday's paper. Mark just smiled and waved.

Mam greeted him with a broad grin. "My lad's in the paper again last night. Why didn't you say? Too modest, I don't think!"

"Mam, you were snappy with me because I was late back and then you slammed the door."

"Oh yes, never mind that now. Give your Mam a hug."

Mark dutifully hugged Mam. Then he went to the bathroom because he needed to pee. The disgusting yellow was still there and it still hurt to pee.

. . .

Over the next few days Mark wrestled with himself. The pain and the discharge slowly eased and by Thursday evening he seemed symptom free. But as his symptoms departed his urge for sex returned. He had not even felt like having a wank while the gonorrhoea was rampant, but now he felt the need again. Having a wank was a temporary release only. Mark felt guilty, yet drawn to The Vault, but he stayed away for the week.

. . .

He went as normal to the chippy on Saturday. Soon he was in his robotic routine of load, peel, drain, chip, bath. Load, peel, drain, chip, bath. Load, peel, drain, chip, bath. His thoughts meandered while he worked, and it helped pass the time. 'Do I still need to be doing this?" he thought. It was only one pound but he recognized that even so, that was good pay for a Saturday boy. Did he still need it when he could earn much more at The Vault? But then if he returned to The Vault, he needed the cover story to keep Mam from asking too many questions. And if he didn't go back to The Vault he would need the Saturday money even more.

His reverie was interrupted by a call from Frank downstairs. "Mark, come down here. Someone here to see you!"

It was three in the afternoon and he was almost finished. The shop was due to open at four.

"Who is it?" called Mark. He did not want anything more to do with Terry Perkins.

"A friend of yours!" was Frank's shouted reply.

Reluctantly Mark descended the stairs. He was surprised to see Tommy there, looking rather nervous. Mark felt relief it was not Perkins.

"Hello, Tommy," greeted Mark, with relief in his voice. "What brings you here?"

"I thought you might still be here so I thought I'd call in to say hello," said Tommy, uncertainly, glancing between Mark and Frank.

"I'm not quite finished," said Mark, "Maybe another quarter of an hour to finish off and clean up."

"He can go up with you to chat while you do that," offered Frank, waving toward the stairs with the knife he was holding which he used to gut the fish.

Mark nodded. "Come on then," he said to Tommy. He led the way back up to his room. The peeling machine was still rumbling away.

"What's that?" asked Tommy.

"It peels the tayties," explained Mark, stopping the machine and taking out the now peeled potatoes. "The next step is to dig the eyes out by hand and then chip them."

"I'll help you," said Tommy, picking up the hand tool and the first potato. While Mark reloaded the machine from the nearly empty last sack, Tommy dug out two pieces and then put the potato in the chipper. He pulled down the handle and the chips fell out underneath. Mark watched this, surprised at Tommy's apparent strength.

"You seem quite strong," said Mark. "It's usually quite stiff to do."

Tommy smiled at the compliment. "Maybe it's helping my dad in the shop," he replied. "A side of beef or half a pig can be quite heavy and chopping them - you have to be strong I suppose." Tommy smiled at Mark, their eyes met. Mark felt arousal coming; he was drawn to Tommy and the feeling seemed mutual as Mark remembered his kiss on the cheek. He put his face close to Tommy's, watching his face for any signs. But Tommy put his hands up round Mark's head and pulled him closer. Then Tommy was kissing Mark on the lips. Mark put his arms round Tommy as he let the kiss continue. Tommy's hand slid down Mark's back and squeezed his bum. They moved apart.

"I like you," said Tommy, simply.

"I like you, too," answered Mark, wondering where this might lead.

"I've never done that before," said Tommy. "Have you?"

"Was that your first time?" asked Mark. "It didn't seem like it. You knew what you were doing."

"Yes, never done anything with a boy before - or a girl for that matter," admitted Tommy. "What about you? You didn't seem to mind."

"I didn't mind. I liked it but I was surprised when you sort of took control. But I did have a boyfriend before we moved here." Mark thought he could safely talk about Tony but not the men.

85

"Lucky you," said Tommy. "I wish I had a boyfriend."

"Well, you have one now," said Mark.

Tommy's eyes widened. "Really? You'll be my boyfriend?"

Mark nodded. He wasn't sure how this would work out but he liked Tommy. He had thought on the first meeting in the dim back lane that Tommy was a bit shy and unsure but now in the light of the room he seemed different. Smaller than Mark - so were most boys his age - but that slim figure held a hidden strength and he was more assertive than Mark had expected and something in him responded to that.

"You mustn't tell anybody," said Tommy.

"I'm not stupid," said Mark. "Of course not."

The two boys together finished off the remaining potatoes and cleaned up while Mark explained where the fire had started and filled in some details for a curious Tommy.

Frank appeared to collect a pail of chips from one of the baths. "You two getting on OK?" he asked.

The boys both nodded as Frank went back down to the shop.

They went downstairs to find the shop already open with fish and chips hissing away in the fryers with that unmistakable smell of a fish and chip shop. There were a few customers waiting. Mark was instantly recognized.

"Well, here's the young hero," said one woman.

"He's taller than he looks in the paper," commented another.

"He lives in my block," said another woman, whose face was vaguely familiar to Mark. "Are you and Tommy pals now then?"

"Yes," said Tommy, firmly, while Mark just nodded, uncertain about Tommy's assertiveness.

Before anything else could be said, Frank opened the till and then went out to the back room, beckoning the boys. He quickly handed Mark a one pound note so that Tommy wouldn't see. "Didn't want that lot seeing me pay you, Mark," he said.

86

"Thanks," said Mark, pocketing the note. Turning to Tommy, he said, "Come on," and led the way out through the small yard and into the back lane. They stopped, looking at each other.

"When can I see you again?" asked Tommy.

Mark thought. He wanted to see Tommy again. A thought occurred to him. "Can you come round mine tomorrow afternoon. Meet my Mam."

Tommy looked disappointed but said, "OK then, yes."

Mark smiled. "But she goes out about three o'clock to one of her office cleaning jobs. Get it ready for Monday morning. So after that it'll be just us in the flat for a few hours."

"Good," said Tommy. And then, "Oh, I didn't mean I didn't want to meet your Mam or didn't like her or anything. It's just I'm glad we'll be alone."

"That's OK. I know what you meant," said Mark.

"See ya tomorrow then," said Tommy.

"Yes. Top floor, Calvert House. There's four doors on the landing, five if you count the one up to the roof."

"Can you go on the roof?" asked Tommy.

"Yes. I do sometimes in the good weather. Take a book up and read."

"How will I know which is your door?"

"It's the green door."

"Have you got an old piano and play it hot?" joked Tommy.

It took Mark a moment and then he remembered the song. "No, but I think you're hot," he blurted out before he could stop himself.

Tommy laughed. "Maybe you'll find out tomorrow."

"See ya," said Mark, surprised at Tommy's growing confidence. They parted and Mark walked home to Calvert House.

# Chapter 16 Friendship

"Are you going out tonight and leaving your poor Mam all alone again?" asked Mam in mock distress.

"Not tonight, Mam," said Mark, "you'll have to put up with me this evening. I'll go to the chippy later and see if Frank can stand me a couple of fish lots."

"He should, seeing all the work you do there. Never mind saving his shop from burning down," said Mam.

"He gave me money for that, and he does pay a whole pound for work. By the way, I've asked a friend to come round tomorrow, if that's OK."

Mam's face took on a look of panic and she looked round the living room. "What? Here?"

"Yes," said Mark. "This is where I live, isn't it?"

"I'll have to clean up," said Mam in a panicked voice as she looked round the living room that appeared perfectly acceptable to Mark's eyes. "Who is it?"

"His name's Tommy," said Mark.

"From school is he?" asked Mam.

"No, he lives above the butcher's next to the chippy."

Mam seemed to relax a bit. "That lad from the butcher's. I think I've seen him. I thought it was going to be one of your posh friends from school."

Mark did not think that his school friends were especially posh, but neither did he think that Tommy should be so arbitrarily demoted. "I'll tidy up in the morning, He's not coming until the afternoon."

Later Mark went back to the chippy, returning with two fish and chips and mushy peas for Mam. He paid for them but allowed Mam to think Frank had given them on the house. They spent the evening eating, drinking tea and watching television.

Once in bed, Mark thought about Tommy coming round the next day and, once Mam had gone to work, what might happen.

. . .

Mark was restless on Sunday afternoon. Would Tommy come? Might he think better of it? Worried about being found out for really being a homo?

There was a knock at the door. Swiftly Mark got up to answer it. Through the spyhole he could see it was Tommy. He opened the door and there he was - this slight, smaller boy with brown hair and pale blue bespectacled eyes.

"Come in," said Mark, smiling, which was returned.

"So this is Tommy," welcomed Mam. "I recognize you now from Hedley's butcher's shop but of course I didn't know your name was Tommy until our Mark told me who you were. When Mark said he had a friend coming round I never thought it was you coz I thought it was one of his friends from school. But anyway, here you are. Take your coat off and have a seat."

"Thank you, Mrs Martin," said Tommy politely.

Mark took his coat. "I didn't remember me telling you my surname."

"It was in the paper," said Tommy simply.

"Oh yes," said Mark. "I keep forgetting."

Tommy sat on the sofa. Mark sat next to him. He felt a mounting excitement and relished the closeness to Tommy, another queer boy, sitting right next to him; like being next to Tony.

"I'm sorry. Tommy," said Mam, "but I have to go to work soon so Mark will have to look after you on his own."

"Mam," said Mark, "Tommy doesn't need looking after. He's not a baby!"

At that Tommy stuck his thumb in his mouth and pretended to cry. Mam looked nonplussed.

"Ok, Tommy," said Mark, "maybe you are." He gave Tommy a playful nudge in the side with his elbow.

"Well, if you're not here when I get back I'm sure we'll meet again. I'm glad Mark has found a friend here. His school is two buses away. If you want anything to eat, help yourselves. Not that there is much, like," Mam finished.

"It's fine, Mam," said Mark. "We'll be all right."

Mam put her coat on, took her bag and was gone.

89

The two boys sat on the sofa.

"Which school are you at then?" asked Tommy.

"Bilthaven Grammar School," explained Mark. "What about you?"

"Just the secondary modern at the top of the High Street. It's just a walk, no buses. So that's one thing. I guessed you were brainy from what was in the paper and that. And then when your Mam said it was two buses I sort of knew, really."

"You seem quite brainy to me," said Mark, for want of anything better to say. Tommy smiled.

There was a moment's awkward silence. Suddenly Tommy took hold of Mark and kissed him, pushing him back on the sofa. Mark liked this assertiveness and allowed Tommy to push him back. Tommy stopped, looking down at Mark. He smiled.

"Are you sure you've not done this before?" asked Mark.

"Never," said Tommy. "but I've thought about it a lot and I've wanted to for ages. And now I've met you. Like it was meant to be."

"What else have you imagined?" asked Mark.

"I've dreamt about being naked in bed with someone. Someone like you," said Tommy. He kissed Mark again, and felt Mark's hard cock through his trousers.

"Let's make dreams come true then," said Mark. "Want to go to my bedroom?"

Tommy stood up and took Mark's hand to pull him up. As they stood up, it didn't matter that Mark was taller than Tommy. To Mark at that moment, Tommy seemed tall. "Show me the way then," said Tommy, confidently.

They went into the hallway, Mark wondering where the virginal Tommy got his self assurance from.

Tommy looked round the bedroom. "Whose are all these books?"

"They're mine," said Mark, thinking this was obvious.

"Have you read all of them?"

"Yes," said Mark. "Well, some are reference books so you read the bits you want. Like you don't read a dictionary just from front to back, you look things up in it."

"I suppose so," said Tommy, looking along the book titles.

"Or like the phone book. The storyline is shit," joked Mark, trying to put Tommy at ease. He sensed that Tommy was a little less self assured when faced with the tangible evidence of Mark's academic level.

"We don't have a phone," said Tommy.

"We haven't either," said Mark, seeking to level things a bit. "It was just a joke."

"There's one for the shop, but I'm not allowed to use it," replied Tommy.

Tommy turned away from the books, and sat on Mark's bed. He bounced up and down slightly as though getting the feel of the mattress. "So this is your bed. It's wider than mine. Do you sleep naked?"

"I wear pyjamas," said Mark.

"I don't," said Tommy. "You should try sleeping with nothing on. It feels great."

"Maybe I'll try it sometime," said Mark.

"Try it now," said Tommy, a tone of authority returning to his voice.

"Now?" repeated Mark, rather surprised at Tommy's suggestion. He knew something would happen in his room with Tommy but he hadn't really thought exactly how things would progress. A kiss or two perhaps, maybe wanking. But Tommy was going for it all straight away. Mark wondered why he felt this uncertainty after his experiences in The Vault. This was different. Tommy was his own age, there was no money involved, this was a friendship. Or a kind of friendship anyway.

While Mark was thinking, Tommy had started to undress. Mark did likewise. Naked, the two boys looked at each other, both were getting erections. Mark wondered what to do next. He had started to feel so sure when with the

91

men but somehow this was different. It was more personal and so in a way, more important.

"You've got a nice body," said Tommy.

Mark looked at Tommy. He could see now that despite his slim figure, he looked quite strong, as had been evident at the chip shop. "So have you," he said. "Let's get on the bed."

They lay side by side on the bed, turned to face each other, then Tommy was kissing Mark with a real passion. Mark felt his tongue probing and he opened his mouth to allow this. He felt his cock being taken and gently wanked. With a further burst of passion, Tommy pushed Mark on to his back and was half on top of him, kissing his face, his neck, his shoulders.

"Are you sure you've never done this before?" asked Mark, breathlessly.

"Ever so sure," answered Tommy, "but I've thought about it and thought about what I would like to do. And now I am doing it. Is that OK?"

Mark simply nodded. As he felt Tommy taking control of him he felt that somehow this was right. Maybe not what the world would think but for him, it was right. He reached for Tommy's hard cock. Not too big but it was extremely hard.

"Do you want me to suck that?" he asked.

Tommy's eyes went wide, and he simply nodded, lying back off Mark. Moving down, Mark licked that hard cock with and then took it in his mouth, working it. Tommy spasmed and sighed.

Then he pushed Nark off. "Not that way," he said. "Can I go inside you?"

Mark simply nodded, mesmerized by the assertiveness of Tommy. "But we need some Vaseline or something."

Tommy frowned. "I suppose we do; I hadn't thought of that. Did your boyfriend go inside you?"

Mark nodded again. "I don't think we've got any."

"Turn over, Mark. I'll try anyway."

92

Despite his reservations, Mark lay on his front. He was aware of Tommy doing something and looking round he saw Tommy was using spittle on his cock. Then he pushed it against Mark who tried to relax. It hurt but Tommy pressed on slowly until he was in as far as he could go. Mark once more felt that sense of fulfilment he got when being fucked. Now he wanted Tommy to carry on. "It's good," he said.

Tommy started to move while Mark's arousal heightened. He felt Tommy come as the movement was easier and his cock rapidly softened. He felt Tommy withdraw.

"Are you OK?" asked Tommy, anxiously.

"Yes," replied Mark. "you were great, but we'll get some Vaseline next time."

"So there will be a next time, then?"

"Yes, if you want it," said Mark.

"I want it as often as possible. I'm glad you moved here."

Mark handed Tommy a box of tissues. "I'm glad I've met you, Tommy. I never expected this."

"Does this mean we're really boyfriends now?"

"I suppose it does. But the sex has to be secret, of course."

"Definitely," said Tommy, and lying next to Mark, kissed him and brought Mark off.

Mark felt totally under Tommy's spell. He felt enslaved almost, like he never had with Tony, and realized he liked that feeling.

# Chapter 17 Conflict

Mark decided he would buy himself the portable radio he had promised himself. Armed with money from his Post Office carefully concealed in his bag, he stopped on the way home from school in the city centre before he got the second bus. He emerged from Dixons with a Roberts R200 all transistor radio in bright red.

"I bought this cheap from a boy at school," he told Mam.

"Does it work? Switch it on and let's hear it," said Mam with enthusiasm. "It looks brand new."

"Yes," said Mark, thinking quickly. "He was given it as a birthday present but he already had one so he wanted to sell it. I gave him ten pounds because it's a good one. No valves now, all transistors."

The radio came on and they listened and twiddled the knobs on top to try different stations.

"That's a lot of Saturdays," said Mam, warily.

"Yes, but don't forget the extra Frank gave me after the fire."

"Of course," said Mam. "You deserve it, Mark."

Mark was happy the radio was explained to her satisfaction.

. . .

He told himself he would have to go back to The Vault on Monday so Pip could go with him for the follow up check. So that need reconciled his internal conflict and gave him the excuse he needed.

But it was with some anxiety he cautiously entered the usual bar. He saw Gordon, Fred and Tom. Here was also a boy, fair hair but not as fair as Mark's, not as tall as Mark but more solidly built. Mark thought he looked rather scruffy. Something about him exuded hostility when he saw Mark. He fixed Mark with a hard stare from cold, grey eyes.

"Hello, Mark," called Gordon. "Come and sit down. Coke?"

Mark went over and sat down. Normally he would have enjoyed sitting next to another queer boy, enjoying the closeness, but not now, not next to this other boy. "Yes please, Gordon," he said, sitting the other side of the table.

Gordon quickly returned with a pint of beer in one hand and a coke in the other. "I'm glad you've come, Mark," he said. "Pip left me instructions for you this evening."

"Where is Pip?"

"He's had to go away on business, but he's asked me to go with you this evening if you turned up."

Mark nodded, sipping his coke.

"Where's he going?" asked the boy.

"Mark, this is Peter," said Gordon. "Peter, this is Mark."

"I know who he is," said Peter sharply. "I've seen the paper. And you've talked about him."

"Hello. Peter," said Mark in as friendly a tone as he could manage.

Peter stared, glared even, at Mark and just lifted his drink and took a sip. He did not reply. There was a moment's awkwardness before Gordon said, "We'll go as soon as you've finished your coke."

"Are you alright now?" asked Fred, anxiously.

"Yes," said Mark. "All cleared up now."

"No thanks to you, Fred," said Gordon.

"I've been as well," said Fred defensively. "Mark, I honestly didn't know."

"Has he had the pox?" asked Peter, leering at Mark. He was smiling for the first time. Although there was hostility, Mark could see once he smiled what the attraction of Peter was.

"Yes, Peter, and it was me I'm afraid," said Fred.

"If you fucked him he must be cheap," said Peter.

"Peter, that's not fair," said Tom. "Fred came in to a bit of money and decided to treat himself."

"And he treated him as well by the sounds of it," retorted Peter, indicating Mark.

"Are you coming, Mark?" said Gordon. Mark finished his coke, and putting on his jacket, made for the door, followed by Gordon.

Once outside, Mark asked, "I don't think Peter likes me very much."

"Don't worry. Perhaps a bit jealous of you and your heroic exploits."

"Does he do the same as me?"

"More actually," replied Gordon. "He'll go both ways, if you get my meaning."

"He fucks as well as gets fucked?" queried Mark.

"Yes, he tops as well if required."

"Has he fucked you?" asked Mark.

"Mark, how would you like it if I discussed your sexual activities with other people? So I am not going to discuss what I do with others."

Mark felt himself flush. "Point taken," he said.

"Right," said Gordon, "Let's get the bus to the hospital."

To Mark's surprise, Gordon came as far as the waiting room, but Mark went to see the doctor alone after only a short wait this time. To his relief it was the same doctor. He examined Mark again and confirmed the swab had shown gonorrhoea. He said that he was all clear. The blood test had come back negative for any other infections.

On the bus back to the city centre, Mark asked, "How long is Pip away for?"

"We never know. Could be weeks."

"Where's he gone?"

"He's always a bit cagey about his business. He has a car dealership but he also gets a lot from another business. All we know is it's something to do with shipping and he goes around Europe and to the far east. It must be a good business because he's never short of money. But we don't pry. None of us talk much about our lives away from the group."

"Is the far east, is that like Japan?"

"He's never mentioned Japan, but Indonesia has been mentioned. Do you know where that is?"

"Yes," replied Mark. "Used to be the Dutch East Indies."

"Clever lad," responded Gordon. "I didn't know that much, although I know where Indonesia is on the map."

"I read a lot," said Mark. "Come to think of it, I don't know much about you."

Gordon smiled. "I think of all the group, we know more about you than the rest of us put together, thanks to your fire fighting exploits."

"What about Peter? What do you know about him?"

"Not much. He says he's sixteen, and we think he lives on the Marlborough Estate. But that's about it. He's mentioned a brother or brothers I think."

Mark had heard of the Marlborough Estate, a large council estate that had a reputation for being very rough. Not the sort of place one would go unless one had to, especially after dark.

As they walked from the bus stop to The Vault, Gordon said, "When we get back I'd like to take you upstairs."

"I've sort of got a boyfriend now," said Mark. "He doesn't know about this of course. I don't want to catch anything again."

"How old is he?"

"My age I think. He lives not far from me."

"Have you done anything with him?"

"Yes. Yesterday actually. He did what you do."

"He fucked you?" asked Gordon, rhetorically. "You are one horny kid. So do you not want five pounds?"

Mark had thought Gordon had meant in return for going with him to the hospital, but the prospect of more earnings tempted him.

"How did he get on," asked Tom of Gordon when they re-entered the bar.

"I **am** here," said Mark. "All clear, actually."

"Yes, sorry, Mark," answered Tom. "I don't know why I asked Gordon."

"Do you want a coke before we go upstairs, Mark," asked Gordon.

"It's getting late so let's go up now."

"Gordon, I'm here. I've been here all evening," said Peter with evident annoyance.

"I've promised Mark the fiver already, Peter," replied Gordon. "Another time."

"A fucking fiver," snarled Peter. "I bet he's not as good as me." Peter glared at Mark.

"Different, that's all. And not as versatile."

"Just a little fairy, is he," said Peter.

"Peter, calm down," said Tom. "I'll go up with you later."

Gordon got the key from the Bar and led the way to the third floor and the brown room.

As they lay naked on the bed, Mark said, "The doctor said I should use a Durex."

"What for?" asked Gordon. "Are you worried about getting pregnant?" he laughed.

"No, but he said that wouldn't have caught the clap if I had. I mean I suppose if Fred had."

"It's fine, Mark," said Gordon. "I know I've not got anything like that. You can trust me."

Mark felt that to be true and was now feeling very aroused so allowed Gordon to enter, sighing with the stimulation and pleasure it gave him. After Gordon came he brought Mark off by hand.

"You know when you get the key from the bar, do you have to pay for that?"

"Of course, a handy extra income for the pub," replied Gordon. "It's three pounds for an hour."

"So each time we've done this it costs eight pounds all together?"

"Yes, Mark, which reminds me, here's your five pounds," answered Gordon, reaching off the bed and retrieving his wallet from his jacket. Still naked, Mark took the five one pound notes and, reaching over his side of the bed, put them in his pocket.

Then there was a gentle tapping on the door. Gordon frowned. "Who is there?" he said quietly after getting up and standing close to the door.

"It's me, Gerry," came the reply. "Is Mark in there with you?"

"Yes he is."

"If you've finished, I wondered if he's up for another with me."

Gordon looked at Mark still lying on the bed. Mark nodded. Another five pounds!

"He says yes," said Gordon. "Wait a moment."

"Stay there, Mark, you might as well," suggested Gordon as he got dressed. He then unlocked the door and Gerry entered. Mark was pleased to see him.

"Shall we split the room cost?" said Gerry. "There's still twenty-five minutes left."

So the deal was done, Gordon left and Gerry quickly undressed. "You're still as beautiful as ever," he said to Mark as he climbed onto the bed and hugged Mark close to him.

Mark was a little concerned because he had already come, but as Gerry kissed and caressed him, his arousal returned. Once more Mark enjoyed the penetration, the feeling of being dominated. He realized that this had attracted him to Tommy. The fact that Tommy was his age and not as tall had made that feeling even more sharp. Then he felt guilty about allowing Gordon and Gerry to fuck him while thinking about Tommy, and then guilty because of Mam. So he simply lay still and waited for Gerry to finish.

. . .

Later he arrived home to find Mam watching television. "You're late," she said. "I don't know what you get up to on your town trips. I hope it's not stealing or anything."

Mark felt the guilt again and feeling himself flushing moved behind Mam's chair so she wouldn't see his fair skin redden. "No, Mam. I sometimes meet up with some friends from school."

"And get up to mischief I expect," said Mam, but Mark could detect the smile in her voice. "Have you had anything to eat?"

"No. But I've a bit left from Saturday's money, " he lied. "The Chinese will still be open, if you fancy something?"

"Yes, I'll be the downy empress again," said Mam.

"Dowager," smiled Mark.

"Who gives a shit? I'll have the same as before. I liked that. But you've got school in the morning so better get your skates on."

# Chapter 18 Control

After school the next day, Mark opened the history book and extracted the Post Office book and most of his accumulated money and went round to the High Street and deposited it. He looked at the mounting total with satisfaction. He was happy with the way things were going, despite having had the clap, but even that had been sorted out within a few days. Mark now felt more confident about continuing as he viewed the balance in his secret account.

Walking back he waved at Frank through the chippy window, now open for the evening trade. Frank waved back while serving a customer. Looking through the butcher's window, the meat trays in the window were mostly empty and he saw Tommy with a striped apron on, wiping down the surface of the counter. On an impulse he went in.

"We're about to close," said Tommy as he looked up. "Oh, hello, Mark."

"I just saw you through the window," said Mark.

Tommy looked round and, picking up a bag, dropped some sausages and a couple of pork chops in it and handed it to Mark. "Quick, put that in your bag."

"I haven't got my bag," said Mark. "I've been home already."

"Well, stuff it in your pocket then. Hurry up," said Tommy quietly but urgently.

Mark stuffed the bag in his coat pocket. "Gimme another bag," he said.

Tommy handed over a bag and Mark transferred the chops which made the load in his pockets easier.

"Is that a customer, Tommy?" called a man's voice from a back room. The voice was followed by its owner, evidently Tommy's father. Mark could see the likeness. "Oh, hello. It's Mark isn't it. Come to see Tommy, have you?"

"Yes, Mr Hedley," said Mark. "I was on my way back home from the Post Office and I saw him through the window so I just came in. Just to say hello, really."

"Well, I'm glad Tommy's got a new friend. He doesn't seem to mix well so I'm glad he's met you. Especially a brave lad like you."

Mark could see Tommy squirming as his father described his lack of friends. He decided to try to offset this a bit. "I met Tommy in the back lane and he seemed to mix well then. I like him so I bet he's got lots of friends really."

"He's too shy for his own good," said Tommy's father. "He doesn't have friends. I hope you can bring him out of himself a bit more."

"I'll do my best," smiled Mark, but thinking of Tommy's assertive dominance once they had been alone together. Thinking about that made Mark start to feel aroused. He was glad he had his coat on to hide that fact.

"Do you want to come round tomorrow night?" asked Mark of Tommy, remembering Mam would be out until late cleaning.

"Grammar school boy, aren't you?" asked Mr Hedley. "Don't you lot get a lot of homework? More than Tommy here, anyway."

"Yes," said Mark, "but not so much tomorrow and Tommy could bring his round to mine and we could do it together." The ambiguity of that phrase struck Mark and he added, "The homework, I mean. Help each other." Mark felt that flush coming but Tommy's face was stricken. Mark cursed his stupidity. But his father seemed unaware.

"Is that OK, Dad," asked Tommy.

"Yes, but not too late back."

"See you tomorrow than, Tommy," said Mark, and fled from the shop, bearing his illicit load but his mind full of Tommy's impending visit the following evening.

. . .

"Mam, look what I've got," said Mark, pulling the sausages and pork chops from his pockets.

Mam's eyes went wide. "Where'd you get that lot? Have you nicked it?"

"No, Mam. I saw Tommy just closing up the butcher's so I went in to say hello and he gave me this lot."

102

Mam looked at the sausages. "Real pork, not beef," she said. "Mark Martin, you have the luck of the devil. You put out fires and get in the paper, you find money on buses and now your pals with the butcher. You'll do OK in life, I reckon. Give your Mam a hug."

Mark hugged his Mam. "I'll only do well with good GCE results. So I've got homework to do."

"You do that, son, I fancy the pork chops. I'll call you when it's ready."

Mark went to his bedroom, and got out his homework. But Tommy was on his mind so he quietly slid the bolt on his door and lay on the bed, trousers and pants round his thighs while he masturbated, thinking of Tommy, but also of Gordon and Pip. Peter came into his mind and he found the boy's obvious dislike for him oddly stimulating. He imagined Peter taking him and fucking him remorselessly. His orgasm was very powerful. Cleaning up, he wondered why he found his own victimization so arousing. 'Something wrong with me?'

He started on his homework sitting at his bedroom table but had not got far when Mam called that the pork chops were ready. She had set out the table again, and there were baked beans and boiled potatoes. Mam seemed very happy and as Mark looked across the table at her while they ate he wondered what she would think of his strange, double life.

. . .

The following evening Mam left for work just after tea so he was alone in the flat when Tommy arrived, with his homework to do.

Mark opened the door to let Tommy in.

"Hi Tommy, glad you could come round."

"Where's your Mam?"

"Gone to work already," answered Mark.

"Let's go to the bedroom, then," said Tommy.

"What about the homework?" asked Mark.

Tommy's reply was assertive now. "Bedroom first and I've found some Vaseline so we can try that. Then you help

103

me with my homework and if there's time, I can fuck you again after that." Tommy was already walking towards Mark's bedroom.

"You seem to have it planned," said Mark, taken aback by Tommy's forthright manner. He was in charge and he knew it. Mark found that exciting but also slightly worrying in some way, unsure where all this was leading.

"Yes," replied Tommy. "If we left the sex until later we'd be thinking about your Mam getting back, but if we are doing homework when she gets back, that looks better." He closed the bedroom door and slid the bolt. "Extra caution," he added.

"What about the second fuck you wanted afterwards though," countered Mark.

"That's why you help me with the homework because you're brainy. It'd take me ages but you can do it quickly so we get time for another fuck."

Mark was still taking in Tommy's confidence when he felt Tommy undoing his belt. Mark stood while Tommy undid his trousers and pulled them and his pants down to his ankles. Mark's physical response was immediate.

Tommy smiled, standing back and looking at Mark still standing there. "You get undressed now."

As Mark did as he was told, he said, "What about you?"

"You first," demanded Tommy, sitting on the edge of the bed watching as Mark took off all his clothes. "Come here."

Mark stepped and stood in front of Tommy, sitting still fully dressed. Tommy took hold of Mark's cock and then ran his hand round his balls and pushed his hand between Mark's legs, feeling along his perineum and stroking his bum. His hand caressed Mark's scrotum and his cock. "Lie on the bed," Tommy ordered.

Mark again did as he was told without comment. He was finding this obedience to Tommy exciting. He felt Tommy's hands on his back, sliding down his spine and over his arse and then between his legs, stroking his thighs and reaching under for his cock. Mark's arousal was now on the verge of climax. "I'm almost going to come," he whispered.

"Not yet," said Tommy, who took his hand away. Mark saw Tommy quickly undressing. Naked, he bent down to his bag and got out a small jar of Vaseline. He smeared some on to his stiff cock and climbed on the bed. "You can come when I say," he said as he knelt astride Mark's thighs. Mark felt a quiver of excitement at Tommy taking control of even this most intimate part of him.

As Tommy pressed into Mark, he said, "You were right, the Vaseline is much better. I'm going to enjoy this."

"Good," said Mark, "I'm pleased."

Tommy didn't hurry; he moved slowly and steadily, extending the pleasure for as long as he could. Sometimes he would stop. "Getting too close," he explained, "don't want to come yet. This is so good."

"It is for me as well," said Mark. He now felt as though he wanted this to carry on forever, Tommy inside him, his hard cock stimulating Mark's internal erogenous areas.

Mark lost track of time as Tommy continued, Mark responding with counter movements of his own but then Tommy's pace quickened. "Can't stop this time," he muttered, as he now thrust quicker, deeper and harder. Several deep, powerful thrusts and Mark felt him soften. "Bloody hell," said Tommy. "Brilliant."

"Stay there," said Mark. He didn't want to lose the feeling of Tommy inside. So Tommy lay on top of Mark while he softened more and then he was gone.

"Thanks, Mark," said Tommy, climbing off Mark and off the bed. He took tissues from the box and wiped himself, looking round for a wastepaper bin.

"Under the table," said Mark, turning over and sitting up. "What about me?"

"You can come later," said Tommy. "I want you to look at my homework."

"Better get dressed," said Mark.

"We'll do the homework naked," said Tommy flatly. "So when I hand it in I can think about you naked doing it for me."

"You said I would help you, not do it for you," said Mark.

"Same thing," said Tommy. "I'll write it of course but you tell me what to write. What's the point of having a brainy friend if he doesn't help you?"

Mark sat at his table, Tommy on the end of the bed next to the table, both still undressed. Tommy got out his homework. "I don't get it," he said. "What's it mean, angle of incidence and angle of re something?"

"Refraction," said Mark. "It's to do with light passing from one medium to another."

"You lost me already," said Tommy with a laugh.

"It's why a stick looks bent when you put it part way underwater, " explained Mark.

Tommy picked up a pen. "You read out what I'm supposed to write."

"But you won't learn that way," argued Mark. "Not if I just do it all for you."

"I'm too thick to learn all that stuff, I'm not a brainbox like you." He smiled at Mark. "So just do as I say."

Mark saw the smile, and his resolve melted. He would obey Tommy. He looked at the problem. He saw at once that they had made the angles simple, he could do them in his head. So he told Tommy what to write. He saw the writing in his exercise book was very child-like, and he watched as Tommy laboriously wrote down the solution to the problem. He looked at Tommy afresh. His academic limitations were laid out before Mark and he had not encountered this before. Even Mam wrote quicker and better than Tommy. Tommy kept stopping and asking how to spell some words.

"I'm no good at spelling," Tommy said.

"Let me look at the book," said Mark. Tommy gave Mark the book. He scanned back through the pages. He could see numerous spelling mistakes. He gave the book back.

106

"I think you had better not spell all the words correctly," Mark advised. "They'll know it's not your work if everything is suddenly right."

"Clever boy," said Tommy, "trust you to think of that. It's great having a boyfriend like you."

Mark sighed and continued to dictate while Tommy wrote. "That's it then, Tommy," he said.

"That's real quick," said Tommy. "That leaves us plenty of time. You can come this time too."

"Thank you, Tommy," said Mark, but the sarcasm was lost on Tommy.

This time after Tommy came, he took hold of Mark and brought him off, even wiping Mark clean with tissues.

"We'd better get dressed," said Mark.

"Yes, we should," answered Tommy. "What nights is your Mam out? I can bring my homework round those nights."

"I can't keep doing all your homework, Tommy," said Mark. "I have my own to do, you know."

"You'll manage, doesn't take you long anyway."

"Also," continued Mark, "if you only come when she's out, she might suspect something."

"See!" said Tommy. "I wouldn't have thought of that. So I'll bring my homework round every night. You're a real pal, Mark."

Mark didn't know what to say, so he just nodded. He knew Tommy liked him but he also knew that Tommy was using him. Part of that felt oddly good.

# Chapter 19 Homework

Tommy was as good as his word. The following night he arrived with homework.

"Hello, Mrs Martin," he said. "Mark's agreed to help me with my homework."

"That's good, our Mark's a kind lad. But, Mark, what about your own homework?"

"I'll be all right, Mam," said Mark. "Tommy doesn't get a lot anyway."

"It's good you're helping your friend, Mark, but make sure you get your own done."

"I will, Mam. Come on, Tommy."

"Nice to meet you again, Mrs Martin," said Tommy happily.

In the bedroom, Tommy put his bag down, slid the bolt and then unexpectedly kissed Mark on the lips. Mark resisted at first but then felt Tommy's tongue exploring and he allowed Tommy, who then reached down and fondled Mark's arse.

"We can't do anything now," whispered Mark, once he had disentangled himself.

"I know that," said Tommy, "but that was a thank you for being such a great boyfriend."

"Just say friend, not boyfriend," said Mark. "It might get overheard."

"But you are my boyfriend?"

"Yes, Tommy. After the last few days, I think so. So what is your homework?"

"In my bag. I got a good mark for the stuff about light, thanks to you."

"Yes, but did you learn anything about the refraction of light?"

"Doesn't matter. When the fuck am I ever going to need that?"

Mark gave up. Tommy produced his homework. Mark saw the same immature handwriting, peppered with spelling mistakes, some of which the teacher had corrected. It was history tonight, about the Romans. It was fairly basic stuff and Mark was able to provide a reasonable answer from memory even though his own studies were of more modern history. He knew that were it his own homework he would do more research and go in to more detail but he felt he was doing enough and anyway, such a detailed piece would not be typical of Tommy. The longest part was waiting while Tommy painfully, slowly wrote down what Mark was saying. Mark started to grow impatient but Tommy kept smiling at him and his gratitude was evident.

At last it was finished. "Tommy, I've my own homework to do. You can stay, but I need to concentrate."

"I'll stay then. I like being with you, Mark. Being near you, like. I'll just lie on the bed and watch you."

"You could try some of my books if you want," offered Mark.

"No, not really into books. I'll just watch."

Mark got out his own homework and started to work his way through the algebra.

After a while Tommy got up and looked at the books. "Are any of these books any good?"

"Tommy, I'm trying to work," said Mark.

"Sorry," said Tommy. He was quiet for a while. "How can you add up letters and that? You can only add up numbers."

Mark was aware of Tommy looking over his shoulder at the equations. "The letters are variables. They stand for numbers."

"So why not just use the actual number then?"

"Because you can change the numbers but still use the same equation."

"That sounds daft to me," said Tommy.

"Please Tommy, I have to concentrate. Go back on the bed and keep quiet."

Tommy laughed. "That's what I say to you when I'm gonna fuck you,"

"Tommy!" yelled Mark.

"Sorry, Mark. It's just I've never had a brainy friend before."

"Your Dad said you don't have any friends, brainy or not!" snapped Mark.

Tommy didn't reply. After a second, Mark looked up and saw tears in Tommy's eyes. Mark instantly regretted his barbed retort.

"Tommy, I'm sorry. I didn't mean to upset you."

"But you're right," replied Tommy. "You're the first real friend I've ever had, who likes me for what I really am. But now you use your clever brain on me."

"But Tommy, you use your brilliant body on me," responded Mark, smiling at Tommy. "So we're even."

It worked. Tommy smiled back. "Yes, we're even. You are cleverer than me, but it's me on top of you in bed."

"Keep your voice down," warned Mark. "But you're right. But now I must work."

After a few moments there was a knock at the door. "Do you lads want a cuppa? Kettle's boiling," called Mam through the door.

Mark was about to say no when Tommy called out, "Yes please, Mrs Martin. Milk and one sugar."

As Mam retreated along the passage, Mark said, "Tommy, I need to work."

"Cup of tea won't hurt," said Tommy. "And when your Mam offered, it would be rude to say no."

Mark resigned himself to more interruptions. "Better take the bolt off then," he said.

"Good thinking. See? You are clever," said Tommy sliding off the bed and moving the bolt back.

Another knock and Tommy opened the door. Mam entered carrying a small tray with two mugs of tea and a plate of custard cream biscuits while Tommy returned to the bed. "Here you are, This is yours Tommy, with the sugar, this is yours, Mark. Don't make a load of crumbs with those biscuits mind. How are you getting with the homework? I must say, Tommy, you don't look as if you're working very hard, lying on the bed. That won't get your homework done."

"Thank you. Mrs Martin," said Tommy, sitting up and taking his mug and a biscuit. "I've already done my homework, and Mark is doing his now."

"Trying to, anyway," muttered Mark, as Mam crossed the room and. putting the tray on the table, moving aside some opened books to do so.

"Mam!" said Mark, testily. "I'm using those."

"You've got to have your tea somewhere. And you, Tommy, don't leave crumbs in Mark's bed or he'll be wriggling all night." Mam laughed at the vision she had created.

"I'll be careful, Mrs Martin," Tommy assured her.

Mam left the room.

"I wish I could make you wriggle all night," said Tommy.

Mark sighed and resumed his homework, trying to ignore Tommy crunching biscuits and watching Mark. He found it hard to concentrate with Tommy's fixed gaze on him. But he soldiered on.

"Mark, mind if I have another biscuit?"

"Help yourself, Tommy," said Mark wearily.

Tommy came over to the table, again peering at Mark's work. "I know a bit about that," said Tommy. "It's about rain and that. At first I thought it was a bike on a lake when the teacher said water cycle."

"Yes, Tommy. The same water goes round and round and we use the same water over and over again. There's only a fixed amount of water on Earth."

"What about when it rains?"

"That's water the sun has evaporated from the sea, and the water in the sea has come from rain. So we drink it again."

"Even water that's been down the toilet?"

"Yes," said Mark, "all water."

"That's fucking disgusting," said Tommy, screwing his face up. "I'm never gonna drink water again."

111

"Shut up and drink your tea, Tommy," said Mark smiling, half to himself, at Tommy's reaction.

"What happened to the letters instead of numbers?"

"Astonishingly, Tommy, I managed to finish that. I'm now doing homework for another subject."

"You get more than one subject? You should move to my school. We only ever get one."

Eventually Mark finished his homework. As he put all his books back in his bag, Tommy said, "Come and sit on the bed with me."

Mark did so. Tommy put his arms round Mark and kissed his cheek. Mark saw emotion on Tommy's face, his eyes were moist. "I love you, Mark. You're a brilliant friend. I'm so glad you moved here," he said, his voice trembling with emotion.

Mark wondered how Tommy could be so assertive and controlling for sex but was otherwise more timid and vulnerable. He leaned over and kissed Tommy on the lips, a kiss that grew increasingly intense. Mark felt Tommy's hand feeling his cock through his trousers.

"We can't do anything like that," said Mark as his cock stiffened. He felt across to Tommy's, he was hard.

In response, Tommy undid his belt and pulled out his cock. "The bolt's on, suck it," he commanded. Mark had time to wonder if Tommy's forceful manner was directly connected to his cock. But he felt Tommy's hand on his head, pushing him down. Mark did Tommy's bidding but worrying in case there was a knock at the door.

There was not and Tommy was naturally pleased with the result. "You're the best boyfriend ever," said Tommy. "But I'd better go. Thanks for everything, not just the homework."

. . .

Inevitably Tommy returned in the following evenings. The pattern was the same, Mam brought tea mugs, Mark did Tommy's homework and then his own while Tommy watched. There were changes. Mark examined Tommy's books and found he could do a pretty good

112

imitation of Tommy's writing. So instead of Tommy slowly writing down what Mark dictated, Mark wrote it in Tommy's hand which made it so much quicker.

Tommy watched this, fascinated. "You write dead fast," he commented. "Even when doing my writing."

"It saves time," said Mark. "I need to get my own homework done, remember?"

"Leaves more time for you to suck me off as well."

"Yes, Tommy," said Mark. Even though Mark never came doing that, he still got aroused and felt pleasure when Tommy pushed his head down to his erect cock.

On those evenings when Mam was out, Tommy took charge and they were both naked and Tommy fucked Mark. Sometimes Mark didn't have time to finish his homework after obeying all Tommy's commands and had to sit up late, often gone midnight, to finish his own. It was irritating but he wanted Tommy too much to complain. He grew to love what he thought of as the two Tommys. The quiet, shy boy of normal life, and, once that cock was hard, the forceful and dominant Tommy. Almost two separate people.

# Chapter 20 Guilty Feelings

Two weeks later on Saturday evening, having told Tommy he would be out, Mark set off for The Vault, although tired from his day at the chippy. He was hoping Pip would have returned and also he was becoming obsessed by his mounting bank balance. As he rode the trolley bus into the city centre, he wondered if Peter would also be there. 'I've not been for a while, maybe he thinks he's scared me off.'

Entering the bar, he saw the group at the table, including Pip. Gordon, Gerry and Fred were there.

"Hello, Mark," said Pip. "Gordon tells me you went back for the appointment and everything was sorted."

"I did," said Mark sitting down beside Pip, "and was given the all clear."

Pip patted Mark's thigh. "Good lad. Coke for you?"

"Yes please," said Mark. He then noticed a half drunk pint of beer and another drink on the table in front of spare seats. "Whose are those?" he asked, indicating the drinks.

"Tom and Peter," said Gordon, and pointed upwards.

"Yes," said Pip, arriving back with Mark's coke. "Their hour is about half done I would think."

"Does Tom like Peter?" asked Mark. "Just that he's never asked me."

"Tom likes a bit of rough, and our Peter is certainly that," said Gerry.

"Perhaps you are too sophisticated for Tom's taste, in that way, at least," said Pip. "Also, Peter is what we call versatile. In fact he likes topping more than being bottom. Probably why he asks for more than you do."

"You mean money?" asked Mark. He hadn't really thought about it before and had just accepted the five pounds that Gordon had offered him at first.

"Yes, because he'll go either way. Some of us like both, especially from a young buck like Peter. Some, like you I suppose, only want to be bottom. Tom for example. He's never asked you upstairs, has he?"

Mark shook his head and thought about that for a moment as he sipped his coke. He wanted to ask how much Peter got paid but drew back from that. He changed the subject. "How was your trip? Someone said you had gone to Indonesia," asked Mark

Pip thought for a moment. "Yes, near enough, anyway, Mark. It was successful."

"Pip's always very quiet about his foreign business dealings," said Gerry. "None of us are quite sure what he does, but it pays well."

"And that's how it will remain," smiled Pip. He turned to Mark. "What brings you here tonight? Are you up for going upstairs with me when Tom and Peter come down?"

"I came to see if you were back, and yes, I'll go upstairs with you, for the usual amount," said Mark.

"No freebies from Mark," laughed Gerry.

"He's got a good business head, I think," said Pip.

"Who gives freebies?" asked Mark. "Does Peter?"

"Peter? Not likely. He'd probably slit your throat just for asking," grinned Gordon.

Mark quietly thought that fitted with his impression of Peter so far.

Tom and Peter entered the bar, both smiling, but Peter's expression changed to a scowl when he saw Mark.

"I see he's back," growled Peter to the group in general, but looking steadily at Mark. That steely glare made Mark feel uncomfortable. Peter continued, "So who can I help next?" He looked round the group, expectantly.

"Actually, Mark and I are going upstairs," said Pip. "Agreed before you came down, Peter."

"So I'll just sit here and let these buy me drinks while you take your cheap fairy slut."

"If I'm a slut, what does that make you, then?" demanded Mark angrily.

"Keep your voice down, Mark," said Pip.

"I can use my cock for more than wanking," retorted Peter triumphantly, sneering at Mark.

"Enough, you two," said Gordon.

115

"Come on, Mark," said Pip, and he led the way upstairs. On the second floor a door opened and a man and woman came out onto the carpeted landing, man and wife, almost certainly.

"Good evening," said Pip as they passed.

"Good evening," answered the man while his wife smiled at Mark, who tried to smile back. 'If only they knew where we are going and what for," thought Mark.

Pip loitered on the landing and only when the couple had gone down the stairs did he open the door marked private and go up the lino stairs to the brown room.

"Why did you wait?" asked Mark.

"We have to be discreet," replied Pip. "The landlord of this place is queer and so he's OK with queer people and he lets us use the room because it's safer than cottaging, but any whiff of what goes on, especially with lads like you and Peter, and all hell would break loose."

"I thought it was because you pay him," said Mark.

"That too," smiled Pip as he unlocked the door to the brown room.

Once inside, Pip took Mark and kissed him while undressing him. Mark relaxed, the slow removal of his clothing was intensely stimulating and he felt that sense of surrender coming over him as he moulded into Pip's body. They kissed and caressed each other before Pip took out the Vaseline and then carefully entered Mark who willingly submitted.

Both satisfied, as they lay together, Mark asked Pip about his trip. "Do you often go to Indonesia?"

"I have to go every now and then," said Pip. "I'm a sort of partner in a business based in that part of the world."

"What sort of business?"

"We transport materials around the islands."

"So does it make a lot of money, then? The others said you're rich."

Pip laughed. "I'm certainly not poor, Mark, but even though I have the car dealership I don't have a Daimler with gold plated bumpers!" Mark understood the reference to the infamous, extravagant Lady Docker.

"Why don't you have a car if you're rich? "

"I do have a car, Mark. Just not a golden Daimler."

"But when we went to the hospital, we took a taxi there and a taxi back. Remember? You took me home."

"Of course I remember. The car was having some work done on it so was in the workshop."

"I bet it's a nice car," said Mark.

"I like it," said Pip. "Austin Healey 3000, if you know what that is."

"Oh, lovely," said Mark. "I bet it's red."

"It is, Mark. Maybe I'll give you a ride in it one day."

"I'd love that," said Mark, enthusiastically, and leaned over and kissed Pip on the cheek. "I'm glad I met you."

"I'm glad I met you," replied Pip. "I'm glad Gordy picked you up instead of some pimp. There are some really evil people out there."

"Like what?" asked Mark.

"Mark, you're such an innocent! There are men, gangsters really, who use boys like you. They make them have sex with people they choose and some of them come to real harm. Beaten and even tortured for sexual turn-on. Maybe even killed."

"Don't they pay them?"

"Yes, but the gangsters keep most of the money. And if the boys object, or try to leave, they are given even worse treatment as a lesson to them and the others. They get them hooked on drugs as well."

"But you aren't like that," said Mark.

"Which is why I said I was glad you met Gordy. You could have got sucked into one of their bad networks, like Peter."

"Peter?"

"Yes, he did manage to break away but he suffered quite badly. He was just twelve then but Peter knows some pretty bad people as well and the pimps were persuaded, not too gently I think, to let Peter go."

Mark tried to absorb this. "I knew I was lucky to meet you," he said quietly.

"Yes, Mark. Time we got dressed," said Pip.

Back in the bar, Mark was given another coke which he drank sitting at the far end of the group from Peter, who seemed to be talking to Tom all the time. Mark looked at Peter with renewed curiosity.

Pip said, "I have to go now." And to Mark, "thank you, Mark. A pleasure as always. Oh, I almost forgot," he finished, stuffing a five pound note into Mark's jacket pocket.

"I would have reminded you," smiled Mark.

Pip then left.

"A pleasure as always," came Peter's mimicry across the table. "Back door wide open, then?"

"That's unfair, Peter," said Gerry. "Mark's done nothing you haven't done yourself."

With that Peter shrugged and turned back to Tom. Gerry turned to Mark, saying quietly, "I know you just been up with Pip, but if you're still willing, there's another five for you."

So Mark was happy to return with Gerry and was another five pounds richer.

On the trolley bus home, he felt a little sore so resolved to leave sex for a few days. 'Oh fuck, Tommy will be round tomorrow,' he remembered. But then he found himself looking forward to Tommy's visit while Mam was out.

. . .

Perhaps as a way of assuaging his guilty feelings, he decided to treat Mam again.

"Hi, Mam," he said as he went in.

"You're late back, Mark. I worry about you. Do your posh friends' mams not worry about them?"

'So she thinks I've been with school friends.' "No, Mam," he answered. "We are capable of looking after ourselves."

118

"That's what you think, smart arse," said Mam. "You're still just a kid, even though you think you know everything. I know you're a clever boy, Mark, but you're still just a boy."

This conversation was not going the way Mark had planned. "Mam. Set the table and put the kettle on. I'm going to spend some of my chipping money on a Chinese for us. It'll still be open."

"Mark, you're the best son ever," said Mam.

"But still just a boy," countered Mark, but laughing at Mam's swift change of tone.

"Fuck off to the chinkies, you daft idiot," she said playfully.

"Mam, that's superfluous. An idiot is by definition daft, so there's no need to say that; and anyway, a minute ago I was clever."

"Super what?" frowned Mam. "Anyway, hurry back. You've made me realize my belly thinks my throat's been cut."

That made Mark remember the comment about Peter slitting a throat. He shuddered slightly as he went back down the stairs.

When he returned, Mam had the table and teapot ready and they ate their meal, chatting and they watched television together until close down.

. . .

The following afternoon as expected Tommy arrived. Mark saw his smiling face, full of pleasure at seeing him. Mark remembered that Tommy had said he loved Mark, and the look on Tommy's face told Mark it was not just a throwaway phrase. So he felt guilty again for his activity at The Vault, with a sense of betrayal, not just of Mam now, but of Tommy as well.

"You hungry?" he asked Tommy. "Fancy a Chinese?"

"Got no money," said Tommy.

"My treat," said Mark.

The two boys ate well, and Mark brought back a third meal for Mam when she came back. He wrote a note saying

119

to warm it in the oven in case she was late back from work and he was already in bed.

Once in the bedroom, Tommy quickly took charge. "I want to make love to you," he said.

Mark was surprised by his use of the term "make love" but he was aware that it was how Tommy felt. And indeed his love making was very tender and loving and Mark began to see a new aspect of Tommy. Then he felt guilty again because he knew he didn't feel as strongly about Tommy. He fancied him, he was a friend and the sex was great, but did it extend as far as love? But then he reasoned that by doing Tommy's homework for him, he was compensating for that, in his mind at least.

"Teacher said my spelling's getting better," announced Tommy while lying on Mark's bed watching Mark do the homework.

"I keep forgetting to make mistakes so it's more like your work," said Mark, trying to think of typical spelling errors Tommy might make.

"Don't worry about it," said Tommy. "Only a few more months of school for me. Shouldn't think I'll do well in the exams but I do know how to butcher meat. I expect you'll be staying on."

"Yes," said Mark. A thought occurred to him. "What year are you in?"

"Fifth, like you," said Tommy.

"No, Tommy, I'm fourth year. Won't do GCEs until my next year. How old are you?" Mark had never thought to ask.

"Fifteen," said Tommy, with a frown. "How old are you?"

"Fourteen," said Mark.

The boys looked at each other for a moment.

"I never thought I was older than you," said Tommy. "Just shows what a brainbox you are if you can do my homework better than me and not even in fifth year. Or maybe it just shows how thick I really am."

"I don't think you're thick," said Mark. "Maybe not as good at schoolwork but there's more to life than that. I wouldn't know how to cut up animal carcasses or which bits come from where. That's a real skill, and useful as well. Probably more useful than knowing the causes of the French revolution."

"Specially for a butcher," smiled Tommy. "Hurry up and finish my homework, young kid. I want to fuck you again."

. . .

Life for Mark settled in to a kind of routine. Three or four evenings a week, Tommy came round, sometimes while Mam was there, when she wasn't their sex grew more and more intense as both boys continued to mature. Usually twice in the week Mark would go to The Vault and his secret savings account grew very full.

# PART TWO 1963

## Chapter 21 Winter and Work

By the time Mark was swotting up for his GCE exams in the Spring and early summer of 1963, he had amassed a considerable amount in his Post Office account.

. . .

**Austin Healey 3000**

True to his word, Pip had later offered Mark a ride in his Austin Healey sports car, and they had ended up at Pip's home, a secluded, large house in what Mark thought was a posh area on the edge of the city, West Farm Estate.

"Do you like my house?" asked Pip, smiling as Mark wandered round, wide-eyed at the luxurious surroundings.

"It's great," Mark said. "Are you a millionaire?"

"Probably, if you add up all the assets here and abroad."

"Wow," uttered Mark quietly, looking around.

"Let me show you the bedroom," suggested Pip.

As they went up the stairs, Pip patted Mark's bum and said, "Usual payment?"

Mark liked Pip and thought he was attractive so he had agreed. "Makes a big change from that brown room," remarked Mark, looking round the large bedroom and the king size bed with soft bedding.

After they had sex together, instead of rushing back downstairs as they would at The Vault, they lay together in that big bed and Mark fell asleep.

"Mark, time to go," Pip was saying, cuddling Mark. "I should take you home."

Mark had quickly dressed and had been dropped near Calvert House but out of sight. If being seen getting out of a taxi was bad, the sight of the expensive sports car would have raised even more eyebrows.

. . .

Over the coming weeks and then months, Mark's visits to The Vault became fewer and being taken to Pip's home was more common. With Pip paying Mark well, he felt less drawn to The Vault, although he missed Gordon. He reasoned also that with Pip he was safer from infection and discovery. After each meeting they would arrange the timing and pick up point for the next one. The pick up and drop off points were varied for safety's sake. Pip gave Mark his phone number in case there was a problem with a planned session and so a new arrangement could be made. Both knew, but neither said it, that what they were doing was illegal with possible serious consequences for both; Pip prison, and for Mark, being taken from Mam, and probably his school and put in some kind of children's home. But all seemed to be going well and Pip and Mark became close.

Mark also continued his relationship with Tommy, doing his homework and helping with his school leaving examinations, about which Tommy was not especially concerned as he intended to work with his father in the butcher's shop. After leaving school in June 1962 that's what Tommy had done. To Mark, this seemed a waste but for him it was something of a relief because he had to work hard in the run up to his own GCE exams and now no longer had the additional burden of Tommy's homework. Tommy would visit at times when Mam was out and rarely when she was there now because he didn't need Mark to do his homework.

This helped Mark devote more time to his studies, but still looked forward to Tommy coming (in both senses of the word) because he liked Tommy and he knew that Tommy more than liked him, loved him even.

Mam had commented on Tommy's fewer appearances but Mark just said he was busy with the shop business, which she accepted. By the time she returned from her job, Tommy had usually come - in all senses - and gone again. His visits to Pip he explained by saying he was visiting school friends to work together toward the GCE exams.

"I hope you're not doing their work for them. I think you helped that Tommy too much. You're a soft touch, Mark," she had said.

Mark decided not to tell Pip about Tommy or Tommy about Pip. He thought it was safer to keep things in separate compartments.

Like everybody else on the planet, they had an anxious few days during the Cuban missile crisis but the Soviet ships turned back.

Through the bitter winter of 1963 with its heavy snow and consequent travel problems, Mark worked hard at revision. He was sometimes late for school or even failed to make the journey at all if the buses weren't on. But this was not for lack of determination. Anxious to meet an essay deadline on one day, he walked from Calvert House into the city centre because his own bus failed to arrive, the bus to his school was late. He arrived very late, cold and tired.

"Mark Martin, you look exhausted," said Mr Farnsworth. Mark stood in the classroom doorway shivering. He saw that more than half of the desks in the classroom were unoccupied.

"I had to walk a lot of the way, sir," replied Mark. "My bus didn't come."

"You need to get warmed up. You look very pale, Martin, even for your fair skin. Robson, can you move seats so Mark can sit by the radiator, please?"

Ethan moved and Mark sat down. He placed his hands on the radiator.

124

"Don't do that, Martin," said Mr Farnsworth, "you need to warm up gradually."

Ethan put his hand on Mark's. "Your hands are like ice blocks," he said. "Have you not got a pair of gloves?"

"Yes, but they're not very thick ones. Still let the cold in."

"Actually," interrupted Darren, "that's wrong. They didn't let the cold in but failed to keep the heat in. Entropy or something."

"Get some decent ones, leather is good," advised Ethan. Mark just nodded in reply.

"We need to get on," announced Mr Farnsworth, returning to the topic of the subjunctive mood in English grammar.

"I wish I were warmer, sir," said Mark, which drew a laugh from the class and a smile from Mr Farnsworth.

"Very apposite, Martin," Mr Farnsworth replied with a smile.

After a time the shivering stopped as he started to warm up while the lesson continued.

At lunch break, which was soon because of Mark's lateness, some went outside to throw snowballs about but Mark had already had enough of the snow so went with Ethan and Steve to the library after their school lunch.

"What did you come for?" asked Steve. "Half the class didn't make it."

"I've history this afternoon and I've got to hand in the essay on 1848 to Mr Raynor. Today is the deadline."

"I've got Geography then," commented Steve.

. . .

Mark and Ethan made their way to the room where History was taught. There was a gaggle of pupils milling around in the corridor.

"The door's locked," said someone.

Just then Mr Hardy, a science teacher, came along looking harassed. "Are you lot Mr Raynor's fifth year history class?" he asked, looking around the group.

"Yes, sir, but the door's locked," someone offered.

"Yes, I'm sorry for the delay but I was looking for the key," said Mr Hardy.

"Where's Mr Raynor?" asked one of the girls as they filed into the classroom behind Mr Hardy. There was an air of puzzlement among the pupils.

As they sat in their usual seats, Mr Hardy addressed them. "Mr Raynor lives someway from the school in a village in the county."

"Which one, sir?" chimed in Ian McLaren; a boy noted for mischief.

"If you think for one moment, McLaren, I'm going to tell you that, think again," responded Mr Hardy sharply.

While Ian McLaren grinned, Mr Hardy continued. "At the moment, the village is cut off by large snow drifts and I'm told the power is off there too. But he did phone and one of the things he mentioned was that you have an essay due in today on" here Mr Hardy looked at a small notebook "European Turmoil 1848." He frowned. "What happened in 1848?"

"There were liberal revolutions in many European countries, another one in France, across Germany and the Chartist movement here were going to march on Parliament to present a petition," said Mark.

"How typically British," remarked Mr Hardy with a smile. "Revolutions all over Europe but here we present a petition."

Ian McLaren raised his hand.

"Yes, McLaren?" said Mr Hardy.

"Sir, if the power is off in Mr Raynor's village, how could he phone the school?"

Several pupils started to smile at this, including Mark and Ethan.

"McLaren, are you deliberately awkward? The telephone system does not require mains electricity. You should pay more attention in science lessons. The power lines are down but luckily not the phone line."

Ian McLaren looked abashed and flushed slightly.

Mr Hardy continued. "On the subject of 1848, and thank you Martin for your explanation, Mr Raynor has asked that your essays be handed in today so if you get them ready I will collect them."

Amid a rustling of paper as essays were retrieved from bags, Janice Boyd asked, "Sir, how will he get them to be marked?"

"I will leave them in his docket in the staffroom and he said that the road should be cleared by the morning so he will collect them then. Now for the rest of this period, I suggest you do some history work on whatever topic you are working on now while I mark some science books."

"Second Empire, sir," came Danny's voice from the back.

"Second Empire?" said Mr Hardy. "What happened to the first one?"

"Defeated at the Battle of Waterloo in 1815, sir," said Mark.

"Ah, now that I do know about. The end of Napoleon. But I confess I wasn't aware there had been another French Emperor."

"Yes, sir," said Mark, warming to his theme. "Louis Napoleon was Napoleon's nephew and in the revolution of 1848 which deposed King Louis Philippe he became the first French President. But in 1852 he was crowned Emperor like his uncle. So his reign is called the Second Empire. He was overthrown after France was defeated by Prussia in 1870."

"Clever clogs," muttered Ian McLaren, but audibly.

Mr Hardy ignored McLaren. "Russia, you say?"

"No, sir," said Mark. "Prussia. Prussia was a powerful kingdom across northern Germany, its capital was Berlin. In 1871, Prussia took over all of Germany and the King of Prussia was made German Emperor. In German that's Kaiser. It was the first time that Germany was one country. That was the Second Reich."

"Well I know about the Third Reich," said Mr Hardy, "but I'm not even going to ask what was the First Reich."

"The Holy Roman Empire, sir," said Mark. "But that was never a unified state in the modern sense."

"Very well," said Mr Hardy. "I can see, Martin, that your history is better than your chemistry."

"Yes, sir," said Mark, chastened.

"Get on with some work quietly now, please."

. . .

Within days Mark had bought himself good leather gloves and while shopping he saw a thick padded coat with a fur lined collar and hood so he bought that as well.

"You'll have no money left if you spend at that rate," was Mam's contribution.

"I've been saving up," said Mark. Mam shrugged and fortunately accepted that.

"The winter was very bad when you were born, Mark. I could have done with a coat like that then. We'd just had the war and then that fucking winter."

"I don't remember, Mam. I was quite young," laughed Mark.

# Chapter 22 All Change

Thankfully March brought a steady thaw, not so fast as to create much flooding but even the most ardent snowball fighters and sledgers were glad to see the snow go. Mark's life revolved around schoolwork, Tommy, schoolwork, Pip, schoolwork, the chippy and schoolwork.

Mam complained. "Mark, I never see you these days. Always either out or with your nose stuck in a book."

"Mam, it's important I get good GCEs for going on to my A levels, and maybe university."

"University? You?" said Mam, aghast. "Mark, only posh people go to university. That school's given you ideas."

"Mam, isn't that the point of school and education? - To give people ideas? And if you ever came to the Parents' evenings you would know about this."

"Don't be smart with me, Mark. I work in the evenings and you can look after yourself. I wouldn't know what to say anyway. You know well what I mean. You'll be out of place at a university."

Mark didn't want to argue so he just said, "You're probably right, Mam. But time will tell."

"Most lads your age are thinking about leaving school and getting a job. I have a hard enough time now finding enough money to get by. So you expect me to keep you for another however many fucking years?"

"Two years at most, Mam. I'd get a grant for university. And as for the next two years while I do A levels, I'll contribute money."

"What from? One fucking pound from the chippy? How far do you think that will go?"

Mark could hardly say he was earning much more from Pip. "I'll ask Frank for a pay rise," he said, lamely.

"And pigs might fly," said Mam.

"Well, I'll get a better Saturday job then," replied Mark, exasperated.

"Nobody's going to pay a kid more than a pound."

"Mam, I'm sixteen, but you still think of me as a kid," retorted Mark.

"You're a kid until you're twenty-one. You were lucky to get that much from Frank. Ask for a big rise. Without you when you first started a couple of years ago he wouldn't have a fucking shop. He owes you."

"Yes, Mam," said Mark, wearily.

"Well, he'd better, or you're leaving school, no argument," said Mam. "Sorry, Mark, I know you like your schoolwork, but we have to be realistic. You'll do OK, you're a bright lad, I know that."

Mark felt shock at that. Mam had always supported him, always said how proud she was of her clever son. That she might stop him staying on had never occurred to him, he had just taken it for granted. But thanks to The Vault and Pip in particular, he had a way out.

"Don't worry, Mam," answered Mark. "I'll sort something out. I've got the Easter holiday which will give me time to look for a better job."

"I know you will, you're a good lad," said Mam. "Give your old Mam a hug."

As they hugged, Mark wondered if she would still think he was a good lad if she knew about the source and size of his pot of gold.

. . .

Mark was nevertheless worried about maybe having to leave school. At his next visit to Pip he talked about this, recounting his conversation with Mam as they lay in his big bed.

"Mark, that would be a terrible waste. I think you have real potential," said Pip as he cuddled Mark close to him.

"Thanks," said Mark. "I am determined to do well and to stay on for A levels. But it might not be possible."

"You should do. Mark, you're a clever lad and will do well with the right encouragement."

"Yes, but Mam isn't very encouraging. Not unless I give her more money."

130

"I am encouraging you," said Pip. "Come and work for me at weekends."

"Like this, you mean? In bed, all weekend?"

"Not all weekend. At my car showroom."

"I forgot you had that. Doing what? I'm too young to drive."

"General helping out, cleaning the cars, sweeping up. As for driving, we can teach you enough so you can move the cars around on site."

"You know Frank pays me a whole pound for Saturday at the chippy. I'm going to ask him for a pay rise."

"I'll pay you ten pounds a day. Provided you tell nobody else at the showroom what you're getting. If you do a Sunday as well, that should give you more than enough to keep your mother happy."

Mark was silent out of sheer astonishment. Then he gripped Pip in a tight hug and kissed him on the cheek. "I don't know what to say. Thanks, that's brilliant."

"I think I've fallen in love with you, Mark. I want to help you. You are such a nice lad, clever, good looking and a good lover, too. I would still want us to have sex, if that's what you want. And I'll still give you your money for that as well."

Mark's head was in a spin. He liked Pip, he liked the sex with Pip and now he had the prospect of what was to him untold wealth. Lying close to his benefactor, he felt a surge of arousal again. "Let's do it again now," he whispered.

Pip was happy to oblige and Mark sighed as he felt the entry, feeling Pip inside him, feeling his climax and then his own. Mark felt really happy.

"I'll have to tell Frank I'm leaving the chip shop," he said to Pip.

"Of course. Go on Saturday and tell him it's your last shift. Then I'll meet you on Saturday evening if you want."

Mark simply nodded.

. . .

"Mam, I've got a new weekend job. It's more money so I can help with the money and stay on at school," said Mark gleefully.

"A new job? What about Frank at the chippy?" queried Mam, looking up from the *Daily Mirror*.

"I'll tell him I'm leaving when I go next Saturday," said Mark. "Tell him it's my last day."

"He won't like that, Mark. Where's this new job?"

"It's a car showroom in town. Saturday and Sunday and also more money each day."

"How much more? And how did you get that job? We don't know anybody who has a car," argued Mam.

Mark hadn't thought this through and so had to think quickly. "There's a boy in my class. It belongs to his dad. "

"What's his name?"

Again Mark thought quickly. "John," he said, using the first male name that came into his head. He needed a surname. John Lennon came into his head. Too obvious. George Harrison. "John Harrison. I think I've talked about him before," he added hopefully.

Mam shook her head. "I don't remember that one but you're always going on about these posh grammar school kids. Ethan something I remember. And a Steve and Eddie I think. You never seem to talk about any girls though."

"I'm too busy with schoolwork to think about girls," said Mark. "Maybe after my exams," he added to deflect any thoughts about his sexuality.

"Well, you won't be peeling taties at a garage, anyway," smiled Mam. "So what are you doing there?"

"Just general stuff, Cleaning the cars, sweeping up. They'll teach me to drive so I can move the cars around. I'll be ready when I'm seventeen then. Probably make the tea and so on."

"Good idea, Mark," replied Mam. "Put the kettle on, I could murder a cuppa."

Mark was glad she didn't remember to ask how much his pay would be.

. . .

132

On Saturday, the first day of the Easter school holiday, as he went to the chippy, he tried to pluck up the courage to tell Frank he was leaving. When he went into the shop instead of his usual cheery greeting, Frank looked serious.

But Mark decided to press ahead straight away. "Hello, Frank. I've got some news for you."

"It can wait, Mark. I've got something to tell you, I'm afraid. My wife has been very ill for some time now and needs constant care. I've decided to sell up. I can use the money to get by. I'm not that far off from retirement age anyway. I got a good deal so I bit their hand off. Paki family but they seem decent people."

Mark was shocked, Frank had seemed an eternal fixture in his universe. But as he knew too well, things change. "I'm sorry to hear about your wife, Frank," said Mark. "I thought she hadn't been in lately." 'How can I tell him now?' thought Mark.

"Thank you, Mark. I'll pass that on. But I am sorry to say it's not good news for you. I said I had a good Saturday boy but it looks like they've got teenage sons of their own so, sorry Mark, today's your last day." Frank looked at Mark with a look of genuine sorrow.

Mark's mind was whirling. Should he protest as though he really wanted to keep the job? An idea came to him. "It's not a problem, Frank, honestly. I've got my GCEs coming up soon so in a way I could really use the time. And I've saved up some money anyway."

"Well, Mark, you've been a really good worker, quite apart from your fire fighting when you started. If you need a reference for another job later, I'd be more than happy."

"Thank you, Frank. When do the new owners take over?"

"Monday. It was signed off this week. I know I should have called round to Calvert House to tell you but I didn't know which flat is yours. It'll be a wrench, but times change and we have to move on."

'How true' thought Mark. But he said, "Let's make today a good one then."

. . .

As they drove to Pip's house in the Austin Healey after Pip picked up Mark after work, Pip asked, "How did it go telling Frank?"

"I didn't have to. He told me. He's sold the business and the new owners have got kids my age so they'll be helping in the shop. So he was sorry today was my last day there."

"Odd sometimes, how things work out. Why did he sell up?"

"His wife is ill and needs looking after and he's near retirement age anyway. I never thought about how old he was, but I didn't think he was that old."

Pip laughed. "So you think someone in their fifties is old, young Mark?"

"Dunno. Hadn't thought about it much. I suppose so. But then maybe not."

"So, are you ready to start work for me tomorrow," said Pip.

Mark smiled. "Before. Tonight at yours, tomorrow at the showroom."

"I'll get you home in good time and pick you up at the junction in the morning. Nine o'clock. I've told the staff you're my nephew but not anything about pay. If anybody asks, just say Uncle Philip pays you out of pocket."

"I forgot your posh name is Philip," said Mark. "Don't they call you Pip then?"

"Not if they value their lives," laughed Pip. "It's Mr Middleton as far as they are concerned."

"Is that your name?" asked Mark, surprised. "I never knew it before." Mark thought for a moment. "Wait, that big, massive showroom, Middleton Motors; is that you?"

"It is, Mark. I'd like you to dress reasonably smartly. Trousers, not jeans. Shirt and tie. Do you have those?"

Mark thought for a moment. "Wow! That's the biggest garage in Bilthaven. Yes. School trousers and shirt, I've got another tie besides my school tie."

"Excellent," said Pip as they pulled into the driveway of his large house.

Later, Pip dropped Mark off near Calvert House. Mark had an extra five pounds in his pocket and the prospect of much more to come.

# Chapter 23 Showroom

"Where've you been?" demanded Mam when Mark walked into the flat at after seven o'clock. "You can get your own tea now."

"It was my last day at the chippy so there was extra to do," lied Mark, glibly. "It was also Frank's last day because he's sold the chippy so the place had to be left spick and span."

"Sold it?" said Mam, surprised. "Why's he done that?"

"His wife's ill and he wants to retire. But it'll still be a chippy."

"So when do you start at the garage?"

"Tomorrow," said Mark. "It's Saturday **and** Sunday, one reason why it's more money."

"How much more?" asked Mam.

Mark had thought about this. To be truthful would lead to all sorts of questions. "It's two pounds a day, so that's four pounds for the weekend." Mark of course did not mention the five pounds for his evening 'work'.

"I said you would sort something out, now didn't I?" smiled Mam. "You're not just clever, Mark Martin, but a lucky bugger as well. Sit down and I'll get you your tea."

Mark smiled to himself.

. . .

Mark was up bright and early on Sunday morning. He had spent all Saturday evening revising so he felt he was entitled to go out all day. After downing some cereal and instant coffee, he walked along to the junction, away from prying eyes at Calvert House, although he suspected that most of the residents, like Mam, would still be in bed. As he stood in the cool early April sunshine, there was no sign of Pip. His watch said five to nine so he leaned on a fence and waited.

At exactly nine, he saw the red sports car approaching. Mark noticed Pip had the top down.

"Good morning, Mark," he said as Mark got in. Mark noticed Pip was wearing a dark suit, white shirt and striped tie. He had not seen Pip in a suit before and Mark thought he looked very sexy in it.

They set off and Mark was surprised he was not cold. Pip explained the cold air went over the windscreen and with the heater on, they sat in a pocket of warmer air.

"Remember, Mark, you're my nephew so call me either Uncle Philip or less probably, Mr Middleton. Probably better if your name is Mark Middleton. I know it's been a long time since the fire but the name Mark Martin might ring some bells."

"Yes, Uncle Philip," said Mark smiling, as he watched Pip driving with renewed interest.

"When will I learn to drive a car?" asked Mark.

"Bloody hell! We've not even arrived yet and you're already making demands," said Pip, but he was laughing and gave Mark's bulge a quick squeeze which had the effect of starting to make Mark erect. But the stimulus stopped and things subsided a bit.

They pulled into the car park next to the showroom. Mark noticed Pip headed straight for a parking space near the entrance. Other cars were there but the closest space was free. Then as they drove in, Mark saw the sign that said 'Reserved. Mr P. Middleton'.

"You've got your very own parking space," said Mark, unnecessarily.

"Boss's perks," said Pip as they got out. Pip quickly put the tonneau cover on. "In case it rains later," he explained.

As they walked to the showroom door, Mark felt suddenly nervous. A man, perhaps forty or so in a suit, saw them coming and opened the door for them. "Good morning, Mr Middleton," he said.

"Good morning, Mr Shaw," answered Pip. "This is my young nephew, Mark, who is working here at weekends to help out in the showroom."

Good morning, Mark," said Mr Shaw, holding out his hand which Mark then shook.

137

"Good morning," said Mark, uncertainly. He looked at Pip, who seemed to read his mind.

"Don't worry, Mark. Mr Shaw, who is the Sales Manager, will look after you. The showroom is his domain, But I know you're a hard worker and a bright young man so just do as Mr Shaw asks and all will be fine." He turned to Mr Shaw. "I'll leave him in your capable hands. No special favours, just treat him as though he is no relation." Pip then left, walking off through the showroom, behind a desk labelled 'Reception' and then disappearing through a door.

"Well, Mark, is this your first job?" asked Mr Shaw.

"No, I worked in a fish and chip shop," said Mark. He immediately wished he hadn't in case it made Mr Shaw remember him. (But it was two years and as Frank used to say, "Today's news is my wrapping paper for chips tomorrow.")

"I hope you find the motor trade more interesting than filleting fish," replied Mr Shaw. "Let's start. Do you know how to make tea and coffee?"

"Yes," said Mark. He was shown over to a worktop unit at the side. There was a kettle, teapot, tea caddy and tea strainer, cups and saucers, a small sink and a gadget Mark hadn't seen before; round and the bottom part was a glass jug. "What's that?" he asked.

"Coffee machine. Filter coffee. I thought you said you could make coffee," said Mr Shaw with a frown.

"I thought you meant instant coffee."

"Don't worry, Mark. I'll show you." Mr Shaw demonstrated how to load the ground coffee and the water. "Press the button and off you go. Now boil the kettle ready to make tea. Customers will come in and look around the cars. Your job is to smile and offer them a free tea or coffee. If they accept, it makes them stay longer and start talking to the sales staff. Do mention the word free so they are left in no doubt."

Mark nodded. He understood this.

Mr Shaw continued. "Start with four coffees, five if you want one. I like mine black, Mr Skelton over there has

138

his white, no sugar," he said pointing over to a brochure laden table where a young man was sitting, who waved at the mention of his name, "Rebecca over there behind the desk likes it white with two sugars and Mr Middleton white with one sugar. Then however you like yours."

Mark tried to remember all the combinations. As the coffee gurgled through, he got out five mugs from a shelf under the  work unit. Then he had a thought. "Mugs or cups?" he called after Mr Shaw, who was walking back across the large showroom.

"Mugs for staff, cups and saucers for customers," he called back.

He took two mugs of coffee over to the table where Mr Shaw and Mr Skelton were sitting and talking.

"Where are the customers?" he asked.

"We don't open until ten on a Sunday," replied Mr Shaw.

"Do you sell lots of cars on Sundays?"

"Not one," smiled Mr Shaw. "Customers come in to look round, perhaps test out a car they're interested in but the law prevents us from actually selling anything on Sundays. Archaic, but there it is."

"The idea is a leisurely, no pressure environment for the customer. Perhaps a test drive. The hope is that they like us so much that they'll come back in the week and buy the car," added Mr Skelton, smiling at Mark.

Mark was looking at the shiny new cars in the showroom. "They are all Fords," he said. "Do you only sell Fords?"

"New, yes," replied Mr Shaw. "We are a Ford main agent. We sometimes take trade-ins and if they are good enough, we put them in our used car lot."

"What if they are not good enough?"

"We send them to auction," answered Mr Shaw. "Now, don't keep Rebecca and Mr Middleton waiting for their coffee," said Mr Shaw.

Mark took two more coffees to the reception. "I hope this is how you like it," said Mark.

"I'm sure it's fine," Rebecca answered.

Mark guessed she was about thirty. He noticed a wedding ring on her left hand. "Where is Mr Middleton?" he asked.

"Probably in the workshop or his office. No, it'll be his office. Silly me. The workshop isn't open on Sundays."

"I don't know where that is."

Rebecca showed Mark through the door, up a few stairs into a passage and then into a big office. One window looked over the showroom, another over the car park. A smaller window looked over the workshop, which was quiet at that moment.

"Come in, Mark," said Pip, who was sitting behind a big desk. "They've got you on coffee duty then."

"Yes," said Mark. "I had to learn how to use the coffee thingy though."

Pip smiled. "Mark, have you not seen when I make us a coffee at my home I use a similar device?"

Mark shook his head. "Never noticed."

"Well, now you know. Off you go; I'm certain Mr Shaw will have more for you to do."

"Pip, I was thinking. I'm off school the next two weeks for the Easter holidays. I could come in more days."

"I'll think about it," said Pip. "And call me Uncle Philip here. You never know who might overhear. Off you go."

Back in the showroom, ten o'clock came but no customers came in. So Mark looked round the cars. He was especially taken with the Ford Capri and its sporty looks. He sat in it and pretended to be driving it, moving the steering wheel from side to side.

"You'd be all over the road like that," smiled Mr Shaw. "You only need very slight adjustments to the steering when driving along. Barely noticeable; unless turning of course."

"When can I learn to drive? Uncle Philip said I would learn so I could move the cars round," asked Mark hopefully.

"Did he now?" said Mr Shaw. "We'll have to see. Earn your spurs in here first."

Mark had a book about King Arthur and the Knights of the Round Table so he understood. He replied, "Can I learn in this, the Capri?" He beamed at Mr Shaw in anticipation.

"A brand new Capri! Not likely," laughed Mr Shaw. "Maybe a used Anglia from the lot, an older model, a 100E. Side valve engine, three speed gearbox, but perfectly good to learn on. For what you would need here anyway."

"What's side valve mean?" asked Mark.

"You are impatient. All in good time. You can learn about engines as well. Maybe get you some time in the workshop if Mr Middleton agrees."

"Oh, I think he will agree," smiled Mark.

Customers started to arrive to browse the cars. Mr Shaw gave Mark a nudge. "Don't let them get away, Mark. And remember to say it's free. Be polite and smile."

Mark approached a couple who were looking at a Cortina, Ford's new medium size family car. "Good morning," said Mark. "Would you like a free tea or coffee while you look at the car?"

The couple looked at each other and nodded. "Yes, that would be nice, thank you," said the woman. "Teas please, milk, no sugar."

"Coming right up," said Mark, and went over to his worktop.

"What a nice young man," he heard the woman say quietly to her husband.

Mr Shaw gave Mark a thumbs up sign on his way over to talk to the couple about the Cortina.

As the day went on, Mark was kept very busy by the influx of browsing potential customers making teas (remembering to use the tea strainer) and coffees. He took a short lunch break over a sandwich with Pip in his office.

"Are you enjoying it?" asked Pip.

Mark nodded while chewing his sandwich.

"You seem to be making a good impression," said Pip. "Well done. I knew you would."

141

# Chapter 24 Testing Times

"Well, then? How did it go?" asked Mam. "Crashed any cars?"

"I didn't drive any cars today. Made coffee and tea all day for the customers."

"Good idea, Mark. I could just do with a cuppa before I go to work."

Mark wanted to explain about the customers using Sundays to browse because the cars could not be sold, and how his job was to keep them in the showroom so the salesmen could get the customers interested and maybe make an appointment to return and buy. But he realized that Mam was not interested in the detail. Resigned, he went to make his umpteenth pot of tea that day. He sat and drank his tea with Mam but was feeling very tired. They watched Bruce Forsyth's "Sunday Night at the London Palladium". He felt he should do some revision even though it was the holiday but when he went to his new desk he decided instead to lie on the bed for a few minutes.

He was woken by knocking - the flat's front door. 'Answer that, Mam, please' he thought. He looked at his watch. 'She'll have gone to work.' He lifted himself off the bed and went to the front door. Through the spy-hole he saw Tommy. 'Of course, Sunday night. Come for his fuck.'

"Hi Tommy," he said, opening the door.

Tommy came in, and Mark shut the door. In the hallway, Tommy turned and kissed Mark and hugged him tight. "I am so horny," announced Tommy. "I was waiting until I saw your Mam go for the bus, then I knew you'd be on your own."

Mark went towards the living room but Tommy grabbed his shoulders and steered him into his bedroom.

"Tommy, I'm tired. It's been a busy day. I've spent all day at work at the showroom."

"I've spent all day, my only day off, thinking about you and waiting for tonight. Don't let me down, Mark," said

Tommy, fondling Mark's bum and then feeling his hardening cock. "See! You do want it."

"Do you not want to hear about the showroom and the cars?" asked Mark in an attempt to deflect Tommy.

"Yes, if you like, but later. Get undressed now!" he finished moving into assertive mode. Mark weakened as he always did when faced with a dominating male, and especially Tommy. And Pip of course.

It did feel good, being in bed, naked and close to Tommy.

"You seem fitter than ever," commented Mark, running his hands over Tommy's increasingly muscular frame.

"It's hard work in the shop. Not just sitting around all day looking at cars."

"There's more to it than that, "objected Mark.

"Yes, but you're not lifting the fucking cars up, are you? Try heaving half a cow about!" retorted Tommy. "Turn over."

Mark obeyed and it felt just so right when Tommy entered.

Afterwards, they both relaxed. Mark asked, "What do you do in the shop?"

"Chop the meat up. Got to know all the different parts of each animal, where the different cuts of meat come from and that. Serving customers as well. So got to know the prices, although me dad puts the price labels on. I'm getting quite good at adding up, and doing takeaways to give change."

"What do you use to chop up the meat?"

"A meat cleaver of course, what do you think? Fucking sharp too."

"Aren't you scared of missing and chopping your hand off?"

"No, coz I wear a special metal glove. Sort of like fine chain mail. Made of stainless steel. I hit me left hand once and it fucking hurt but the cleaver didn't get through the glove, just left a whacking great bruise. So what about you? Drive around all day?"

"No, they will teach me to drive, this holiday I hope."

"You're not seventeen yet are you?"

"No, but I can move the cars on site, just not on the public road."

"I forgot you had school holiday. I'll get Good Friday and Easter Monday and that's it, while you're lazing around. At least I won't have to go in the fucking army now National Service has been ended."

"I'm going back tomorrow so maybe then. I make tea and coffee for the customers and talk to them nicely."

"Is that all? Cushy number! You getting as much as you did in the chippy?"

Mark thought 'Keep the story straight.' "Two pounds a day."

"Twice as much for half the work," laughed Tommy. "You land on your feet every time, Mark Martin."

. . .

The used car lot was beyond the car park with its own entrance from the main road. On Monday lunchtime, Pip took Mark round there to find a suitable car. As Mr Shaw had predicted, a trade-in Anglia 100E, with the side valve engine was selected. Behind the used car lot was a large unpaved area but with what seemed to Mark an ash covering.

"What's this place," asked Mark.

"We use it as overflow parking space if needed, but otherwise nothing. I have plans to build a new, bigger workshop here and use the present workshop to extend the showroom. Now let's see if you can move this car without hitting anything."

"There's nothing here to hit," said Mark.

"Exactly," replied Pip, with a smile.

Mark made the little car jump around while he mastered the clutch and was soon driving round in a big circle in first gear. Changing gear caught Mark out as the second, middle, gear made the car leap forward.

"That's a very useful gear for getting away from the traffic lights," laughed Pip.

"What's the top speed of this car?"

"Maybe seventy. A bit more with a following wind," Pip added. "When you've done a bit more I'll give you a proficiency test to see if you can be let loose with other cars."

Back in the showroom, Mr Shaw set Mark on cleaning out a Ford Corsair demonstrator that had been out on a test drive and the interior had got a bit soiled. So cleaning cars and making the drinks kept Mark on the go. The work in the chippy had been tiring and repetitive, but this was tiring because of the constant changes of role, the need to keep smiling at the customers, some of whom looked at this boy with disdain, taking their free drinks without a word. 'Ignorant people' thought Mark while he smiled nicely at them.

The problem with this was that Mark returned home at night tired, especially as he was working every day. On some evenings when Mam was out he went to his bedroom and ignored the knocking at the door which he knew was Tommy. He felt bad about that because he knew that Tommy loved him and while he perhaps didn't love Tommy in the same way, he liked him and enjoyed the sex with him.

"Where were you night before last? I knocked a few times. You're not avoiding me, are you?" asked Tommy. Mark saw pain on his face. 'He actually does love me' thought Mark.

"Of course not, Tommy. Sometimes I'm so tired I fall asleep on the bed. Maybe that's what happened."

Mark thought 'I'm always lying to people, even Tommy, never mind Mam.' Mark felt uncomfortable about that because at heart he didn't like lying. But he knew the truth would hurt, so he justified it to himself that way.

Tommy's face brightened up, so Mark could not resist his demands once more.

. . .

By the end of the Easter holiday, Mark was considerably richer. On his final day, Pip put him through his paces in the little Anglia, with tests on careful manoeuvring, reversing etc, and then some time in a much bigger Ford Zephyr. Pip was pleased with the test.

In some ways it was a relief to get back to school. He felt he hadn't done enough revision during the Easter holiday what with the garage and Tommy's demands. He had never quite understood that Mark still wanted to do schoolwork during the holidays. Now back at school, Tommy was more accepting of Mark's need to study for the impending GCE exams. Sometimes Mark would tune in to Radio Luxembourg and have the music in the background. He liked the Beatles and the Roy Orbison song "In Dreams".

Inexorably the GCE exams drew closer. Mark worked very hard, going to Pip's only after work on Saturday and seeing Tommy only on Sunday evening, despite Tommy's protestations. In bed he asked Pip if he could drop Sunday work until after the exams.

"Of course, Mark. You must do well in the exams, a clever lad like you must do yourself justice. I'll do whatever I can to support you." Pip held Mark close and squeezed him, kissing his neck. "I love you, Mark Martin," he whispered, caressing Mark's stiff cock and balls.

Mark wasn't sure what to say. Were his feelings for Pip love? So he just kissed Pip with a grateful passion.

All too soon the exams started. His best subject, History, went well. He had to answer five questions, three from one section and two from another. As advised he spent the first few minutes of the two and half hours reading through and selecting the best questions. He noticed some others were writing straight away. Hadn't they read the instructions carefully enough? Ian McLaren was one, he saw. Ethan and Eddie were reading like Mark. He could not see Danny without turning right round. 'Concentrate on your own exam.' From section ten he chose to write about Prussia between 1806 and 1830, Napoleon's dealings with Russia and from section eleven, about races and nationalities in the

146

Habsburg Empire and the changes up to 1867, the Crimean War and the Franco-Prussian War of 1870. Once he had started the words just flowed from his brain onto the paper.

Mark was confident of the English exams but was stumped by the first, composition paper. Of the six titles offered for him to write about, none of them struck a chord. In the end he decided on "A Channel Crossing" but rather than write about a cross channel ferry, he wrote a story about the D-Day landings from the viewpoint of an ordinary British soldier landing on Sword Beach. Mark named him Tommy! He had a pal called Timothy. He was running out of time in the hour exam, so had to finish quickly by the simple expedient of ending with "The Waffen SS had retreated. They entered the small village. The destruction seemed complete. There were bodies, some burnt inside their homes. Others lying bloodied where they had been shot. The slaughter of a defenceless coastal community. Men, women and even children lying in their own blood. None showed any sign of life. As Tommy, along with Timothy, edged through the shattered and burnt out houses of the village, once happy family homes, Tommy never saw the sniper who, with an accurate headshot, killed him instantly. The End." Mark had to hope it would do.

The second English exam was more structured. He made short work of the compulsory précis and comprehension questions and for his third he chose the mainly grammar based answer based around a letter from a farmer to some campers. He finished with time to check over his work. He felt he had done enough to pass.

He had to smile to himself in French because the first translation piece was about a Madame Martin. It made him think of Mam. Again he felt he had done enough.

That evening at home, he greeted Mam with, "Bonsoir, Madame Martin. Comment allez-vous?"

"What are you talking about, you dafty," she smiled.

"One of the questions in the French exam today was about a Madame Martin."

"Don't be silly. Put the kettle on, there's a good lad."

One by one the exams passed and Mark could at last relax. He was pleased when Manchester United won the FA Cup because it was the team's comeback from the Munich air disaster five years before. No more school work until September. Now the wait until August for the results.

# Chapter 25 Confrontation

There was no requirement to attend school for fifth years once the exams were over. With Pip's blessing and encouragement, Mark spent most days at the showroom, extending his range of work which now included fetching the demonstrator cars from their garage and driving them round to the front, suitably valeted, for potential buyers to test drive. He thoroughly enjoyed this work and he became obsessed by the rising sums in his post office account, now in the hundreds of pounds. But, he reasoned, he would need that to subsidize Mam so he could stay on at the Sixth Form to study for his A level exams and hopefully university after that.

Some evenings he spent with Pip, usually those when Mam wasn't working, and with Tommy when he had the flat to himself.

"Mark," complained Mam. "You're never here. I never see my lad these days. You work all the days and I don't know why, but you always seem to be out the evenings I'm not working. Are you fucking avoiding me or what?"

"Of course not, Mam," said Mark. "But I'm not a kid any more."

"So you keep telling me." Mam suddenly smiled. "I get it. What's her name?"

Mark hesitated. "Er, Pippa," he said. "She's at school," he continued, warming to the lie. "She lives on that posh estate out west, West Farm Estate."

"So that's where you've been going? What about her mam and dad?"

"What about them? I like them," Mark replied, mentally casting Pip in the role of the mythical Pippa's father.

"But do they like you?"

"Yes, Mam, they seem to. anyway."

"Of course they do," smiled Mam. "Who couldn't like my lovely, sexy lad."

149

"Mam!" exclaimed Mark in protest at her explicit reference to his sexual attraction.

"Well, I just hope you're careful. Take precautions and that," advised Mam, now grinning broadly and looking Mark up and down.

"Mam!" shouted Mark again, flushing red. "It's embarrassing."

"I'm your mam. I used to change your nappies."

"I'm going to my room," said Mark, and fled as he heard Mam chuckling behind him.

. . .

The summer passed by, evenings with Pip or Tommy, days at the garage. Mr Shaw was concerned that Vauxhall were going to launch their new small car, the Viva, just before Ford's new Anglia, and feared lost sales as a result.

At last in August, the GCE results were out. Mark scored A grades in English Language, English Literature and History. B grades in Mathematics, Physics, Biology, French and German, a D grade in Chemistry. All GCE passes therefore.

"Mam! I got three As, five Bs and a D," said Mark happily.

"Well done, love. That's good, is it?" she asked.

"Yes, Mam, it's good," explained Mark, wearily.

"Well then, you should be able to get a good job with that lot," chirruped Mam.

"Mam, I told you before. I'm not getting a job. I'm staying for Sixth Form to do A levels and then apply for university."

"So how long have I got to work my knuckles to the fucking bone to keep you?" snapped Mam.

"We talked about this. I got the better weekend job so I can give you some money for my keep while I stay on," said Mark, starting to get angry. He glowered at Mam, standing close and now towering over her.

"Well you'd fucking better," Mam said. "You'd better keep that job or it's straight down the employment exchange for you."

"I'm surprised you know where that is," retorted Mark. "Maybe you should try it."

"You cheeky little sod," shouted Mam, raising her hand to strike Mark, which he easily deflected. "I've worked my socks off for you and that ungrateful hussy of a daughter. And this is the thanks I get?"

Mark calmed down a bit and felt he needed to offer an olive branch. "Mam, it's because of you that I've been able to do so well in the exams. You might not always understand what I'm on about, but you've always cared for me and looked after me. I do love you, Mam."

Mam softened, and Mark saw her eyes water. "Is that true, Mark. Is that what you really think?"

"Of course it is, Mam. I know you still think of me as a ten year old which is annoying, but without you, where would I be?"

"Come here, son. Give your Mam a hug. And well done in them exams."

Mark gave Mam a hug. "Shall I go and get us a slap up meal from the Chinkies to celebrate?"

Mam smiled. "That would be lovely, Mark. I'll boil the kettle while you're out."

. . .

"Me Mam and Dad are going to Blackpool next week. Taking me sister but I didn't fancy it," said Tommy as they lay in Mark's bed one evening.

"Why not?" asked Mark. "I've never been to Blackpool."

"Coz I thought that while they were away I'd have the flat to myself and so you could spend lots more time with me. Maybe stay over all night."

The thought of spending all night in bed with Tommy, sleeping with Tommy, appealed to Mark. "I could make some excuse to Mam," he offered.

"No need, Mark," said Tommy, pulling a face. "They've got my uncle coming to look after the shop for the week rather than close up. He'll be staying in the flat. And what's more, Dad did this because I know the business so I'll have to help my uncle. He's not a butcher so I guess I'll have to do more work."

"That's a shame, Tommy. Lost your trip to the seaside."

"I've been before. Have you never been to the seaside?"

"Yes, Tommy, I've been to the beach at the coast here," said Mark. "But before Mam and dad split up we went to Majorca for a holiday."

Tommy frowned. "Where's that?"

"It's an island, but it's part of Spain. I learned some Spanish there."

"Spain! Abroad?"

"Yes," affirmed Mark.

"I've never been abroad," said Tommy. "You're dead lucky, Mark."

"Yes," said Mark, smiling at Tommy. "Lucky I met you."

"Do you mean that?" said Tommy, his face lit up.

"Of course," answered Mark.

"Right then," said Tommy, switching to master mode. "On your front."

Mark was happy to comply.

. . .

Pip was really pleased with Mark's GCE results. "Excellent, Mark. I'm proud of you. I expect your mother is too."

"I think so," said Mark. "She doesn't really understand how important it is though. We had a bit of a row about me staying on as well."

"But you are going to, aren't you?" said Pip, concerned.

"Yes, thanks to you, really. When I said I would give her some money for my keep, she said it was OK."

"I'm really glad about that, Mark. We must have a celebration for your great results."

A few days later Mark was surprised to be taken to The Vault. When he walked in with Pip, everybody was there; Gordon, Gerry, Fred, Tom and even Peter, sitting next to Tom. They had even arranged for a small buffet.

"Hello, Mark, Congratulations," said Gordon.

"Thank you," said Mark, surprised by all this.

"Yes, well done, Mark," said Gerry, coming and giving Mark a hug.

"Drinks all round," said Gordon.

"I've ordered us a bottle or two of champers," said Pip. "It is a celebration."

"Come and sit down," said Gordon to Mark.

All the men were very friendly to Mark, despite his absence from The Vault for some time.

"We've not seen you here for ages," said Gerry. "We've missed you."

"I've been working a lot," said Mark. "And studying for the GCEs of course."

"Well, we can see your hard work paid off," said Tom.

"He's been working at the showroom," said Pip. "Charming the customers and doing odd jobs around the place."

"I learned to drive as well, although I'll have to wait before I can drive on the road," said Mark.

"So Pip, that's where you've been hiding him," said Fred.

"Not just at the showroom, knowing how Mark and Pip get on," said Gordon with a grin. The men laughed.

Mark flushed and Pip just tapped his nose, smiling. As good as an outright admission they'd been fucking.

Peter was looking hard at Mark, seeming very resentful. He was now older and bigger. Mark found that slightly unnerving.

"Champagne for all, including Mark," said Pip. "A toast. To Mark."

"To Mark," was repeated as the toast was drunk. There was food and drink in plentiful supply. The evening drew on and Mark started to feel rather light headed.

"Pip, I feel a bit funny," he said.

"Champagne gone to his head a bit," said Gordon.

"I'll take him out the back for a breath of fresh air," said Pip.

They stepped out into the back yard. There were stacks of empty beer barrels waiting to be collected. Mark sat on one. There was some light from the pub and the street lights outside the big gates on to a back lane.

"Are you feeling any better?" asked Pip. "Fresh air should clear your head a bit." He put his arm round Mark and hugged him.

Mark smiled at him. "Yes, thanks. And thanks for this and everything," he added.

"I'm happy to help," said Pip. "You know that. Are you coming back in?"

"I'll sit for a few more minutes," said Mark, enjoying the cool summer evening air.

"OK," said Pip. "Come in when you're ready." Pip got up and went back in.

Mark sat and took deep breaths. Life was good. He became aware of another presence. He saw a lit cigarette and now smoke from behind the stack of barrels. Peter emerged smoking.

"Think you're clever, do you?" said Peter, his voice full of quiet menace. "Think you can just waltz back in here after months of being Pip's bum boy and just pick up where you left off?"

"They're just having a party for me, what's wrong with that?"

"I'll tell you exactly what's wrong with that. I was number one at The Vault long before you showed up with your fireman's hat on and I'm still number one here. So you can just piss off and don't come back!"

"And if I don't?"

Peter produced a knife, it snapped out of its handle with a sharp click. "You won't be so pretty very soon."

# Chapter 26 Class Differences

Mark looked at the knife, the blade glinting in the street lighting. He looked at Peter, older, but Mark was as tall, if not heavy set like Peter. Mark didn't fancy his chances in a fight.

But he answered, "And if you did anything with that, what do you think that lot in there would think of you then? I doubt you'd be number one very long; or any number in fact."

Mark's words seemed to hit home with Peter who hesitated before replying. "Listen, you arsehole, you've been warned. That's what I'm saying," said Peter softly.

Mark turned and went back to the rear door of the pub. He looked back and Peter was still standing, outlined against the light from the back lane, still smoking. There was now no sign of the knife.

"Are you feeling better, Mark?" asked Pip.

"Yes, thanks. Are you giving me a lift home after this?" asked Mark.

"Yes, if that's what you want."

"Something I need to talk to you about, but when we're alone."

"Is everything all right, Mark?" asked Pip with concern.

At that moment Peter came back, drew a few more drags on his cigarette before stubbing it out in the ashtray and sitting back next to Tom.

"Yes, I'll tell you later," said Mark quietly.

The evening carried on with a light and convivial atmosphere. The buffet food was all eaten. It was at closing time when they left. It was a short walk to where Pip had parked his car.

As they got in, Pip said, "Could you stay at my place tonight? You know how much I want you."

This threw Mark into a turmoil of indecision. He wanted Pip too, but he wondered what Mam would say if he were out all night. He would say he had stayed with Pippa.

"Yes, I'd like that," he said.

"Then you can tell me what's on your mind," said Pip as he drove the sports car deftly through the city streets.

"Would you like a drink?" asked Pip as they went into the house.

"I think maybe I've had enough tonight," said Mark.

"I was thinking of coffee, or perhaps just water," said Pip. "Water is good because it rehydrates you and helps prevent a hangover. But I can make coffee. You know how to do that now," he added, smiling.

"Maybe both, then?" suggested Mark.

"Drink some water while the coffee is on the go then."

Mark drank a glass of water sitting in Pip's large, modern kitchen. They then moved to the large living room and Pip drew the curtains, and they sat on the large sofa with their mugs of coffee.

Pip put his arm round Mark. "Come on then, what is it?"

Mark paused. He took a sip of his coffee while he thought.

"It's Peter," he said at last. "After you went back in from the back yard at The Vault, Peter was there smoking. He threatened me, said he was number one with you lot and I should piss off. Then he had a flick knife and said I had been warned. Said I wouldn't be pretty much longer."

"Oh dear," said Pip. "I'm sorry. I'm sure he wouldn't really do anything though. Just trying to scare you away."

"Well, I did say that if he did that, you lot wouldn't have any more to do with him so it would be counterproductive for him, although I didn't say it like that."

"He probably wouldn't have understood," said Pip. "But don't worry about it. Tom knows Peter best, I'll have a word. It'll blow over, you'll see."

"He called me your bum boy and called me an arsehole."

"Mark, you're better looking than he is, you're cleverer than he is and now anyway, richer than he is. So his only response is to call you names. Stop worrying about Peter." Pip leant in and kissed Mark. "You're a lovely lad, Mark. Worth ten of him."

"I'm tired. But I want to thank you for the party, It was a really nice thing to do, you and the others."

"Let's go up and you can thank me in bed."

They stood up and for the first time Mark saw that he was as tall as Pip. Mark lay on the bed while Pip undressed him. He became very aroused despite the quantity of champagne he had drunk.

"I need the toilet," said Mark and he walked, now naked, to the en-suite bathroom while Pip watched him across the bedroom, taking in his youthful fit body. When Mark emerged from the bathroom, Pip was already in bed. Any inhibitions diluted by the alcohol, their love making was even more passionate than normal.

"You're fantastic," said Pip.

"So are you," replied Mark.

They fell asleep.

. . .

"Where the fuck were you all last night?" screamed Mam. "I was worried sick."

"I'm fine, Mam," said Mark. "I stayed over at Pippa's after work yesterday."

Mark had arrived home after a day in the showroom, so some thirty-six hours after he had left home.

Mam was not impressed. "So I'm sitting there all night worried to death while you're off shagging some lass?"

"Well, we haven't got a phone so I couldn't ring up to let you know. What else could I do?"

"What else? What else? I'll tell you what else, Mark Martin. You could've fucking come home, that's what else!"

Mark realized that Mam's fury was really an outward manifestation of her love for him. "Mam, I'm sorry. It was thoughtless of me. Maybe I should've called in here first to let you know. But some friends had laid on a little party for me to celebrate my GCEs and it went on late."

Mam seemed mollified by Mark's apology and explanation. "I don't know, Mark. You just seem to be growing up too quickly. What happened to the little boy I used to have? Now it's parties, work, shagging around and talk about university. I can't keep up."

Mark thought how the world he was moving into was so different from Mam's. Quite apart from being queer and that world, he was moving in different social circles. 'I'm less working class and more middle class these days' thought Mark. Even his friends at school, such as Ethan, Steve and Eddie, were middle class. Of the group at The Vault, only Fred was probably working class, the rest middle class judging by wealth and attitudes; Pip certainly.

"Mam, it's OK," he said. "The world is changing, it's the nineteen sixties. I'll be fine. I've got a good brain and in time I'll use it to look after us."

"You're a good lad at heart, Mark. I know that. But I hope you're careful with this lass. Having a kid now would really screw up your university plans and that."

"Don't worry about that, Mam. No chance of pregnancy."

"Glad to hear that. I don't suppose you've got enough for another Chinky treat, have you? Make up for last night?"

"Of course, Mam. I'm starving, actually. I'll nip round now while you get things ready here," said Mark.

"Sounds like a good deal to me," smiled Mam. "Give me a hug before you go."

. . .

The new school term approached. Mark remembered he'd need a new school uniform. He had outgrown his shirts, trousers as well as the school blazer. His relatively new winter coat still fitted. But Mark was left with the problem of either asking Mam for money for the uniform or buying it all himself. In the end he decided to buy it himself even though Mam might query the cost and how he could afford it. He was giving her an extra five pounds a week for his keep so he reasoned she should not ask too many questions. There was a sixth form tie, but he would get that at school on the first day of term.

So he kitted himself out with good quality stuff. His school friends seemed to assume that he was in the same income bracket as most of them, unaware that he and Mam lived in a small council flat. Mark wanted them to continue to think that, fearing that they would look down on him if they knew.

At home he was trying everything on in front of his mirror. He went into the living room.

"Mam, what do you think?" he said.

"Very smart. Give us a twirl."

Mark turned right round. "Do you mind if I look in your long mirror?" he asked, thinking of the full length mirror in Mam's bedroom.

"Of course you can," she answered. Mam got up and they went into her bedroom. Mark looked at himself in the mirror. 'I am rather smart' he thought to himself.

Just then there was a knock at the flat door. Mam went to answer it while Mark continued to preen himself.

"Mark, it's Tommy," she called. Then more quietly, "Hello Tommy. Haven't seen you for a while, where've you been?"

"I'm working full time now in the shop," Mark heard Tommy reply. He walked into the hallway.

"Hi, Tommy," he said. "Not seen you for a bit. Are they back from Blackpool?"

"Yes. It went OK with me uncle. I had to do most of the work though, and of course the freezer was almost empty but Dad's fixed that. What about you? Looking very smart. You going out?"

"No, it's my new school uniform, ready for next week. I'm going to get changed out of it now. Come along," said Mark, heading to his bedroom. Mam went into the living room.

Once in his bedroom, Mark explained," Tommy, she's not working tonight."

"I know, but they're all out at the pictures tonight to see that new film, something, 'Jason and the Astronauts'.

Mark laughed. "Argonauts, Tommy. It's set in ancient Greece and there weren't many astronauts then." He thought Tommy was definitely working class.

"Yes, that's what I meant. But I thought you could come round mine for a couple of hours. Have to be gone before they get back though."

"Did you not want to see it?" asked Mark as he got changed.

"Yes, but not if I could have you round mine. So hurry up."

"Yes, Tommy."

They walked down the familiar back lane. The back of the chippy looked the same and the clean patch on the wall that Mark had scrubbed more than two years ago was still discernible. They crossed the yard of the butcher's shop.

"Is that your bike? Is it a new one?" asked Mark, noticing a Raleigh racing cycle leaning against the wall.

"Yes, but I don't ride it so much these days. Don't get the time. But maybe we could go on bike rides together," Tommy finished enthusiastically.

"I haven't got a bike," said Mark. "Nowhere to keep it now. I had one when I was little though."

They entered the building and once inside, up stairs to the flat. It was bigger than Mark had expected, based on the upstairs of the chippy. It had been built on at the back to give more rooms. But Tommy went straight through into his bedroom. Despite all the time he had known Tommy, this was the first time he'd been in Tommy's room. It was smaller than Mark's, there were Airfix models and posters on the walls, mainly of Paul McCartney and Bob Dylan.

"You like them?" asked Mark.

"Yes, I think they're both good looking," replied Tommy.

Mark smiled. "So it's not the music that you like then?"

"Yes," answered Tommy, a touch defensively. "That as well. Let's not waste time, Mark. Get undressed."

Mark looked at the narrow single bed as he undressed. "Is there room for us both in there?" he asked.

"Yes," said Tommy now in assertive mode. "I'll be on top of you so there'll be enough room."

That comment made Mark's arousal complete and he desired Tommy more than anything. So here he was, in this strange bed, Tommy's own bed, in Tommy's room, being steadily fucked by Tommy. His capture and submission was total. Mark could hardly contain his own climax as Tommy thrust towards his. Tommy came before Mark, so Tommy held a tissue around Mark's cock as he wanked him to completion.

It was tight as they lay on their sides facing each other in the narrow bed. Tommy kissed Mark. "I love you, Mark. When you've finished school can we live together?"

That took Mark completely by surprise; not just the suggestion, but the naivety of it. "I expect I'll be going to university. That could be anywhere."

"Doesn't have to be. There's a university here."

"I want to try for Oxford or Cambridge," said Mark.

Tommy looked ashen. "They're miles away. That means I wouldn't see you for three years!" His voice was now anguished.

"Tommy, they have long vacations, holidays. More than school holidays. So I'd probably be back here then."

"Probably? Only probably? You'll make new friends, maybe another boyfriend, and forget about Tommy."

Mark felt Tommy's distress. He was glad he hadn't told Tommy about Pip. He kissed Tommy hard. "I would never forget you, Tommy. Anyway, that's two years away and it might not happen. Let's cross that bridge when we come to it."

That thought cheered Tommy up, to the point where he fucked Mark again. Mark was dressed and gone before Tommy's family returned.

# Chapter 27 More books

Mark walked into school on the first day of term and the new school year feeling confident. He had all new uniform on, he had transferred his coveted Laudatum badge to his new blazer and he knew he looked smart. Mark liked the Sixth Form immediately. Most of the idiots had not stayed on so the atmosphere in the new much smaller classes was very different. More mature, staff treating the students more like equals with open discussion around the topics. His chosen A level subjects were History, English and Politics, the last Mark chose because it looked interesting and made a good match with History. It was a fairly new option and he was in a group of just six students with his History teacher, Mr Raynor. Mr Farnsworth was teaching the English group so he was comfortable with teachers he knew and also who knew him. He looked forward to the coming year of Lower Sixth.

The workload was heavy with a lot of reading in all subjects but Mark liked reading and had always read a wide range of books so this was not onerous for him.

He had so many new books he bought a new bookcase and spent time carefully arranging the books organised by subject and day of the week according to his timetable. Mam helped him move stuff around in his bedroom to make space for the new bookcase.

"Why don't you get rid of some of these old books," Mam suggested, casually picking up a few and tossing them onto the bed while they moved things around; in the process nearly giving Mark a heart attack when she threw *Europe in the XIX Century* by D.G.O. Ayerst, in which his Post Office Savings book was concealed, across to the bed. Luckily Mam's eyes didn't follow the book to its destination and so didn't see the savings book now protruding. Mark swiftly put it back inside.

"Mam, don't just throw my books about," he complained. "Books should be treated with respect."

"I know you love your books, Mark," she said. "I don't know how you have the patience to read them all."

"They're interesting to me, Mam," said Mark.

"You're an odd one, Mark," said Mam. "I don't know where you get it from. Not from me, that's for sure. Or your dad."

"You said Granddad had loads of books," suggested Mark.

Mam's face softened. "Yes, he did," she said wistfully. "He was a proper bookworm like you, so that must be how you got it."

"Got it?" smiled Mark. "Mam. It's not a disease."

Mam picked up a book and, opening it at random, started to read, hesitantly, "*Give me that man that is not passion's slave, and I will wear him in my heart's core, ay in my heart of heart, as I do thee.* What the fuck does that mean? It makes no sense."

"It's Shakespeare, Mam."

"Couldn't he write proper English then? How are people supposed to understand that?"

"He's saying that he likes his friend so much because he thinks logically rather then emotionally."

"So why the fuck doesn't he just say that then?"

"That was the way English was spoken back then." Mark decided Mam was never going to be a Shakespeare fan. He had to admit to himself that he found it hard to follow at times but no way was he going to admit that to Mam.

A similar reaction was forthcoming from Tommy. "What you got all those new books for?" he asked when calling round.

"They're the books for my A levels.."

Tommy picked up a slim book. "*The Prince*? Is it about Prince Charles?"

Mark laughed. "No, Tommy. It was written about four hundred years ago by an Italian called Machiavelli. It's about how to be a successful ruler of a country."

"Well, if he was that good at ruling he's a king, not just a prince," reasoned Tommy. He flicked the pages. "What's monarchy?"

"It's a country where there is a king or queen. Like here. Britain is a monarchy because we have a Queen."

"What if there's not one?"

"Then it's called a republic and instead of a king or queen it has a president, like America or France."

"How come you know so much?" demanded Tommy, frowning at Mark.

"Because I read so many books I expect," answered Mark.

"Are there any books about being a butcher?"

"I'm sure there are, Tommy. There are books about everything. Do you want to read a book about being a butcher in your spare time?"

"Fuck off," laughed Tommy. "I'm too busy being a butcher to waste time reading about it. And in my spare time I want to come here and fuck you. So less talk now, come on, I'm horny."

. . .

Marks' life continued to follow much the same pattern as before, seeing Tommy some evenings, working at the showroom with his savings mounting up. Once or twice he and Tommy went into town but stayed well away from The Vault. At the bus station on one such outing, Tommy spotted the photo booth.

"Let's get a picture of us both," said Tommy. They squeezed in the booth and pulled the curtain. They grinned into the screen as the flashes went off. Suddenly Tommy turned to Mark and kissed him on the lips, probing him with his tongue. Mark resisted at first but soon submitted to Tommy's advance. The camera flashed again twice more.

"What did you do that for?" asked Mark as they separated.

"The only way we can get a photo of us," said Tommy.

164

Outside the booth they guarded the output slot carefully and retrieved the photos the moment they dropped.

"Two me, two for you," said Tommy, putting his two carefully in his pocket. Mark did the same.

Apart from Tommy, Mark was spending time at Pip's, sometimes overnight, when he told Mam he was staying with 'Pippa'.

"I hope you're still being careful, Mark. So when am I going to meet this Pippa?" she asked on one occasion. That gave Mark pause for thought.

"I don't know, Mam. Like me, she's busy with A levels. She's doing the same ones as me so we work together a lot of the time."

"So you don't just spend all your time shagging, then?" grinned Mam. She gave Mark a playful punch. "You're a randy sod, Mark Martin."

"Mam! Stop it," said Mark. 'If she only knew' he thought.

Mark's status at school rose rapidly one day when after spending the night with Pip, he was dropped off at school in the Austin Healey. That drew envious attention from some others.

"Is that your dad?" asked Ethan curiously. "I thought it was just you and your mother."

"It is," said Mark, wishing he could pass Pip off as his dad.

"He didn't look old enough to be Mark's dad," commented Steve. "Unless he started very young," he added with a grin.

"No, it's my Uncle Philip. He owns the garage where I work," said Mark, trying to bring some consistency into the fabricated world he seemed to live in.

"Is that why you moved up here then, coz you've family here?" asked Ethan, to which Mark just nodded, glad of the explanation.

165

"I wish I had a car like that," said Steve as they walked toward the school entrance. "Get loads of lasses that way."

"You've already got a girlfriend," remarked Eddie.

"Oh, yes, the lovely Gemma," said Mark.

"Hey you," grinned Steve. "Hands off, Get your own girlfriend."

"I've already got one," said Mark, instinctively as self-protection mode kicked in. But this comment drew sudden interest from the others.

"You're a dark horse, Mark," said Ethan. "You've not mentioned that before."

"It's nobody you know so what was the point?" responded Mark.

"Come on then," urged Steve. "Tell us all about her. What's her name?"

Mark thought, keep it the same. "Pippa," he said, thankful he had described Pip as Uncle Philip, not Pip.

"So what's she like?" asked Eddie.

"Not as tall as me, she's got fair hair, beautiful blue eyes, and a lovely figure," said Mark, warming to his theme and building up an image of Pippa in his mind.

"Big tits?" asked Steve.

"Trust you to think of that," said Ethan.

"No complaints," said Mark with what he hoped was a knowing wink.

"Does she live near you?" Steve continued.

"She lives on West Farm estate," said Mark.

"Oh, rich girl is she?" said Steve. "What does your mam think of her?"

"My mam hasn't met her. She just says to be careful when we have sex, shagging as she says," replied Mark.

"Are you having it with her, all the way?" asked Ethan, eyes wide.

Mark felt the need to strengthen his heterosexual credentials so replied, "Yes, don't you?"

Steve butted in, "Ethan hasn't got a girlfriend. We think he's a bit queer. And his dad a copper, too." Steve was laughing as he said this in a way that indicated he wasn't serious.

"No I'm not," said Ethan indignantly. "After Jackie I'm just taking a break."

"Oh yes, Jackie," laughed Steve.

"Jackie in our class?" asked Mark, but at that moment they went in through the doors into the crowded corridor and the moment was lost.

So Mark became known as something of a quiet Casanova, a reputation he did not dispute. But the exchange did make him look again at Ethan, rather attractive. But far too risky to make any kind of approach. He knew that being identified at school as queer would make life intolerable. He wondered how many of his male classmates and others were secretly hiding their true sexual inclination.

The group was together again at lunchtime. As sixth formers they weren't pushed outside but could pass time in the school library.

Steve once again raised the question of Pippa. "You don't live at West Farm, do you?" he queried of Mark.

"No," said Mark, wondering where Steve was going with this. "I live at Northside, near the famous chip shop," he added with a smile hoping to deflect further questioning about Pippa.

"Oh yes, the one you tried to burn down," laughed Steve.

"Very funny," said Mark, giving Steve a poke.

"No lasses in Northside?" questioned Ethan.

"I expect so," said Mark. "But I met her at the showroom where I work at weekends."

"You got friends near where you live," asked Danny.

Mark immediately thought of Tommy. "Yes, Tommy Hedley. His dad owns the butcher's next to the chip shop, that's how I met him. Same age as us, but he works in his dad's shop now."

"Do you get free meat, then?" joked Steve.

"Actually, I do sometimes," said Mark.

"This Tommy person sounds useful to know," said Steve. "When we meet up in the city you must bring him sometime."

"He probably wouldn't come," said Mark, "and anyway, he works six days a week."

# Chapter 28 Responsibility

Mark did mention this idea to Tommy. "I was talking about you to my friends at school and they said I should bring you into town to meet them one evening."

Tommy's face was one of sheer horror and fear. "You've been telling them about me? About us, what we do?"

"Tommy, of course not that. We were talking about friends and they asked what friends I had in Northside so I said you. Obviously I didn't say anything about sex."

Tommy let out a sigh of relief. He shook his head. "No, I don't fancy that. I'd feel stupid with all your clever friends."

"Tommy, you're not stupid. I told you that before."

"But they'll talk about things I don't know about, like you do sometimes."

"But when I do, you don't feel stupid with me, do you?" said Mark comfortingly.

"No, but that's because it's you. And anyway, if they guess I'm queer, that would spoil everything for you."

"Why would they guess that?"

Tommy pulled a face. "Other boys do. They called me homo remember. And you had to clean that off the wall way back."

"Is that why you've never had many friends?" asked Mark.

"I've never had **any** friends. Not since I was in the junior school anyway. It's too risky."

"But you made friends with me," said Mark.

"Yes, but only after you told me that you were a homo as well, remember. In the back lane?"

Mark thought back and realized that was true. He felt a real sadness for Tommy. 'What an isolated life he must have led. No wonder he had latched on to me so much' thought Mark. "Yes, I remember now," he said. "So do you just sit in at home all the time?"

"No. I get away on my bike as much as I can. Out into the countryside, in the forest." Tommy paused, and then

169

continued wistfully, "I like the forest, hidden by all the trees. I feel safe there. It's quiet and cool, even on a hot day. You can hear birds but not people. It has lots of different moods. You get like this sunlight through the trees making patterns. When it's wet you can hear the rain; it falls different on different trees. At night the darkness is like a kind of cloak round you."

"Tommy Hedley, you're amazing."

Tommy smiled. "In the summer we can go there together. I'd like to strip you naked and make love to you with the trees all round."

Mark was astonished. "Naked? Outdoors?"

"It's OK. I know places where nobody would know."

"Have you undressed naked when you've been there alone?" asked Mark.

Tommy flushed and nodded. "It feels great, the air round your body. Round your cock and that as well. It makes me feel like I'm together with the trees. I think that they have a way of talking to each other.  I love them and it sounds daft, but I feel like they're loving me back. It's like a feeling I can't describe."

Mark felt quite emotional at this. "Tommy, have you ever written about this? That's a lovely description of your feelings."

Tommy looked at Mark, now back in his real world. "Me? Write? You know me, I'm too thick for that."

"You just proved you're not, Tommy."

"I am, Mark. You have to do my homework for me. At home I like making construction kits, Airfix models."

"Tommy, I'm so sorry. But you have a friend now."

Tommy looked at Mark, his eyes moist. "I love you, Mark. I don't know what I would do without you now. I'm scared of you going off to university and leaving me alone again."

Mark's heart went out to Tommy. He felt the weight of responsibility for Tommy's happiness on his shoulders.

"That's ages away yet, Tommy, and it might not even happen."

He kissed Tommy who then kissed him back and switched to dominant role.

. . .

Once more life settled into a routine for Mark; school, some evenings with Pip, usually twice a week with Tommy. Weekends at the showroom. Mark was also taken into the workshop at half term and spent most of the days that week in borrowed overalls learning about cars and engines, including police cars. Mark was informed they had the contract to maintain the police fleet. He at last found out the difference between side valve, regarded now as old fashioned, and overhead valve engines. He learned how to change spark plugs and set the points gap correctly in the distributor. He would sometimes drive the customers' cars from the workshop round to the front car park to be collected, remembering to put paper coverings in the footwell and on the seat. These were left in the car as a form of advertising because they had the garage name and the Ford logo on them.

Christmas came and went, a low key affair. Tommy had managed to give Mark a pork joint with lovely crackling.

"Mark, I never know these days what to get you," said Mam as they ate. "I did think of a big packet of Durex so that you behave responsibly but instead I got you this."

She handed over an envelope.

"I'm glad it's not Durex, Mam," said Mark. He saw Mam's look of expectation as she watched him open the envelope. Mark steeled himself to express joy whatever was in it. To his surprise it was a book token for ten pounds.

"Mam, that must have taken ages for you to save up for that," he said, genuinely pleased.

"I didn't know what to get but you've always got your nose buried in a book and I didn't know what book to get you so the lass in WH Smith's suggested a book token so you can choose your own book. But don't get school books, get at least one to read for fun."

"Thanks Mam," said Mark and got up and went round the table to give her a hug. "Here's yours," he said, handing her a wrapped up box. "I hope you like it, Happy Christmas."

He watched as she unwrapped the set of perfume, cologne, soap, bath salts. talc etc. from Paris. It was expensive so having received the book token, he was glad he had spent as much on Mam's gift.

"Mark, that's really posh stuff. It says it's from Paris. Does that mean it's French?"

"Yes, Mam. All the way from France just for you."

"I'm going to smell really posh with this lot. You're a good lad, Mark."

Mark smiled.

He decided to treat himself to a camera. Several of his friends had Brownie cameras, but the new Instamatic camera had come out which made loading the film much easier. So he chose that.

. . .

Back at school in the New Year and Mark's routine resumed. He was enjoying life, and his savings pot was growing. Mark thought that he would be able to live well at university. Maybe even have his own car.

In February Mark turned seventeen and Pip arranged for him to have driving lessons from the British School of Motoring. The vehicle was a Ford Cortina, which suited Mark because he was used to the type having driven them at the garage. The instructor was a middle aged man called Mr Dobson.

Ford Cortina Mk1

"You have your provisional licence?" asked Mr Dobson. Mark showed him the licence. "I will now show you the controls of the car," continued Mr Dobson.

"I know those," said Mark confidently. "I've driven a Cortina before. I work weekends at Middleton Motors and I drive the cars round there."

"Very well," said Mr Dobson. "Let's see how you get on."

Mark put the car in first gear and set off. But immediately there was the blast of a car horn and the car came to a sudden stop as Mr Dobson slammed on the brakes using his dual controls. Another car overtook with the driver glaring across at Mark. Mark felt himself flush red.

"You failed to use your mirror before setting off, you failed to check over your shoulder for passing traffic and you failed to give a signal. Had I not been ready for your overconfidence and stopped the car, you would have caused an accident. Driving on the road is not the same as driving round a garage car park. There is a lot more to think about. Now, show me the indicator."

Mark sat, feeling stupid and acutely embarrassed. "I'm sorry, Mr Dobson. It's there," he said, pointing at the switch on the right of the steering wheel.

"Let's start again, a valuable lesson having been learned. Into first gear, check the mirror and a quick glance over your shoulder to check any blind spot, give a signal and if clear only then move off."

This time Mark set off along the road. He realized that driving round the garage area he had never reached fourth gear or gone faster than about twenty miles an hour maximum. There were other cars, lorries and buses all doing their own thing, pedestrians who seemed intent on suicide, road signs to look out for - it all got very tiring. At the end of this first lesson he was exhausted.

173

"I think you'll do well," said Mr Dobson, dropping Mark off at the showroom. "You know how to control the car which is a good start because all your attention now can be on what's going on around you. Remember, Mark, driving carries a heavy responsibility. I'll see you next time."

Feeling chastened, Mark got out. "Thank you, Mr Dobson," he said. "I'm sorry about the bad start."

"Let's not worry about the start now. It's where you finish that matters. I think you have the makings of a good driver."

Tired but happy, Mark went into to see Pip.

Mr Dobson's prophecy proved correct. After just six lessons, Mr Dobson suggested Mark apply for the driving test. Mark got both Pip and Tommy to test him on the *Highway Code* until he felt confident about answering questions on it. By the time the test came round, Mark had three more lessons and Mr Dobson was satisfied Mark was ready. Mark felt less confident.

"Got my driving test in the morning," said Mark to Tommy as they lay in his bed while Mam was at work.

"They letting you off school then?" asked Tommy.

"Not really, but they seem to turn a blind eye if we stay off for half a day for it."

"That's weird," said Tommy. "Turning a blind eye."

"I suppose they know that because tests are hard to get students will stay off anyway. Except during exams I think."

"No," said Tommy. "I mean saying that about a blind eye."

"It comes from Admiral Nelson who put his telescope to his blind eye so he could ignore a signal not to fight."

"If he was an Admiral he could do what he wanted," argued Tommy.

"Tommy, I haven't got the time or energy to explain all that now," said Mark, and then kissed Tommy before he could complain.

"You'll pass the test, you're brainy. I can't afford driving lessons, never mind pass a test. I've never passed a test in my life coz I'm thick."

"Not that again, Tommy. You're clever in different ways to me, that's all."

. . .

Tommy's prophecy came true and at the first attempt, Mark was awarded the coveted pink pass certificate that would upgrade his provisional to the little red booklet of the full licence.

"Well done, my clever boy," said Mam. "Shame you haven't a fucking car though," she added laughing. "You should get that garage to give you one." She used Mark's camera to take a picture of him holding the licence, a copy of which was sent to his dad and sister.

. . .

"Got my test next week," said Ethan, eyeing Mark's pass certificate enviously. "I bet I won't pass first time though, like you." But he did. So did Eddie.

Much to his annoyance, Steve failed his test by mounting the kerb when reversing both when reversing round a corner and also in the three point turn. Mark, Ethan and others were sympathetic. Learning to drive seemed to be a compulsory rite of passage for seventeen year olds, boys especially.

Pip of course was delighted. But his delight stopped short of letting Mark loose in the Austin Healey 3000. "When you've got a bit more experience, then maybe and demonstrated responsibility on the road."

# Chapter 29 More Responsibility

Spring turned to Summer and the end of Mark's time in the Lower Sixth. But a couple of weeks before the end of term Mark was asked to see Mr Harris. He wondered what he had done wrong, and that fear of discovery was always at the back of his mind. But the other students all seemed normal with him so he tried to put that fear aside as he smartened himself up and nodding to the duty prefect sitting outside, he knocked on the door.

"Come in," he heard Mr Harris call from inside. Mark entered. Mr Harris was sitting behind his desk looking at some papers so Mark just stood in front of the desk and waited.

Mr Harris looked up after a moment. "Sorry, Martin," he said. "Sit down over there." He pointed to the chairs round the coffee table. It took Mark back to his Laudatum award years earlier. He touched the badge in his blazer lapel with the memory.

Mr Harris got up and came over. "I wanted a quiet word with you, Mark, before any announcement is made." He smiled at Mark, who had noticed the use of his given name rather than his surname. Mr Harris was evidently trying to put Mark at his ease which only made Mark more nervous. "We are going to offer you the appointment of a prefect from September, but not only that but the position of Head Prefect. How do you feel about that?"

Mark was rendered speechless. He had not really expected to be a prefect in Upper Sixth, even less to be Head Prefect.

"I can see that's come as a surprise, Mark," said Mr Harris.

"Yes, sir," said Mark. "I mean, there's others who've been at this school longer than me. I joined in fourth year, sir, if you remember."

"I do remember, Mark," answered Mr Harris. "And since then your record has been exemplary, all your teachers think highly of you, your academic record has been excellent and according to all the reports I have received you appear to have the respect of your fellow students. It's an appointment on merit, Mark, not Buggins's turn."

Mark wasn't sure who Buggins was but the context was clear. "Thank you, sir. I don't know what to say, really."

Mr Harris smiled. "So I see you accept. Congratulations."

"Thank you, sir," repeated Mark.

"There is a more delicate matter I need to talk to you about however."

Mark's heart started to race, was this it? 'But he wouldn't make me Head Prefect if he knows I'm a homo.' Mark waited.

"I understand that you live with your mother, just the two of you?" he posed.

"Yes, sir."

"It's a shame she never comes to our Parents' Nights to be told how well you're doing."

"She works in the evenings, sir. But I tell her what I'm doing and she gets the reports of course."

"Yes, of course," said Mr Harris. "It's a small flat I believe and I imagine that money is a bit tight."

Mark simply nodded.

"The prefect blazer is not cheap, Mark. I can see that the one you have on looks quite new, but as Head Prefect you would need a new one with the white edging. I am prepared to supply the prefect blazer for you in return for your current blazer, provided you don't ruin it before the end of term. As you know we carry a stock of good quality second hand uniform to help some pupils who find the cost difficult. Perhaps we should have offered you this before but as you say, you joined the school later so we were less aware of your needs. I only saw recently that you are receiving a free school lunch. But I can see your mother has made the effort to kit you out well and that deserves its own reward. Nobody would be told of course. How do you feel about that?"

"I didn't know about that system, sir," said Mark.

"As I say, it's completely confidential. Only those pupils we approach learn of it. Free meals are a useful guide but we do take other factors into account."

"I do have a weekend job, sir, so I helped to buy this uniform," offered Mark.

"Even more commendable, Mark. You show initiative and the right spirit. And yes, I remember your work at the chip shop of course," smiled Mr Harris.

"I left there a while ago sir, I work in a garage now, Middleton Motors. The chip shop was sold and anyway I get more at the garage."

"That's where I get my car serviced," commented Mr Harris. "So how do you feel about the blazer exchange? The Head Prefect badge is supplied by the school of course."

"Yes, sir, thank you sir," said Mark, thinking to keep an eye out for Mr Harris's Ford Zodiac.

Mark left the office in something of a daze. Appointment as a prefect was a surprise but Head prefect was a shock.

"Hello? Earth calling Mark Martin." It was Ethan who punctured Mark's reverie in the corridor.

"Sorry, Ethan. I was miles away. Just had something of a shock."

"How shocking," quipped Steve.

"Mr Harris said I'll be a prefect next year."

"Congratulations, but it's not that surprising," said Ethan.

"Yes, but he said I will be Head Prefect."

"Now that is shocking," said Steve, in genuine surprise. "Double congratulations. Do we all have to walk five paces behind you from now on?"

Mark smiled. "No, of course not. It's just I wasn't expecting it. There's only fifteen prefects out of all the Upper Sixth so I wasn't really expecting that, never mind Head Prefect."

At that moment the duty prefect Mark had just seen outside Mr Harris's room approached the group.

"Hello Tim," said Eddie. "Come to congratulate Mark?"

"What for?" said Prefect Tim, with a puzzled frown. "No, Mr Harris wants to see you, Ethan. And you, Eddie."

The group all looked at each other. Ethan and Eddie were offered, and accepted, appointments as prefects in September, two of just fifteen.

Steve received no such offer. He tried to hide his disappointment but was genuinely glad for his friends. "We all meet at Taylor's at seven tonight for a party," he said, Taylor's Club being a favourite meeting place in the city. "End of term celebration as well."

. . .

"We're having a bit of a party at Taylor's later," said Mark. He wondered what Tommy's reaction would be but to his surprise, Tommy appeared interested.

"What for?"

"Coz I'll be Head Prefect next term, some of my friends is also to be prefects and anyway, it's almost the end of term."

"Why are you the head one then?"

"Tommy, I don't know why, but there it is," joked Mark, using the tagline of comedian Harry Worth. "It's a mystery to me as well. There's only fifteen prefects so it's good to be made one, especially Head Prefect."

"I always said you're a brainbox," said Tommy. "OK, I'll come."

Mark was surprised but also pleased that Tommy was coming out of his shell a bit.

Taylor's was busy, full of noise and young people. Mark and Tommy went in, looking around.

"I've never been in anywhere like this before," said Tommy.

"I've only been a few times before," Mark assured him, as he scanned the crowd for familiar faces.

"Mark! Over here!" Darren's voice.

Mark looked in the direction of the call. Then he spotted a few classmates, including of course Ethan and Steve.

"Who's this?" asked Steve, looking at Tommy but in a friendly way.

"This is Tommy Hedley, he lives near me," said Mark.

"The butcher boy," said Ethan. "Welcome Tommy."

"Brought any sausages?" asked Steve with a smile.

"No, sorry," said Tommy. "I didn't know I was supposed to."

"Steve's teasing you, Tommy. Don't worry," said Mark. "What's everybody drinking?"

"You're not eighteen yet," said Tommy. This was greeted with roars of laughter.

"Don't worry, Tommy," said Mark. "You **are** eighteen and I look it, so no problem."

"Is Tommy eighteen?" asked Eddie. "I thought he was a bit younger."

"He's older than me, if not as tall," said Mark.

"Not many people our age are as tall as you, Mark," said Ethan.

Over light beers, the group chatted away, interested in Tommy and asking him questions about being a butcher, one thing Tommy could talk about with authority. Mark took a couple of photographs and hoped they would come out. It was an enjoyable and convivial evening.

On the bus on the way back to Northside, Tommy seemed happy. "I like your friends," he said. "They don't seem posh like I thought."

"They're a nice bunch," said Mark. "I wouldn't be friends with them if they weren't."

"That one with the fair hair, Ethan is it? Is he like us?"

"Like us?" said Mark, puzzled.

"You know," and dropping his voice to a whisper, "Homo."

"No," said Mark. "I know he's had at least one girlfriend. Why do you think he is?"

"I don't know, just a sort of feeling. He looked at me funny once or twice, like he was fancying me."

"Well, you are very fanciable, Tommy," answered Mark with a smile, "But I doubt if that was why he was looking at you."

As they parted at the bus stop, Tommy said, "Thanks, Mark, for the night out. It's the first time I've done anything like that. Never had any friends to go with, you see. But now I have you."

"Yes, Tommy, you have me. In all ways," he added.

At school, they relived their evening at Taylor's, recounting the various silly things that had been said and done.

"Tommy seems nice," said Ethan. "I never knew there was so much to being a butcher."

"You **would** like him, Ethan," said Steve, laughing. "I think he's a puff like you."

"Fuck off!" replied Ethan, giving Steve a play punch.

"Is he one, Mark?" asked Darren.

"How would I know?" retorted Mark. "He's not going to advertise it even if he is, which I don't think he is, anyway."

"Maybe he's Mark's bum boy," said Steve jokingly.

Mark felt himself flushing red, obvious with his fair skin.

"Mark's blushing, now," said Danny.

"It's just annoying, all this," said Mark. "He's a nice lad even if he is queer. So what?"

"We're just joking with you, Mark," said Eddie. "Calm down."

The moment passed but it set Mark off feeling insecure. Something had flowed between Tommy and Ethan at some subconscious level that neither was aware of. The summer holiday was coming and Mark pushed it out of his mind.

Mr Harris called all the prefects-to-be to see him on the last day. They were given their prefect badges; Mark's said Head Prefect. There were eight boys and seven girls.

Mark now remembered that when he was in fifth year, the Head Prefect had been a girl.

When they were dismissed, Mr Harris said, "Mark, will you wait behind a moment, please."

There followed a discussion about the extra role of the Head Prefect and then he was given a bag.

"Your prefect blazer is in there, Mark. It's the same size as the one you have on now, which I want you to bring in next term. It's been cleaned and looks as good as new."

"Thank you, sir," said Mark. "Am I the only prefect being given a blazer like this?"

"No, Mark," smiled Mr Harris. "But I am not going to tell you who else has, just as yours is a secret."

Mark nodded.

Leaving school, Eddie saw the bag. "What you got there, Mark?" asked Eddie, smiling.

"Just some stuff Mr Harris gave me."

"Like this, I guess," replied Eddie, and then Mark saw he too was carrying a similar bag.

Mark laughed and put a finger over his lips. Eddie laughed and did the same.

# Chapter 30 Cottaging

Mark knew most of his friends were going away for a summer holiday, usually for two weeks, many heading for Devon or Cornwall, others going north to Scotland. Mark and Mam hadn't been away since the split, in fact the family holiday to Majorca has been the last, and that had turned out rather fraught because, looking back, Mark could recognize the tensions between his parents were building even then.

Mark took the bull by horns. "Mam, we haven't been away for ages. Don't you feel like a break?"

Mam laughed. "Yes Mark, let's fly to America on one of them 707s to New York. We could call in to see that LBJ fellow while we're there. Hey, we could drop in to see Elvis too, have a cuppa with him." By this time Mam was laughing so much she could hardly get the words out.

Mark was angry. He was serious about having maybe just a few days away but as usual, Mam didn't take him seriously. "Mam! I'm seventeen, not seven!" He turned and went to his bedroom.

Mark was sitting in Pip's office with a coffee during a break and recounted this episode.

"For this summer?" asked Pip. "You've left it a bit late, Mark. Places get booked up. Where were you thinking of?"

"I don't know, really. It's a daft idea. As you say, it's too late."

Pip was thoughtful for a moment. "Leave it with me. What about your mother's work though?"

"I hadn't thought about that. I suppose she'd not want to risk losing her jobs."

. . .

Mam didn't look happy. "Mark, have you got any more money? The offices where I clean are shutting for two weeks next week. You know they pay me out of pocket, so for two weeks we'll only have the social."

183

"Yes, Mam, I'll help out." Mark paused. "Does that mean you won't be going to work at all for those two weeks?"

"The offices won't need cleaning if they're closed, will they, dafty," retorted Mam. "but I knew you'd see us right. You're a good lad, Mark Martin."

Mark reported this to Pip at his house after work.

"Interesting. I may have the solution. A friend of mine has a cottage he lets out at Callingham-on-Sea. It's a nice little village with a nice beach. Two bedrooms. What do you think?"

"I bet Mam would love that, just get away from Calvert House. How far away is it?"

"About eighty miles I think, down the coast."

"Is there a bus or train? How would we get there?"

"Mark," said Pip, with a smile of anticipation. "I was thinking of letting you use one of the demonstrators. Perhaps a 1200 Cortina?"

Mark was stunned. "Me? They cost over six hundred pounds! What about the other people at the showroom? Won't Mr Shaw mind? I mean, do all the staff get this?"

"Certainly not, Mark. But you are my nephew, remember."

"Nepotism," said Mark, grinning. He was so excited. "But what if the cottage is already let out?"

"Let me make a phone call," said Pip. Mark watched as Pip made a call, enquiring about the cottage. He smiled at Mark as he listened. Mark heard Pip ask for the booking.

He put the phone and smiled at Mark. "It's not let, Mark. I asked him to hold it."

"Can I afford it?" asked Mark. "I don't know how much cottages cost."

"Yes Mark, you can. Like the car, my treat."

Mark leant over and kissed Pip. "Thanks, Pip. Mam won't believe this."

"She will when she gets there," said Pip. "I love you, Mark. I wish you were my son, or if I had a son, that he'd be like you."

"But we couldn't have sex if I were your son," said Mark, as Mr Farnsworth's work on subjunctives flashed through his mind.

"I suppose that would be a bit odd," laughed Pip.

'Isn't it odd, anyway?' thought Mark, but said nothing.

. . .

"Mam, We're going away next week for a holiday."

"Says who? You booked that flight to America?"

"Not America, Mam, but a place called Callingham-on-Sea. It's about eighty miles down the coast and we have a cottage booked just for us. For you and me, Mam. What's more, we'll have a car for the week."

"Have you gone stark, raving bonkers, Mark Martin?" said Mam. "What the fuck are you on about?"

"It's from the garage, Mam," said Mark, thinking quickly. "It's a kind of bonus. The sales of cars have gone up since I was there and P... Mr Middleton says it's because of the way I am with the customers, keeping them there."

"All you do is make them fucking tea and coffee!"

"Yes, Mam, but I smile at them and charm them into buying a car." Mark hoped that Mam would swallow this explanation.

"I'll believe it when I'm there," said Mam cautiously.

"Mr Middleton thought you'd say that," smiled Mark.

. . .

Mark was busy cleaning out a Cortina demonstrator for its next run when Mr Shaw approached him. "You'd better make a good job there, Mark. This one's yours next week. Just make sure you bring it back in one piece. And yourself of course."

"Yes, Mr Shaw," said Mark, grinning.

On Saturday morning after a night at Pip's, they went in the Austin Healey to the garage.

"All ready for the lad to go, Mr Middleton," said Mr Shaw.

There was the smart green Cortina. Mark looked at it, hardly believing this was happening.

185

"Come to the office, Mark. Some paperwork to sign for the car hire. It's to make sure you're insured and covered by the AA policy in case anything goes wrong." Together using a road atlas, they planned the route, Mark making notes. "No, Mark, take the road atlas with you."

Later, driving away from the showroom, Mark felt on top of the world. Life was so good. There was a lot of Saturday morning traffic so he had to be careful. He had done some road driving since passing his test under trade plates, but this was different. He felt the responsibility of the car, he didn't want to let Pip down. He decided not to go straight back to Northside; instead he drove out to the school. The gates were closed of course but he felt good. It occurred to him that there was a more direct route to Northside from school rather than go the bus way via the city centre.

As he drove though the nice looking estate not far from the school he saw a familiar figure waiting at a bus stop. Ethan! He stopped the car. Ethan's look of surprise when he saw Mark at the wheel amused Mark. At a sign from Mark, he opened the passenger door.

"Where are you going?" asked Mark.

"Just into town. Is this your car?"

"For the next week, yes," answered Mark. "Get in, I'll give you a lift."

As they drove into the city centre, Mark explained the upcoming holiday and the loan of the car. He dropped Ethan off and drove home, pleased that at least one of his school friends had seen him in the car.

Mam was thrilled to be driven by her son in a nice new car to the cottage. They had packed up some food in the car.

"Bog roll!" shouted Mam. "What if there's no toilet paper?"

"Mam, I'm sure there will be," said Mark. "Mr Middleton said everything would be there."

Now Mark was driving steadily towards Callingham-on-Sea. He had his route notes and was looking out for relevant signposts. The journey took just over three hours, arriving late afternoon.

"I think it's that one," said Mark as they pulled up outside a small house on the cliff top road at the edge of the village. The key he had been given fitted, and they went in.

"Mark, this is dead posh," said Mam, looking around the well appointed interior of the cottage. "There's towels and bog roll here too," she added as she investigated the bathroom and toilet. Then she went to the kitchen. "This is very posh, Mark. The kettle's posher than ours. We needn't have brought it. Why don't you try it out, Mark. After all that driving, I need a cuppa."

"I don't remember you driving, Mam. Unless you were dreaming while you were asleep," said Mark, amusement tinged with annoyance. But he made the tea anyway.

"There's a posh TV," said Mam as she sat down in a comfortable chair with her cuppa.

"Mam, stop saying posh all the time," said Mark, thinking she would have a fit if she saw Pip's house.

"Well it is," said Mam. "Turn it on."

So Mark turned on the television. The first thing that came up was a western. Mark sighed. "Mam, it's a dual standard TV," he said.

"What's that mean?"

"It can get that new BBC2 channel," he explained.

"Let's have a look."

'Anything but cowboys' thought Mark. He switched over. A man talking about buildings. They watched for a few moments

"I'd heard it was just for posh people. Turn it back, Mark," said Mam.

"There you go, posh again," said Mark as he switched back to the cowboys. Mark already was beginning to wonder if spending a whole week in just Mam's company was going to work out. He had good intentions but Sartre said that's what the road to hell was paved with.

187

"Let's get something to eat at that nice looking pub we passed," suggested Mark.

"You can't go in a pub. You're not eighteen yet," said Mam.

Mark thought 'If only she knew.' But he said, "I can with you if it's to eat a meal. Anyway, I can pass for eighteen easily."

As they walked the short distance in the early evening sun into the centre of the small fishing village, looking out across the blue sea, Mam said, "Tomorrow we'll find the funfair. I like the dodgems. I'll drive better than you."

"What funfair?"

"The funfair. There'll be one round here somewhere, It's the seaside, isn't it?"

Mark sighed. This was not going to be an easy week. He realized by just how much he had outgrown his mother in so many ways.

In the event the week passed by happily. They ate each evening in one of the two pubs in the village; each had a good restaurant attached. There were boat trips along the coast to nearby villages which they could explore, they went for drives in the countryside.

"I never knew England had so much green countryside," Mam commented on one trip which had taken in hills and forests as well as farmland.

"You don't get out enough," answered Mark.

"But I am now, thanks to you, my clever son," smiled Mam.

Mark smiled as he steered the Cortina carefully back to Callingham-on-Sea.

Mark's photos came out well. Mam at the cottage. Mam by the sea. Mam in the restaurant. Mam in the car. Mam walking in the forest. Mam on a boat trip. And a blurry one of Mark with the car.

# Chapter 31 In Command

Back in the Calvert House flat, suddenly their trip seemed to belong to a different world.

"I wish we could've stayed away forever, Mark," said Mam. "It was lovely spending so much time with my clever son. You're a good lad."

"Thanks, Mam. Yes, it was nice, wasn't it. Maybe we can do something like it again sometime."

"We could go back to that island in Spain and you could learn more Spanish."

"Mam, both  the cottage and the use of the car were from the garage. I don't think they have a dealership in Majorca. And I think I've forgotten any Spanish."

Mark soon had to turn his attention back to school. He returned the Cortina to the showroom, and it was back to work there and in the workshop for the remainder of the holidays, spending time with Pip ("Mam, it's been a while since I saw Pippa.") and of course Tommy was happy to see him back home.

"I've missed you," said Tommy, as he steered Mark to the bedroom when Mam was back at work.

"I've missed you, too," answered Mark, realizing he really had.

"So we need to catch up then" demanded Tommy, switching to dominant mode. Mark felt that same thrill he always did when someone took charge of him sexually, the more so because Tommy was smaller than him although about the same age.

"Have I left me watch here?" asked Tommy afterwards. "Can't find it anywhere."

Mark shook his head.

"I think I lost it that night when I went out with your mates. Not seen it since that I can remember."

"Sorry, Tommy. Nobody said anything. Was it expensive?"

"No, just a cheap one off the market, but it's a nuisance."

189

Mark made a mental note of that with Christmas coming up.

The remaining couple of weeks of the summer break passed and it was the new term. Mark had his prefect blazer with its white edging, and his Laudatum badge proudly in the lapel. He pinned on the Head Prefect badge. He felt proud looking at himself in the mirror and he got Tommy to take a photograph of him to send to dad. He was nervous about his new role, not just as a prefect but as Head Prefect. He felt extraordinarily self conscious walking into school wearing the new blazer with its white edging.

He met Ethan as they walked in through the main entrance, a prefect privilege.

"Ethan, I honestly have no idea what to do next."

"You'll think of something," remarked Ethan.

Mark saw the chair outside Mr Harris's office. "I just have. Ethan, you're duty prefect today for Mr Harris."

"Wow! That was decisive! Yes, sir," grinned Ethan, plonking himself down on the chair.

At that moment, Mr Harris emerged from his office. "Mark, welcome to your first day as Head Prefect. One of your jobs is to establish a roster for the duty prefect each day."

Mark smiled and pointed to Ethan sitting on the chair.

"Oh," said Mr Harris. "I'm sorry, Robson, I didn't see you there. Well. Mark, you seem to be on top of things. Any problems, let me know. There's bound to be a settling in time."

"Thank you, sir. I will." With a wink at Ethan, Mark set off for the prefects' common room, a sanctum he had rarely entered before. Eddie was there already, trying to plug in the kettle. "Want a coffee, our Lord and Master?" he asked Mark with a grin.

"Thank you," said Mark looking around the prefects, most of whom seemed to be there.

"I thought I saw you with Ethan," said Jackie. "What have you done with him?"

"I sat him on the duty chair outside Mr Harris's office," said Mark. "I think as far as possible, we will alternate girls and boys each day for that. Jackie, will you do it tomorrow? By then I should have a roster for that and other things. If you find your duties, especially the Head's runner which is an all day job, clash with important lessons, I can adjust it later. Is everybody happy with that?"

There was assent round the room. As Eddie handed Mark a coffee mug, he said, "That's good, Mark. Stamping your authority from the start but not dictatorial. You're going to be OK."

"Thanks Eddie. That means a lot."

And so it proved. Mark was able to make some minor adjustments to the rosters so that prefects could attend all vital lessons. He included himself in all the rosters. All were now only a few months away from A levels and Mark too wanted to do well so could understand their concerns.

Mark rather enjoyed his position. He realized that the new intake regarded him with some awe, having just left their primary schools and now in their big new grammar school with its strange ways. He asked Mr Harris if he could call a meeting of all the first years to talk to them, ideally without teachers present so they would be more at ease.

"An excellent idea, Mark. Why haven't we done this before? Help them settle in."

Mark roped in Ethan, Jackie, Eddie and Debbie for this. Entitled 'First Year Forum' all first years were invited to this one lunchtime in the school hall. The turnout was very high, maybe because it turned out to be a very cold and wet day even for September.

Mark opened the proceedings. "My name is Mark Martin and for reasons I am still unsure of, I have been made Head Prefect. How many of you had prefects at your primary school?" About half the children raised their hands. "Maybe some of you were prefects. So most of you know that prefects are not people to be afraid of. One of our main jobs is to keep you safe at school and to maintain discipline so that everybody can get the most out of their time here. As

191

you can see, there are no teachers here because we want you to talk freely and ask any questions."

Mark then introduced the others and explained how the prefect system worked in the school.

A hand went up tentatively. "Yes?" said Mark.

"Please sir," said a young boy, "What's that gold badge you're wearing? I've seen some others with that but not all are prefects."

"First, you don't need to address prefects as 'sir'. That's for the men teachers. This badge is called a Laudatum badge which is a Latin word to do with praise. It's awarded for special achievements. One of the other prefects who isn't here now has one because he's very good at gymnastics and has been picked for trials for the England gymnastics team. Another because she is very good at horse riding and has won medals in show jumping."

"Is sport why you got yours," asked the boy more confidently.

"No. Mine wasn't for sport," said Mark, but before he could move on, Eddie stood up.

"Mark got his for being a very brave hero," said Eddie. "He was working in a fish and chip shop a few years ago and was on his own when it caught fire. Instead of panicking he called the fire brigade and then went back to the fire and put it out himself, saving the whole row of shops from being burnt down to the ground."

Mark flushed red and glared at Eddie, but all the children started clapping and cheering. Mark took a theatrical bow.

As the applause subsided, several hands went up. "How old were you then?"

"I was fourteen," answered Mark.

Another child, "I live in Northside, the chip shop there had a fire while I was in the juniors. It's called Frank's Fish'n'Chips."

"Yes, I live in Northside," said Mark, "I had a Saturday job with Frank back then. But he doesn't run the shop any more but the new owners kept the name."

192

That exchange had the effect of breaking the ice and then questions about all aspects of the school came thick and fast. The meeting was judged a great success and was only finished when the bells rang for afternoon lessons. Mr Harris said Mark's idea would be repeated next September and possibly before that, at the start of each term.

The rest of the school term went well. Mark enjoyed his role, and also his studies. His teachers said he was on course for good A level grades, easily enough to get to university.

It was early December one evening when Tommy said, "I can't afford to buy you a posh Christmas present, but my dad says it's OK if I give you a turkey for your Christmas dinner."

Mark was stopped in his tracks by that. He hadn't yet given much thought to Christmas, apart from helping put up large Christmas trees with decorations in the school entrance, assembly hall and at the showroom.

"You don't have to give me anything for Christmas, Tommy," said Mark. "You gave us pork last year I think."

"I want to. I love you, Mark, so you're getting a turkey. But I thought I'd better tell you before in case your mam went out and bought one."

Mark thought about it. He hadn't had a turkey for Christmas dinner since Mam and Dad split and they moved up here. Two Christmases had seen just muted celebration. Mark decided it would be nice for Mam and he would make it special.

There was a big Christmas party at school which the prefects largely organized, Mark recognized that the girls had taken the lead on this. He bought Mam a new winter coat which he knew she would think was posh but like it because of that. Mark remembered that Tommy had lost his watch so he bought him a new one. Not from the market this time though. It was an Omega chronometer.

On Christmas Eve morning Tommy arrived, with his dad carrying a large turkey. "We need to see if it will go in your oven," explained Tommy, "or we can swap it for a slightly smaller one."

"Fits a treat," announced Mr Hedley in the kitchen.

"Thanks so much, Mr Hedley," said Mam. "It's very good of you."

"Mark's been a good friend for Tommy, his first real friend. Really brought him out of himself so I'm glad to help, Mrs Martin."

Mark went to his room and retrieved the wrapped watch and handed it to Tommy. "Promise you won't open that until tomorrow," said Mark.

Tommy promised.

Mam loved her coat. "What did you get for Pippa?" she asked.

The question took Mark by surprise. "Er, some French perfume and a scarf," he improvised.

"You never talk about her much. Just say you've stayed there," said Mam. "When you talk about school and that it's always Ethan, Steve or Eddie and them."

"I thought you didn't like me to talk about me shagging, as you call it," said Mark lightly.

Mam laughed. "You're a rogue, Mark Martin."

"I must take after you then," said Mark but with a smile.

"Cheeky sod," laughed Mam back.

For days afterwards, they ate turkey, more turkey, then turkey sandwiches and finally a thick turkey broth that lasted three days. Mark had to admit Mam got full value from that bird.

# Chapter 32 Tick, not Tock

It was Boxing Day when Tommy appeared.

"Hello, Tommy. Want a turkey sandwich?" said Mam jokingly.

But Tommy simply shook his head. Mam was oblivious but Mark immediately sensed that Tommy was unhappy.

"Let's chat in my room," said Mark as brightly as he could. He led the way and closed the door. "What's the matter, Tommy?"

Tommy looked anxious. He took the Omega watch out of his pocket in its box and handed it to Mark, who took it, frowning.

"Me mam and dad say I've to give it back," he said.

"Why? Doesn't it work?"

"It's not that, Mark. They say it's too expensive. They're asking how you got so much money when your mam has tick at the shop. They're asking where you got that much from."

"Tommy, I honestly didn't know Mam had tick at your shop. But it's OK, I'll sort out the tick. I'll have words with Mam. Keep the watch. I bought it for you."

Tommy shook his head. "They're wondering why you spent so much money on me. Asking if there's more to us than just being friends. Mark, I'm scared."

Mark gave Tommy a hug, he made to kiss him but Tommy backed away. Mark thought for a moment. "Tommy, years ago my dad bought me a bundle of Premium Bonds. I'll just say that in the summer one of them came up for a thousand pounds. That's how I took Mam away on holiday, hired that car and bought you the watch."

"If I say that, they won't believe me," said Tommy, shaking.

"Then I'll tell them," said Mark, decisively. "Let's go round now."

"I'd rather just give you the watch back. It's too posh for me anyway. You have it."

"Tommy, I bought that for you. It'll be OK. How much is the tick?"

"About three pounds I think," answered Tommy.

Mark went to his desk and took five pounds out of the drawer. Reluctantly, Tommy accompanied Mark round to Tommy's flat.

"Hello, Mark," said Mr Hedley, cautiously. "I'm sorry I had to send Tommy back with the watch but it's hugely expensive and we can't accept it."

"Honestly, Mr Hedley, it's fine. Ages ago my dad bought me ten premium bonds and last summer one of the numbers came up for a thousand pounds. That's why I took Mam away for a week to our own cottage and hired the car. She deserved a treat. I wanted to get Tommy something nice for Christmas as well. He's my only friend in Northside and I knew he'd lost his watch, maybe when he came on a night out with me that time."

Mr Hedley frowned. "I follow that, Mark, but it seems strange that after such a lucky win, your mother since hasn't paid her bill at my shop."

"I'm sorry about that, Mr Hedley. I didn't know. Mam's not very good at handling money, but I hope this is enough to clear the debt," said Mark, offering the five pound note.

Mr Hedley took the note. "This will more than cover it, thank you, Mark. So she has a bit of credit now. But that still leaves the matter of the watch. Omega."

Mark had hoped he'd said enough. "Sorry, Tommy, I really didn't want to say this but the watch isn't brand new. I bought it at the pawnbroker in High Lane. I was walking past and I saw it and I thought of Tommy. So I got it quite cheaply really. But it's still a good watch."

"I see," said Mr Hedley. "I did wonder why an eighteen year old boy would buy such an expensive present for another eighteen year old boy. You understand one has to be careful?"

"Of course," said Mark, hoping Tommy wouldn't blab that he was still seventeen.

"Mark's top of his school," said Tommy. "He's the Head Prefect as well."

"You're obviously a very intelligent and capable young man, Mark," said Mr Hedley. "I am sorry that I seem to have misjudged the situation."

Mrs Hedley, who had sat saying nothing, spoke up. "So our Tommy can keep the posh watch then," she said firmly.

"Of course he can, dear," said Mr Hedley.

As Mark and Tommy walked round to Calvert House, Tommy asked, "Did you really buy this at the pawn shop?"

"No," said Mark. "It is brand new, Tommy. You're worth it."

"Did you really win a thousand pounds on those premium bonds, then?"

"No, Tommy. My dad did buy me some, but they've never paid out a penny. It's from what I earn at the garage."

"Mark, I feel so much better. Is your Mam in?" he asked hopefully.

"Yes, Tommy. It's Boxing Day, remember. But she'll be working tomorrow," he added with a smile.

But Tommy answered, "I will be too. I'll head back home then. Thanks, Mark."

"Come round soon, Tommy. Mam will be out again evenings soon."

Back in the flat, Mam asked, "Where's Tommy?"

"At home, Mam," answered Mark. "How come you've got tick at the butcher's shop? Especially when they gave us such a nice turkey for Christmas."

"Mark, that's none of your business," said Mam, defensively.

"It is, Mam, when I'm giving you money to help with the shopping," replied Mark angrily. "You shouldn't have need for tick."

"Sometime maybe I've left me purse at home and that," offered Mam weakly.

"I gave Tommy a nice watch for Christmas and his dad is asking how, when you owe money. It's embarrassing,

197

Mam. Tommy was told to hand the watch back, and he's my only friend in Northside."

"I'm sorry, Mark. I know you and Tommy get on well. I'll pay the tick off next week."

"I've already done that. I also said that one of Dad's premium bonds paid up which is how we went to the cottage and had the car as well as buying the watch. So make sure you go along with that if you get asked."

"You said that was from the garage."

"Yes, Mam, it was, but I don't want everybody knowing that."

"What about the lad's watch?"

"He's keeping it now I explained," said Mark. "Is there tick anywhere else?"

Mam looked sheepish. "A couple of quid at the corner shop," she admitted.

Mark dug in his wallet and gave Mam three pound notes. "Pay that off tomorrow, please Mam. And no more. If I'm not giving you enough, say so and we can work it out."

With that, Mark turned and went to his room, bolting the door. He needed space to think about things Tommy had said. More than just friends? Mark found that disturbing.

Mark worked at the garage, spent time with Pip and also with Tommy when Mam was at work. There was less of this because many offices were shut right from before Christmas into the new year.

For New Year's Eve to welcome in 1965 the gang had agreed to meet at Taylor's, if only to escape their parents watching *The White Heather Club* to see in the new year.

The venue was packed with young people. Mark had suggested Tommy go with him again, with which, to Mark's surprise, Tommy agreed. Amid the throng. Mark saw Eddie and Darren and made his way over to them.

"Hi Mark. Hi Tommy," said Eddie. At that point Ethan, Steve and Danny arrived, along with Jackie and Debbie. The music was loud but in their shouted conversation they all greeted Tommy as one of the gang. Mark could see on Tommy's face the pleasure that gave him. The evening went well, much beer was consumed and everybody was feeling very jolly. As midnight approached, the television in one corner was put on while Big Ben's chimes heralded 1965. Everybody formed into circles and, linking arms, sang along to *Auld Lang Syne*.

"Happy New Year!" they all shouted at each other, swigging more from their glasses.

Mark noticed Tommy was physically shaking. "What's the matter?" he asked.

"It's them," he said. "Bullies who were at my school. Let's go." He indicated a group of young men near the bar. It became obvious that as Tommy saw them, they saw him.

They came across to where Mark and Tommy were. "Well, if it's not little Tommy Hedley, prize puff of Northside. Who let you in here, you little bender?" demanded one of them, thrusting his face into Tommy's.

"He's with us," said Eddie. "Leave him alone."

"So, are all you lot queers, then?" said the bully scornfully.

Most of the group seemed unsure of what to do in this situation. While they hesitated, the lead bully looked at Ethan. "He looks like a homo," he announced to his bully pals who were leering at the group. "Are you the butcher's bum boy? We know he's got one in Northside."

"I don't live in Northside," said Ethan, but he glanced at Mark as he said it, as did one or two others. This was not lost on the bullies.

"So this is the one," said the leader, sneering at Mark. "Where've I seen you before? I know your queer face from somewhere."

"Leave him alone!" shouted Tommy, suddenly defiant. This simply made the bullies laugh. Then one started to sing,

*Puff, the magic dragon lived by the sea*
*And frolicked in Tommy Hedley's bed in a land called* Northside

This made the bullies laugh. By this time Tommy was close to tears.

199

Mark was frozen but Steve shouted, "Why don't you lot piss off and leave people alone?"

Just when Mark thought it could get no worse, it did.

# Chapter 33 Missing

Maybe the singing had attracted his attention but with both horror and fear, Mark watched Peter come over to them. He was a little unsteady on his feet, his over consumption of alcohol was obvious.

"If it's not the famous Mark Martin with all his fairy friends," he announced.

"Who's this?" asked Eddie.

"Just someone I know," said Mark.

The bullies looked on with interest at this new ally. "You know these homos?" the leader asked Peter.

"Are they all queers?" asked Peter laughing. "No, I just know this tall cunt here," he said, pushing his hand on Mark's chest. "Rents his arse to anybody who pays."

Mark knew that if he accused Peter of the same it would confirm his own guilt. He didn't know what to say.

"Mark, what's he talking about," asked Ethan.

"I'm talking about Pip Middleton, that's what. Martin's his bum boy. Has been for years."

"Shut up, Peter," shouted Mark. "You're talking rubbish."

"You work at Middleton Motors, don't you?" asked Ethan.

"Not just cars he services, though," laughed Peter, thinking his own joke the funniest thing he had heard.

"What about this one?" the bully asked Peter, pointing at Tommy.

"Na. Don't know that one. Looks like a puff though," said Peter, still laughing.

"You lot should be ashamed of yourselves," intervened Debbie. "This is supposed to be a New Year celebration."

"See you later, Hedley," said the lead bully, making a cut throat motion. The bullies then sauntered away.

"You too, moron," snapped Debbie at Peter.

"I'll see you soon, Mark," said Peter, drawing his fingernail slowly down his cheek to remind Mark of his earlier threat. He left too.

The group were now all looking at Mark. "What's all that about, Mark?" asked Eddie.

"It's rubbish," said Mark, but even as he said it he knew his voice carried no conviction.

"He said Pip Middleton. Is that your uncle?" asked Steve.

"I really thought you'd bring Pippa here tonight, but instead you bring Tommy. Does Pippa even exist, or is that this Pip?" demanded Eddie, a note of hostility edging into his voice.

"Fuck me, the Head Prefect who we all admired and looked up to, turns out to be a homo," said Danny.

Mark didn't know which way to turn or what to say. His world, his respect, his position; it was all destroyed in what seemed like a sudden, massive explosion. He was exposed not just as being queer but now seen as a liar, deceitful and a betrayer of his friends.

"I'm going," said Tommy, his voice full of emotion. "I've had enough of this all my life and I'm fed up with it. It's never going to stop, is it? Are you coming, Mark?"

Mark looked round his friends, fellow students, mainly fellow prefects. The look of reproach on their faces was mixed with disgust on some. "Yes, Tommy," said Mark. "Let's go."

Outside on the street they were careful just in case the bullies - or Peter - were still hanging around. The city centre was full; mainly young people celebrating, mostly inebriated and underdressed for the bitter cold of the early morning.

"Who's Pippa? You never said about a girlfriend," said Tommy.

"There is no Pippa," replied Mark. "I made her up to avoid suspicion. I suppose I should have realized that when I never took her out like the others did with girlfriends sometimes that it would be found out."

"So who's this Pip? Someone at the garage?"

"Yes, Tommy, he owns it."

"So why did that rough boy say what he did about you and this Pip? Have you been having sex with him?"

Mark wondered what to say, but Tommy deserved an end to lies. "Yes, Tommy, sometimes. It's one reason he pays me well." Mark immediately regretted that last bit.

"So it's true; you let men fuck you for money. All the time I was making love to you, other men were paying you?" Tommy was in tears by now.

Mark didn't know what to say.

"I loved you, Mark Martin! I even thought that maybe somehow, one day, we could be together. But when you're queer, what's the point of having dreams? Eh, Mark? What's the fucking point of anything any more? I wish I'd never met you!"

Before Mark could think of something to say, to reach out to Tommy, to reduce his distress, Tommy was gone, running into the night.

"Tommy!" shouted Mark, as he set off after him. But he was lost in the crowds. Mark searched but could not find Tommy. He ended up walking all the way to Northside and Calvert House. Mam had left the bolt off and the flat was silent. He went to the bathroom and then to his bedroom. Automatically he got ready for bed, looking at the bed, the bed he had shared so many times with Tommy. He climbed in, pulled the blankets over him - and wept.

. . .

"Mark, are you OK?" Mam was rattling the door. "I wish you wouldn't keep bolting the door. What if you were poorly?"

"I'm fine, Mam," called Mark. "It was a long night." Mark realized that he had in fact slept although it didn't feel like it.

"Too much to drink," taunted Mam. "You're not eighteen until next month."

'Next month? Oh, yes, it's January now.' "I just want to sleep, Mam."

"Seventeen and coming home with a hangover. Whatever next?" he heard Mam say as she retreated.

Mark stayed in bed on New Year's Day as long as he felt he reasonably could. But his bladder and hunger got the better of him in the end so he dressed and got himself some cereal for breakfast. He barely spoke to Mam. He wanted to think. He was now dreading returning to school on Thursday. He knew he would be the talk of the Upper Sixth, then the Lower Sixth and then the whole school. How could he carry on as Head Prefect if everybody was secretly - or maybe not so secretly - hating him? With all the background chatter it would be bound to reach Mr Harris eventually.

But first, Tommy. 'If only I hadn't asked Tommy to go to Taylor's on New Year's Eve.' It had been a mix of liking Tommy's company and wanting to give him some social life and a good night out for New Year. He walked round to the shops. Although it was Friday, all were closed of course on New Year's Day including Hedley the Butcher. Mark walked round the end of the row and went to the back gate. It was closed and locked. The wall and gate was higher than Mark, but he crossed to the other side of the back lane from where he could see the back windows of the upstairs flat. He thought he knew which was Tommy's room now, but the curtains were drawn. At other windows there was no sign of any movement or habitation. 'Maybe they've all gone out for the day' thought Mark. He waited for a while in case there was movement. But it was freezing, the puddles were frozen, so Mark left. He reasoned that tomorrow, Saturday, the shops would be open and Tommy would be at work. He would make an excuse to see him and make everything right with him.

. . .

Someone was banging on the front door of the flat. Mark stirred and looked at his watch. Ten past seven. He heard Mam coming out of her bedroom shouting, "Hold yer horses, I'm coming. Who is it at this time in the morning?"

There was a muffled reply and then Mam, "Wait a moment, Mr Hedley."

Mark heard the bolt being withdrawn. Mr Hedley? Mark was suddenly fearful. Had Tommy told his parents about being queers and what they had been doing? Mark decided to remain in his warm bed, but listening as best he could.

"Mrs Martin, is our Tommy here?"

"No, Mr Hedley. Not that I know of anyway. Unless he's with our Mark."

Mark quickly decided the best thing to do was get out of bed, just in time because Mam was knocking on the door. "Mark, is Tommy in there with you? His dad's here looking for him."

Slipping his dressing gown on over his pyjamas because of the cold, Mark called, "No, Mam. Tommy's not here. Just me."

Mr Hedley's voice, "Does Mark know where he might be?"

Mark opened his bedroom door. Mam and Mr Hedley were standing at the end of the passage to the hallway.

"I'm sorry, Mr Hedley," said Mark. "I've no idea where he is. I haven't seen him since Thursday night. Well, early hours of Friday morning I suppose after we left Taylor's. Hasn't he been home?"

"Yes, he came home very late but when he got up late on Friday he seemed upset and then he went out on his bike and we've not seen him since. Do you know why he was upset, Mark?"

"Some boys that knew Tommy from school were at Taylor's and just after midnight they were having a go at him, calling him stuff."

"Stuff?" questioned Mr Hedley. "What stuff?"

"They were calling him a homo and things like that and he got upset. My friends stuck up for him but he decided to leave."

"That again! So did you stay on after he left?"

"No, Mr Hedley. I left with him but he was still upset and ran off and I lost him in the crowds. It was very busy on the streets. But I don't think he would get his bike out just to come round here."

"No, you're probably right. He often goes off on his bike but he's been gone all night and it's freezing. We're worried to death about him. Have you any idea where he might go?"

Mark shook his head. But then he remembered something. "Tommy once told me he liked to ride in the forest. He said he liked the forest surrounded by trees."

"Maybe he's fallen off and hurt himself," suggested Mam.

"Possibly, Mrs Martin. Mark, did he say which forest?"

"No, sorry, Mr Hedley," answered Mark. "He just said the forest."

"Very well. Please let us know if you hear anything."

"Yes, of course," said Mam. "Won't we Mark?"

Mark nodded. Mr Hedley left.

"I wonder where the lad's got to," said Mam. "I hope he's OK."

"Yes, Mam," said Mark.

"I'll put the kettle on," said Mam.

Mark went through the motions of getting dressed. He was worrying enough about his friends and school; now he was worried about Tommy as well. As he dressed he remembered it was Saturday. He was due at the garage.

# Chapter 34 Discord

"Hello, Mark," said Mr Shaw as Mark walked in. "Happy New Year!"

"Thank you, Mr Shaw," said Mark. "Happy New Year to you. Is Uncle Philip in?"

"Yes. He asked me to send you up as soon as you got in."

Mark climbed the stairs to Pip's office and knocked.

"Come in, Mark."

Pip looked serious as Mark sat down. "Mark, have you spoken to Peter recently?"

"I saw him on Thursday night at Taylor's; first thing Friday I suppose because it was after midnight. Why? What's happened?"

"Did Peter mention my name in relation to being queer?"

"Yes, Pip, he did. He said I was your bum boy and had been for years. He was drunk though. How did you hear about that?"

"It seems that there was an off-duty policeman in Taylor's who overheard some argument among a group of boys about some being homos. I suppose you were in that group."

"Yes. I was there with friends including one from Northside. These bullies knew him and called him a fairy and it led to an argument that drew Peter over to us. I hadn't even known he was there before that. It was very crowded. Have the police been here?"

"Not yet, Mark. I had a phone call from a friend in the police. We maintain the local police vehicles remember so I have contacts."

"I saw them in the workshop."

"We will try to contain this, Mark. Your name wasn't mentioned but I'll have to warn the men at The Vault. It's too dangerous to continue that. In fact, I think I'll ring Gordon and Gerry now. The others don't have phones."

Mark sat while Pip made phone calls. He could hear Gordon's shock as Pip outlined what Peter had said. He said he would contact Fred and Tom and another name that Mark didn't recognize. Much the same conversation followed with Gerry.

At last Pip put the phone down. Only then did he see that he had used a switchboard line rather than his direct line. "Fuck!" he said. "That was risky. Fingers crossed."

"Will it be all right now?" asked Mark anxiously.

"I hope so, Mark. It's the end of The Vault for us I think. Now we just carry on as normal."

"Is it the end for you and me?"

"Oh no, Mark. I've told you, I love you. But it means we must be more careful and not give Peter any more ammunition. What an idiot! Off you go, Mark. Use your charm to entrap more potential buyers."

Reassured, Mark returned to the showroom and started making the coffee and preparing the tea. Buoyed up by Pip's confidence, he felt better. He was thinking what he would say on Thursday. Peter was a drunken idiot who had been sacked by the garage and had always been jealous of Mark. Yes, Mark had suspected Tommy was a homo but he was still a nice lad and when he had got upset Mark felt he should leave with him to support him as a friend. Pippa was away over Christmas and New Year with her family or otherwise he would have brought her. I'm not a homo but I've no problem with boys that are. Yes, that might work. They'd all had a lot to drink so details might be hazy. He'd talk to them all first thing on Thursday back at school and nip this in the bud. Feeling more at ease, Mark got on with his day.

After work, Pip took Mark to his West Farm home. They ate, talked more, Pip trying to settle Mark's worries. Mark said his friend had run off after the taunts and had stayed out all night. His parents were worried. They made love and Mark told Pip what he would say at school on Thursday. Pip thought it would work so Mark was even calmer. Pip dropped Mark off near Calvert House as usual.

"You're late back," said Mam. "Have you had anything to eat?"

"Yes, Mam. I've been to Pippa's. I had something to eat there."

"I hope you remembered to say thank you, Mark. Posh people like that set a lot of store by good manners."

"Yes, Mam, of course I did. Have you heard anything about Tommy?"

"No, so he's probably back home safe and sound," said Mam. "No news is good news, they say."

Mark wondered what to do; should he go round to see if Tommy was back? Mr Hedley had obviously been unaware of their falling out. Mark racked his brains to think of anywhere that Tommy might have spent the night but it was true, Mark had been his only friend. He decided it was too late now to go round. If Tommy had returned, would Mr Hedley have called round to let them know? Maybe not if Tommy had said the friendship was broken. Sunday was their only day off so they probably wouldn't welcome an early morning call before he went to the showroom. So it would have to be Sunday evening. He watched some television with Mam before turning in.

Sunday at work passed normally enough. It was quiet perhaps because of the icy weather. Talking to Pip at lunchtime, Mark asked, "Do you mind if I just do tomorrow and Tuesday? School starts on Thursday but I think I'll need Wednesday to get things sorted out."

"Of course, Mark. Whatever you think is best. Let's hope it goes well for you at school. I'm sure it will. Any news of your missing friend?"

"No, but I've not been round to see. Mam thinks he's back because no news is good news, as she said."

"I expect she's right." At that moment the phone rang on Pip's desk. He frowned. "Direct line," he muttered. He picked it up. "Philip Middleton." Pip listened intently, his face changing to one of concern, even fear, Mark thought. "Yes, very well. Thanks for letting me know, I'll tell him, and look after yourself." Pip put the phone down.

"What's happened?" asked Mark, putting his sandwich down.

"That was Gordon. It's Peter. He's very angry that the Vault group has finished and he's blaming you. It means no more money for him. Making all sorts of threats. Saying the whole Marlborough gang will be after you."

"How is it my fault?" said Mark, feeling a stab of fear in his gut. "He was the one who shot his mouth off at Taylor's."

"Knowing Peter, it'll just be talk, but it will pay to be careful for a while. I think this week I'll pick you up and take you back so you're not waiting for a bus in the city centre. Does he know where you live?"

"He knows it's Northside. Probably knows Calvert House because of the papers after the fire."

"All the more reason for me to ferry you about for the time being at least."

Pip took Mark to West Farm where they ate a nice meal and made love. Being naked in bed with Pip made Mark feel safe and protected and was able to relax.

As they got dressed, Pip said, "I'll take you back in a minute, Mark. I just want to catch the local weather forecast to see if there's any end to this cold snap."

It was still the short Sunday local news summary when the television came on. The newscaster said, "Some breaking news. Reports are coming in of a body of a young teenage man being found in Gorbeck Forest. Police are not looking for anyone else in relation to this death. The name of the dead teenager has not been released but his family are being supported by family liaison officers. More on this in our summary tomorrow morning. So, over to the weather."

"If the police aren't looking for anyone else, sounds like a suicide," commented Pip.

Mark felt a sharp pain in his gut. "Tommy," he said shakily.

"Your friend from Northside?"

Mark simply nodded, as now tears streamed down his face.

"Mark, you don't know it's him, No name was given."

"Pip, you don't understand. He was in love with me, we had sex. He was in a terrible state after Peter said about us. I'm sorry but I never knew how to tell you. I just know it's him."

"I can't say I'm not disappointed you couldn't tell me about him, Mark. It breaks our safe, closed circle. But I suppose as a teenage boy, I am not too surprised. I think I'd better take you home now."

. . .

"Mark! Where the fuck have you been," was Mam's greeting when Mark walked into the flat.

"At work, then at Pippa's," answered Mark.

"Shagging again when I've had the police here about Tommy and you!" snarled Mam, obviously very upset, or angry, or a mixture; Mark wasn't sure.

"Tommy and me? What did they say? Where's Tommy?" asked Mark, but he felt deep down that his premonition had been right.

"Tommy's killed himself in the woods or something but he had a letter on him and it was about you," cried Mam. "There was a photo of you and him as well. The cops said you were kissing him. What have you been up to, Mark?"

"What did the letter say? Have you seen it?"

"No I haven't seen it, just what the coppers said. What's going on?"

"On Thursday night, New Year's eve, we were at Taylor's and these bullies that remembered Tommy from school started going on at Tommy, saying he was a queer and that. Tommy was upset and he left. I chased after him but lost him because it was very crowded. I haven't seen him since."

"So why would Tommy write a note about you, Mark? Are you bent as well? Why were you kissing him? The coppers said it was a sort of love letter."

"Mam, I knew Tommy was queer but I liked him anyway. He told me he loved me though."

"Well, the cops want to speak to you about it."

211

"Speak to me? Mam, I didn't kill him. I didn't know it was Tommy until you told me just now."

"What do you mean? Didn't know what was him?"

"I just saw a bit on the news on TV at Pip's about a body found in Gorbeck Forest, but they didn't say who it was."

"Who the fuck is Pip?" demanded Mam.

Mark cursed himself for the slip. "Pippa, I meant, obviously, Mam."

"I think you've been hiding things from me, Mark, and maybe for a long time, and I'm too thick to see it."

Mark was about to reply when there was a loud crash from the hallway.

"What the fuck now?" shrieked Mam. They went into the hallway but there was nothing to be seen. Cautiously Mam opened the front door on to the landing - and screamed. Mark rushed to her, looking around the landing and down the stairs. But Mam was pointing at their green front door. Embedded in it was a meat cleaver which was holding a sheet of paper. On it were words written in blood.

*Mark Martin*
*killed our Tommy*
*Rot in hell pervert*

# Chapter 35 Downfall

"Mark, I'm not having this! Go to the phone box and call the cops. They want to speak to you anyway, but this is a fucking threat."

"Mam, Tommy's dad might be waiting for me with another meat cleaver. What then?"

"You run like fuck. Now go and call the cops. I'm supposed to be at work later. Offices open tomorrow."

Reluctantly and cautiously Mark descended the stairs and went outside. 'Fuck, forgot my coat' he thought as the icy cold hit him. But he decided against going back and instead made his way carefully over the frozen ground to the phone box. As he got closer he saw that someone was already in it but luckily as he got near they came out, nodding and giving an automatic smile at Mark, which he tried to return. He got through to the police and explained what had happened. Having established that nobody had been hurt, they said officers would be round when available. It was a busy night it seems. Mark returned to the flat.

"Are they coming?" asked Mam as he entered the hallway.

"Yes, Mam. But not straight away. When they can. They're all busy."

"Busy?" snapped Mam. "I'll give them fucking busy! I've got an axe in me front door and a note in fucking blood against me son. And they'll come when they can? Bastard cops!"

"Mam, it's no good ranting on. We'll just have to wait. Shall I put the kettle on?"

"Yes, Mark. Do that."

So they sat and drank tea while watching television and waiting for the police.

Time passed, and eventually Mam said, "Fuck this, Mark. I've got to get to work. It's you they want to talk to anyway." She went to the bathroom and then put on her coat.

"Mam, do you have to go?" asked Mark, now nervous about being alone with Mr Hedley, possibly ready to take his grief out on Mark.

"Just don't open the door to anybody except the police and you'll be fine." With that, she left.

Mark waited alone in the flat. He paced around, unable to settle. He tried to have a wank but there were too many thoughts flying around in his head and he got nowhere. Television provided no distraction.

Late, and there was an authoritative knock on the front door. Through the spyhole he saw two men but not in uniform.

"Who is it?" he called.

"Police," answered one of the men. "We've come about this note on your door and about Thomas Hedley."

Mark wondered if somehow these were thugs sent by Mr Hedley or even from the Marlborough estate. "You're not wearing uniforms," he called. "How do I know you're police?"

Mark saw the man pull a face and he got out a card which he held to the spy hole. Mark had never seen a police warrant card but it looked official. He opened the door.

"Are you Mark Martin?" said the first man as they entered the hallway.

"Yes," answered Mark.

"I am Detective Sergeant Williamson and this is Detective Constable Crawford. Can we sit down while we talk to you?"

Mark went into the lounge and the two sat on the sofa, Mark in an armchair.

"Who do you think left the note on your door?"

"Tommy's dad I think. He's a butcher so he has meat cleavers and blood. And it says, our Tommy."

"And why do you think he blames you?"

"I don't know," said Mark. "I wasn't with him. I didn't kill him. I liked Tommy."

"It seems he liked you a lot too, judging by the letter and photo we found."

214

"Can I see the letter?" asked Mark.

"No, it's evidence and it's at the police station, not with us."

"What did he do?" asked Mark. "Stab himself or something?"

"From what we can work out, he leaned his bicycle against a tree and used it to climb up to tie a rope round a branch and his neck and then kicked the bicycle away. It was lying beneath him beside the tree."

"He hanged himself?" said Mark, trying to stifle back tears.

"I'm afraid so, Mr Martin. Can you tell us where you were on Friday, New Year's Day?"

"I was here, slept in a bit and then just stayed in. Oh, I did walk round to Tommy's to see if he was back, but I got no answer. We'd had a bit of a fall out on Thursday night. Well after midnight really. It looked like everyone was out. So I just came back."

"Was anybody with you here on Friday?"

"Just my mother. It's just the two of us now."

"How old are you, Mr Martin?" asked Crawford.

"Seventeen," said Mark. "Eighteen in February."

Sergeant Williamson pulled a face. "I'm sorry, Mr Martin. I thought you were older. We may have to talk to you again with your mother present. That's all for now. We'll have a word with Mr Hedley about the damage to your front door. I think you can remove the blade now."

The two detectives left. Mark pulled the meat cleaver from his front door and screwed up the note.

Mrs Simpson appeared from her door opposite. "That the police, Mark?" she asked, seeming excited. "I saw the note earlier. Is that about the lad they found in the forest?"

Mark simply nodded and went in, shutting the door. Through the spy hole he saw Mrs Simpson with a smirk on her face as she went back into her own flat. 'Nosey cow' thought Mark.

He went back inside. The police interview had gone well enough, he thought. He imagined Tommy with the noose around his neck, standing on the crossbar of his beloved bike and then kicking it away and hanging there. Was it a quick death? Hanging was supposed to be instantaneous but he doubted whether Tommy used a proper hangman's knot. He had read about Albert Pierrepoint, the official hangman, and remembered that the person's weight had to be used and the height of the drop had to be carefully calculated. So it was likely that Tommy choked slowly to death. Mark lay on his bed and wept. Poor, poor Tommy. Just for loving him. Mark decided the world was a cruel place. What was the point in having dreams if you were queer? Tommy was right.

He was woken by noise. It sounded like a gun going off. There was shouting and other voices. Mark went out onto the landing in time to hear another loud bang from below, echoing up the stairwell. It really sounded like a gunshot.

"Martin! Where's Mark Martin?" an angry voice shouted.

Had Mr Hedley got a gun and was coming for Mark? He started to shake and cautiously peered over the stairwell. Peter! And he had a gun!

"Top floor, the green door," he heard a female voice say. Mark was now churning with fear. Peter was coming to kill him. How had he got a gun? But then, Peter lived on Marlborough estate and everything people said about it seemed true.

Peter looked up. For a second their eyes met. Peter raised the pistol, Mark saw the flash and the bang. Peter was now running up the stairs. The flat offered no safety now Peter knew which was his. Mrs Simpson's door briefly opened as she peeped out and then firmly shut again. The roof! Mark opened the door and climbed the stairway, closing the door behind him. He did the same with the top door. There was snow on the flat roof and he was leaving footprints. He was shivering now with both cold and fear. He went round behind the top of the lift shaft next to the brick structure that housed the roof access door. He waited but

216

couldn't hear anything? Was Peter in his flat? He was glad Mam was at work or Peter might have shot her. But then if Mam had been there, Peter might have done nothing. But then Peter had a gun and had fired it so he was already in trouble and unlikely to back down. Thoughts streamed through Mark's mind as he cowered on the cold roof. He could see lights of other buildings and streets, hear traffic from the main road.

The roof access door opened. Peter emerged, pistol in hand. He saw the footprints and laughed. "You can't hide up here, Mark. I'll find you." Then he saw Mark. "Got you now, Mark Martin," he said quietly. Somehow that was more frightening than had he shouted. It demonstrated control and calculation. Mark backed away as Peter came towards him across the snowy roof. But Peter followed, backing Mark up at the corner of the roof where there was a low, knee-high parapet which ran round the top of the block of flats. "Don't feel so cocky now, do you?" said Peter. "I've got the gun and you've got fuck all. Look at you, shaking like the little fairy you are."

"You've done it as well," said Mark.

"I've done what you've done but much more. But now thanks to you, not any more. I needed that money. If you live up Marlborough, you'd know why."

Mark shook his head. "It's your fault, not mine. You shot your mouth off in front of everybody at Taylor's. You can't blame me."

"That was just the end, it started when you turned up at The Vault. So when I saw you with your queer pal, that was it."

"Tommy? He's dead now, thanks to you, you bastard!"

"Well, you're about to join him," snarled Peter. "Get on your knees."

Mark didn't move but Peter jabbed him with the pistol. Slowly Mark knelt in front of Peter.

"Maybe I should get you to suck me off first," laughed Peter. "Blow me before I blow you away."

217

"Fuck off, Peter," said Mark, steeling himself. He then felt the metal of the gun against the top of his head. Peter then stepped back slightly and the gun moved away. As Mark looked up at Peter, he heard the shot, the flash hurt his face. All he could do was push Peter's legs. Mark realized that Peter had somehow missed but after Mark's push he was overbalancing, trying to regain his balance. But he slipped on the icy surface, toppled against the parapet, and without a sound, he was gone. Mark froze for a second. Gingerly he looked over the parapet. There on the ground among the bins Peter lay, the white snow around him being slowly discoloured by an expanding pool of blood from his head. It looked black under the street lighting. Mark knew immediately that Peter was dead. Mark knew immediately that he had murdered Peter with that push.

"Oh fuck! Oh Christ!" Mark looked around. 'Got to get away before anybody finds him'.

He ran down the stairs to his landing. All was strangely quiet. He ran to his room, trying to think what to take. His backpack. He stuffed some clothes into it. His Post Office book. He would need money. In his drawer he saw his passport. That went in the bag. From the bathroom he retrieved his toothbrush, back to the bedroom for his hairbrush. In his wardrobe he saw his school blazer with its white edging, the Head Prefect badge and his Laudatum badge. "Fucking hell," he said as tears came to his eyes. All gone now, everything gone. 'Hurry up' he told himself. 'Mam, what about Mam?' Grabbing a sheet of paper he quickly wrote a note.

*Sorry Mam. It's all gone wrong so I've had to go. None of it's your fault. It's mine because as you guessed I'm a homo. So now I have to go, I love you, Mam. Mark xxx.*

He put on his coat and good shoes, and grabbing his bag, peered out of the front door. Nobody about. Was Nosey Simpson watching through her spy hole? He stuck two fingers up in case. He closed the door quietly and crept down the stairs, He made it out of Calvert House, he hoped without being seen. Out of Calvert House for the last time. With tears in his eyes he ran away as fast as he could. Get the bus into town - and then what? 'Idiot! Pip. Phone Pip.'

In the phone box he scrabbled for some coins and dialled the number. It was now late, he hoped Pip would answer.

"Hello?"

At that familiar, safe voice, Mark started to sob.

"Mark? Is that you? What's the matter?"

"Pip," stammered Mark. "I've just murdered Peter. He had a gun and I pushed him off the roof and now he's dead."

"Where are you, Mark?"

"In the phone box."

"Yes," said Pip. "Go and pack a bag and I'll pick you up at the junction as soon as I can. Try not to be seen."

"I've got a bag packed," said Mark. "I can't go back to Calvert House now. They might find his body any minute."

"I understand, Mark. It's a shame because I would have said bring your passport."

"I've got that," said Mark. "I was thinking of going to France."

"Why France?"

"It's nearest abroad."

"Good, go and hide near the junction and wait for me."

The phone went dead. Thank God for Pip. Mark walked through the cold night to the junction. He looked for a hiding place. There were some bushes along one side so he squeezed in and waited. It was cold and even in his warm coat the stillness made him shiver. Or was it fear?

He heard the Austin Healey before he saw it, the deep throb of its twin exhausts clear in the night air. And there he was, his saviour, Pip.

He climbed in and they set off. Mark realized he was now on the run. A new chapter in his life had begun.

# PART THREE 1965

# Chapter 36 Flight

Pip drove swiftly through the night but near his home he cut the engine and coasted past his house.

"What's the matter?" asked Mark.

"Just checking there are no police waiting," replied Pip. After which he started the engine and drove quietly onto his driveway.

"Somebody's here," said Mark, noticing a Ford Cortina parked to one side, He recognized it as a demonstrator from the garage.

"No, that's our transport. This car is too noticeable." Pip put the Austin Healey in his garage, closing the door. They went into the house directly from the garage. Mark noticed a large rucksack and jacket in the hallway.

"Is that yours?"

"Yes," answered Pip. "We can't stay here. Police have been to The Vault and Tom has been arrested. It looks like before he came to you Peter went on a rampage of revenge."

"Are we sleeping here tonight?"

"No, Mark. As I said we can't stay here. We're leaving now. Go to the bathroom, we've a long drive ahead of us. What happened to your face?"

Mark looked in a mirror in the hallway. His right cheek looked red and sore. "I think it was when Peter fired the gun close to my face."

"How did he miss at that close range? But then you pushed him and he fell."

"Yes, but I didn't mean to push him over the edge," said Mark.

"Go to the loo then, I've a phone call to make."

Mark went into the downstairs toilet off the hall. He heard Pip talking on the phone. He heard something about "an extra person" and "extra fuel".

The call ended and Pip and Mark arrived in the hall together.

"Come on then, Mark. Time to go."

The grandfather clock in the hallway said almost half past one. Monday now. The clock's date window had still not quite changed to four. It seemed like a week! Outside they put their bags in the Cortina. Mark saw it was one with the larger 1500 cc engine.

"Where are we going?" asked Mark.

"Down south, well away from here. I've had an escape plan ready for some time but I thought I'd be alone and didn't think it would be because of The Vault. There are things you don't know about me, Mark. I'll explain as we go."

But after about half a mile, Pip pulled the Cortina into the side of the road and stopped.

"Mark, I can't do this. I shouldn't be taking you away with me like this. I love you, Mark, and I was taking advantage of the situation to basically kidnap you. You should stay here in England, be with your mother. And you've a sister and father too."

"No, Pip. I don't want to be hanged!"

"Mark, you won't be hanged. You're only seventeen for a start and from what you told me you were scared and acting in self defence. Peter's death was an accident brought about by his own actions, not yours."

"But everybody knows I'm queer now so they'll all hate me anyway. And if I stay here I'll have to give evidence against Tom, maybe Gordon, Gerry and Fred as well. I know what we did was against the law but everybody will find out and anyway, you were all kind to me. I was never forced. So the police can do without me. I want to be with you, Pip. There's no life for me here now. It's like poor Tommy said, queer people can't have dreams. Please, let's go."

Pip leaned across and kissed Mark.

"Ouch," said Mark. "That's my sore cheek."

"Sorry. Right, Mark, off we go." Pip started the engine and they set off.

Pip drove carefully out of Bilthaven and once on the main roads, with a bit more speed. "We have to be careful of ice," he said, "although the main roads should be gritted."

221

Mark noticed that the road did appear to be just wet in the headlights. Neither spoke much. The miles passed by and the weather seemed to get a little warmer as they drove south, above freezing at least. Pip now drove fast, using the power of the car to its full. There were sections of dual carriageway and Pip pushed the car at high speed, up to a hundred miles an hour. There was little traffic, just the occasional lorry trundling through the night.

Mark woke up when he felt the car slowing and on gravel. Blinking he saw they were at a petrol station and truck stop. "Why are we stopping?"

"I need to pee and you might as well. We need petrol and if you're hungry, something to eat. I also need a break from driving, but we've made good time."

It was just gone four o'clock when they went back to the car and it was still dark.

"I can drive," said Mark. "I've just had a sleep."

Pip paused. "OK, Mark. I know you can drive, just don't be daft. At least it doesn't seem frosty here."

"But I don't know the way. I don't even know where we're going."

"Mark, in case we get stopped it's better that you don't know until we get there. There are other people involved."

"From the other business you have?"

"Yes, Mark, but I don't want to say more at the moment. I'm asking you to trust me. I'll tell you when I can."

"Yes, Pip, I do trust you. I have to now, I suppose anyway."

Pip smiled. "That's hardly a ringing endorsement, Mark. Right, I'll direct you to the new M1 motorway which will take us to the edge of London. From the end of the motorway I'll either drive or direct you."

Pip navigated Mark, watching him drive and was happy that Mark could handle the car on the road.

"I did have a Cortina for a week in the summer," Mark reminded Pip.

"Of course you did. And it came back in one piece I remember."

They came to the motorway, joining it near Northampton.

"Can I drive on a motorway?" asked Mark.

"Of course you can. It's just a glorified dual carriageway. Learners can't, but you can."

Soon the car was speeding south. With little traffic Mark found the driving easy. The Cortina ate up the miles. Pip was quiet and when Mark looked, he was asleep. He enjoyed the drive and extra power of the larger engine. He topped a hundred miles an hour at some points. He just wished he could enjoy it to the full but always at the back of his mind was the image of Peter lying dead on the ground by the bins. He shuddered thinking of it.

*End of Motorway 1 mile*

Seeing the sign Mark slowed down and gave Pip a thump.

"Well done, Mark. When you come to the end I'll tell you which way to go."

It was a built up area but Pip obviously knew the way. Soon they were on a very straight road.

"Is this London?" asked Mark. "I've never been to London."

"Sort of, Mark, it's the outskirts I suppose. We're near a place called Harrow. Soon you'll come to the North Circular Road, A406. You will need to turn right."

There was more traffic now.

"Where's everybody going at five o'clock in the morning?" queried Mark.

"They might ask the same about us," parried Pip.

"I would too," responded Mark. But he was finding the increasing traffic on the strange road harder. "Can you drive, please."

Mark found a place to pull in and they changed seats. Pip drove confidently along the North Circular.

"Is that the Thames?" Mark asked as they crossed Kew Bridge.

"Yes, this is Kew."

"I've heard of Kew Gardens, it's been on television. Is that near here?"

"Not far," answered Pip. Mark got the impression Pip didn't want to talk so he just sat and watched the buildings go by. He was feeling anxious now his mind was not occupied with driving. He thought of Mam; she'd get home and find his note. It was still dark at six o'clock, the more so because of heavy cloud cover. Had they found Peter yet? Now he wished he hadn't written he was a homo. He had been rushed. But it would upset Mam. Maybe make things worse for Tom and perhaps Gordon and Gerry if the police were after them as well. But he forced the thoughts from his mind, it was too late now. He noticed Pip had turned off and now they were on the A23. Progress was now slower and Pip kept glancing at his watch.

"Are we late?" he asked.

"I hope not, but it'll be tight," answered Pip.

They passed signs for Gatwick Airport. "Is that where we're going?"

"No, Mark. Too dangerous for us to go there. They may be looking for us by now. I hope not yet, but it pays to be safe."

Soon Pip turned off the main road and drove down some country lanes. There was a hint of light on the eastern horizon. Through a gate way and Mark could see a small aeroplane ahead. Pip drove up to it and stopped. A tall grey haired man came towards them.

"You made it, Philip," he said. "Is this the extra passenger you mentioned?"

"Yes, Oscar, my nephew, Mark."

"No time to waste," said Oscar. The bags were transferred from the Cortina to the plane. Mark sat behind Oscar and Pip. He didn't know what to say so he said nothing. He had to rely on Pip completely. Oscar started the engine. In the quiet of the predawn it seemed deafening to Mark. The plane moved round and Mark could see some buildings. There was a windsock. The plane then surged

224

forward across the smooth grass and soon was in the air. It banked round sharply and Mark could see the little airfield and make out the Cortina where they had left it. He looked out as the plane climbed. There were towns below, street lights marking where the roads were. The plane stayed quite low and Mark could see cars moving around. Then everything below was dark and featureless. Peering down he saw a light, It was a ship! They were over the sea! His flight from justice had well and truly begun.

# Chapter 37 Lamb Stew

Mark was relieved when the little plane was once more over land. They seemed to be flying very low over endless countryside as it got light. Pip and Oscar were talking through headsets, but Mark couldn't hear what was being said. He felt shaky and nervous. What was going to happen to him? Pip was saying very little to him, all he had said was that he would explain everything later.

The plane made a tight turn and Mark could see it was going to land. He clenched his fists to brace himself but the landing was soft on grass. It came to a stop but the engine was still running. Pip spoke to Oscar, they shook hands and Pip indicated to Mark he should get out. They got their bags out and Pip took hold of Mark and guided him past the back of the plane, away from the propeller. With a sudden burst of power the plane surged forward, and making a wide turn, raced back down the field and was airborne and climbing away.

"Welcome to France," said Pip. But then he saw the anxiety on Mark's face. He put his arms round Mark and hugged him. "We'll be OK, Mark. Think of it as an adventure."

"Adventure stories have an ending. I'm scared, Pip. I don't know the ending. Maybe I should go back home."

"Mark, I did say you didn't have to come. I offered you the choice. If you really want to go back, I can arrange that but I can't go with you. Not now."

Mark cried. Yet he knew that his only friend in the world now was Pip. Tommy had seen that homos dare not dream, that he had no future. Wiping his eyes, Mark turned to Pip, and nodded. "Sorry, Pip. It's just it's all happened so quickly. My head can't take it in."

"I understand, Mark. I will look after you."

"How?" Mark looked round. They were in a field, in France. It wasn't an airfield, Mark saw, just a field. But as he thought this, a man appeared through some trees.

"Bonjour, Monsieur Philippe," he called.

"Bonjour, Marcel," answered Pip, shaking hands.

"Et le garçon?" said Marcel.

"May we speak in English?" asked Pip. "for my sake as much as for Mark."

"Bonjour, Mark," said Marcel, offering his hand, which Mark took.

"Mark is my nephew, and is travelling with me."

"C'est bon," said Marcel. "but first some food and then sleep. When must you be at Orly?"

"Tomorrow afternoon, Tuesday afternoon."

"Is it still Monday?" asked Mark.

Pip smiled. "Yes, Mark. It is."

Marcel led the way back through the trees to a road and a parked car. It was a short drive to what Mark assumed was a farmhouse. It looked old, with wooden beams in the walls but not black and white like old houses in England.

"Where's this?" Mark asked Pip nervously.

"It's all right, Mark," said Pip, giving Mark a hug. "It's safe here."

"Where are we though?" persisted Mark.

"In France, near Rouen," said Pip. They entered the house to be greeted by a smiling woman.

"Bonjour, Monsieur Philippe," she greeted Pip, and they exchanged kisses on the cheek.

"Bonjour, Madeleine," responded Pip.

"My wife has some food for you after your journey," said Marcel.

"Where's the bathroom?" asked Mark, which he was promptly shown.

When he returned, Pip was just finishing a phone call. "I managed to get through to Rebecca to say I wasn't well and wouldn't be in for a few days."

"Are we going back after a few days?" asked Mark, puzzled.

"No, Mark. I'm trying to buy us some time. I hope she assumed I was calling from home."

"Please, give me your passports," said Marcel. "they will need entry stamps for France so that your journey may continue."

Pip and Mark handed Marcel their passports. Marcel then left the farmhouse, returning after about half an hour. "They will be ready by the morning. He does excellent work."

Madeleine produced some ointment which she rubbed gently into Mark's sore cheek. It made Mark think of Mam, and he felt a tear run down his cheek. Madeleine said something soothing in French too quick for Mark to catch, but he felt better.

A large pan of stew, Marcel said the meat was lamb, was produced. Mark was very tired and was falling asleep at the table, nearly dropping his head into his bowl of stew.

"I think he needs to sleep," said Marcel.

"Moi aussi," said Pip.

Madeleine said something in a worried voice to Marcel.

"My wife is sorry that there is only one bed because we did not know about Mark. But it is a double bed," translated Marcel.

"That's fine," said Pip. "Mark and I can share."

As they prepared for bed, Mark noticed that under his shirt Pip was wearing a belt with pockets.

"What's that?" he asked.

"It's a money belt," explained Pip. "I'm carrying a lot of cash, mostly American dollars, which are accepted in most places or I can change for local currency. Also a small amount of gold."

"What? Real gold?"

"It wouldn't be much use if it wasn't?" smiled Pip.

Mark thought to himself that Pip should have said, "if it weren't", and then he thought of Mr Farnsworth and the lessons on the subjunctive verb form.

Pip noticed the sudden sadness on Mark's face, and gave him a hug. "Did that remind you of something?" he queried tenderly.

228

"School," said Mark. He remembered walking with pride around the school, Head Prefect, looked up to by others. How those first years had looked at him with awe. Pip just hugged him again and withdrew a small ingot from a pocket at the back of the belt. For its small size, it felt heavy to Mark. He gave it back to Pip who returned it to the belt.

It was a large, old fashioned double bed but it was comfortable enough. The room was cold but under the thick covers they warmed up. Very quickly the two fell asleep, arms around each other.

Mark woke up alone in the bed. The room was dark. He found the bathroom and returned to the bedroom to get dressed.

"You're awake," came Pip's voice, as he came in through the door while Mark was pulling on his clothes.

"What time is it?"

"Almost half past eight. You've slept almost twelve hours."

"What's going to happen?"

"Now, Madeline has made some more food for you. Later we will get some sleep and early tomorrow, we leave for Orly."

"What's Orly?" asked Mark.

"It's the airport in Paris. Marcel will drive us there."

Mark's head was full of questions, so much so he took a moment to decide which to ask first. "How do you know Marcel?"

"He is part of my other enterprise, Mark. So we work together."

"So where are we going from this Orly place?"

"We will journey to New Guinea where I have work as you know. But I will take care of you, Mark. Nothing will change that."

Mark nodded.

"Sit down a moment, Mark. I have something to tell you."

Mark sat on the bed, Pip next to him, arm round him.

"Mark, I've just listened to *Radio Newsreel* on the BBC Light Programme. You can pick that up here."

"What did it say?"

"Most of it was about Vietnam and a plane crash in Russia. But it was on about Peter and you, Mark. It said the police were looking for you. But, and I'm not sure how you'll take this, Mark, but the gun Peter had was a starting pistol, It could only fire blanks. It did say he had terrorized the block of flats where you lived though."

"A starting pistol? Like at athletics? There's one at school."

"Yes, Mark. So it wasn't that he missed you, he was trying to scare you."

"He did that all right," said Mark. "Does that change anything?"

"Not really. They still seem to think you pushed him off from what I could gather."

"Pip, I'm scared. It wasn't supposed to be like this. I've got my A levels in a few months."

Pip simply shook his head and hugged Mark.

They ate (more stew) and baguette with fresh butter. There was red wine and some kind of creamy dessert. Mark ate well and felt a bit better, but still tired.

In bed, they decided to sleep, but as they held each other arousal came and quietly and gently, they made love, Mark finding comfort feeling Pip within him again.

As dawn broke on Tuesday morning they were eating fresh croissants with that same butter and freshly made coffee.

Back in the Citroën DS, Marcel drove them through the French countryside. Pip was in the front with Marcel and Mark was in the back. After a few minutes, they stopped in a small village. Marcel went into a house and returned a few moments later with the two British passports. "He does good job, eh?"

Pip looked inside, as did Mark. There was a new stamp. It didn't mean much to Mark but Pip was pleased, "Marcel, that looks really good." He took a bundle of francs from his wallet which Marcel took into the house. When he returned, they set off again. Mark felt a little car sick, but said nothing. He blamed the butter.

After about an hour and a half, Mark noticed a sign for Versailles. "Are we going to pass the palace at Versailles?" he asked.

"I'm sorry my young friend," replied Marcel. "We are close, in fact I think it is behind the trees to our left but we have not the time to visit."

Mark sat back in his seat. He had read about the 'Sun King' and would have liked to see this bit of history.

Not long afterwards, they arrived at Orly airport. They retrieved their bags from the back of the car, and Pip bade Marcel farewell.

In the airport, Pip was buying tickets for a flight to Athens.

Mark followed the French enough to understand this. "Why Athens? That's Greece. I thought you said New Guinea."

"Yes, Mark, but there are no direct flights so we have to change flights anyway. But Athens is a good place to make any trail go cold. They would not expect Athens so it buys us more time."

By midday they were airborne in the Air France Caravelle on their way to Greece.

# Chapter 38 Elgin, second thoughts

"Can we see the Parthenon while we're here?" asked Mark as they taxied towards the terminal building.

"I wasn't planning to stay in Athens, just find our next flight and go." But the look of disappointment on Mark's face softened his resolve. 'Poor lad' thought Pip. 'This must be a nightmare for him. Still seventeen but so brave'. "Very well, Mark, you missed out on Versailles so the Acropolis, here we come."

Mark smiled at Pip. It occurred to Pip it was the first time Mark had smiled since he had picked him up at the junction.

"There's the sea just there," commented Mark as he looked out of the window.

"We haven't got time for the beach and the Acropolis," grinned Pip as he retrieved their backpacks from the overhead locker.

One inside the low airport terminal, Pip booked their flights for the next day, this time to Tehran in Persia. Mark didn't question this now. He knew the series of short hops was designed to make the trail harder to follow. Pip also bought some drachmas.

Outside, they found a taxi and managed to communicate that they wanted to go to the Acropolis. The driver said it was about eight kilometres. 'Five miles' thought Mark. There was a lot of traffic and progress was slow. By the time they arrived in the city centre it was already starting twilight.

"Our flight tomorrow isn't until mid afternoon again," said Pip. "I think we'd better find a hotel and do your Parthenon in the morning."

"My Parthenon?" laughed Mark. "I'll remember that!" The first hotel they tried was full, and the second.

"Of course, it's the Orthodox Christmas this week," said Pip.

"Christmas?" said Mark, surprised.

"Yes, Mark. The Orthodox Church uses an older calendar and they celebrate Christmas on the seventh of January."

"That's Thursday," said Mark, thinking of the start of term at school.

"We'll be gone from Greece by then," added Pip.

At the third full hotel, the receptionist spoke good English and made a phone call.

"A small hotel five minute walk from here. I have reserved one room for you, all they had left."

"Thank you," said Pip.

The receptionist showed them where the hotel was on a street map which he then gave to Pip. "Tell them Marinos sent you."

The hotel was basic but it was just for one night. There was a double bed, a wardrobe with drawers and a wash basin. The bathroom was along the passage. They had a quick wash and set out through the now busy streets as night fell quickly to find food. They were off the main tourist beat and found a taverna in a side street that seemed to have only local customers. The menu was in Greek of course. A young waiter approached, smiling and saying something in Greek.

"I'm sorry," said Pip, "Do you speak English?"

"Sure thing," replied the waiter with a strong American accent. "I'm from Boston."

"Thank you," said Pip. "Can you translate some of this?"

The waiter started to run through the menu quite fast. Neither Pip's nor Mark's tired brains could cope.

"What do you recommend?" asked Pip.

The waiter thought for a moment, looking at Mark as well. "I guess you're from England. Maybe the souvlaki with a mixed salad on the side?"

"That sounds fine," said Pip.

"What's souvy stuff?" asked Mark.

"I think it's various meats on a skewer."

Pip was right and both found it very tasty. They ate well, drank retsina and ate honey balls for dessert.

It was quite late when, slightly worse for wear, Mark in particular, they made their way back to the hotel. More relaxed, they cuddled and had sex before falling asleep.

They woke early which was good in one way because they accessed the bathroom easily. They found the hotel did serve breakfast so they ate fried eggs with omelette and bacon. It was just after nine o'clock when with their packs on they found a taxi to take them to the Acropolis. Pip was secretly worried that it might be closed off because of the impending Christmas but his fears were unfounded.

As they wandered around near the Parthenon with its views across the city, Mark was lost in thought. Pip watched him and felt his love for this boy, no, young man, fill his soul. He knew he was totally in love with Mark. He knew Mark didn't feel as strongly about him but knew Mark liked him a lot. Whether that was love or maybe moving towards love, Pip wasn't sure.

Mark picked up a small marble stone from the ground. "I've got part of the Parthenon," he announced.

Pip smiled. "You'd better drop it though. They probably have rules about walking off with bits of the Parthenon; especially English people."

"Like Lord Elgin," chuckled Mark. "Anyway, you said it was my Parthenon." He slipped the small stone into his pocket.

"Naughty boy," joked Pip.

"You should know," retorted Mark, laughing.

Soon it was time to be heading back to the airport south of the city. At three o'clock they were taking off aboard the Olympic Airways flight to Tehran.

It was dark when they landed but Pip immediately looked for an onward flight.

"It says Hong Kong there, that sounds exciting," suggested Mark.

"Probably too exciting, seeing as how it's British territory," said Pip drily.

"Oh yes," said Mark, crestfallen.

234

"Apart from which, we've lost a day while you were raiding the Acropolis and stuffing half of it in your pocket."

"Call me Elgin," joked Mark. "What's Shah mean?" he added looking up at a large portrait of a highly decorated man.

"Emperor. He's the Emperor of Persia, or Iran as it's called."

"It sounds a bit like Tsar," commented Mark.

"There's a flight to Bangkok in about two hours. I'll try for that." Pip managed to get two seats on that flight. They ate at the airport and later were heading east on the nearly eight hour night flight to Bangkok for much of which they slept.

The time difference meant that it was the early hours when they arrived in Bangkok. Pip immediately set about looking for their next flight.

"How many more flights will there be?" asked Mark, feeling unaccountably irritated.

"I hope just one more," answered Pip. "The quickest route would be via Hong Kong so I think we'll have to go south to Malaya then east to Port Moresby."

"Where's that?"

"New Guinea. That's where the boat is."

"They're cannibals there, aren't they?" said Mark in alarm.

Despite Mark's distress, Pip had to smile. "Very unlikely. There may be some still in the deep interior but not in the towns. Technically it's ruled by Australia, but it's largely self governing."

"I am so mixed up," complained Mark. "What country is this and what day is now?"

"Thailand and early Thursday morning here," answered Pip, scanning flight information.

"Thursday! Is that the seventh of January?"

"Yes, Christmas Day soon in Athens," said Pip, trying to cheer Mark up.

235

Mark's lips were trembling. "First day of term. I should be at school. I'm the Head Prefect! What the fuck am I doing half way round the world?"

"I'm sorry, Mark. I'll do my best to make it all right. I promise. Actually, it's still Wednesday evening back home. Not that I expect that's much comfort to you."

"But you can't make it all right! Nobody can make it all right. I killed Peter and now look at me! I've lost everything, absolutely everything. I was supposed to be going to university. That's what I was saving up for with your money and the others. Tommy was right. Don't dare to have dreams, Mark Martin!" He started sobbing. People around stared.

"Jet lag," he explained as he cuddled Mark's shaking body.

Pip bought tickets to Kuala Lumpur. On the flight Mark was now feeling depressed. The enormity of his situation hit home with the realization that his friends would be going into school. They would know he was wanted for murder and he wondered what they thought. He remembered he had posted a duty roster for the coming term and as far as he remembered Jacqui was duty prefect. He wondered who would be Head Prefect in his place. He hoped it would be Ethan. The others liked him and although he had a quiet, gentle nature, Mark thought he would be good. But all these thoughts made him withdraw into himself and when Pip tried to talk to him, he didn't respond.

At Kuala Lumpur airport they had to wait for the flight to Port Moresby. They bought some food which Mark ate automatically. Some outlets were closed. They were told that some had moved to the new airport due to open soon. Mark wondered what was the matter with this one. He pulled a face and said nothing.

"I'm sorry, Mark," said Pip.

"What for?"

"You're sulking. All this. Dragging you halfway round the world."

"Like you said, I could have stayed behind, but I'd still lose everything because I'd be locked up. No A levels, no university. So at least I'm not in prison, which is where I'd be without you, Pip."

"We'll enjoy life together, Mark. I do love you. I don't ask that you love me but I do think you like me."

"Yes, of course I do. My feelings are all jumbled up. I loved Tony. I missed him but then I met Tommy and you. I know Tommy loved me. I feel so guilty about him. Maybe if things were different he'd be alive."

"You're not to blame, Mark."

"But if I hadn't asked him to come to Taylor's with me on New Year's Eve those Northside bullies wouldn't have told everyone he was queer. It was just me, and we'd worked out an explanation for what Peter said."

"But Peter came looking for you to get revenge for the end of The Vault, so what happened on the roof might still have happened anyway."

"Perhaps," said Mark. "But Tommy wouldn't have hanged himself."

"That's true," answered Pip. "But you'd still either be in prison or here with me. Not with Tommy."

"But at least he wouldn't be dead, would he!" snapped Mark.

"I'm sorry, Mark," said Pip, responding to Mark's distress.

"Stop saying that," said Mark.

Pip didn't reply. He looked at Mark, how he had grown up since they first met those years ago. At one level Pip knew he still sometimes thought of Mark as the fourteen year old he first met even though he was almost eighteen.

Their flight was just under two hours to Singapore where they changed planes for the seven hour night flight to Port Moresby.

# Chapter 39 Arrival and Argument

As they ate their airline food, Pip turned to Mark and asked, "Mark, have you ever heard of an E-boat?"

Mark, busy chewing, shook his head, then, swallowing, asked, "No, I don't think so. Why?"

"Because you're going to be on one soon. It's about time I filled you in on the nature of what I have called my other enterprise."

"I was wondering when you would," said Mark. "Something to do with an E-boat?"

"Yes, we operate one. E-boats were German fast patrol boats, about a hundred and fifteen feet long. They carried torpedoes and guns and their role was quick in-and-out attacks of Allied shipping, especially in the Channel and the Baltic. After the war some were taken by the Dutch navy which is how we got ours."

"Is that because Indonesia used to be the Dutch East Indies?"

"Yes, but it was occupied by the Japanese in the war so after the war, they declared independence. The Dutch tried to hang on but gave up, in 1949 I think. But they retained West Irian, the western part of New Guinea, until a couple of years ago when it was given to Indonesia. Anyway, that's how our E-boat got there."

"So is it like a motor torpedo boat, a bit like Kennedy's PT boat?"

"Very similar idea, Mark. How did you know about Kennedy's boat?"

"When he was shot there was a lot on TV about him. There's an Airfix kit of the boat as well. Tommy had one. He had a lot of plastic models. Do you still have torpedoes?"

"No. The armament was removed. We converted it to carry goods. There was a large crew cabin at the rear of the boat and that is where we store the cargo. E-boats had a large crew for their size but we don't need many."

"What kind of cargo?" asked Mark.

Pip paused. "All sorts, Mark. Whatever things people want taking from one place to another. Sometimes mail parcels. We're cheaper than by air, especially for heavy stuff. But to be honest, that's a cover. The profitable things we carry are to support people who are fighting against the dictatorial Indonesian government to gain their independence."

"Support? How? You mean guns?"

"Yes, Mark. Guns, ammunition, even mortars, but that's rare."

"Why?"

"I tell myself it's to fight for democracy but it does pay extremely well. The rebels pay us very good money. That's what financed Middleton Motors, where the investment came from to extend and modernize it. Quite apart from buying expensive sport cars."

"So where do these rebels get the money from?" asked Mark.

"Good question. I've never gone into it, the less one knows about such things, usually the better. But probably from the Soviet Union."

"Russia? They're communist!" exclaimed Mark.

"Keep your voice down," cautioned Pip. "The PKI is the Communist Party of Indonesia. But they are also opposed to Sukarno who has made himself a dictator. The problem in West Irian is that the PKI is fighting the rebels as well as Sukarno. They want to be the government of Indonesia. Sukarno uses the PKI guerrilla war as an excuse for his repression. There are even rumours that Sukarno funds the PKI to keep the threat alive so he can stay in power."

"He gives money to the people who are fighting against him?" said Mark, incredulous.

"It's politics and power, Mark."

Mark sat and thought about this. "Did you start up this business with the boat?"

"No, Mark. I have an older cousin, who is German. The two parts of the family lost touch during the war, but my cousin Willy got back..."

"Willy?" interrupted Mark, laughing.

"Wilhelm, and you know enough German to know it's said with V sound. Anyway he got back in touch. He had been in the Kriegsmarine in the war and had ended up in command of an E-boat aged just twenty-three. Had Germany won the war he would probably have gone far in the German Navy. He loved E-boats. He didn't want to stay in Germany after the defeat so he set off to travel the world. In Indonesia he saw an ex-Dutch E-boat for sale so bought it. I think at first he wanted to run fast passenger ferry services round the islands but when the chance of earning much more money came up he took it. I was looking for money to build up my father's garage and he offered it."

"So you're a gun runner? Basically a pirate?" enquired Mark, trying to absorb all this.

"Maybe. But we don't fly the Jolly Roger. Perhaps we should," smiled Pip.

"You should call the boat *Revenge* after Blackbeard's ship," offered Mark.

"It already has a name, *The Flying Dutchman* which was also a pirate ship. But Wilhelm has it in German of course, *Der Fliegender Holländer* or DFH for short."

"My German's not too bad," said Mark.

"Don't worry, he speaks reasonable English."

"What will I do on the boat?"

"I've told them you're my nephew, as usual. Willy accepted that, probably because of the loss of contact during the war. I said you were in trouble and needed some time away from England."

"Yes, like the rest of my life," said Mark bitterly.

"You'll be with me," said Pip. "I suppose the best description would be as a deckhand. General helping round the boat and trips ashore."

"Will I sleep with you?"

"Ashore, yes of course. On board, probably not. I'll talk to Wilhelm about it, but he's the captain, so it's up to him."

Early on Friday morning, they landed at Port Moresby. The first thing Mark noticed even before he left his seat was the heavy rain. It was bouncing off the wing.

"It's raining really hard," he observed to Pip.

"It's a tropical climate here and there's a lot of rain," Pip informed Mark. "We'll have to get you some lighter clothing otherwise you'll bake in the humidity. And we'll get some sun cream as well. With your fair skin you'll burn very easily."

"Sounds a real fun place," said Mark.

"Don't worry, it's much more comfortable once we're out at sea."

"When will that be?"

"I'm not sure, Mark. That depends on Captain Meissner. It depends what cargoes he's got lined up."

"Who's that?"

"My cousin, Wilhelm, Willy."

Mark laughed as he got his bag from the overhead locker. "I can't get used to that. I'll giggle every time I call him that."

"No problem. You call him Captain."

"Does he know you're a queer?"

"Yes. He is too."

"How much older than you is he?"

"Eleven years. Come on, we're getting off."

As they stepped out of the aircraft, the heat and humidity hit Mark like walking into a wall, despite the rain. They scurried quickly into the terminal building where they passed through passport control without a problem.

Pip breathed a sigh of relief. "No worldwide hunt for us yet, then Mark. I did think there was a slight risk that our details would be circulated. But I think we covered our tracks."

"All the different airports?"

"Yes. Right, next job a taxi to my favourite hotel here, a shower, change of clothes, food and set up a meeting with Wilhelm."

"The Captain, you mean," said Mark, with a smile.

241

"He's my cousin, but not yours."

"If I'm your nephew then he's maybe some cousin of mine as well," replied Mark, logically.

"Good point, Mark. But stick to Captain for the time being after you meet him and the others."

"Who was Jackson?" asked Mark.

"Jackson?" responded Pip, puzzled. "Oh, the airport name. I have no idea, Mark."

The journey from the airport took about fifteen minutes. Mark was already sweating with the heat, in the high seventies Fahrenheit (mid twenties centigrade, Mark estimated) and the humidity, probably at a hundred percent.

The hotel was close to the harbour and Mark looked to see if he could find DFH but Pip went straight in and so Mark followed.

"Mr Philip," greeted the receptionist. "Glad to see you back again."

"Thank you," said Pip. "Is the room ready, we could do with a wash and change."

"Yes, of course, everything as you like."

They went up a flight of stairs to their room. It was more modern than Mark was expecting with its own bathroom. Pip turned on an air conditioner to cool the room.

"Time for a shower, for us both, I think," announced Pip.

Coming out of the bathroom the room was now much more comfortable. Drying himself off, Mark felt Pip put his arms round him, and turning to him, kissed him and stroked Mark's bum. Mark felt his arousal starting which Pip of course noticed.

"I want to make love to you," whispered Pip in Mark's ear. He eased Mark onto the bed. Mark felt that relaxation of submission coming over him and allowed Pip to stroke and caress him, both now fully aroused.

"I love you, Mark," whispered Pip. "I may be almost twenty years older than you, but I want us to be together forever."

Mark simply nodded, part of him wanting the same, another part of his brain thinking that now he had no other option. Did he love Pip? He wasn't sure. He wasn't sure what love felt like. Had he really loved Tony Jarvis? Perhaps. And Tommy, poor dear Tommy? Looking back, probably.

"What are you thinking about?" asked Pip, concerned and noticing that Mark's erection was softening.

"Nothing," answered Mark, automatically. "Actually I was thinking about Tommy."

"You miss him?"

"Of course I miss him!" said Mark sharply. He got up and stood beside the bed. "I miss Mam, I miss school, I miss Ethan, Steve, Eddie, Darren - all of them! I was Head Prefect. People looked up to me! Now I'm a murderer getting my arse fucked on the other side of the world!" Tears now streamed down Mark's face and he sat on the bed, howling his grief and loss. Pip went to put his arms round him, but Mark shrugged him off. Pip just sat next to Mark, feeling the boy's distress and feeling powerless to do anything about it.

"I might just as well kill myself. Everything's ruined," cried Mark.

"No, Mark. Please don't ever think that. I know things look desperate now but there is adventure and fun ahead, and we'll be together, always. Give it time, life is too precious to end on a whim. As for Tommy, think that nobody can hurt him now."

Mark's thoughts were of what might have been. "I'd walk through the school in my white edged blazer, Head Prefect badge on one lapel, Laudatum on the other. I knew the younger kids liked me, especially since I arranged that meeting, but they still looked at me with some awe in their faces. It felt good," sobbed Mark.

He turned round and lay on the bed, face down. "If I'd said no to Gordon that first meeting when I was fourteen I'd still be Head Prefect and on course for university. So come on then. Fuck me. That's what you want, isn't it?" There was bitterness in his voice.

Seeing Mark's young, naked body lying ready, Pip was tempted but instead he lay next to Mark, stroked his fair hair and kissed the back of his neck.

Mark turned his head to face Pip. "I'm sorry, Pip. My head's in a mess, and I'm scared. What will become of me?"

"Don't be scared, Mark. I am here to love you and look after you. and I never want to fuck you if you don't want it. It's all been so sudden for you. Only about a week ago you were having a new year party with those friends and Tommy then everything changed. I'm sorry, Mark, so sorry. I wish everything could be back the way it was, but Peter just ripped everybody's lives apart."

"Do you know what's happening back home?" asked Mark. "Mam will be worried about me."

"No Mark. And the Light Programme doesn't stretch this far. I had thought of sending a telegram to Gordon, but it would give away where we are if someone else saw it. And I don't even know if he would receive it. For all I know they could all be in prison now."

"You're not, and I'm not, thanks to you, Pip." Mark reached for Pip's cock and drew it towards him.

"Are you sure?" said Pip.

Mark nodded. Once more it felt right and Mark forgot his troubles as Pip made love to him, the sensation, both physically and mentally consuming him. If this was to be his life from now on, then maybe it wasn't so bad.

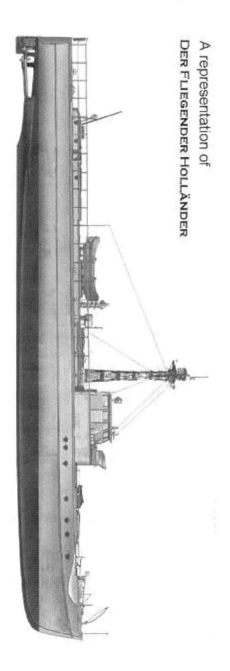

A representation of
DER FLIEGENDER HOLLÄNDER

They woke up, Pip cursing. "Oh fuck! I didn't mean us to fall asleep." He looked at his watch. "Come on Mark, get dressed. Willy will be wondering where we are."

"I know where your willy is," quipped Mark, reaching for Pip's cock. Pip was glad that Mark seemed a bit happier, able to make jokes.

Pip looked out of the window. "At least the rain has stopped. We must get you sun cream and better clothes. In the meantime dress as best you can."

They used the bathroom and were getting dressed when there was a knock on the door. Cautiously Pip opened it. Mark heard what he thought was the receptionist. "Mr Philip, Mr Wilhelm is in the lobby. He is asking for you."

"Yes," said Pip. "Tell him we will be down shortly."

Mark didn't know what was expecting - perhaps a tall blond Aryan with a muscular build. But in the lobby, Pip went up to a small, dark haired slight figure wearing a naval style cap, white shirt open at the neck and light coloured trousers. The two embraced.

"You have much to tell me, Philip," said Wilhelm Meissner. "Especially how a person who has not brothers or sisters has a nephew. I think this handsome young man is he?" he added with a knowing smile.

"Willy, this is Mark. Please, as far as everyone else is concerned he is my nephew."

Mark shook hands with Meissner. He stepped back so as not to make his height advantage too obvious.

"Philip, I must say I am envious. I am assuming you fuck him?"

Mark flushed, but Pip just nodded. "I've told him on shore but not possible on the boat."

"Maybe," said Meissner, looking Mark up and down. "As part owner, I have made the space for you, not in crew space but opposite my cabin. Also when you have said that you were bringing a young man, I arranged for the extra bunk."

"Won't that make it a bit obvious?" said Pip.

246

"A kind uncle looking after his young nephew?" Then he roared with laughter. "Philip, you forget. Most of them fuck any boy they can find on the islands. They know I have Jules."

"Opposite your cabin? The armoury?" queried Pip.

"We have made a space aft for the weapons in the magazine space so you shall have your cabin with your nephew," answered Meissner, who was laughing. "I wouldn't put him in the crew's cabin, he's too lovely for that."

Mark looked from one to the other, trying to absorb his new world. He looked questioningly at Pip.

"Mark, the captain says he made us our own cabin. Originally it was a radio room I think, then used as an armoury, but now, it seems, for us."

"Doesn't it have a radio now?" asked Mark.

"Yes," said Meissner. "But modern sets are much smaller than wartime so the radio is now in the wheelhouse, also my cabin. We have radar as well now. The boat has been made much more modern since I bought it. So the space is for you and your new uncle Philip," he ended with a laugh.

"I need to get some clothes for Mark," said Pip. "The ones he has aren't really suitable for this climate. Also some sun protection. Also I need to open a bank account for him."

"We have clothes already on the boat," said Meissner. "Come, it is late." He led the way outside to where a taxi was waiting. They were driven down through the town, where they stopped at a bank. An account was opened for Mark but with Pip as operator until Mark was eighteen.

"Am I going to get paid?" asked Mark. "How much?"

"Of course. How much depends on how much the boat earns. Everybody gets a share of the profits. So you will get a small share. It's paid in American dollars."

"Do you get a share?"

"I am part owner so my share is second biggest after Captain Meissner."

"Philip, at first the boy's share must come from you, or it means the rest get a bit less. They would not be pleased

247

with him for that. Later if he earns it, we can change that," said Meissner.

Pip nodded. "Yes, Willy, I see that. It's fine by me."

Then the taxi took them along a curving road along the shore until they arrived at some jetties and warehouses.

Then Mark saw his future home. Long, low and sleek, painted pale grey, the boat lay alongside a pier.

"Welcome to my Schnellboot, Mark," said Meissner with a smile as they traversed the gangway.

"Fast boat," translated Mark. "Why are they called E-boats?" he asked.

Meissner frowned. "They are not," he said. "That was the English name for Enemy Boat. For us they are S-Boot, Schnellboot."

Mark felt the captain's annoyance. "Es tut mir leid," he apologized.

Meissner's face was suddenly wreathed in smiles. "Er kann gut Deutsch! Ich mag ihn schon."

"I was hoping you'd like him, Willy," said Pip. "he's a good lad and I love him dearly."

Mark felt uncomfortable at this open declaration of love, it stirred up his confusion again. But then they were aboard. "Is it made of wood?" he asked, surprised.

"There is a metal framework, light alloy I think, and then a wooden hull laid on that. One reason why it's so fast, it's light," offered Pip.

Mark looked around. To his right was the bow of the boat and the wheelhouse or bridge. There were fenders stored on deck in front of that. He could see where the torpedo tubes had been and to his left, the studs where the holders for the torpedoes had been.

"A better mast for the radar," said the captain, gesturing towards a lattice mast behind the bridge. "Also for the whistle." At Mark's puzzled look, he added, "For the fog and to give signals."

As he was taken towards the stern of the boat, he saw some portholes low down in a slightly raised deck section, the air intakes and exhausts for the engines below and two large rubber dinghies, lashed firmly down.

"Our lifeboats," said the captain. "But we never need them because we are faster than everything else." He was smiling as he said this. Mark made no comment.

"Here is where the stern gun was once for anti-aircraft," explained the captain further, "but now it is a hatch for the hold beneath. Once maybe fifteen men were there, but we do not have so many now."

"Why not?" asked Mark.

"We do not need gunners, torpedo men, signallers, radio men and men for warfare," explained the captain. "We have changed the boat in some ways since I bought it, to make it good for its new use." Mark could sense the pride he had in this boat, his love for it even.

He led the way down a companionway into the hold. Mark wondered how fifteen men had once lived in this space.

"Tomorrow this will be full. We take mail and supplies to Rabaul," said the captain.

"What's there?" asked Mark, indicating a hatch to the rear.

"A fuel tank and the gear for the rudders. Come, meet Jules."

Turning forward, they were on a narrow walkway. A young, dark skinned and dark haired man wearing an apron came out of the door to the left. He and the captain smiled at each other.

"This is Jules. He is from Algeria but he is very nice. He also is a good cook which is lucky because we have to eat the food he makes. What is it tonight, Jules?" the captain concluded by asking.

"Goulash with rice," answered Jules, who was looking at Mark with interest.

Indicating a door opposite the galley, the captain said, "This is the stern head."

Mark looked in. It was a small washroom and toilet. "Head?" he repeated, puzzled.

"The heads are the name given to the toilets on vessels like this. Navy language," explained Pip. Mark thought he had a lot to learn about his new life.

"Come," said the captain. He led the way forward through another hatchway between two large fuel tanks.

"Each hatchway like this is a watertight door. The boat has many watertight compartments," explained the captain.

"I hope they go up to the top," said Mark, smiling, and thinking of the film, *A Night to Remember* about *RMS Titanic*.

"Of course," said the captain curtly. "Why must they not?"

"On the *Titanic* they didn't and the water overflowed from one to another making the boat sink and about one thousand five hundred people drowned," said Mark.

"Why are English so obsessed by this ship?" asked the captain. "Nobody thinks about *Wilhelm Gustloff* where maybe between eight and ten thousand people drowned. Maybe because they were German?"

"I'm sorry," said Mark. "I haven't heard of that."

"No, because you are English. It was January 1945 and was carrying refugees. This too, do not say **the** *Titanic*. It is the name of the ship. We do not say **the** Mark Martin, do we? Also, learn this. *Titanic* was not a boat. It was a ship. Do not call ships boats. It shows you are ignorant."

"I am trying to learn," said Mark.

The captain's expression softened. "You are young boy. Think like this. A ship can carry a boat, but a boat cannot carry a ship."

Feeling chastened, Mark followed them to one side into the next section where there was a big diesel engine in the centre of the boat. From his time in the workshop Mark could see it had twenty cylinders in a V layout. A very powerful engine! They walked between it and the hull of the boat. Light came from a row of small overhead portholes that Mark had noticed on the deck. A smaller engine was running.

"Why is that engine running when we are not moving?" asked Mark.

"It is auxiliary engine to make electricity for us. We need lights and power and also for the gyrocompass which must have power at all times. But this main engine drives us when we are cruising and it drives the centre screw," said the captain.

From the other side of the engine a man appeared, wearing just shorts. He was tall and fair but now his skin glistened with oily sweat.

"Ist alles gut, Lothar?" asked the captain.

"Ja, Kapitän, sie läuft gut," the man replied.

"Mark, meet my old comrade and the best engineer afloat, Lothar Steiger."

Steiger did not offer his hand but just looked at Mark with what Mark could only consider a look of contempt. Mark felt uncomfortable.

Through another bulkhead door and to his surprise he was now between two more twenty cylinder diesel engines on either side.

"These drive the outer screws when we need speed," said Pip.

"How fast can this boat go?" asked Mark.

"About forty-five knots," said Pip. "That's about fifty miles an hour to you. That is very fast on water."

The gangway then led forward between what Mark was told were two more of the fuel tanks.

"How many fuel tanks are there?"

"Seven," answered the captain. "Enough for twenty-fours at full speed. Three days at economy running."

Mark looked at Pip. "How many gallons is that?"

"I'm not really sure, Mark," said Pip.

"You English and your gallons," laughed the captain. "Now here on the left, the port side is where your cabin has been made and on the starboard side is my cabin. But first we finish the tour."

Next was the forward cabin. "Here six men would sleep, officers and petty officers. Now all crew are sleeping here." There were eight bunks, four either side, and a table in the middle. There were portholes either side. A small compartment provided a private bunk. Some bunks were obviously not in use and had items stored on them.

"Mike is our navigator and Giorgio is for the helm and has the first aid duty but they are on shore now."

Going forward again through a bulkhead door Mark was shown the forward head (another toilet) and the shower room. Beyond that was the locker for the anchor chain.

Then back through the crew cabin and up some steps up to the wheelhouse.

"At one time the bridge was open to the air but we spend much money here to make it enclosed. It rains a lot here. Also we have the modern instruments, the radio, the depth sounder and the radar. Of course also the wheel."

The captain looked expectantly at Mark and Pip.

"it's a wonderful boat, Willy," said Pip. Mark nodded his agreement.

"Now you have seen all of *Der Fliegender Holländer*," said the captain. "He is good boat, yes?"

Mark nodded more, trying to be enthusiastic. So much to take in. He was now feeling very tired and also very hungry. "Pip," he said. "When did we last eat? I don't know which I feel more, tired or hungry."

"Soon we eat Jules's goulash, he is a wonderful cook." said the captain.

Mark and Pip retired to their small cabin. There were two bunk beds, two lockers, two small armchairs, two portholes and that was pretty much it. The lower bunk bed was wider than the top.

"Is that wider for both of us?" asked Mark with a grin.

"I think it's so people can sit without banging their heads on the top bunk. At least it's our own space," said Pip, sounding optimistic. "I always slept in the crew cabin before."

"I have my uses then," smiled Mark. "I'm having the top bunk," he announced with a tone of finality.

252

"That's fine," said Pip. "but I hope that some of the time you'll share the bottom bunk with me. They are not the narrowest of bunks."

"All I want to do is sleep right now," said Mark.

"After we've eaten," said Pip.

So they went to the forward crew cabin where everybody ate round the table. Mark met the other crew members. There was Giorgio, a short Italian who talked a lot and Mike, an American who spoke very little. 'The Quiet American' thought Mark, remembering the Graham Greene novel. Jules brought the food which Mark ate voraciously, thinking it was very nice. But then maybe his hunger by that time was so great anything would have tasted delicious. Steiger, the engineer, grumbled about having to squeeze seven people round the table better suited to six, looking at Mark as he did so.

After using the 'heads' and a quick wash, Mark returned to his cabin. While Pip was out of the cabin doing the same. Mark undressed and climbed to the top bunk. When Pip re-entered the cabin, Mark was already asleep.

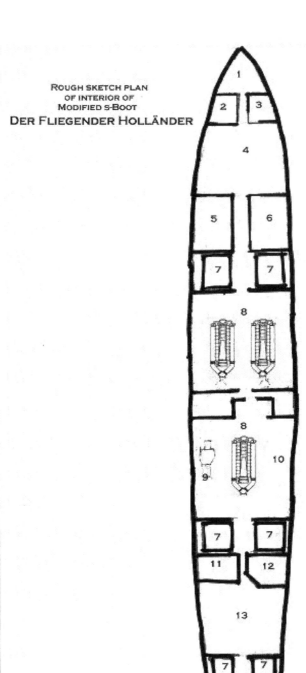

ROUGH SKETCH PLAN
OF INTERIOR OF
MODIFIED S-BOOT

# DER FLIEGENDER HOLLÄNDER

1. ANCHOR LOCKER

2. WASHROOM

3. HEAD

4. CREW CABIN

5. MARK'S & PIP'S CABIN

6. CAPTAIN'S CABIN

7. FUEL TANK

8. ENGINE ROOM

9. AUXILIARY ENGINE

10. WORKSHOP AREA

11. GALLEY

12. HEAD AND WASHROOM

13. HOLD

14. RUDDER GEAR

# Chapter 41 Learning the Ropes

For a moment Mark wondered where he was. He had been dreaming he was at home in his own bed with Tommy. Now he listened to the low throbbing of the diesel generator. There was a dim light in the cabin from the curtained portholes. Mark leaned over to see Pip, but his bunk was empty. He wondered what time it was; his watch had stopped and anyway, it would be reading the wrong time zone. He climbed down and dressed. He remembered he had been promised some better clothes but so far they had not been given to him. He stepped out into the walkway. The door opposite to the captain's cabin was shut. He wondered what it was like. He heard voices to his left and went into the main crew room.

"Good morning, Mark," said Pip. "You seem to have had a good sleep. I was about to come and wake you."

"Yes, I think so," answered Mark. He went through to use the head before returning to the crew cabin. He was introduced to the two crew members he had briefly seen at the meal.

"Mark, this is Mike, the boat's navigator and first officer," Pip said, indicating the fit looking, middle aged man with fair hair in a crew cut, who simply nodded at Mark. "And this is Giorgio, the helmsman and because he was a navy medic, he gets to be our first aider."

The small, plump man stood up and came to Mark and hugged him. "Welcome here," he said warmly.

"Giorgio is Italian," said Pip by way of explanation for this effusive greeting.

"What time is it?" asked Mark, sitting on the end of one bench.

"Almost eight," replied Pip.

"What day is it?" Mark followed up with, to the amusement of the others.

"Does he have a brain?" asked Steiger tartly.

"He's done a lot of travelling the past few days," explained Pip to the group. "It's Saturday Mark."

"The ninth then," said Mark, at which Pip nodded.

Then Jules appeared with breakfast which was porridge and bread with butter and marmalade.

"Eat up, Mark, there's a lot to do today before we sail," said Pip. "One of which is to sort you out with some more suitable clothes."

Mark nodded because it was already getting hot.

At the end of the meal, Mark and Pip went to their cabin. Giorgio arrived with some light Khaki clothing, shorts and shirts, also a large brimmed hat. "You tall boy but I think these fit you so now be a lot cooler when it hot," he said before departing.

Mark changed into the khaki clothes. They weren't a bad fit. "How do I look?" he asked Pip.

"Gorgeous as always," said Pip. He reached out and kissed Mark, with a growing passion. Mark pulled away, nervous about being discovered.

"What if someone comes in?" he said anxiously.

"They won't, and anyway, I think they know you're more to me than just my nephew."

"Don't they hate queers like everybody else?"

"When the captain is queer and shares his cabin, and bed, with Jules, the cook? And they have all been known to find willing boys ashore. If they hate homos they keep quiet. Probably the least tolerant is the Chief Engineer, Lothar Steiger."

Mark smiled. "He's the **only** engineer. I thought he didn't like me," said Mark. "Why does the captain keep him?"

"They served together on these boats in the war. They go back a long way together. When their boat was attacked and sunk by the RAF they survived days on the life raft together before being picked up by another S-boat. Steiger was wounded but Willy kept him alive."

"Wow," said Mark. "What's first officer mean? Isn't that the captain?"

"It means first after the captain. Mike's second in command."

256

"Is Mike American? He didn't seem especially friendly."

Pip laughed. "Mike says little so it's hard to know what he thinks. But he knows these waters very well. He was here in the war and I think he's stayed here ever since."

"There are no books," said Mark. "I miss my books."

"I packed one or two but we'll get you some books," said Pip. "All in good time."

"Pip, I was thinking about Mam. She'll be so worried. I know you said it was risky to send a telegram to Gordon, but I wondered if you sent one to that Frenchman, Marcel, was it? He might be able to find something out or even get a message to Mam; a letter maybe?"

Pip was thoughtful. "Clever boy, Mark. That might just work. He could post a letter, perhaps more anonymously from Paris, to your mother. It would have to be one way though, he couldn't put an address on it that would start a trail back to us, and to this boat. I'll think about it."

"I've got my Post Office Savings Book," said Mark. "It's got all my money in it. I can't use it here though, can I?"

"No, Mark, and even if you could, it would give where we are away."

"Then Mam should have it," said Mark. "If we post it to Marcel, he could post it to Mam."

"As I said, I'll have to think about it," responded Pip. "In the meantime there's work to do."

Mark was set to work. He was handed a mop and a bucket with a rope tied to the handle by the captain.

"You wash down all the deck," the captain said curtly. The smiles from yesterday had gone. 'Have I done something wrong? Aren't I welcome here suddenly?'

"Where do I get the water from?" asked Mark.

Meissner shook his  head and simply pointed over the side as he walked away. Mark felt foolish. He realized what the rope was for. He decided to start at the bow and work towards the back of the boat. He noticed the deck was quite dusty. He was still mopping the front section when to his disquiet he saw Pip leaving the boat along with Captain

Meissner and Mike. He felt a moment of panic at being separated from Pip.

But Pip saw him and called out, "We're just going to sort out the cargo, Mark. Won't be long."

Reassured, Mark continued his deck swabbing, working his way to the stern. Despite his lighter clothing, it was hot work as the heat of the day built up.

Later the captain, first officer and Pip returned with a truck. This was unloaded into the hold at the rear of the boat. Mark's job was in the hold with Giorgio and Mike to receive the boxes and bags passed through the hatch by Steiger, Pip and Jules. Some crates were heavy, others were lighter, mail sacks. Some were bulky but surprisingly light. Mark was told it was Balsa wood. There were some boxes that seemed personal in nature.

By the time the boat was loaded and fully fuelled it was mid afternoon. Mike took a flag from the locker and hoisted it up the mast; red and yellow diagonal stripes.

In response to Mark's querying look, he said, "Means we're carrying mail. Makes us look official." He ended with a rare grin.

Jules fed them eggs and rice and announced no more hot food until they reached Rabaul.

Mark was excited as they cast off and he felt the power of the centre diesel as the boat pulled away and headed out to sea,

Mark was sitting on deck behind the bridge where the captain, first officer and Giorgio guided the boat out to sea.

"This is better," said Mark to Pip who sat beside him. It was cooler as the boat picked up speed. "How long will it take to get to this Rabaul place?"

"We should be there on Monday morning. I expect we will just be doing about eighteen knots. The cargo isn't due there until Monday so there's no point in wasting fuel by going at top speed."

"So are we just using the middle engine?" asked Mark.

"Yes," answered Pip. "If Willy calls on all three engines, you'll know about it."

"How far is it to Rabaul from here?"

"About a thousand miles," answered Pip.

Already the boat was clear of the harbour and meeting the swell of the open sea but the boat kept a steady speed, Mark watching the wake as the bow pushed through waves and the trail left behind. The sun shone on the sparkling sea. Despite wearing his hat, Mark squinted against the sunlight off the wave tops.

"I should have thought to get you sunglasses," said Pip. "Wait there while I see what I can find." He went below while Mark enjoyed the breeze on deck. Pip returned wearing sunglasses and carrying another pair which Mark put on. He sat down next to Mark, leaning against the deck housing, and put his arm round him, pulling him close. "Are you all right, Mark?" he asked.

Mark nodded. He felt strangely at peace. "I could get used to this," he said quietly.

Pip squeezed him gently. "I love you, Mark. We'll try contacting Marcel when we get to Rabaul."

Mark smiled.

At that point the captain approached them. "You were supposed to swab the boat down," he said sharply to Mark.

"I did," said Mark, puzzled.

"Stand up when I speak to you," Meissner said. "We are working now, and I am your senior."

Mark struggled to his feet, as did Pip.

"You missed the upper deck housing, come with me." Mark and Pip followed the captain to the raised housing above the galley, the rear head and the hold. "This was not done properly," said the captain.

Mark remembered he had not done that because he hadn't realized it was included. "I'm sorry. Shall I do it now?"

"If you dip the bucket over the side now at this speed you will be pulled into the sea, and I would not come back for you. Maybe the sharks get you first anyway. Philip, please educate the boy." The captain then left.

Mark was by now almost in tears, which Pip sensed. "Calm down, Mark. It's all right."

"But he was horrible. He was nice before we set off. Doesn't he want me here?"

"One thing to learn about Wilhelm is that this boat is his life. In fact I think he loves it more than life. Once at sea he becomes the S-Boat commander again of twenty years ago or more. But he is a very good captain. But if you ever did fall overboard I'd make damn sure he'd go back for you. I'll have a word with him."

Mark looked at the bridge and could see Meissner and Mike in conversation and Giorgio at the wheel. Despite Pip's assurance he felt ill at ease. Maybe because of that anxiety he felt the rise and fall of the boat more acutely.

"Pip, I think I'm getting seasick."

"Best stay on deck then so you can see the horizon. Your brain can then account for the motion better than if you were down below. It will wear off when you find your sea legs. Did you know that Nelson was seasick at the start of every voyage?"

"Lord Nelson?" said Mark. "Maybe I'll be a sailor yet, then."

Pip smiled and hugged Mark. "I'll get you some seasick tablets that will help."

# Chapter 42 Letter

Later, Pip went to the bridge when just the captain and Giorgio were there. Mark could see Pip talking to the captain, both looking occasionally in Mark's direction. When Pip returned to Mark, he said he had asked Meissner to be more understanding and give Mark time to get used to things.

Over their evening meal of cold meats, bread and butter, Giorgio spoke to Mark. "Tomorrow the captain he say I show you the helm, how to steer the boat. Then you can help me."

"God help us if the kid is at the helm," said Steiger. "Can he read the compass?"

"That what I teach him as well, Lothar. Why you so mean to him?"

"I just think having the boy here could be a liability," replied Steiger.

"Mark's a clever lad," said Pip. "He is a quick learner, Lothar."

"I'll do my best," said Mark, feeling as ever uncomfortable in Steiger's presence. "Who is steering the boat now?" Mark asked Giorgio.

"The captain," replied Giorgio.

"Which is why he is the only crew member not here at the moment," said Steiger, as though stating the obvious.

"Time for me to go," said Mike. "I've got first and middle watches."

"Do you ring bells?" asked Mark.

"What does he talk about now?" demanded Steiger.

"I've read in stories about things like eight bells in a dog watch," said Mark.

"That's old fashioned stuff, Mark," intervened Pip before another remark from Steiger. "From the days of sailing ships. The dog watches are in the evening, like now. Now we just use our own watches and clocks. There is an accurate chronometer on the bridge used to calculate longitude."

"By the time difference from Greenwich Mean Time," said Mark. "Fifteen degrees of longitude for every hour."

"Is right," said Giorgio, grinning at Mark as he got up. "I go to bridge now."

Steiger left as well.

"Maybe make a navigator out of him yet," said Mike as he departed forward to the head and washroom.

Mark tried to stifle a yawn but Pip said, "Mark, I think you're in need of some sleep. It's been a busy day."

"Good idea," came a voice from the hatchway. It was the captain, but he smiled at Mark, which made him feel better. "Philip and Mark, you have the forenoon watch."

"Eight o'clock until midday," said Pip.

"Now I clear up," said Jules in such a tone that meant everybody out of the way.

Pip and Mark went to their cabin.

Mark spent some time writing a letter to Mam he hoped would be sent from Rabaul. He knew he could never get a reply but he wanted to tell her he was safe.

Dear Mam

I know you must be worried about me. But this is really me writing, not a fake. To prove it, remember me being the emperor and you the dowager empress of China. Now you know it's really me.

I love you Mam, always will. I am sorry about everything. You guessed in the end I am a homo but it's not what I chose. Just the way I am, like having fair hair and blue eyes and being tall. I didn't choose those either. I think you will have heard about the boy called Peter coming to the flat with a gun looking for me. He was blaming me for things I can't write about now but he was a homo too. I tried to hide on the roof but he followed me and he was holding the gun to my head and said he was going to kill me. I pushed him and he slipped on the ice and fell off the roof. Mam, it wasn't deliberate, I didn't mean to kill him, just stop him shooting me. I found out later it was only a starting pistol but I thought it was real.

262

I think if you get this letter it will come from France, but I can't tell you where I am because then I might get caught and locked up or hanged. But I am being looked after and I am fine. It's quite good here and I am learning to be a sailor.

Mark stopped and thought about what else to say. Had his comment about being a sailor given too much away? Probably not, there was a lot of ocean on the world. Then he remembered he had his post office savings book. It was no use to him now.

I am sending you my post office savings book. It's where I was saving up to help you and for going to university. All that's gone now so I am sending it to you. There's a lot of money there so I hope you can get it out. I won't need it now.

Mam, I was so proud of being Head Prefect and having that gold Laudatum badge. Walking round the school with that and the Head Prefect badge, it was wonderful. Even though it's all come to nothing I will always remember that. I would like it if you could somehow let Ethan Robson know you've heard from me and that I'm fine and that I did not kill Peter on purpose. But don't do that if the school finds out or they will tell the police and they will then question you.

Please don't worry Mam. You told me I am a lucky bugger so you know I'll be OK. Give my love to Dad and Sis. I will try to write again.

I love you, Mam

Mark xxx

"What do you think, Pip?" he asked, showing Pip what he had written.

Pip read the letter. "It's a lovely letter, Mark. I think it will help to put your mother's mind at rest; a little bit anyway."

Mark smiled at that approval from Pip. He folded the letter carefully.

They heard Mike on the bridge talking to Giorgio, Meissner and Jules going into the captain's cabin.

"Let's go to bed," said Pip. "I'd like to make love to you, and we are on watch at eight o'clock."

"O eight hundred hours," said Mark with a smile.

Mark and Pip went to the head and the washroom, and feeling cooler, took a brief turn on deck. The night sky was clear and Mark thought he had never seen so many stars.

"The sky is amazing," he remarked to Pip.

"It's usually cloudy so you're lucky to see this tonight. But now let's go below."

Mark agreed , looking forward to the closeness and love making with Pip.  It was a shame that afterwards he would have to climb to his top bunk instead of falling asleep with Pip. Although the lower bunk was wider, sleeping two overnight was not really practical.

. . .

Mark woke up to feel the boat still moving, rising and falling, the throb of the diesel engine further back in the boat making itself felt. Pulling the shade aside he looked out of the porthole across the sea as far as the horizon. There were clouds in the sky but blue patches as well. Six-fifteen according to his watch. 'Are we still in the same time zone?' he wondered. He peered over the edge of his bunk.

"Good morning, Mark," said Pip, making Mark jump.

"I didn't know you were awake."

"Do you want to climb down and join me?"

"I need the toilet," replied Mark.

"The head," corrected Pip with a smile.

"I'll never get used to all this," said Mark, clambering down the metal ladder fixed to the bunk, and nearly losing his balance with a sudden roll of the boat. He recovered quickly.

"Good, Mark," observed Pip. "You're getting your sea legs. Hurry back."

He met Jules emerging from Meissner's cabin. "Hello, Mark. I'm going to make the breakfast now. Eat it at seven."

"Thank you, Jules," said Mark, turning left toward the bow.

"No, come with me, Use the stern head so you don't disturb sleeping crew."

"Who's on the bridge now?" asked Mark.

264

"Giorgio. He has morning and forenoon."

So Mark followed Jules between the fuel tanks and the two silent outer engines and round the running centre engine steadily throbbing away. "Where is Mr Steiger?" asked Mark, not wanting to meet him.

"Maybe asleep," said Jules as they went past two more fuel tanks and arrived at the galley on their right, with the aft head opposite. Ahead was the hatchway into the hold.

"Why is the galley so far from the crew room? You have to carry the food past the engines and that."

"You forget that before where we now carry the cargo is where most of the crew sleep when this was a navy boat."

"I forgot that," said Mark.

Coming out of the head, Mark saw Jules busying in the galley.

"Today I make porridge, the sea not too rough," he said. Jules stepped out and in the narrow passageway, put his arms round Mark, and stroked his bum. Mark recoiled, not because he thought Jules unattractive - the opposite in fact - but he knew he was the captain's and anyway, he was Pip's.

"Not good, Jules," he said. "I'm with Pi - Philip."

"You are beautiful boy."

"Thank you, Jules. You are nice too." Mark turned and headed forward back to his cabin.

When Mark recounted his encounter to Pip, Pip said, "That's naughty of Jules. If Wilhelm found out I don't think he'd be very pleased. You played it well, by the sound of it."

"Is it right that the captain and Jules sleep together?"

"Yes, Mark. They've been a couple for a long time now."

"Is that what we are? A couple?"

"I really hope so, Mark. For many, many years to come. I love you and just want to care for you and be with you."

"And fuck me, as well," laughed Mark as they cuddled up naked in Pip's bunk.

But Pip was serious. "Mark, I only want that if you do. I never, ever want you to do anything you don't want to do. I love you too much for that."

"I'll let you into a secret, Pip," answered Mark. "Of all the ones in the closed circle at The Vault, you were my favourite."

"What about Gordon?"

"Yes, I liked Gordon. He's second but you were soon the first."

"That's sweet of you, come here." Pip kissed Mark and ran his hands over his body, causing Mark to become highly aroused and, applying Vaseline, drawing Pip into him.

# Chapter 43 Solo

After the promised porridge and coffee, it was time for the forenoon watch. That included Mark and Pip. They were taken by the captain to the boat's bridge. Mark looked around, remembering what he had been told when being shown round.

Giorgio was at the helm and through the windows Mark could see ahead - nothing but sea.

"Welcome, Mark," said Giorgio with a welcoming smile that warmed Mark's heart. "Today I teach you how to pilot the boat, yes?" He looked at Meissner as he said this, who nodded.

"What sea is this?"

"This is Coral Sea. Big navy battle here in 1942."

"Where's the bell thingy?" asked Mark, making a pushing motion with his hand.

"What do you mean?" asked Pip.

"I've seen in films when the captain wants to go full speed ahead he pushes a lever round and it tells the engine room what speed is needed."

"Now we have a better system," said the captain. "These three levers are for the engine throttles. Lothar has made this system. It is hydraulic like the brakes on your car."

"This is so that if necessary one person can be here alone driving the boat," supplemented Pip.

"Come, Philip," said the captain. "We have to talk about Yangap." Pip and Meissner left the bridge which was cramped with four of them.

Giorgio set about teaching Mark all the various instruments; the radar screen, which showed no other vessels for miles around, the depth sounder which was off because they were over deep water, the compass. set in double gimbals. which showed that now, having rounded Normanby Island, they were travelling due north, the throttles, of which only the centre one was in use. There was a row of fuel gauges. There was even a dial that showed the

267

angle of the rudders. Mark tried to remember everything and in his head it all seemed part of an interrelated system which made it easier.

"It's a bit like driving a car," he said. "But where are the brakes?" he added, laughing.

"You a funny boy," answered Giorgio. "But also the sea can be bumpy, not like the autostrada."

"You've not driven in England," quipped Mark.

"You have many things that affect you. The wind, the sea currents. You have three rudders, three propellers sometimes, the depth of the water sometimes. And near the coast you have the tide as well that can try to push you. When you try to come alongside the dock all these forces can try to push you the wrong way."

"It seems very complicated. I thought it was just standing here and holding the wheel," said Mark ruefully. "Why are there two speedometers?"

"Is not like the wheel of car on hard road. Water moves as well as the boat so we have two different types. One uses tube and air pressure, called Pitot. The other has little wheel that spins. Sometimes they agree, but usually we have to estimate based on what they say."

"I said it was complicated," said Mark.

"Now you take the wheel. You steer so the boat stays going north on the compass."

"Isn't there a difference because magnetic north is different from true north?"

"No, Mark," smiled Giorgio. "Only the best for the captain. This is gyro compass so gives true reading. North is real north. But of course we are in the south part of the Earth."

"That's clever," said Mark as he took over the wheel. He soon found that the boat would wander off its bearing so constant correction was needed. "It's a bit like steering a car," he said. "You have to keep adjusting it."

"You doing well, Mark," smiled Giorgio. "I like you."

"I like you, too Giorgio," said Mark. "but not that way."

"I not mean that way," said Giorgio. "I'm not strange man like captain and Jules or your Uncle Philip. But I like you. You will be a good helmsman. You have natural feel."

"Thank you, Giorgio," said Mark. He was fascinated by the dials and how the rudder indicator moved as he turned the wheel to keep heading north. Then there was a ping noise.

"What's that?" asked Mark, worried in case he had done something wrong.

Giorgio pointed at the radar screen. As the line swept round, it picked up an echo. "Maybe clutter but looks strong."

Mark and Giorgio watched the echo. After a while, Giorgio said, "I think it a ship. He goes south maybe eight knots. He about fifteen kilometres away." He picked up binoculars and studied the horizon to starboard. "I not see him. He too far away, I only see about eight kilometres with binoculars."

"Shall we tell the captain?" asked Mark.

"No," said Giorgio. "Is not a problem for us. Now try throttle for engine. Take middle lever and push forward but not quickly."

Mark pushed the centre lever, which was already further forward than the other two, slowly forward. He felt the boat push forward and pick up speed. The background engine noise rose in pitch.

"Is good," said Giorgio. "now slowly back to where it was before."

Mark obliged. Then Steiger was on the bridge. "What's the problem?" Then seeing Mark at the helm, "You're letting the boy play with Mathilda."

"I teach him the boat," explained Giorgio. "He just try the throttle."

"Does the captain know?"

"Yes, Lothar. His idea."

With a tut, Steiger left the bridge.

"He doesn't like me," said Mark.

269

"Only person he like is the captain," said Giorgio. "Captain kept him alive for days in little rubber boat when he wounded after boat sunk in war. He die otherwise."

"I heard something about that," replied Mark. He continued to steer, keeping his eye on the compass and other instruments. His eye caught the chronometer. It read almost two o'clock in the morning. "Is that the time in England?"

"Yes, at zero longitude. they all sleeping now after Saturday night out," smiled Giorgio.

Mark glanced at his watch. Almost twelve noon. "So that must mean we are about one hundred and fifty degrees east," he said, thinking 'Even I can work out ten times fifteen degrees'.

His forenoon watch had gone quickly. He had enjoyed it and felt he had learned a lot. He had forgotten to ask who Mathilda was.

Mike appeared carrying what Mark recognized as a sextant.

"Mike come to work out deviation from course," explained Giorgio.

"I think I've kept us on course," said Mark. "I've done my best."

"Not problem, but while compass always say north, maybe current and wind push boat to side. So you think boat going just forward, maybe also a bit sideways, like a crab. Is called leeway."

"So much to learn," said Mark, thinking each time he thought he had mastered it, another factor came into play.

Mike came on to the bridge and took a rolled up chart from a cupboard at the side, looked at the chronometer and disappeared below, grunting at Mark. "Probably miles off course now," he muttered, to himself but audibly.

Mark pulled a face. 'I'm no use at this' he thought.

A few minutes later Mike appeared again, returning the chart to its place. "How long has he been at the helm?" he asked Giorgio. 'I **am** here' thought Mark.

"Most of forenoon," answered Giorgio.

To his surprise, Mark felt Mike pat him on the shoulder. "Almost bang on course, very little leeway. Well done, kid," Mike said with a rare smile.

"Thank you," said Mark, choosing to ignore the kid remark. "Giorgio is a good teacher." He was happy he had just learned what leeway was.

"You're being taught by one of the best," said Mike, before disappearing below. Giorgio beamed with pleasure at that.

Jules appeared at the companionway. "The lunch is prepared," he said. "Just bread with butter and cheese or chocolate." He disappeared. Mark thought chocolate sounded good.

"I go for my food," said Giorgio. "I was here at four o'clock this morning."

"Who will pilot the boat?" asked Mark.

"You will."

"On my own?" Mark felt panicky.

"Yes. You have the boat."

"Yes," said Mark.

"No, said Giorgio. "It's the handover so there is not doubt. You must answer 'I have the boat' so I am sure."

"I have the boat," said Mark.

"Yes, you good on helm. And we are just in cabin. So try not to hit anything," he finished with a smile.

"There's nothing here to hit."

"Exactly, my young friend," replied Giorgio as he descended the companionway.

Suddenly Mark was back at Middleton Motors, getting his first driving lesson from Pip. He felt emotion welling up inside him at all he had lost. So much had changed in such a short time, reaching the heights and then plunging to the depths. Thinking of which, Mark concentrated on his job. While he was enjoying it, he could see how it could be boring after a time. The endless sea, the drone of the diesel, hypnotically watching the compass and the other instruments.

271

After ten minutes, the captain came and stood beside him. He said nothing but watched Mark. Although not as tall as Mark, he felt the captain's powerful presence next to him. The man somehow exuded authority.

"You like this?" the captain said eventually.

"Yes, it's good. I think I'm getting the hang of it now." Meissner frowned.

"I mean I'm starting to understand it," explained Mark, thinking perhaps the captain didn't understand the idiom.

"Giorgio said you learn quickly. You want the afternoon watch as well?"

"Yes please," said Mark, pleased with the captain's apparent confidence in him.

"Good. I still need to talk with Philip about a new job. But do not be silly. If you do not know something, then call down. You have the boat."

Mark remembered, so he replied, "Ich habe das Boot." Meissner smiled and went below.

So Mark, just seventeen years old and newly at sea, found himself in sole control of the boat as it sailed across the Solomon Sea at a steady eighteen knots, the maximum using the single, middle engine. His thoughts wandered a bit as he continued. He wondered what Ethan and the others would say if they could see him now, directing this powerful boat on his own. 'Is it only just over a week since I was with them at Taylor's?' he mused. Then he thought about Mam. He found himself missing her so much. Her constant desire for a cuppa, the way she never seemed to understand what he was talking about, the loving look in her eyes though and the hugs which he bridled against at the time; but what would he give now for the chance to hug Mam again? A tear rolled down his cheek, which he wiped away with his hand.

# Chapter 44 Stormy Weather

"Left you in charge alone, Mark?" came Pip's voice from the companionway as he entered the bridge.

"Yes. The captain asked if I wanted to stay on for the next watch as well."

"Wilhelm? I had assumed Giorgio. Mark, that's really good for him to trust you like that."

"He stood and watched me for a while," explained Mark. "but I have to call if I need help."

"Yes, Mark. And do so. There's no shame in calling for help. Well done. I am still planning with Wilhelm so I'll leave you to it. Oh, I brought you this plate. I guessed you'd opt for chocolate spread rather than cheese. The spread is from East Germany so tastes a bit nuttier than the English version. Don't spill the coffee."

With that he was gone. Despite the sea breeze it was warm but Mark ate his bread and spread and carefully drank his coffee.

After a while, Mike came up. "OK, kid?" he said.

"Yes thanks," said Mark. "Actually, can you take it for a few moments? I need to use the head."

"Sure kid. You gonna be long?"

"No. just for a pee," said Mark.

He turned away, then remembering, "You have the boat."

Mike laughed. "You got it, kid. I have the boat."

On his return, much relieved, Mark reversed the procedure. "I have the boat."

With a smile, Mike answered, "You have the boat. You'll do OK, kid. But as the senior, I should hand the boat to you first rather than you take it."

'Something else to remember,' thought Mark as he settled in to the routine. He noticed the dark clouds building up ahead and to his right. 'Starboard, I mean.' But it didn't seem to make a difference so he kept on. As time went by he noticed the swell on the sea getting more pronounced, but he kept on course as the boat rose and fell. He thought someone would come to the bridge, but nobody did. Yet he didn't feel the call-for-help threshold was passed so he carried on. It got more difficult to maintain the heading with more correction needed, and it was getting windier too but he managed, getting the feel of how the boat handled.

The clouds filled the sky and it started to rain as the sea got rougher. Mark was beginning to think that he should call for help.

Behind him he heard the captain. "Ich habe das Boot."

"Sie haben das Boot, Sir," he said, stepping back from the wheel.

"No. Stay there and steer," replied Meissner.

Puzzled Mark held on to the wheel. Then Giorgio was beside him. "When the captain is on the bridge he always have the boat, even if someone else is on the helm," said Giorgio. "But he commands and you steer where he says."

Mark nodded, adjusting the increasingly active wheel. 'Something else to learn.'

It was now raining heavily. Giorgio reached forward to a switch and a round part of the centre screen started spinning, throwing off the water allowing Mark to see ahead. "Is called Kent screen," said Giorgio.

Mark felt more secure with Giorgio beside him as things got rougher. The boat was now rising and falling more noticeably. The waves were now coming at an angle causing the boat to roll as well. The corkscrew motion was uncomfortable.

"Starboard twenty degrees," said the captain. Guided by Giorgio, Mark brought the boat on to its new heading, now the bow was facing the waves directly, some of which broke over the bow. Mark found it easier to steer going directly into the waves.

Meissner nodded his approval. "You steer well, not much yaw. It seems we have an extra helmsman. But it is now the end of your watch. Go and rest."

"Yes, sir," said Mark. He realized he had automatically said 'sir' again when being told to do something. School training. But it wasn't out of place, he thought. Not when addressing the captain.

He found Pip in their cabin, who grinned at Mark as he came in. "Well done, Mark."

"I was wondering if anybody would come as the weather got worse," he replied, holding on to the bunk ladder for support against the boat's motion.

"I was in Wilhelm's cabin because we had business to talk about, but he has a compass in there and he kept saying how well you were doing, particularly as the weather got worse."

"I didn't know that," said Mark. "But I'm tired now and need a lie down."

As Mark made to climb the ladder, Pip said, "Lie with me. For a time, anyway."

Mark wanted to rest but he also wanted to please Pip. So he and Pip lay on his bunk, Mark feeling Pip's arms round him, offering safety, security and a future. He fell asleep.

. . .

Mark awoke to feel the boat thrusting and heaving through the waves. "What time is it?"

"Eight o'clock. End of the second dog watch, start of the First watch."

"Shouldn't first watch start at midnight?"

"You're too logical, Mark," said Pip, hugging Mark.

"Why is it called the dog watch?"

"I don't know. There are various theories, but anyway it's time to eat."

"I need to pee first."

"Me too, be careful standing up, hold on."

Jules had prepared a meal of cold meats, frankfurter style sausages, salad and boiled potatoes.

"Isn't it dangerous boiling potatoes in rough weather?" asked Mark.

"They are canned potatoes, so I heat in the can and make a hole for the steam in the top," said Jules.

""He's an enterprising guy," said Mike. He finished his meal quickly and left for the bridge. The captain came down and ate his while the potatoes were still hot.

"At sea the evening meal is usually at this time so everybody gets the chance to eat it while it's hot," explained Pip.

Mark just nodded because his mouth was full of food. The captain said very little and left. Mark was very tired and happy to retire to the cabin.

"I'd like to make love to you again," said Pip.

"Pip, I'm so tired. Maybe in the morning?"

"Of course, Mark. Like I said, I never want you to feel forced."

Mark climbed up to his bunk and was soon asleep, despite the movement of the boat.

Mark awoke to find the boat was steadier. There was daylight through the portholes. He pulled aside the curtain and looked out. Land! In the distance he could see forests and beyond tree covered mountains. Mark guessed the boat was still doing the same speed and he felt there was just the one engine running as before. Needing the head, he climbed down from his bunk.

Pip was awake and smiled at Mark. "Hurry back," he smiled. Mark could see the love in his eyes. It reminded him of Mam and the way she looked at him sometimes. Upset, he went forward to the head, going quietly through the crew cabin where some of the bunks still had the privacy curtains drawn. Mark didn't know who slept in which one. He passed Pip on the same mission on his way back to the cabin, who just put his finger to his lips. In his cabin, Mark checked his watch; a quarter to seven.

Pip returned to the cabin. "Share my bunk with me for a while. Over an hour before breakfast." He came to Mark and kissed him. Mark felt the arousal coursing through his body and made no resistance as Pip eased his shorts down. Mark stepped out of them, naked now. Pip did the same and they got into the lower bunk.

276

"I have often thought about what I would do if I had to leave England in a hurry," he said as they cuddled and fondled each other. "As you know I had plans in place but I never thought I would have a beautiful young man like you with me. You make it so much easier and better."

"I didn't even have a plan," said Mark. "I never expected it at all. Then Peter and his stupid big mouth."

"Well, he paid the price for that," said Pip.

Mark stiffened. "Pip, I didn't kill him on purpose. You saying that makes it sound like revenge, like I meant to murder him."

"I didn't mean it like that, Mark. You know I didn't."

"No, but now you said that, that shows it's what people back home will be thinking. That I'm a ruthless murderer." Mark was now upset. Although he could feel Pip's hard cock against him, his own arousal fled. "Sorry, Pip. I know you want it now but that's upset me. Wait until tonight, please."

Of course," said Pip. "As always, it's up to you."

So they lay and cuddled, Pip stroking Mark's hair. "You need a haircut," he whispered, kissing Mark's cheek. Mark was about to reply when there was a tap on the door and then the captain entered. Mark flushed with embarrassment at being caught in bed with Pip but the captain said nothing about it and did not seem surprised.

"Mark, you will eat breakfast soon. You are on helm for the forenoon. Giorgio needs rest, he has been at the helm all night through the storm."

"Yes, sir," answered Mark.

"Good morning, Philip," said the captain as he left the cabin.

"We'd better get up then," said Pip.

Jules was still preparing the breakfast for the watch change at eight so Mark went to the bridge companionway. "May I come up?" he said.

"Yes," came the captain's reply.

Meissner was on the bridge with Giorgio. Mark thought he looked tired.

"Breakfast yet?" enquired the captain.

"Not yet but I thought I'd come and see what was going on first. What's that land?"

"New Britain," said Giorgio. "We at Rabaul this morning."

Mark thought, Monday morning. His friends - were they still friends or did they think he was a murderer - would be getting ready for school. 'Don't be silly' he thought. 'They were probably still watching Bruce Forsyth or something, maybe just going to bed on Sunday evening.' Looking at the compass he could see the heading was sixty-five degrees. At a call from below he descended to eat his breakfast. He then went to the head and was about to return to the bridge when Pip pulled him into their cabin.

"Pip, I said tonight," protested Mark.

"I know, you're on watch in a few minutes, but I wanted to hold you and kiss you and say how proud I am of you. They way you've handled yourself since coming here. I had thought you'd be just a passenger but already you've made yourself a valued member of the crew. It just makes me love you even more." With that he kissed Mark who felt the need to fight off getting horny and that need to surrender.

"Thanks Pip. I love you."

Pip's face was emotional. "Mark, that's the first time you've said that to me. It means so much."

Mark smiled and went to the bridge.

"Mark, you have the boat. Maintain sixty-five degrees. Call if you need help. We both are going to eat and rest."

"I have the boat, sir. Sixty-five degrees."

The captain smiled slightly and, followed by Giorgio, left the bridge. Once more, Mark was in sole charge of the boat. On the radar screen he could see the land to port, which he could also see from the bridge. There were no echoes apart from that. A bit concerned, he noticed the fuel gauges were much lower now, some were reading empty. There was now a gentle swell and blue sky with patches of

278

cloud. As the boat made its steady progress, Mark felt a kind of contentment.

# Chapter 45 In the Dock

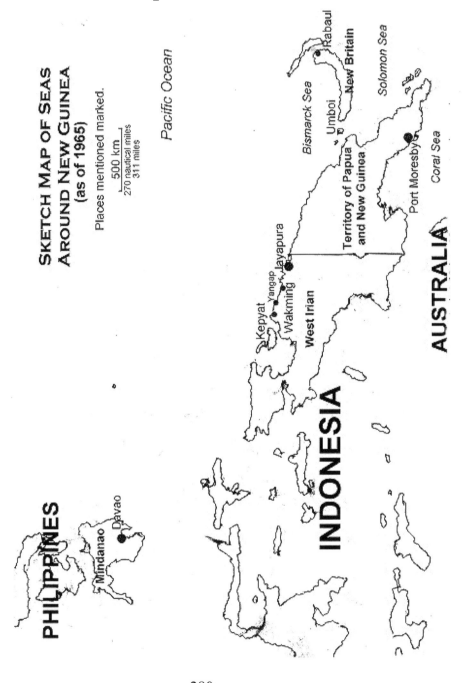

SKETCH MAP OF SEAS AROUND NEW GUINEA (as of 1965)

Places mentioned marked.

500 km
270 nautical miles
311 miles

Pacific Ocean

Rabaul
New Britain
Solomon Sea
Bismarck Sea
Umboi
Territory of Papua and New Guinea
Port Moresby
Coral Sea
Jayapura
Yangap
Kepyat
Wakming
West Irian
INDONESIA
AUSTRALIA
PHILIPPINES
Mindanao
Davao

It seemed an age later when Meissner returned to the bridge with Mike.

"I have the boat, Mark, but stay there," said the captain.

"You have the boat, sir," repeated Mark.

Through binoculars they studied the southern coastline of New Britain. Mike took a chart from the locker. Checking through binoculars again, Mike tapped the chart. "Here, Captain," he said.

Meissner nodded. "New heading, Mark. Steer fifty-five degrees."

"Fifty-five degrees, sir," repeated Mark, thinking those navy war films were coming in handy. More use than westerns. Then he felt that sadness but concentrated on turning the wheel, watching the rudder indicator and the compass until the compass indicated they were on the new heading. He thought about *The Battle of the River Plate* which he had enjoyed, the hunt for the German pocket battleship, *Graf Spee*. It suddenly occurred to Mark that the very boat he was now driving had once flown the swastika flag. That made Mark shudder. Was the captain a Nazi? Had he been a Nazi? All these thoughts wandered through his mind as he maintained his fifty-five degree heading.

The captain and Mike were concentrating on the chart. Occasionally Mark would be given a new heading until they were once more heading north. Before long Mark noticed land on both sides showing on the radar, although it was only visible to port.

The captain announced, "Cape Gazelle. New heading, Two eight five."

"Two eight five, sir," said Mark. He looked at the compass. Almost a ninety degree turn to port. He gently turned the wheel to bring the boat round to head more or less due west.

"He has nice touch, no?" It was Giorgio coming to the bridge. With four of them it was a bit cramped.

"You've done well, Mark," said the captain, "but time for Giorgio to take over to enter Rabaul."

281

"Captain, he is good. I stand here with him and teach him some more?"

Meissner thought for a brief moment. "Yes, he must learn, but under your orders, Giorgio."

Mark thought he saw Mike raise his eyebrows but nothing was said. Turning north again they entered a bay with land on either side.

"Ten knots," ordered the captain.

Mark panicked briefly wondering what to do, but Giorgio pulled the throttle back and Mark saw the rev dial of the active engine fall back and the boat slowed down. It made its way up the wide bay until Mark could see a town ahead.

"Is that Rabaul?" he asked. "That looks like a volcano," he joked, indicating a conical shaped mountain.

"It is, and he has a twin the other side," said Giorgio pointing in the other direction. "Thirty years ago they both go bang together and destroy much. Deep down they are linked."

Abashed, Mark said nothing. There were several ships moored in the bay, but none directly in his path. There was a big mountain behind the town which was along the side of the bay to their left.

For the first time, Mark saw the radio used. The captain though was speaking in a language Mark did not recognize. The call finished and the captain smiled.

"Start outer engines," he ordered. Giorgio pressed two buttons on the control panel. Mark heard the engines start up and immediately the boat felt more alive, like a big dog straining on its leash.

"Stop centre," ordered the captain again. Again Giorgio cut the centre engine.

"I take it now, Mark. You done very good," said Giorgio. And then to the captain, "OK if he stay and learn?" The captain just nodded. Mike left the bridge.

"Now we run slowly on outside engines. Makes the boat turn better," explained Giorgio to Mark, who was however, none the wiser. So he just watched.

282

"Dead slow," came the command. The throb of the two engines died down to an idle as the boat approached a jetty. Some men came out and waved, which the captain acknowledged. "Deploy fenders," he called. Pip and Jules took the stored fenders from the foredeck and put them over the starboard side of the boat, securing them to cleats.

"Giorgio, take us in," said the captain. Mark watched fascinated as Giorgio adjusted the steering, allowing the boat to slow. He used the throttles also, at one point putting the port screw in to reverse which made the boat turn sharply; even Mark could see that it was more than could be done by the wheel alone.

"One screw astern, the other ahead, make boat turn," said Giorgio by way of explanation. Barely moving, the boat came alongside the jetty to starboard, just touching some big rubber tyres hanging off the jetty. Giorgio briefly put both engines in reverse, or astern, and the boat stopped. Before it could start moving backward, he put them to neutral. Mark saw Pip, Jules and Mike on the starboard deck catching ropes thrown by the men on the dock and making the boat fast. Some others were wheeling a gangplank toward the boat. Once the boat was secure, the captain said, "Stop engines." The boat went eerily quiet. Then Mark heard the sound of the small generator starting up.

"Giorgio, that was really good," said Mark. "I'd never have thought about using the engines like that."

"He's the best," commented the captain as he left the bridge.

A truck came along the dockside and stopped near the boat.

"Come," said Giorgio. "We unload cargo."

Another battered truck came along with what seemed like a makeshift crane mounted on the flatbed. As Mark quickly discovered, it was indeed just that. Again with Giorgio and Mike, he was in the hold, helping to lash the crates to ropes from the truck crane. It was hot work and now they weren't at sea, the heat and humidity took their toll. Sweat was pouring off Mark but he worked hard and did

283

his best, if only to avert criticism from Mike. Mark only felt really secure on board with Pip and Giorgio.

It was now early afternoon and Mark remembered the letter and post office savings book. "Pip, can we get the letter sent to Marcel from here, please?"

"Yes, Mark. We are here overnight so I'll try to get us into the hotel."

Just then, Wilhelm interrupted them. "Philip, come please. Kiap here."

"I won't be long, Mark, I promise."

While Pip was gone, Mark made sure he had the letter and the post office savings book safe. He looked at the record of his deposits, a few withdrawals. They brought back memories. But he steeled himself and drew solace from the thought that if Mam got his money, to her it would be a fortune.

"Sorry, Mark, but that was important," said Pip on returning. "Put some overnight things in your bag. Hotel for us tonight."

"What's kiap?" asked Mark, as he put extra things into his bag.

"I'm not sure why the name is that. Maybe from the German Kapitän. The north of the island was once German territory, remember, under the Kaiser. Kiap is a sort of local admin officer from the Australian government. Willy knows him well so we smoothed the path for supplies and refuelling."

"Why Australia?" asked Mark, worried. "Won't they report us to the British police?"

"This is under Australian administration, but don't worry. We keep the local Kiap happy," said Pip, making a money gesture with his fingers.

As they went ashore, a small, rusty old tanker was driving on to the dock. "Our fuel," said Pip.

"I noticed the tanks were very low," said Mark.

"You don't miss much, do you, Mark Martin," smiled Pip.

284

"Don't say my name like that," said Mark. "I'm wanted."

"Of course you are, by me," replied Pip.

Although it was by now mid-afternoon, the post office was still open. They had to fill in a customs form, enclose the letter and the precious savings book, as well as a letter for Marcel explaining what to do and giving the Calvert House address. Once sealed, Mark briefly touched the envelope to his lips in a brief kiss before handing it over. Pip paid for the postage for air mail to France.

"When will that get there?" he asked.

"Probably next Monday, perhaps by Friday."

As they left, Mark felt a sense of relief that he had done his best. He imagined Mam opening the letter and reading it, happy to know he was safe and happy with the money.

"If Marcel posts it to Mam on Friday, she might get it next Monday."

"Ever the optimist," said Pip,

They took a taxi to the hotel. It turned out that Pip had already arranged this from Port Moresby but hadn't told Mark in case they were delayed.

It seemed quite luxurious and their room was air conditioned! Bliss! In the room, they showered and lay naked on the bed. Their love making was slow and gentle and afterwards, Mark fell asleep in Pip's arms.

They woke to find it was dark. Early evening.

"I'm hungry, nothing since breakfast," said Pip. "I bet you are, too."

"Starving," announced Mark.

They dressed and went to the restaurant. They ate well, and drank a bottle of wine between them.

Then back to bed and a deep sleep, with an alarm call booked for seven.

# Chapter 46 Spring

Mark woke before the alarm call. Tuesday morning, but still Monday evening back home. He thought about Mam, he thought about school. He tried to visualize how Monday had gone. Ethan kept coming in to his mind. What did they think of their Head Prefect now? 'Probably ex-Head Prefect' he thought. He turned and looked at the sleeping Pip next to him. 'Where would I be now without you? Probably caught and locked up, awaiting trial for murder.' Mark leaned over and kissed Pip on the cheek, which woke him up.

"Are you all right, Mark," he said sleepily. "What time is it?"

"Just after half six," said Mark, standing up and walking to the window, It was light outside now. Pip watched Mark, admiring the teenager's naked body, taking in the fair skin, tall, slim body, nice arse and ample cock. Pip thought to himself that he didn't deserve such beauty as this. But all he said was, "Time for a cuddle then before we have to start the day." In the cool comfort of the big bed the cuddle developed into more. Mark felt Pip inside bringing him closer to an uncontrolled and fiery climax, as they came together.

"I've messed the sheet," said Mark.

"I'll leave an extra tip, don't worry," Pip assured him. "Shower and food. Nothing against Jules's porridge but we'll have a good breakfast."

At breakfast in the hotel restaurant Mark was surprised to see Wilhelm and Jules. Pip was less surprised. "I half thought they might," he said to Mark. So they joined them at their table.

"Who's left on the boat?" asked Mark.

"Only Giorgio. Lothar and Mike are in town somewhere, probably found ladies for the night, How is it you say? Sowing oats?" said Wilhelm. " We must go back by ten o'clock. The boat is fully fuelled and stocked and we have the pick up to do."

"Are we not getting cargo here?" asked Mark.

286

Wilhelm and Pip exchanged glances. "Full of questions, this boy," said Wilhelm.

"It's one of our special jobs," said Pip. "I told you about them once."

Mark understood the reference to carrying weapons so just nodded.

"We used too much fuel coming here," said Wilhelm. "There is too much drag. Lothar went into the water yesterday evening and there is too much growth on the hull. So soon we must get the boat cleaned."

"Bali?" queried Pip.

"Is the best place. And good for a break as well."

Mark had heard of Bali as a beautiful place so was now looking forward to seeing it.

By ten o'clock, they were all on board and ready to cast off. Mark was on deck with Pip and Jules. It was cloudy and already very humid. The captain, Giorgio and Mike were on the bridge. Steiger was below with his beloved diesels.

"Mark, come," called the captain.

Pip gave Mark a nudge to obey but Mark needed no reminder. "Yes, sir?"

"Mark, this you must learn. You are on the helm for rest of the forenoon watch."

Pip and Jules went forward and lifted the fenders over the bow against the pier.

Mark felt a moment of panic because the boat was still alongside the jetty, but Giorgio patted his shoulder. "Is good, Mark. I show you spring line."

"Ready, helm?" demanded the captain.

""He ready with me, captain," replied Giorgio.

"Start all engines," ordered the captain.

Under Giorgio's guidance, Mark pressed the buttons to start all three engines. He heard them splutter into life.

"We have spring line from midships bollard to dock at stern," said Giorgio. Mark realized that the Spring line was a rope from the middle of the boat to a bollard on the dock near the stern of the boat. "Now you see how this work."

The captain looked impatient but simply said, "Dead slow ahead centre only. Slight starboard rudder."

Mark gently pushed the throttle for the centre engine and turned the wheel. As the boat edged forward he could see how this worked. Held by the spring line which became very taut, the forward motion was transferred into sideways motion as the stern swung away from the dock, the bow up against the fenders against the dock.

"Wow," said Mark. "That's magic." The stern of the boat was now pointing out into the harbour.

"Rudder amidships. Slow astern centre engine," commanded the captain, peering out at the dock. As the boat moved slowly backwards, the spring line slackened which was then lifted off the midships bollard by Jules and dropped over the side from where it was hauled by men on the dock. The fenders were hauled inboard and stowed. Mark checked the rudder indicator to make sure all were lined up centrally. The boat was moving backwards slowly out into the harbour, the captain looking astern from the side of the bridge. Mike was watching Mark closely and occasionally nodding approvingly. Mark could see they were now some way from the dock.

"Centre neutral, port half astern, starboard half ahead," Meissner's order. Giorgio nodded at Mark who made the changes. Instantly the boat started to swing round to port, almost 'on the spot'. Soon it was facing in the opposite direction, south down the large harbour of Rabaul toward the twin volcanoes.

"Stop outer engines, make for fifteen knots on centre engine." Mark did what was ordered.

"Heading one seven aero," came the order. As the boat increased speed to fifteen knots Mark adjusted the course to almost due south.

"Spring is good, eh, Mark?" said Giorgio. "Captain, OK if I leave Mark here now?"

Meissner nodded. Then he said, "Well done, Mark." So then Mark piloted the boat out of the vast harbour, passing close to the eastern volcano called Tavurvur and then east and finally north again on a heading of three four zero or twenty degrees west.

The captain left the bridge, saying to Mike, "You have the boat."

"I have the boat," said Mike without looking up from his chart. Mark assumed he was staying on the helm. Then Mike turned to Mark. "You have the boat. If I'm not back call me or the captain in one hour, or if you are unsure of anything."

"Yes, sir," answered Mark. "I have the boat." Once more Mark was alone on the bridge, moving three knots more slowly than before, wondering where they were going. He hadn't liked to ask. But he felt he was becoming a real seaman.

A few minutes later he heard Pip from the short companionway to the bridge. "Permission to come to the bridge?"

Mark laughed. "Permission granted!"

"How's it going?" Pip asked as he stood beside Mark. "This is something I've never done. I know Wilhelm is impressed with how quickly you've got the hang of this. Giorgio says you're a natural seaman, with a good feel for the boat."

"Really?" said Mark. "I liked the way they used the spring line to get off the jetty, and especially how using the screws in opposite directions made the boat spin round."

Pip watched Mark at work, admiring his young protégé and lover. "You were a natural driver so I'm not surprised."

"Where are we going?" asked Mark.

"To a small inlet on the north coast of New Guinea to pick up the consignment and from there to the drop off in West Irian, which is part of Indonesia."

"How far is it?"

"About eight hundred kilometres so about five hundred miles for the first part. We are due there tomorrow evening."

"Why fifteen knots this time?"

289

"I suppose Mike has calculated that speed will save fuel and get us there on time."

Mark absorbed this information as he piloted the boat steadily northwards. Pip patted Mark's shoulder and left. Just as Mark was thinking the hour was up, Mike reappeared on the bridge. "I have the boat. Stay on the helm."

"You have the boat."

Under Mike's navigation, Mark steered the boat past Kumlakor and then turned west to pass north of Watom Island. Giorgio came to relieve Mark who went below and went straight to the head.

. . .

After a couple more watches at the helm for Mark, the following evening, they were nearing their destination. During his last watch, the captain came on to the bridge.

"I have the boat," said the captain.

"You have the boat, sir," said Mark, wondering why the captain had come up.

For some time the captain said nothing but just watched Mark, making him feel a bit uneasy. Eventually he asked Mark, "You know which sea this is?"

"Part of the Pacific Ocean?" he ventured.

"This is Bismarck Sea," answered the captain. "You know about Bismarck?"

Mark smiled to himself. "Yes, sir. The Iron Chancellor. German chancellor under three Kaisers, sacked by Wilhelm the second in 1890."

Meissner smiled. "Yes indeed. You are well-informed, Mark. Most English people just think of the great battleship but it was named after the man. Also most people forget Kaiser Friedrich. He died too soon. How different Germany's history might have been," he said, wistfully, Mark thought.

"Gut," said the captain. "You have the boat," he said as he left the bridge.

"Ich habe das Boot," said Mark trying to please the captain but he was speaking to an empty bridge.

# Chapter 47 Nacht und Nebel

Later in the cabin, Pip said to Mark, "Wilhelm is pleased with you, Mark. Having an extra helmsman has made a big difference, especially to him, Mike and Giorgio. It eases the burden."

Mark smiled, but then said, "He tells you that, but why doesn't he say it to me?"

"It's not his way, Mark."

"He was captain of one of these in the war, is that right? Fighting for Hitler against us?"

"Yes, and he was very successful by all accounts. He has the Iron Cross. But I think he would see it as fighting for his country rather than for Hitler."

"So is he a Nazi?" asked Mark, in a hushed tone.

"No, Mark. He thought they were barbarians from the gutters of Germany. I think Lothar used to be more inclined to admire Hitler, but not since they were exposed as so evil. But the bond between Wilhelm and Lothar is very strong."

"Because of when their boat was sunk?"

"Yes. Willy fought for days to keep Lothar alive in the life raft. Luckily they were rescued in time. So he is devoted to the captain," said Pip. "He even forgives him for being queer," he added, smiling.

"Doesn't he like queer people? A bit hard on this boat, I'd say."

"Maybe at one time, believing the stereotypes. But he accepts it now as part of human nature."

"He's not very nice to me sometimes."

"Again, Mark, just his way. Don't worry about it."

At that moment there was a call. "Mark to the bridge!"

Mark went to the bridge. It was the brief tropical dusk. They were close to the coast on their port side, which the captain and Mike were studying through binoculars, Mike occasionally seemingly checking against a chart. They were creeping along at about five knots. Mark squeezed in next to Giorgio.

"Watch and learn," said the captain.

"Why are we doing this in the dark?" asked Mark. "Doesn't it make it more difficult?"

"Nacht und Nebel, Mark," said the captain.

"Darkness and Fog," said Mark quietly, remembering his European history and how bad, secret things had happened at night in Nazi Germany. Mark looked at the radar screen to see the coastline and was surprised to see a blank screen.

"Why is the radar off?" asked Mark.

"Radar sends out signal so now we quiet," said Giorgio. "Nobody know we here."

Mark guessed this was because the illegal pick up had to be secret. He also noticed that the normal navigation lights, white on the mast and on the stern, red on the port side and green on the starboard side, were off. As darkness overtook them, a red light was switched on in the bridge. It reminded Mark of the dark room at school. Another pang of loss. But then he saw the depth sounder was on. To him the paper roll was a puzzling squiggle of lines until Giorgio explained it.

"The water now about ten metres deep," said Giorgio, "but soon much less. You will learn also to listen to the noise. How quick it bounce back tells you the depth. That saves the paper."

"How much water does the boat need?"

"Two metres to be safe. But then we have just perhaps as small as ten centimetres left underneath."

Mark frowned. There didn't seem much margin for error.

The captain and Mike seemed satisfied and gave helm directions. As the boat turned to port Mark saw they were entering a river. Mark could see that the water was getting shallower. They moved slowly upstream. Pip, with Steiger and Jules, was at the bow of the boat.

"Three metres," announced Giorgio. Then, "Two point five metres."

292

There was a flash of light from under the trees that lined each river bank.

"Engine to neutral, drop anchor," commanded Meissner.

The three at the front heaved the anchor over the side and secured the cable. The boat was still as the anchor took hold. Steiger went below and the generator started up as the centre engine stopped.

"Was interesting, no?" said Giorgio.

"Yes," answered Mark, wondering what would happen next. In the darkness, and now the rain, he saw two boats coming towards DFH.

"Come with," ordered the captain to Mark. They left the bridge along with Mike and made their way aft. The hold hatch was opened to reveal Jules, Steiger and Pip in the hold. Slowly wooden boxes were lifted from the boats, now alongside DFH, onto the deck and then lowered into the hold. The only light came from the hold. Each box was heavy but manageable by two people. Mark noticed stencilled lettering on the boxes, some in what looked to him like Russian, others looking Chinese. They were obviously guns and ammunition. It was hard work and Mark was sweating and aching by the time all the boxes were loaded and the hatch secured.

A man from one of the boats boarded DFH and was greeted by the captain. Together they went to the hold that was now packed with the boxes. Mark followed out of curiosity. 'Lucky we don't have to go through the hold to get to the stern head' thought Mark.

Seeing Mark there, the captain handed him a crowbar. "Choose a box and open it," ordered Meissner. To his companion, he added, "If the boy opens a box he chooses, it is really random."

Mark gathered this was to check that the cargo was what it was meant to be so he picked a large box and set about prising it open. Inside was a rack with six guns secured in slots in the wood. Meissner lifted one out and inspected it

"Alles in Ordnung," he said. "Yes, all good, all in order."

They moved forward and the captain and his guest went into his cabin with Pip.

"Money talk, Mark," Pip explained as the door was shut.

"Coffee in cabin," said Jules, and taking three mugs into the captain's cabin. Mark went to the crew cabin where everybody else except Giorgio was starting the coffee with bread rolls.

"I take Giorgio coffee," said Jules.

Mark could see that he would then be in the cabin with Mike and Lothar Steiger. "It's OK, Jules," he said quickly. "I'll take it up." He picked up his own and Giorgio's and carefully went up to the bridge.

"Coffee and bread roll," said Mark.

Giorgio was leaning against the binnacle with large binoculars round his neck. "Thank you, Mark."

"Are you on lookout duty?" asked Mark, unwilling to return to the crew cabin.

"Yes, now we have this cargo we must be very careful. Sometimes navy ship see us and come on board for inspection so we must not be seen." He put the binoculars to his eyes and looked out over the stern towards the sea. "No ship there now," he said.

Mark turned to look in that direction. "There's a light, very faint."

Frowning, Giorgio lifted the binoculars again. "Where? Are you certain about light?"

Mark nodded and pointed to where he thought he could see a light out at sea. Giorgio looked as well. "Maybe," he said. "Very faint like you say. You look through binoculars."

Mark took the binoculars and looked. "These are good," he said. He could see the light now, moving slowly to their right. "There's another light below it, green," he said. "It's some way out at sea though and moving that way," he explained pointing.

"Moving east," said Giorgio. "You watch ship while I see captain. If he turns , you shout. You have good eyes."

Giorgio went below and Mark heard him knocking on the captain's door. Mark watched the distant ship and it moved further east. It didn't turn and was lost from view behind the headland at the mouth of the river.

Meissner appeared on the bridge followed by Giorgio. Pip and the guest were just outside.

"Give it to me," Meissner ordered Mark, who handed over the binoculars. He scanned the view seawards. "There is no ship," he snapped. "You must not imagine things, it is too important," he said to Mark.

"I'm sorry, sir," said Mark. "but there was a light with a green light lower down, moving east. It's gone now."

"Is true, Captain," said Giorgio. "I see light as well but not as good as Mark."

"Very well," said the Captain. "Maybe you are right and I am wrong. Is good to keep on lookout. You stay here and use your good eyes."

"Yes, sir," said Mark, wondering if he should say "Aye, aye, sir". He thought better of it.

Mark was left on the bridge with the powerful binoculars. The rain had now stopped so he stepped outside for a better view seawards. He looked at the lattice mast with the radar scanner on top and considered climbing up to be able to see further. He decided against because it was wet and he might slip in the darkness.

There was a burst of activity. The captain, his guest and Pip appeared. There was handshaking and the guest climbed down into his boat and rowed toward the shore.

The captain and Giorgio came onto the bridge.

"I have the boat, Mark," said the captain.

"You have the boat, sir," said Mark, thinking not for the first time, that a ship would have to be big to carry this boat.

"I think Lothar is ready," said the captain. "Start all three engines into neutral."

Mark looked at Giorgio now standing beside him, who with a gesture indicated that Mark do it. He was glad that the waiting was over and was looking forward to the excitement of this clandestine mission. At his touch the engines throbbed into life.

"Up anchor and secure," called Meissner to the foredeck party. "Turn us round, helm," was the next order.

Again Giorgio gestured to Mark. "Like in the harbour, use screws to turn boat," he said quietly.

Mark, watched carefully by Giorgio, put the port engine to half astern, the starboard engine half ahead. The boat was already drifting with the river current and somehow Mark knew the boat needed steerage way. The boat swung round under the influence of the opposing propellers. Mark saw that Giorgio was listening to the depth sounder closely. "Is OK," he reassured Mark. The captain was looking seaward through binoculars. As the bow came round towards the open sea, Mark got the order, "All engines, five knots." Mark adjusted all three throttle controls to suit and DFH crept slowly out of the river mouth into the open sea. The captain carefully scanned the horizon for ships. Mark looked round but could see nothing. The ship he had seen earlier was now over the eastern horizon, or at least where he thought the horizon would be. It was so dark and the cloud cover kept out any starlight and even moonlight. Mike came to the bridge and looked over his charts in the dim red glow of the bridge lighting.

"Course three-two-five, helm." Mike said.

Mark turned the wheel to port until the heading was as ordered.

"Ready captain," said Mike.

Meissner smiled. "Mark, now you may see what my boat can do. All three engines, full power."

# Chapter 48 Interception

Mark pushed the throttles fully forward. "Wow!" he said as he felt the boat spring forward, the engine noise rising to a full throated roar, the bow lifting out of the water as the boat gathered speed. 'This is like a speedboat!' thought Mark as he kept the heading on three-two-five.

After a few minutes, the captain ordered, "Port thirty-five. Heading two-nine-zero."

Without reducing speed, Mark swung the wheel to port on to its new heading. The boat banked against its own wash as it turned at speed. It was exhilarating, the boat hammering through waves in the darkness. The speed of the boat differed on the two dials, one read about thirty-eight knots, the other forty knots. Mark shrugged and carried on. It was interesting but at the same time, monotonous. There was nothing to see which was unnerving, just speeding through total darkness. 'What if we hit something?' he thought. 'But there's nothing to hit' he comforted himself.

Occasionally Mike came to the bridge, looked at the instruments and left. On one occasion he got out a chart and studied it.

"How do you know where we are?" asked Mark. "The radar isn't on to see the coastline."

"Speed and time, kid. It's called dead reckoning. But you have to remember tide and currents as well. We need to be well past Jayapura. It's a busy port."

"How do you know about currents and that?"

"Been here a long time. Trust me, kid, I know these waters." With that he left the bridge.

It must have been about two hours later that the captain and Mike returned to the bridge. Meissner pulled a face when he saw the speed dials.

"Much drag," he muttered. Then, to Mark, "I have the boat, helm," he said.

"You have the boat, sir," answered Mark, but there was no move to take the wheel from him so he stayed put.

Then Meissner and Mike studied the charts.

297

"Slow ahead all engines, make for five knots," the captain ordered.

"New heading, helm," said Mike. "Steer two-four-zero." He was looking closely at a chart and then peering over the port bow towards where Mark knew there was the coast.

"We should be coming to Yangap soon, captain," said Mike, after looking again at his chart in the dim red lighting, and then looking landward.

Mark could see ahead an extra darkness. Land. But nobody said anything. 'Should I shout Land ahoy!?' he wondered. Instead, "Captain, there is land ahead of us. I can just make out something."

"Point," ordered the captain. Which Mark did, pointing just over the port bow. The captain looked through the binoculars. "Yes, Mark. Well done."

"The kid's got young eyes," said Mike.

"Call Giorgio," said the captain. Which Mike did. The captain continued. "You are learning fast, Mark but this is total darkness and Giorgio knows this place."

"Yes, sir," said Mark. "But can I stay and learn more?"

"I expect you to," replied Meissner, as Giorgio arrived and took the helm. He turned on the depth sounder.

The boat crept closer to the coast. The dark shape of the hills of the north coast of Indonesian West Irian loomed closer. Mike was comparing what he could see with the chart. "Depth, please," said Mike.

Giorgio turned on the depth sounder paper output. Thinking about how radar would give them away, Mark asked, "Won't that reveal that we're here?"

Mike laughed. "To the fish, maybe." Mark shut up. The boat moved closer to the shore, now clearly visible. The white of breaking waves could be seen.

"Five metres," said Giorgio.

The boat now moved carefully along the darkened coastline. "Why are we so close, isn't it dangerous?" asked Mark.

"No kid, I know where we are and the land helps mask us against any radar from out at sea."

In the darkness DFH crept along. Mike constantly checking the chart against the land mass and calling for depth readings. They entered a small bay and headed for a light to starboard. As the depth sounder reported three metres, they came alongside a small wooden jetty. In the gloom Mark could see a number of men waiting. The boat was secured and one came on board, greeting Meissner warmly.

"Good to see you again, Captain. Welcome to Yangap," this person said.

"We talk in my cabin while the crates are unloaded." They went below. Mark was about to go to the hold to help when he was told to remain on the bridge.

"You seem to have the best eyes on the boat, kid," said Mike. "Stay here and keep watch, especially out to sea. Any sightings, raise the alarm."

Mark was rather pleased not to be heaving the heavy crates about so remained on the bridge, periodically scanning around the bay and seaward with the binoculars.

The captain and the other man emerged from the cabin; they seemed happy, Mark thought. The captain looked at the bridge, saw Mark with the binoculars and gave an approving nod. They went aft to where the final boxes were being stacked on the jetty. Mark wondered if the rickety structure would take the weight.

At last the job was done, they cast off and with Giorgio at the helm, as dawn broke they headed out to sea. There was an atmosphere of elation, and Mark realized there had been a tension while they were carrying the weapons.

"Now we are heading for Jayapura to seek fuel and a cargo," announced Meissner. Once out at sea navigation lights were turned on and the radar was operating. Mark was left at the helm. "Steer one-zero-five," was the order.

Mark was alone on the bridge when the radar pinged. He saw the echo clearly. Compared to the freighter he had watched before this seemed different. It was faster and coming towards him. He looked to port and thought he could see a ship. He reached for the binoculars and found the vessel. He could tell straight away it was a warship. Time to call the captain.

"Captain to the bridge please!" he shouted. "Approaching warship!"

A clatter of feet led to Meissner and Mike appearing very rapidly.

"Where?" demanded the captain.

"There's a radar echo and I can see it clearly through the binoculars." Mark felt anxious, fear even. Why would some warship be heading for them? Even Mark could see it was adjusting its course to intercept them. "Shall I start the outer engines? Can we outrun it?" he asked.

"No need this time," said the captain. "We are empty, looking for fuel and a cargo."

"Who are they?" asked a still nervous Mark, as he held his course.

"From Sarong. ALRI. Indonesian navy to you.," replied Mike.

## A Riga class frigate

"We know this ship," said the captain. "A frigate given by the Soviet Union, Riga class. They will inspect us. Meantime stay on current heading, stay at eighteen knots. Yes Mark, we could outrun him, but not the hundred millimetre shells he might fire at us."

That did little to calm Mark's anxiety. Word got round the rest of the crew who came out on deck as the frigate drew closer. Now binoculars weren't needed to see the two gun turrets forward of the bridge and the large

300

radar dish. The radio suddenly spoke, making Mark jump. The signal was strong, more than enough to break the squelch setting.

"This is Republic of Indonesia Navy. Flying Dutchman, you are ordered to heave to for inspection."

Meissner told Mark to put the engine to neutral. He then picked up the microphone. "Indonesian Navy vessel, we are in international waters but in a spirit of friendly cooperation, will heave to as requested," replied the captain, grinning.

A different voice answered. "Captain Meissner, you disappoint me. I was looking forward to the chase."

The captain smiled. "Good day, Captain Sutrisno. A pleasure to meet you again. A chase? You know I could outrun you."

"But you know I could outgun you. I think from your willingness you have already delivered your cargo."

"I am heading for Jayapura to find a cargo and to buy fuel. We have no cargo. Business is not good."

"My deepest sympathy," came the sarcastic reply.

By this time the frigate was close and in dawn's early light Mark could see a boat being lowered with four men on board. To Mark's eyes the warship looked huge but he was told a frigate is a small, general purpose warship, the workhorse of most navies.

The boat came alongside, three of the Indonesian sailors climbed aboard using a rope ladder that had been lowered for them amidships.

"Stay here, Mark," said Mike as he and the captain left the bridge to meet the boarding party. Mark could only watch as the captain and Mike, and now Pip spoke to the boarding party. One was an officer, a lieutenant, Mark thought. They walked aft to the hold hatch and went down the companionway. Mark looked across at the frigate. He noticed that B gun turret was pointing at them. Some crew members had lined the rail and were looking at DFH. The funnel, large and backward leaning, had some smoke trailing

301

from it. He was joined unexpectedly on the bridge by one of the Indonesian sailors, followed by Pip.

"Are you all right, Mark?" asked Pip, concerned.

Mark nodded while watching the sailor. A man of perhaps forty or so. Mark found it hard to judge. This man looked at Mark and raised his eyebrows slightly but said nothing. He looked in the lockers and inspected the charts. Mark was aware that the captain and the officer were talking in the captain's cabin. Everybody seemed tense. Mark was also concerned because the frigate now seemed noticeably closer. The man left the bridge without a word followed by Pip and Mark saw all three, Pip and the captain, along with Mike, by the rope ladder. Then the boarding party climbed down into their boat and sped back to the frigate.

Meissner and Mike came to the bridge. "What did the man do here?" asked Meissner.

"Not much," said Mark. "He looked at the charts for a time."

"Yes, trying to see from marks where we have been. But Mike is careful that way." Mike nodded.

"The warship is much closer to us now," said Mark.

"All masses attract each other," said the captain. "This is normal. Start all three engines."

Mark did so, wondering what manoeuvre the captain was considering. He watched the frigate take the boat back on board.

The radio spoke. "Thank you for your co-operation, Captain Meissner. Have a safe journey to Jayapura. I will tell them you are coming."

"He wants to make sure I was saying the truth about Jayapura," smiled the captain. Then into the radio, "Thank you, Captain Sutrisno. Very kind of you." Turning to Mark he said, "Continue one-zero-five, centre engine only to ten knots, Outer engines in neutral.

The frigate was now under way but remained close on a parallel course. It was putting on speed, pulling ahead and creating a wash that made DFH rock.

Meissner smiled. "I thought he would. Same course, full ahead on all engines."

Mark did so and as before the boat leapt forward. Soon they were doing twenty knots but the frigate kept pace. Twenty-five knots and the wake from the frigate made it harder for Mark to steer.

The captain looked through binoculars at the frigate and laughed. "He is watching you, Mark. Maybe he thinks you are too young." But now DFH was pulling ahead of the frigate as the speed crept up past thirty knots towards forty knots, DFH pulled clear of the frigate.

"He thinks he is Fangio," said the captain. "But I am Fangio. Good work, Mark."

Mark smiled. Soon the frigate was well behind and it turned away. After a while, the captain reduced speed to eighteen knots and stopped the outer engines.

# Chapter 49 Night Talk

Halfway through the afternoon watch, Mark was relieved at the wheel by Giorgio. Only then did tiredness hit Mark. He had been at the helm almost continuously since leaving Yangap twelve hours earlier, with quick breaks for the heads and eating sandwiches at the wheel. Plus the stress of the boarding party.

"You young, you have good stamina," said Giorgio.

Pip was in the crew room. He and Jules were playing cards. "Mark, well done," said Pip.

"I need sleep," said Mark. "And the heads." He went aft to the stern head for a little more privacy. Steiger was in the engine room with the centre engine with a cloth and oil can. Mark thought he looked as though he were actually stroking it. Steiger let Mark past but said nothing. Passing the galley Jules was at work, cleaning the cooking range.

"You like boiled potatoes tonight?" he asked Mark as he passed.

"Lovely," said Mark without stopping and going into the stern head opposite the galley. Sitting for some time, Mark found time to ponder the changes in his life. Two weeks ago he could have never imagined where he would be. It hit him that it was Thursday. New Year's Eve had been Thursday. "Fuck you, Peter!" he shouted.

There was a tap on the door. "Mark, are you ill?" Jules asking, concern evident.

"I'm fine, Jules," he said. He finished off and washed his hands. "Sorry, Jules," he said as he emerged. "Just thinking about something."

"Someone called Peter," said Jules.

"Yes," said Mark but then walked forward past Steiger again.

"I hear you did well today," Steiger said, looking at Mark with - what? A sort of respect? But Mark just said "Thanks" and moved on.

In the cabin, Pip was waiting. "Problem, Mark? You've been a long time."

"I'm just tired," replied Mark, undressing ready for a sleep.

"Lie with me for a while," offered Pip.

Mark was so tired that this was as good as climbing the ladder to his bunk. So he and Pip cuddled in the lower bunk. Mark felt Pip's arms round him.

"You can always talk to me," said Pip. Mark didn't reply, Pip looked and saw he was already asleep. So he just lay and held the boy tight, feeling his love for Mark. Was it really just two weeks ago that Mark had come to him, pleading for help? So he held his love while he slept.

. . .

"I was at school," said Mark sleepily.

"Have you had a good sleep?" asked Pip.

"I was at school," repeated Mark. "I thought all this was the dream. I was telling Ethan and the lads about this crazy dream I'd had. It's the other way round, isn't it?" Tears welled up in Mark's eyes. "What time is it?"

"Just gone seven, Food in an hour at the end of the dog watches," said Pip, encouragingly.

Mark was unmoved. "So just gone nine in the morning at home. Registration. Oh fuck, Pip? What am I going to do? I had a future."

"My dear Mark, we'll make a future together. We can make this business work, expand it. You're a good seaman and in time we can get another boat which you will command. I will always love you and look after you."

Mark smiled. "Captain Martin. Sounds good." He snuggled up close to Pip. "Come into me, now."

"Are you sure?"

"Yes. I feel good and safe when you're fucking me."

Pip obliged and he made sure his entry was slow and careful. He loved the way Mark responded and it made him so aroused too.

It was only after that when Mark said, "We're not moving."

"No, Mark. We're moored in the Jayapura roads."

"Moored in a road?"

"Roads are a term for an area of a port where vessels can anchor or tie to a buoy."

"Like you? Tied to a boy?" Mark chuckled.

Pip smiled lovingly. "Where I want to be moored for the rest of my life."

"Aren't we next to a quay?"

"No, we're out in the bay. Willy went ashore earlier to sort business."

"How? Did he swim?"

"They have what I suppose are water taxis, but we are all sleeping on board tonight. This is not such friendly territory as before."

There was a tap on the door and Meissner entered. 'Does he always like catching us in bed' thought Mark.

"Come soon. You eat first because I want you on first and middle watch. Both of you please, Philip."

"Yes of course," answered Pip.

The captain left and they got dressed. They ate their meal of beef stew, including boiled potatoes and carrots.

"I cook this because we stop before I thought we would, " explained Jules.

On the bridge they could see the lights of Jayapura on three sides. Other vessels of various sizes were moored in the large bay.

"Remember this is Indonesia," said the captain, briefing them. "If they come trying to sell stuff, send them away. Do not allow anybody on board. Call me if there gives a problem."

So they settled down for the double watch which would take them to four in the morning. Jules came up with coffee and bread at times. They spent the night keeping each other awake and watching the activity round the harbour. It seemed busy until the small hours. They talked, Pip interested in the details of Mark's life. Mark talked about his earlier life before the split, about the pain caused by the family break up and how his sister, perhaps because she was older, never fully reconciled herself to it or forgave her mother.

Pip described his childhood and how after his birth his mother had never been able to conceive again. His father's early death from cancer and him taking over the small garage. Then his mother's suicide with an overdose of her anti-depressants, so he had thrown himself into the business, expanding it and obtaining the Ford Main Agent status. This was helped by Wilhelm making contact suggesting an investment in his boat. Everybody had advised against it but he had not mentioned the most profitable aspect of course so he had gone ahead and it had paid off handsomely, which he used to expand the premises by buying property around and investing in the latest electronic testing equipment. Also he had been able to buy the house at West Farm Estate and his Austen Healey, all for cash.

Mark had never heard in detail before about Pip's earlier life. "Did your parents know you're queer?"

"I think my mother suspected but she never said anything. Like your Tony, I had a friend as a teenager who I experimented with but never as much as you did with Tony. I found him very attractive but it just sort of faded off. We lost touch after school."

"So am I the first one since him?"

"To be as close to, yes, Mark. I didn't love him. In fact I feel closer to you than I have anybody. But I did have sex before I met you, of course."

"At The Vault?"

"Yes, Mark. Gordy is what they call a paralegal and I met him when buying land to expand the garage. He did some of the legal stuff. One reason why I thought of a telegram to him but your idea was better. Anyway, he introduced me to The Vault group, but we didn't have sex much after that. There was Peter of course. Then you came along and I fell in love with you."

Mark pondered the random chain of events in his life and in Pip's that had led to him being here. If just one thing had been different, everybody's life would now be different too.

Mike came up for the morning watch at four in the morning so Mark and Pip went gratefully to their cabin and to bed. Maybe it was the long and intimate chats through the night but it was Mark who asked for the physical intimacy. So they made love in Pip's bunk before Mark climbed the ladder and fell into a deep sleep.

They were woken by a tap on the door at nine o'clock and the entry of the captain. 'At least we weren't in the same bed this time' thought Mark.

"Good morning," said Meissner. "Philip, I need you to come ashore with me. We have a cargo and mail for Port Moresby. We have a berth at one o'clock so everything needs to be ready for then. Mark, you can sleep more but you may be needed when we berth."

The captain left, and Pip got out of bed and pulled on some shorts. "Going to the head," he said. "Won't be long."

Mark then felt the same need and seeing that Pip had gone forward, decided to go to the stern head, even if Steiger was by the engines. He too pulled some shorts on and also trainers because he would have to go through the engine rooms. As he came out of the head, Jules saw him, eyeing Mark's body.

"Mister Mark, you have no breakfast. Was an hour ago, but I can make more porridge for you."

"Thank you, Jules," said Mark. "For Philip too, I think."

"I bring along soon."

He was as good as his word and Pip, fully dressed, and Mark still in just shorts, ate their porridge at the crew table and drank coffee.

"I have to go with the captain," said Pip. "But I'll see you later."

"I think I'll go back to bed until afternoon watch," said Mark.

Pip smiled. "You're learning the lingo and turning into a real sailor."

308

In his bunk, Mark slipped off his shorts and started to wank, thinking not of Pip but of Tommy. Then those thoughts made him stop and feeling sad, he fell asleep.

Mark was at the helm under Giorgio's guidance as DFH was docked alongside a quay. The town looked large and busy, surrounded by forest clad hills and mountains. Then it was hard work packing the hold with various crates, some mostly commercial, some personal goods being moved. There was also mail, not letters which went by air, but heavier and bulky stuff as before that wasn't so urgent.

# Chapter 50 Confidence

As the final cargo was loaded, Mike came to find Mark. "The captain says I gotta show you how to plot a course. Come with me."

Mark went with Mike to the bridge where he was shown the chart locker and how the charts were stowed in order for easy and quick access. For the next half hour Mark watched as Mike plotted their course from Jayapura to Port Moresby. He asked questions which Mike didn't seem to think were daft ones as he explained how to work out the distance and then calculate the speeds required for different arrival times.

"It is now Friday afternoon, we need to be in Port Moresby on Monday morning. What's the distance?" Mike questioned Mark.

Mark looked at the charts, their course following the north coast of West Irian and then the rest of New Guinea as far as Madang before passing between New Britain Island and Umboi Island before heading south to round the eastern tip of New Guinea to head west and then north to Port Moresby. "One thousand, three hundred and twenty miles?" he suggested.

"Not quite," said Mike. "Nautical miles. Not miles. That's important for the speed calculation, kid. Knots means nautical miles an hour."

"Yes," said Mark, wondering why Mike was taking time to teach him in such detail. But he thought about Pip's idea for the future and being captain of his own boat so he would need this knowledge.

"So how many hours from now, say four p.m. to Monday say ten a.m?"

Mark thought. "Sixty-six?"

"So what speed do we need to average, kid?"

"I'm not much good at long division," said Mark.

"Then get good, kid, and damn quick"

Mark scribbled on some paper. "Twenty knots. But eighteen might do it. Why not get there on Sunday evening?" he asked, thinking of a night in that nice hotel with Pip.

"Uses more fuel and an extra day port fees. Wanna pay the extra yourself, kid?"

"I hadn't thought about those things," admitted Mark.

"You'll learn, kid. You're bright," said Mike. "One more thing though, there's an easterly wind at the moment, so we'll make twenty-five knots to compensate."

Mark nodded. Each time he thought he had mastered something, there was another factor to consider.

It was at about four o'clock that they cast off. Mark was at the helm, Giorgio standing by. Mark panicked because another boat had moored behind them. He noticed the mail flag was flying again.

"So we use spring line again, Mark," said Giorgio. The captain nodded and ordered the spring line fitted.

"Very well Mark, let's see how you do," said Meissner.

Mark gulped and felt nervous but he started all three engines into neutral and then the centre engine dead slow ahead. Jules and Pip were at the bow with the fenders and as before the spring line went taut and the stern swung out away from the boat behind. Once at about thirty degrees from the quay, Mark put the centre engine to slow astern and the line slackened. But nobody did anything. The captain looked at Mark questioningly. 'He's leaving it to me!'

"Cast off the spring line," he called. The line was dropped from the quay and Jules and Pip hauled the line in. "Fenders inboard," he called again. Again Jules and Pip complied, Pip with a big grin on his face.

They were now in clear space away from the quay, so Mark turned the boat using the two outer engines as before. He looked at the captain.

"You know where the ocean is," said Meissner.

So Mark put the centre engine ahead for 5 knots while they were in the harbour area. Once clear of the harbour Mark increased speed and once clear of Tanjung

Suaja headed east-south-east and increased speed to twenty-five knots using all three engines. He was elated that he had done this and furthermore had been trusted to do it on his own imitative. He felt supremely confident now.

Steiger came on the bridge and looked around. "Very fuel efficient exit, Giorgio," he said. "You like my engines."

"Lothar, was Mark all the time, not me," said Giorgio.

"All I said to him was let's see what you can do," added the captain.

Steiger looked at Mark, still at the helm, and grunted, "Well done" and disappeared again. Mark smiled to himself.

With Mark and Giorgio alternating at the helm, they reached Port Moresby in the rain on time at nine on Monday morning. Mark put the boat alongside the same jetty as before. The captain now seemed to have confidence in Mark's seamanship and boat handling ability as well as being confident that Mark would call if he needed to, like when the frigate was approaching. "You had the sense to say it was a warship to make it urgent," Meissner had commented.

Mark and Pip spent the night together in the hotel, a much needed rest for Mark. He was tired, he was learning so much it was as though his brain was saying, 'Give me a break!'

On the Tuesday morning they were back at sea on another mail run. As the days and weeks passed, the work was more or less continuous. Meissner was getting more anxious about the need for the hull to be cleaned; it slowed the boat and used more fuel. But it seemed the jobs kept coming. Mark grew more and more proficient at navigation as well.

February arrived, and after a trip ashore by Pip and Meissner at Port Moresby, Mark spoke to Pip. "Did you go to the post office?"

"Yes, Mark. You know we always do. There's a lot of post pick up and it's my job now to deal with it." He showed Mark the contents of his shoulder bag. There must have been about fifty envelopes in there of varying sizes and colours.

"Have you heard back from Marcel yet? Did he get the letter and post office book?"

"No, Mark. Nothing yet. I would have told you."

"Yes," said Mark, disappointed. "You would have."

"I did go to the bank as well, of course. You're getting quite a rich young man," smiled Pip, hoping to cheer Mark up a bit.

"How much have I got?"

"Just under thirty-eight thousand dollars," said Pip with an even broader grin at Mark's shocked face.

"What's that in pounds?" Mark managed to utter.

"I'd say about fifteen thousand, two hundred and odd pounds," said Pip, still amused by the look on Mark's face. How he loved this boy!

Mark thought for a moment. "Is there a way I can send some of that to Mam?"

"Oh," said Pip. "I'm not sure how you could do that securely. All I can promise is I'll look into it when we get the chance."

"I never thought it would be anything like that," said Mark. "I'd like to send some to Tommy's parents as well. And a bit to Ethan."

"Why Ethan?"

Mark shrugged. "Don't know, really. Probably my best friend at school. I like him, and the lads tease him sometimes saying he a homo. He always says he isn't though."

"I don't see how that could be done safely, Mark. Some of our jobs are very profitable," answered Pip. "I'll let you guess which ones."

"I think I can. So this is where the new showroom, posh house and fancy car came from," said Mark.

"That's right, Mark. And you know now why I never said much about my other business to the lads at The Vault."

Mark nodded. He was lost in thought trying to imagine Mam's face when she found how much money he'd sent.

. . .

At an intellectual level, Mark always knew that there was danger at sea, and even more so when carrying the highly illicit but highly profitable cargo. But this was brought home in early February.

It was another night time run in quiet mode on Thursday, no radar, lights or radio. The weather was poor, with thick clouds and heavy rain. Mark was at the helm with Giorgio squeezed in next to him (he was better at interpreting the depth sounder), the captain and Mike. Hugging the north coast, first of Papua and then into Indonesian waters creeping along the north coast of West Irian. Mark was charged with using his sharp eyes seaward looking for lights while Mike and the captain looked for their destination. The hold was full of explosives and ammunition.

"This is the bay, captain," said Mike.

"Steer two-four-zero," commanded Meissner.

Mark turned the boat to its new heading, entering the large Wakming Bay. Mark had earlier studied the chart along with Mike so he knew the layout of the bay.

"There is one deep channel, the rest is shallow, two or three metres," said Mark, as much to himself as anyone else.

"Better keep to channel," advised Giorgio to Mark. He then was calling out depth soundings and DFH barely moved through the water, Mark adjusting his course to stay in the deeper water.

"Seven metres, called Giorgio. "Good channel."

Mark glanced out to his right. There seemed to be a cloud low and closer than the rain clouds. It was hard to see in the almost total blackness. He looked back at his instruments to check his course and the depth, and then looked again, puzzled by what he had seen. Smoke? Something resolved itself into a hard, black shape against the dark background. Unmistakably a warship, close and totally blacked out.

"Warship to starboard! Close by!" he shouted.

"Verdammt! He has us, blocking the channel," said Meissner, looking through binoculars.

"Not if we go over the shallows," said Mark.

"Not enough water, if we go aground, then he will take us," answered the captain.

"There's at least two metres, sir," said Mark. "At full speed the boat will lift a few extra inches as well. And the tide is in."

Meissner hesitated.

"Permission to start outer engines and go hard to starboard at full speed, sir," said Mark urgently, not enamoured of the idea of spending the next few decades in an Indonesian prison - if they survived.

"Yes, Mark, do it!" ordered the captain with sudden decisiveness.

The engines roared into life and Mark pushed all three throttles forward. As the boat sprang forward, Mark swung the wheel and DFH banked sharply turning to starboard, almost across the bows of the stealthy warship. The noise and sudden whiteness of the wake alerted the warship's captain to their escape plan. Instantly they were bathed in light as the ship's searchlight found them. It was the same frigate.

Mark watched the speed rapidly increasing and the depth rapidly decreasing. The pinging was almost instantaneous. The light was powerful and it hurt to look at it but it did show Mark one or two landmarks on the shore which helped him, using his memory of the chart, to know where he was. Night vision now gone, Mark relied on his memory, They were now doing forty knots and as Mark had thought, and hoped, DFH was riding high on the water.

Using their speed and shallow draught, they escaped across the shoal water, but then the frigate opened fire with machine guns. Bullets impacted the side of the bridge, The captain, Mike and Giorgio crouched down as the side window was smashed. Mark, still standing at the wheel, noted with a strange detachment as a bullet thudded into the binnacle he was standing beside. Hands grabbed him and he fell flat on his face as another bullet whistled past that would have hit Mark were it not for Giorgio who had pulled him down.

The firing stopped, but the boat was now moving at forty knots, close to the shore, in shallow water with nobody at the helm. Cautiously Mark looked up. The frigate was now behind them and appeared to have stopped.

"Oh fuck!" said Mark looking ahead as the others stood up. DFH was doing forty knots straight towards the rocky headland at the mouth of Wakming Bay.

Mark grabbed the wheel and turned hard to starboard again. The boat tilted violently as it banked on its wash that was breaking on to the rocks, they had come that close.

Steiger appeared at the companionway. "Was ist los?" he shouted, gripping the rail to steady himself.

"Sutrisno," said the captain. " But we get away over the shoals."

Just then a shell whistled overhead and a huge waterspout went up, showering the boat.

"Main ten centimetre guns. Zick-Zack-Muster," commanded Meissner.

Mark guessed that meant zig-zag which he did, taking the boat further out to sea. The shelling stopped without further near misses.

Looking back through binoculars, the captain laughed. "He is aground. He tried to follow us. Court Martial for Sutrisno I think. Your quick thinking has saved us, Mark. Well done."

"Thank you, sir," said Mark, smiling.

# Chapter 51 Calculations

Pip was very happy of course not just with the escape from and grounding of the frigate, but with Mark's demonstration of his newly acquired skills in a moment of great stress and danger.

"Mark. I'm amazed. You kept your cool from what I hear, even remaining at the wheel under fire. *The Boy stood on the Burning Deck* has nothing on you. I am so proud."

"The deck wasn't burning," said Mark, puzzled, but pleased at Pip's praise.

By means of coded radio messages the cargo was successfully unloaded at a different rendezvous the following night, DFH having remained concealed in a creek during Friday's daylight. They were told a tug had been sent from Jayapura to haul the stranded frigate off the mud banks where, because of Sutrisno's speed, he had become stuck fast.

Back in Port Moresby the following Tuesday, laundry done, refuelled and resupplied, Meissner was looking for his next job. Meanwhile, Mark and Pip had retired to the hotel to take advantage of the comfort and the wider choice of cuisine.

They made love and talked.

"Was there nothing at the post office?" asked Mark.

"Plenty," replied Pip, "but nothing from Marcel, I'm sorry to say. That's what you meant, isn't it?"

Mark nodded, disappointed. "Is there a new job yet?"

"I think so. I need to see someone, along with Wilhelm for an hour or so. Can you wait here?"

"Of course," said Mark. "I'll get some sleep and read up on the *Manual of Navigation*. Great circles fascinate me."

Pip smiled. "You're a hard worker, Mark. I love the way you're taking this so seriously." With that he left.

Mark settled down with the manual. He reflected that had he been given such a book at school, he would have struggled, but now he had the practical experience and motivation to study and learn it.

He was woken by a knock on the hotel room door.

Mark went to open it and was surprised to see the captain.

"Mark, I have to speak with you," he said. Mark backed into the room and sat on the unmade bed. Meissner sat in a chair.

"Mark, I have some bad news. I was in the car on our way back from a meeting. Philip, Mike and Giorgio were with me because this was an important meeting. Something was wrong with the taxi when we came back down the hill into the town and it went off the road and there was an accident."

Mark felt as though he had been drained of all his blood. "Pip? How's Pip?"

"Mark, do not be frightened. Philip is hurt, so is Giorgio. Not badly but they are now in the hospital. I am slightly hurt and so is Mike, but we are not in the hospital."

"How long will he be in hospital? Can I go and see him?"

"Perhaps for two days only, for both of them. Philip has hurt the neck in the accident. Giorgio bleeding on the head. The driver is more badly hurt but he will live. I will take you now because I believed that you would want to see your uncle," the captain finished with a knowing smile.

At the hospital, Pip was pleased to see Mark, his face lit up when they walked in. He was sitting up wearing a neck brace. He also had some minor cuts and bruises.

"Mark, how are you?" asked Pip.

"It's me who should be asking how you are," retorted Mark with a grin, happy to see Pip not too badly hurt it seemed.

"Just hurt my neck in the accident. Giorgio had a bang on the head, but he'll be all right."

"I am glad you are not seriously hurt, Philip," said Wilhelm. "I am getting the boat fixed but there gives a problem for the wheelhouse window. The rest is minor. My boat is tough German wood and strong."

"Will it be fixed in time for that special job?" asked Pip.

"We will go as soon as the boat is repaired and you and Giorgio are also repaired. Mike is finding the window. Now I will find Giorgio and leave uncle and nephew to talk," said Meissner with a laugh as he left.

"He always makes fun of us," complained Mark. "Do you ever tease him about Jules?"

"Not really. Maybe now and then," said Pip. "I'm so glad you came, I've missed you even for the few hours."

"I was studying the navigation manual but fell asleep on the bed," admitted Mark.

Pip reached out and gripped Mark's hand. "You're a very special young man," he said. The two talked for a time and then Mark left to go back to the hotel with the captain.

It was strange eating in the hotel without Pip but he joined Wilhelm and Jules on their table at their invitation.

"What's this special job?" asked Mark, cutting off a piece of his steak.

The captain frowned. "Not here, Mark, Once we are at sea, the crew will be told."

"I not know either," added Jules.

So Mark ate his meal and they just made small talk,

The following morning after a night alone in his hotel bed, Mark was at breakfast when Pip and Giorgio came in. Pip was still wearing the neck brace and Giorgio had a bandage on his head but Mark was glad to see Pip.

"Just one night? That's good," said Mark.

"Yes, but I'm supposed to wear the neck brace like this for a couple of weeks. It's a bloody nuisance."

"I was worried you'd still be in hospital for my birthday in ten days time," said Mark.

"When is the birthday?" asked Wilhelm.

"February 20th, a week on Saturday," said Mark. "I'll be eighteen then."

"A week on Saturday?" repeated the captain, puzzled.

"He means not this coming Saturday but the Saturday after," explained Pip.

"I must remember that," said the captain. Mark wasn't sure if he meant the way of saying the date or his birthday.

Back at the boat, the captain was annoyed that the window was not yet fitted. Other repairs were going well, mainly just a question of replacing damaged wood and painting. There were only a couple on the hull, most were around the bridge housing which is what the gunner seemed to have been aiming at.

"I wanted to leave this evening, but the extra fuel is not here," grumbled Meissner.

"The fuel tanks are all full," said Mark.

"For this we must have more fuel," said the captain, crossly. Mark shut up.

It was early afternoon, the window had not yet arrived and Mike set off into the town to chase it up. A truck arrived.

"Here is the fuel. Fifty Einheitskanister of diesel, an extra thousand litres," the captain said happily.

"Unity canisters?" said Mark to Pip.

"German name. What we call jerrycans but don't say that in front of Wilhelm or Lothar," Pip replied quietly.

"Shall I open the hold hatch," offered Mark.

"Then where must we put the cargo?" said Meissner, snappily.

So all available hands had to transfer the fifty cans, each weighing about twenty kilograms, from the truck and on to the deck of DFH where they were securely lashed along each side.

Later, Mike returned annoyed. 'What's new?' thought Mark.

"The dumbass motherfucker hasn't finished the job yet," said Mike. "I showed him my Colt and then he promised he would be here at first light."

The captain was even more annoyed. "Another night here, then. If we miss the ship I will come back and shoot the fool."

Mark was then summoned by Mike who had charts on the crew table in the cabin. He indicated a point in the Bismarck Sea about a hundred nautical miles north of Umboi Island.

""Right kid, work out a course to this point, starting eight a.m. tomorrow, 11th, arriving at exactly four p.m. on Friday, 12th. Speed required and estimated fuel consumption for that journey. And if that mother fucker doesn't get the glass fitted in time, you'll have to do it all over again."

Mark collected a notepad and pencil on which to do the calculations. He actually enjoyed the mental challenge and having done part of the route before into the Bismarck Sea he could visualize much of it. He began to see the value of 'knowing the waters'.

Mike came back in some time later. "Well, kid, what you got?"

"We can't do it," said Mark, "We would need to maintain forty-four knots. The boat can't do that. With all the shit on the hull, it struggles to get over forty knots."

Mike frowned, "Fucking motherfucker!" He strode over to his small compartment and emerged holding a Colt revolver, went up the companionway and off the boat. Mark wondered if he should do anything, unsure of what Mike was going to do.

Meissner came in having heard Mike's departure. Mark explained the situation and his calculations, which the captain looked over and agreed Mark was correct.

Mark, feeling stressed, went to his cabin to recover. Pip came in and Mark had to explain all over again.

"Nobody is blaming you, Mark," said Pip. "What you have done is provide accurate information."

An hour later, Mike was back, bringing with him a rather frightened Papuan carrying the frame from the bridge with the new glass in it. Mike stood over the man while it was fitted. After which, the man was offered a drink but having been paid, he fled ashore. There were smiles all round. While the captain sorted out leaving with the port authorities, Mark reworked his calculations.

321

"Based on leaving here at twenty hundred hours we could average eighteen knots to reach that point at sixteen hundred hours on Friday," he announced proudly.

"Why has he gone all military on us?" muttered Steiger. "Easier for Mathilda though," he added as he left for his engines.

"Who's Mathilda?" asked Mark.

Pip smiled. "The engines have names. The centre engine is called Mathilda. The port engine is called Leni and the starboard one is Renata I think."

"He really loves them, doesn't he?" said Mark.

"Good for us he does. They are old now but he keeps them running like new. Wilhelm was right I think when he said Lothar Steiger was the best engineer afloat."

At eight p.m. or twenty hundred hours as Mark now liked to call it, DFH cast off and headed out of Port Moresby onto the dark ocean, all normal navigation lights on. They were on their way to this mysterious special job.

# Chapter 52 Parallel Course

The captain wanted to ensure they were on good time so ordered twenty-five knots on three engines until they would pass between Umboi and New Britain. As they left the harbour and were in clear water, the captain spoke.

"Once we are closer, then can we slow if we need to," he said. "Giorgio, helm please. All others to the crew room."

So the captain, Mike, Steiger, Jules, Pip and Mark gathered round the table.

"Mark, you must be thanked for your navigation work and to Mike for teaching you well. We should now be on time for the meeting."

Mark wondered what meeting in the middle of the sea. It must be another ship, but he resisted the temptation to ask and kept quiet.

"This is a special job because it shows the trust that a certain government has in us, trust we have earned over the months and years. But it must remain a secret which is why until now only Philip and I knew about the information."

Mark looked at Pip. 'He knew all along?'

The captain continued. "At four p.m. on Friday we will meet with a ship at sea and a cargo will be transferred to us. Neither this boat or the ship will stop so it will test Giorgio's skill to maintain position while they lower the cargo into our hold. The weather looks reasonably calm which is lucky."

Mark felt a slight feeling of rejection that Giorgio was designated helmsman for this but he understood why.

"What's in this special cargo and why this transfer at sea?" asked Lothar Steiger, with an irritated tone.

"Lothar, my old friend," said Meissner. "I know you feel that you should be told earlier but it was a condition that only I knew and then Philip as well as part owner of the company. The secrecy is because of the involvement of this other government. They are keen to help their friends in West Irian but cannot be seen to do so. The cargo is explosives, ammunition, guns but also a large amount of gold. Some of the gold is for us in payment, as they cannot be seen to pay through normal banking channels. Any questions?"

Mark could contain himself no longer. "What is this other government?"

"The People's Republic of China," said the captain.

"Communists?" said Mike. "Why are we helping communists?"

"It's business," said the captain. "The party in Indonesia is very strong and is part of the government. But they are planning a coup against Sukarno to take over completely. This shipment, the gold especially, will help. But Mike, do not worry. The coup will fail and the party will be eliminated. Indonesia will not go communist and in the meantime, we will all be much richer."

"I hope you're right, Willy," said Lothar.

"But didn't the Russians support Sukarno against the Dutch to take over West Irian?" said Mike. "And now the Chinese are supporting the rebels?"

"No Mike, this shipment is not for the rebels, it is for the PKI in Java. But as I say, it will fail."

The meeting broke up and Jules went to prepare the evening meal. In their little cabin, Mark tried to make sense of what he had heard.

"I don't understand it," he complained to Pip.

"The politics of Indonesia are very complicated, Mark. Back home I try to keep up but it's not easy. But Wilhelm is here all the time and has contacts who give him bits of inside information. I trust his judgement and so I ask that you trust mine."

"Of course I do," said Mark. "I suppose I have to, really. I know you look after me."

As the boat made its way round the south east of New Guinea before turning north, Mark and Giorgio worked alternate watches, with the captain occasionally providing relief. Pip would spend time on the bridge to keep Mark company, admiring and revelling in Mark's new found expertise which only served to strengthen his love for Mark.

They ran into some heavy weather on Thursday crossing the Solomon Sea towards Umboi. Mark had to deviate from his course to ride the waves better, so the extra five knots that had given them extra time had proven their worth. The storm passed. And Giorgio was at the wheel as they passed Point Ming on Umboi Island during the night.

Friday dawned fine and clear, much to the relief of the captain. Mark had the afternoon watch but while visibility remained good, the sea started to get quite choppy, enough to make steering a little less easy.

The radar pinged. As the bar swept round, there was an echo almost dead ahead.

"Captain! Radar echo bearing five degrees to starboard," he called down.

Meissner came to the bridge and searched ahead through binoculars. "I think that is the ship," he said with a smile. "Steer towards the ship."

The captain watched the radar. "No other echoes, good. We are alone."

Mark altered course directly toward the distant ship. As he got closer, the details could be made out, a black hull with dirty white upperworks and a black funnel. The ship looked run down and rusty.

Mark then heard a scream from the companionway to the bridge. Meissner turned and found Giorgio, hurrying to the bridge had lost his footing and slipped. It was only a few steps but he had managed to bang his head again and was complaining about his wrist.

"My wrist is maybe broken," he cursed.

"Philip!" called the captain. "Come and help Giorgio." Then to Giorgio, "Can you steer?"

Giorgio shook his bleeding head. Pip came and helped Giorgio away to the crew cabin where there was a first aid box. By this time they were close to the ship. Mark could see Chinese writing on the stern, 黑天鹅 and 'Shanghai'. Men were now appearing on the deck. DFH was pitching in the choppy sea but the Chinese vessel was big enough to remain steady. It seemed to tower over DFH.

Meissner looked at Mark. "Can you do this?"

"Yes, sir," replied Mark. "I know this boat now."

"We have to go very close, only a few metres or so but must not hit and must stay in the same place for their crane to lower the crates. We must not lose a crate in the sea."

Mark gulped. 'Only a few metres or so from the ship's side? In his choppy sea?' "Permission to use outer engines, sir," said Mark. "Three screws should help keep us straighter."

The captain raised his eyebrows but nodded. Mark started the outer engines. There was a slight delay. Mark thought maybe Steiger had not been expecting that. With the thrust now spread right across the stern and flow through all three rudders, Mark felt the difference. The Chinese captain had obviously seen the needs of DFH and sounded one short blast on his whistle.

"Careful. He is turning to starboard," said the captain. "Listen for his sounds. One for starboard, two for port. Three if he stops."

The ship was turning into the sea so that Mark could steer straight into the waves, eliminating roll and with only the short, choppy pitch to deal with. Pip, Steiger and Jules were now near the stern, opening the hold hatch.

"I must go to help there. Keep the hold hatch close under their derrick. You have the boat."

"I have the boat, sir," said Mark and then he was alone on the bridge, inching towards the mass of the Chinese freighter, its black rusty hull side sheer to his port side. He saw the derrick being swung out and it seemed to project much more than a metre over the side so Mark was matching the speed of the ship, about ten knots, and trying to keep on a perfectly parallel course, positioning the open hatch below the derrick. He estimated the gap at about five metres. He heard some shouting from the stern but could not make it out. Constantly looking to his side and to the stern to check his position. Not only did he have to keep adjusting the wheel but also the throttles because while the waves did not affect the big ship, they had the effect on DFH of constantly changing the speed as each one slowed and then accelerated the boat slightly. Normally that would not be noticed but now this was critical.

The first crate was now being lowered. One hand on the wheel, the other on the throttles Mark watched as the crate came down and was seized by Pip and Steiger and moved into the hold. Pip and Jules were ordered down into the hold while Meissner and Steiger remained on deck. The crates looked heavy and despite his best efforts swung slightly as they came down. Mark guessed they were heavy. One by one the crates came down. The extra weight could be felt and Mark had to open the throttles slightly to maintain the same speed as the freighter. Another issue was that because the two vessels were so close the water forced between them was pushing then apart, but as the Chinese ship was so much bigger, it was DFH that was being pushed, another force that Mark had to contend with. There was little Mark could do to prevent the pitching of the boat which made lowering the crates through the hatch difficult. All he could do was keep the boat as steady as he could in the right position. In his concentration he lost count of the crates.

The short dusk was falling when to Mark's surprise the last drop from the ship was what looked like a suitcase. The captain seized this and on the deck opened it and looked inside. He then gave a thumbs up sign to the officer seemingly in charge of the operation on the Chinese ship. The Chinese ship gave two blasts on his whistle. The derrick was swung inboard as the ship started to turn to port, away from Mark. He gathered the operation was over, especially when he saw the hatch being fastened down.

The captain and Pip were carrying the suitcase along the deck toward the bridge. It was evidently heavy.

As they reached the companionway and were manhandling the suitcase, Meissner said, "Good work, Mark. Very good."

Pip said, "Mark, that was excellent. Well done."

"Mark, steer due west, two-seven-zero degrees, eighteen knots. I will return soon."

Mark turned on to the new heading, wondering where they were going. He noticed the boat was now riding slightly stern down. He stopped the outer engines and made for eighteen knots on the centre one only. He felt elated that he had successfully steered the boat under what he knew were very testing conditions.

Meissner returned to the bridge. "You did very well, Mark. I am very pleased you have learned to handle my boat so well. You are a natural sailor. I have the boat."

Mark smiled. "You have the boat, sir. Yes, thank you, sir. It was difficult but I enjoyed it."

"I will take the helm, you go below for some food and Mike wishes to talk with you."

In the crew cabin, Mike had charts out. "Right, kid. A new course." He pointed at a spot on the north coast of West Irian, Kepyat. "We need to be there in the morning. Course and speed, please."

"I'll use the rendezvous position until we get a fix," said Mark. "It's near enough." He set to, enjoying the mental challenge once more.

After some minutes, Mark announced, "It's five hundred and forty nautical miles. We'll need to make thirty knots."

"Go tell the captain then, kid," said Mike.

The promised food hadn't arrived so Mark went up to the bridge. Steiger was there.

"Mark," said the captain, "This must be interesting I think. You notice we are stern down because the cargo is very heavy."

"Yes, sir."

"Now we correct this. Lothar will move fuel from the tanks at the stern to forward tanks. But what have you calculated?"

"We need to steer two-seven-eight degrees, west by north, at thirty knots, sir," said Mark.

"Much as I thought," said the captain. "Lothar, we need Leni and Renata again."

"Is good, Wilhelm," said Lothar, "but I must shut down Mathilda for a while. We can make thirty on two engines."

"Mark, go below, eat and rest. You have done well today," ordered Meissner.

Mark went below.

# Chapter 53 Special Job

Mark slept fitfully during that Friday night. The boat seemed to have an uneven motion and at some point in the middle watch he decided to go out and see what was going on. What he found was a rainstorm with gusty winds. Very unpleasant weather. To his surprise Giorgio was at the helm.

"Hello, Giorgio," said Mark. "Are you feeling better?"

"Yes, much better. Wrist not broken, just sprain I am sure. I have strapping on it."

Mark could see that. "I'm glad about that."

"Why you here? Not yet morning watch. Mike come at four o'clock."

"Couldn't sleep."

"You had busy day. Everybody say how well you do with transfer. Maybe I no longer have job," he added with a smile.

"I'm sure you will have, Giorgio." With that Mark decided to go to the head and then back to bed.

"Where've you been?" came Pip's voice as Mark tried to creep quietly into the cabin.

"Use the head, and talking to Giorgio. He's on the helm until four."

"Come and get in with me," offered Pip.

So Mark did, and they made love, Mark falling asleep in Pip's arms. Soon though he woke and climbed to his own bunk.

. . .

Mark woke. He could smell bacon. Bacon! If Jules was frying they must have stopped. Through the porthole he could see that they were anchored near a small settlement of some kind.

On deck he saw they were in a narrow inlet with a village of maybe twenty houses grouped along the shore. Single story with rusty corrugated roofs. There was a small jetty with what looked like three or four fishing boats tied up.

The morning was spent manhandling the heavy crates from the hold into these boats that ferried them ashore. It turned out the leader of the PKI group was not there but had invited the crew to a celebration in another village in the mountains, more secure than this little settlement of Kepyat, hardly worth the name of village.

The morning had not been too bad. The Papuan PKI soldiers, who were buying the supplies the boat had brought, had provided an old truck and an armed escort. Giorgio, Mike and Mark went in an old U.S. army jeep with the convoy up to the PKI base in the mountains. It was a strange war, thought Mark, the rebels fighting for their independence from Indonesia, the Indonesian army, and the communist PKI who seemed to be fighting everybody else. The indigenous native tribes usually kept well away, but he knew they had been known to ambush stray groups, of whom few survived. Cannibalism was still practised and nobody wanted to end up in the pot! The main danger they were told, would be a rebel ambush. Mark was given a pistol which he had no idea how to use. Mike insisted on driving half a mile ahead of the convoy, the theory being that if there were an ambush set up, they would let the jeep pass safely and wait for the escort and truck to appear, and then ambush that. He dismissed the idea of a native attack. On the way into the mountains, in the cool early morning air, the ride was reasonably comfortable. Mark rode in the back, behind Giorgio, who drove, and Mike, the taciturn American. He seemed very much ill at ease with this expedition. Meissner, Pip and the rest stayed with the escort, while Steiger, thankfully, stayed on board working on his beloved diesels and also of course not to leave DFH unattended. Mark was glad to be included in the land party because he didn't fancy being left on the boat with Steiger. The principal worry was the state of the bridges. Attempts had been made to blow some of them up, and the repairs appeared very makeshift. There was also the chance that they had been mined by one side or other, and they would all either be blown up, or fall into the crocodile infested waters below.

331

The main argument when they arrived safely was over whether the escort would take them back to Kepyat, where the boat was. The leader, incongruously wearing a Manchester United top, argued with Meissner. This rather spoiled the meal which had been prepared for them by the Papuans, which was a rice dish, with meat, vegetables and fish, also some throat stinging curry. This meal was taken at a leisurely pace, and they drank much of the local beer with it. This tasted to Mark like lager and was surprisingly good. Meissner forced their hand over the return journey in the end by threatening to bring no more supplies in future. So mid afternoon, in sweltering heat and humidity, they set off back to the boat that was home.

The old truck also belonged in Kepyat it seemed, and its lightened load did not make any difference to its speed - dead slow. As they bumped slowly down the mountain road, the heat grew more and more intense. Every so often they would pull into clearings at the side of the road, under the cover of the trees, to avoid detection by Indonesian aircraft. After the noise of the engines, Mark could hear the noise of the jungle, there seemed a lot of animal noises but he could see none. 'Jungle is noisy' he thought. He didn't remember that much noise from *Zoo Quest*. Rain clouds started to gather with the heat, but did little to diminish the general discomfort. The sweat was pouring off them, especially Giorgio, the little Italian whose chubby physique did little to help him in the heat.

"Now you know why is better at sea," he complained. "This land too hot, too sticky."

Mark liked Giorgio, not least because it was he who had quickly pushed him flat on his face when they were surprised in Wakming Bay by the Indonesian frigate. While the bullets zipped around him, thudding into the woodwork, Mark knew that had it not been for Giorgio's quick thinking, they might well have been thudding into him.

Mike was still not easy to get to know, and in Mark's few weeks with this crazy outfit that he had unwittingly got himself mixed up with, he felt he did not know him any better now than at the beginning. He was from Los Angeles, had served in the U.S. Navy in the war, and hated the Japs. That was as much as Mark knew.

It became obvious that the heat was troubling Giorgio more than anybody. He started complaining long and loud. The heat and the tension was getting to all of them. Everybody was bad tempered.

"You shouldn't be so fat, you fat wop," retorted Mike, sharply.

"Americans, you think you own the world since the war," replied Giorgio crossly.

"You're sore 'cos you backed a loser, and anyway, who would want to own an asshole of a place like this? Christ, what are they fighting for?" said Mike, wiping the sweat from his brow.

"I expect that it matters to them, it is their country," Mark said.

"Christ! Listen to the little motherfucker," said Mike. "Seventeen years old and knows it all! Kid, I was fighting my way round these fucking islands kicking the Nips before you were even thought of. I tell you, they're not worth it."

"Well why did you spend so long fighting here then?" Mark said, rather unwisely.

Mike turned round in his seat, grabbed Mark's sweat sodden shirt, and pulled him close, Mike's angry face just inches from his.

"Don't try to get smart with me, kid. I'll kick your ass all the way from here to L.A. if you give me lip. I was fighting for my country, and I was helping to kill Nips."

He let go of Mark's shirt and relaxed a bit.

"Not that it did me much fucking good. Bloody navy," he said, more to himself than anyone else.

"Leave the boy alone. He know no better," said Giorgio, wrestling the jeep out of a larger than usual pothole.

"Sorry, no offence intended," Mark said, crossly, as he sat back, his pride hurt. Mike had ripped a button off Mark's shirt, so he opened up the front and flapped it to try to cool down a bit.

333

It was then the fateful breakdown occurred. Mark noticed the truck behind had stopped, and so had the escort.

"Stop!" he shouted to Giorgio, "Something's wrong, I think".

Giorgio stamped on the brake, throwing them forward.

"Christ!" yelled Mike. "You trying to kill us, you fat wop? What the fuck's wrong now?"

So saying, Mike jumped out of the jeep and strode back the few yards to the rest of the convoy. Now that the convoy had stopped, the heat was overwhelming. The equatorial sun was high in the sky and totally merciless. Insects started to dart around, taking advantage of this free supply of food. Mark too got out of the jeep and went to see what was up. By this time, the PKI soldiers were peering at the engine, and arguing loudly in their own language. Meissner brusquely tapped the driver on the shoulder.

"Why have you stopped?" he asked.

"The motor, it stop," said the man simply.

"Verdammt!" cursed Meissner. "I can see that, how soon can you repair it?" he asked, resting his hand on his Luger pistol. The gesture did not go unnoticed. The driver stiffened, and some of the PKI men muttered, looking angrily at Meissner and the rest of the group and fingering their own weapons.

"Go easy, Willy," said Mike, "we might need these motherfuckers yet."

Willy smiled at the driver. Mark knew that smile was that of the crocodile, but the driver, not knowing Wilhelm Meissner as he did, smiled back.

"I fix," he said. The tension was gone, and everyone relaxed.

"Maybe I see," said Jules, the Algerian cook who had been riding with Meissner in the truck.

The driver shrugged, and Jules delved into the engine. A moment later, he popped out again.

"Air in the petrol, I think. It will be needed to clear the air from the carburettor. It is the heat", he said to

334

Meissner, leaving an oily mark across his face as he wiped away the sweat.

"How long, Jules?" asked Meissner, curtly.

"Ten minutes, fifteen maybe," he said.

"Do it," ordered Meissner.

"Christ, I can't stand this for a quarter of an hour," said Mike to Mark. "Come on."

He walked back to the jeep, and Mark followed. Later, he wished he hadn't. They got into the jeep.

"Airlock in the carb.," said Mike to Giorgio. "Let's push on."

"Is that a good idea?" Mark asked.

Mike turned and looked at the young Brit sitting behind him. He looked somehow so innocent, so vulnerable, lost in this vicious circumstance that he was only just learning to come to terms with, notwithstanding his now undoubted competence at sea. For a moment, Mike's heart went out to him, thinking of himself at that age. But he knew that he could not allow his feelings to rule him, the price would be too dear. He hardened himself, and turned away.

"Christ, listen to the kid!" exclaimed Mike. "There's no fucker else in this asshole of a jungle for fucking miles. If there was, the motherfuckers would've jumped us on the way up when we had the cargo." He settled in his seat.

"Drive, Georgey!" he said, with a wave of his hand.

Giorgio shrugged, and with a grind of gears they lurched off down the road. It was a relief to get moving again, especially as they now went at a more reasonable speed. The air moving past brought a welcome cooling effect, the disadvantage was the greater bouncing around on the rutted and bumpy road. Still Mark was pleased that he had not waited behind, and was looking forward to getting back on board the boat, even though that would be stiflingly hot until they set sail. At least it was "home".

Giorgio and Mark started to talk, mainly about the women in Port Moresby and Rabaul.

"I show you nice woman," Giorgio said. "Handsome young boy should sex with woman as well." So Giorgio promised to take the youngster to places where he would have experiences he would never forget.

"Yeah," interrupted Mike, "a dose of pox most likely. I didn't think Limeys screwed anyway, apart from each other's asses. Whole damn lot created by immaculate conception," he added laughing at his own witticism. Mark thought about Giorgio's offer. Maybe he should try it, at least once.

Mike was still chuckling at his joke at the expense of supposed British sexual habits when they came round that bend.

"Mama mia!" cried Giorgio.

"O fuck!" said Mike.

"Shit!" Mark said, and that's just what he felt like doing. The phrase "shit scared" is very accurate.

# Chapter 54 Roadblock

Across the road in front of them was a small personnel carrier and a jeep, and facing them were about a dozen uniformed soldiers, with some very nasty weapons pointing at them. Giorgio stamped on the brake and the jeep slewed across the road to a halt, about fifteen yards from the soldiers. Giorgio wrestled with the gears, found reverse and with tyres tearing up the road surface, started to back off. A volley of shots raced just over Mark's head, and he ducked instinctively. The jeep stopped. Mike leapt out and ran towards the cover of the forest at the edge of the road. Bullets zipped off the ground around his feet. He stopped and raised his hands, only about five yards from the jeep.

"Who are they?" Mark asked.

"Indonesian army, Sukarno's men," said Mike in a low voice. "This could be a bastard."

In any army, even the untrained eye can tell the officers from the rankers. There was no mistaking the Indonesian who stepped forward now, smiling to himself. He was more smartly dressed than his men, and was not carrying a sub-machine gun, but just had a pistol holster, with presumably a pistol in it, although Mark was never to see it. The officer had an air of arrogance and self-assurance that frightened Mark. He knew whatever happened next would be up to this man, and he was scared. The officer came towards the three, and his men advanced with him. A wave of his hand ordered Giorgio and Mark out of the jeep, and another gesture to put their hands up. A rapid order, and one of his men relieved them of their weapons, including Mark's pistol. He smiled again, and spoke rapidly, looking from one to the other to see if they could understand. Mark couldn't, and he didn't think Mike or Giorgio could either. At least neither gave any sign. There was a short silence, while the noise of the forest reasserted itself.

Still looking at them, the officer snapped out one word.

"Meissner!"

Mark couldn't help it. The recognition showed on his face, and on Giorgio's also. The officer laughed, and shouted something out to his men. They grinned, and nodded, taking a step closer, leering. Mark's stomach was churning with fear, and he wanted to be sick. He feared the worst, and was not wrong.

"Stupid bastards!" said Mike to Giorgio and Mark.

The officer laughed again, and went closer to Mike. He could not believe his luck, to have three of Meissner's gang of pirates walk straight into his hands. He knew what he was going to do, and how much credit it would bring him.

"You traitors," he said, in a thick accent. "You take guns to enemies of Indonesia."

He stepped back and spat accurately into Mike's face. Mike made to lunge forward, but was jabbed in the gut by a machine gun.

The officer again issued orders and a soldier went into the personnel carrier and returned with a coil of rope. Sections were cut off this, and under threat from the guns of the soldiers, the three captives' hands were tied behind them. The cord bit deep into Mark's wrists and he winced with the pain, but the soldier's reaction was to pull the cord even tighter. Mark could hear Giorgio's breathing, fast and shallow, with fear. His own heart was pounding, and he was trembling uncontrollably. Only Mike appeared unafraid, he seemed only coldly angry. Mark hoped that he could come up with some miracle to get them out of this. He knew this part of the world, he had been hereabouts in the war, and for all anyone knew, ever since. Surely, he could do something? Where was the escort? Why had they not got the engine fixed? What was Jules playing about at? For Christ's sake, hurry up!

Again the officer spoke.

"Now, you pay!"

Another order, and the soldiers turned to the rope again, cut off a length, tied a noose in it and flung it over a branch at the edge of the road, about twelve feet from the ground. Mark's throat went dry. He tried to call out, but all

338

he could do was croak. He looked at Mike, pleading with his eyes, but Mike was still more concerned with hating the Indonesians. Giorgio was stock still, but Mark thought he saw his eyes water. As the soldiers prepared a second noose, Mark fought back tears. Mark thought of Mam; would she ever know what had happened to him? At least he had sent her the money. The officer stood to attention and, facing them, made a formal speech of some kind, while his soldiers grinned at each other. When he had finished, he turned to Mike, whom he had picked as the leader.

"You punish is death," he said.

"Go to hell!" said Mike.

The officer laughed, and stepped close to Mike.

"No, you go," he said quietly.

At that moment, Mike suddenly kicked out and caught the officer straight between the legs. He collapsed, clutching his groin, his face screwed up in pain. A soldier smashed his gun's butt into Mike's face, and blood poured forth as he went down. The soldier guarding Mark gave him a vicious dig with the barrel of his gun, and he nearly fell too. Still on the ground, the officer shouted to his men. One replied, apparently in some disagreement, pointing at the two nooses. A soldier came from the personnel carrier, with a further length of rope, thicker than the previous one. As the officer struggled to his feet, more orders. While a third noose was made from the second rope, the soldiers bound the feet of the captives. Mark thought that he could not despair any further, but he found new depths of fear then. Mike, somehow still alive and cursing, was picked up by four of the soldiers and carried over to the first noose. The noose was placed round his neck, and a small piece of cardboard with some word on Mark could not understand was put on as well. By this time, Mike was silent. He was held up by the soldiers, while another secured the far end of the noose to a tree. Then they dropped him, and he fell limp at the end of the rope, and was still. Mark cried yet more, tears running down his face at the hopelessness of the situation. He

339

thought of poor Tommy, hanging from his tree in Gorbeck Forest. Was it quick?

"Don't weep, English boy," whispered Giorgio, misunderstanding the reason for Mark's selfish tears, "Mike dead before they drop him. He with God now, and soon we will be too."

Mark looked at Giorgio, amazed. He supposed he was a Catholic, he had never thought about it before.

"Fuck your God," Mark said, his anger coming through his tears, frustration and terror. "If he's so fucking wonderful, why is this happening?"

Giorgio looked at Mark. He had become fond of this young man in a fatherly way and respected his rapidly learned seamanship, and knew he did not deserve this fate. Giorgio had no answer, for at that moment, he was dragged over to the second noose, it and a card were placed round his neck, and he was held up, struggling, by six of the soldiers. Mark heard him start to chant a prayer of some kind in Latin or Italian, then they let him go too. He made the most awful croaking noise, and jerked around on the end of the rope.

The officer beckoned to Mark's guard with an order. He was pushed, stumbling and hopping with bound feet to the third noose, and stood in front of the Indonesian officer. Close up, he was a small man, perhaps five foot seven or eight, with hard brown eyes. He looked Mark up and down dispassionately. More orders. The card and third noose were placed round Mark's neck. It occurred to him that their bodies, with their little cards, were supposed to be left for as long as they lasted, hanging there, to prove that President Sukarno would have no mercy on his enemies. The bulky knot was slipped down to Mark's neck. He could feel the soldier pulling on the rope as he dragged it tight over the branch. Mark felt many hands grabbing his body, some twisting and hurting his genitals, as he was lifted high. The rope tightened more, pulling his head up.

Mark screamed out, "Please, no! Please don't!"

Then they let go of him.

The pain was intense. The rope round his neck was choking in a way he could never have imagined. His ears started drumming, his whole head buzzing and ringing. His head was going to burst. He wriggled trying to get free, out of instinct, even though the noose went tighter as he gasped in vain for air. The pressure of the rope seemed to be forcing his throat up into his mouth, his tongue suddenly huge. The pain and panic were total as a sea of blackness started to well up around him. One of the soldiers took aim with a pistol at Giorgio's writhing body and shot him through the chest. Mark saw him take aim at his own helpless body, smiling as he aimed at Mark's genitals. Mark was suddenly aware of a sharp pain, and a blast of heat on his body. There was a strange feeling that he had to make a choice, and suddenly he knew that he had to try to live as long as possible. But as he did so, he entered oblivion.

. . .

Cool water on his face. Incredibly fierce pain round his neck. His throat choking and cracked dry. A miracle as water entered his mouth. Swallowing was so painful. Deep, rasping breaths. Air! More air! Mark spluttered, and opened his eyes. Voices, blurred faces. He was lying on the ground, looking up at the clouds and the blue sky, the beautiful blue sky. The cursed jungle looked like the Garden of Eden. Perhaps it was.

"Er lebt," said a voice. A familiar voice, thought Mark. 'He lives' he automatically translated in his mind.

Gradually, Mark could take note of his surroundings. Somehow, he was alive! He had survived. Had that officer changed his mind and let him off? He didn't mind. He was alive, and would do anything to stay that way.

Slowly Mark's eyes focussed. The nearest face was Pip's. He had been rescued!

"Mark! Mark," Pip was saying. "Speak to me. It's ok now, I'm here. We're here."

Mark looked up at Pip. "I love you, Pip," he said. But speaking hurt.

341

It turned out that Mark was the only survivor. Mike and Giorgio were dead. So were all the Indonesians, some obviously executed after the fight with a bullet in the head. Mark saw the officer sprawled in the road, sightless dead eyes staring at him, blood oozing from his head. His jeep was burning nearby.

Mark didn't know how long he had been writhing at the end of that rope, but when the convoy had come round the corner, the gunfight had been short and swift. Giorgio had indeed been shot, and the attempt to make sure of Mark before rescue had missed, going through his legs, grazing his right thigh. He was doubly lucky, as was later pointed out to him. His noose had been of thicker rope than the other two, and therefore had not choked quite as quickly. The officer's jeep had been hit in the fuel tank and had exploded, probably the blast of heat he had felt as he had gone. Mark was alive because the thinner rope had run out and the speed of Jules's work on the truck. He was still 'complete' because of some Indonesian's poor aim.

They spent some time removing all evidence of the ambush. The bodies of the soldiers were hidden some distance from the 'road' with the expectation that wildlife would soon dispose of them. The Papuan PKI happily seized the personnel carrier while the burnt out jeep was pushed into the thick foliage out of sight from the road and from above.

342

# Chapter 55 Those in peril on the sea

Pip improvised a bed of sorts in the truck and Mark was carried on to it. The bumpy ride was uncomfortable but Pip stayed with him in the back of the truck. It was not made any happier by the presence of Mike's and Giorgio's bodies. Mike's in particular bloodied. Mark tried just to focus on Pip, who held him close and tried to shelter him from the bumpy ride as best he could. Nobody spoke. At last as dusk fell they arrived back at Kepyat village. The villagers watched as the convoy approached, children excited running alongside.

At the small jetty the bodies were lowered onto one of the fishing boats.

"Can you walk, Mark?" said Pip.

It hurt to speak so Mark just nodded. He was helped down from the back of the truck by Pip and a PKI soldier. Leaning on Pip he was put in the same fishing boat, next to the two corpses. Mark thought they were already beginning to smell, and insects were buzzing around them.

Lothar Steiger was on the deck of DFH at its anchorage in the inlet. He waved at the group. Nobody waved back. Meissner was talking to the leader of the PKI group. It seemed a sympathetic chat, and they shook hands. Meissner came over to the boat and climbed in. The Papuan villager or fisherman started the little outboard motor, British Seagull, Mark noticed and soon they were on board DFH.

Lothar's face changed to shock when he saw the occupants of the fishing boat. "Was ist passiert?"

"Help with the bodies first," said the captain. The bodies were heaved aboard in a rather undignified manner. They were placed in the hold along with fifty now empty jerrycans. Steiger had used the time to top up the fuel tanks.

Mark was taken to his cabin. He sat on the edge of Pip's bunk and started crying and screaming, despite the pain. He simply couldn't stop. Pip held him close. "Mam!" he sobbed.

The captain heard and came in. "It is shock," he said. He left and returned with the first aid box, looking through the various tablets.

"Here we have it," he said. "Marsilid. He must take this. It will help. Also he has pain in his neck and throat, he must take these for the pain."

Pip looked at the box. Paracetamol. Mark was now rocking back and forth on the bunk, sobbing. "I want to go home."

Mark was coaxed into taking the tablets.

"Philip, you must get him well. We have no crew now, just myself, Jules, Lothar and you two. I need Mark to be fit again."

"Of course I'll do my best, Willy. He needs rest and time."

"Put him to bed and then come out. You must help more, We must leave here tonight but there is only me to navigate. Lothar can steer a bit and you must learn so that on the open sea, I can sleep."

"I'll do what I can, Willy."

After the captain left, Pip said, "Did you hear that, Mark? Did you understand?"

Mark's sobbing subsided and he nodded. "I feel so tired, Pip. I thought I was dying," he whispered. "I was thinking about Mam and even poor Tommy in the forest. I couldn't believe it when I saw your face."

"You said you love me," smiled Pip, caressing Mark's blond hair.

Mark started crying again. "Pip, I want to go home."

"Let's get you into bed, Mark," continued Pip.

"I need the head," said Mark. "Help me?" He was guided through the crew cabin to the forward head. Odd items belonging to Giorgio and Mike lay around, upsetting Mark. Nobody was in the crew cabin, which was unusual. The boat felt empty. Mark sat for a time while Pip waited outside. Then he helped Mark back to their cabin and helped Mark get undressed and into his lower bunk.

344

"I have to go and help as best as I can, Mark. Try to sleep."

Mark nodded. He now felt very sleepy. Pip left the cabin. Wilhelm was on the bridge, alone. Lothar was on the foredeck.

"Philip, please help Lothar with the anchor. We must leave here."

Pip did as ordered and he heard the sound of the engine starting. He and Lothar stowed the anchor on the foredeck and the boat moved slowly out of the inlet into the open sea. With no illicit cargo on board, full navigation lights were on and the radar was in use.

Pip returned to the bridge. "What can I do to help?"

"Help Jules with sewing in the hold. We have sheets from their bunks which is all we can use to sew them. Tomorrow we bury them at sea."

In the hold, Pip found Jules sewing up the two bodies in their makeshift shrouds. He was weeping as he did it. Their method was basic, to roll the body rather unceremoniously in the sheet and then sew the ends with strong thread.

"If we are careful tomorrow, the sheet will hold," said Jules. "How is Mark?"

"Sleeping, I hope. I feel exhausted myself. I don't know how Wilhelm does it."

"The captain is made of steel," said Jules. Pip could only agree.

After the bodies were sewn up, Jules went into the galley to prepare some food. Their banquet in the mountains seemed a lifetime ago, but Pip realized it was only a matter of hours.

"Philip!" came the captain's call. Pip went to the bridge having looked in on a sleeping Mark. "Philip, it is lucky it is calm. You must steer for a time."

"I don't know what to do," said Pip.

"Make sure the compass stays there at three-zero-four degrees. Watch the radar screen for any echoes,

345

especially fast ones from the south. Call if you see any. Also if you see any lights. I must eat and rest. Do not sleep."

"Yes, Willy. I think I can do that. Where are we going? Bali?"

"No, too far and now too dangerous for us, It is Indonesia remember. We will go to Davao in Mindanao. We can get the boat cleaned there and maybe find new crew. Filipinos are good seamen."

So Pip took the helm, thinking about Mark, the boy he loved, his competence at doing what he was now having to do. The boat surged on through the night. Pip found himself nodding a few times but managed to stay awake. Almost midnight and Lothar arrived.

"I have the boat," he said, putting his hands on the wheel.

"Does that mean I'm off duty for a while?"

"Yes, Philip. You go."

There was a light under the captain's door and he could hear low voices within. Willy and Jules, he thought. In his own cabin, he only partly undressed in the dark and climbed into Mark's bunk. It smelled of him. Pip fell asleep.

The Sunday morning dawned fine with a calm sea. Pip was woken by movement. It was Mark, getting up.

"How are you, Mark?" Pip asked. Mark was standing in the cabin, wearing just shorts. Pip thought him beautiful, but there seemed a determination about him.

"I'm OK, my neck hurts a bit and talking does. Maybe I should steal your neck brace," said Mark. "I noticed you've stopped wearing it. Going to the head, back in a minute."

Pip climbed down from Mark's bunk and was standing in the cabin when Mark returned. "Jules is at the helm," he said. "That's a first," he added with a smile.

Pip was happy to see that smile, but he knew it hid the traumatic memories behind it.

Mark went over and lay on Pip's bunk. "I want you," he said.

"Mark, are you sure?"

"Yes. I need you. When you're in me it's like the rest of the world doesn't exist." Mark slipped his shorts off, Pip did the same. Slowly and gently they made love in the spooning position, both climaxing together, Mark prepared with some toilet roll. Mark relaxed in the calmness that followed orgasm. He felt better.

"That was good. Thank you, Pip. Has Jules been on the helm all night?"

"No. Lothar relieved me, so Jules must have relieved him."

"Relieved you? You mean you were on the helm?" Mark was almost laughing as he said that.

"Mark, I'm not totally useless. All I had to do was keep it on three-zero-four degrees and shout if I saw a sign of any other ship."

"Three-zero-four degrees?" repeated Mark. "That's no bearing for Bali."

"We're going to Davao in the Philippines. Bali is too far and too dangerous now."

"Yes, probably not enough fuel for Bali as well. What speed are we doing?" Mark peered out of the porthole, He could see the wake of the boat. "A bit more than twenty knots I think. I must dress and see what's going on. What's the hurry to use this fuel?"

"He has the boat booked in at Davao so I think he wants to be on time so as not to miss the slot. I think the captain wants the funerals today. I helped Jules sew Mike and Giorgio up in sheets last night."

Mark nodded as he dressed. His watch had stopped. "What time is it? I didn't wind my watch up last night."

"Twenty to eight," said Pip.

"O seven forty hours," smiled Mark.

On the bridge, Jules greeted Mark. "Mark, you OK now?"

"Yes, Jules. Much better today thanks. I have the boat," he added firmly.

"You have boat, Mark. Why?"

347

"Because I want some breakfast," said Mark. "Three zero four?"

"Yes, Mark. You like my porridge? Sea is calm and it swallow easy for you."

"Yes, good idea. Thanks Jules."

Mark noted the boat was doing thirty knots, but the fuel gauges looked reasonable. Then looking back he saw the jerrycans had gone. So he settled down into his familiar routine, trying to shut out of his mind the terrible scenes of the day before.

The captain was pleased to see Mark at the helm. "You tell me if you feel bad. That's also an order."

"Yes, sir," answered Mark.

The porridge went down well, Mark eating his while Meissner took the helm.

At midday, the captain ordered all engines stopped. They all gathered at the stern and the two shrouds were carefully lifted from the hold.

A board was placed under one, Mark thought it was Giorgio.

The captain read a prayer.

Pip said, "Do you know the hymn, *Eternal father, strong to save?*"

"We sing that at school," said Mark. Then, more subdued, "I mean I used to."

The captain shook his head. "You sing it for them."

Mark looked at Pip, who nodded. They sang. The words came back to Mark as each line started.

> *Eternal Father, strong to save,*
> *Whose arm does bind the restless wave,*
> *Who bids the mighty ocean deep*
> *Its own appointed limits keep;*
> *O hear us when we cry to Thee*
> *For those in peril on the sea.*

"That's all I can remember," said Mark.

"It is good," said the captain. "I will send them." He lifted the board and Giorgio slid into the water. He did not sink immediately but soon slid under the surface. The other shroud was placed on the board and again the captain lifted the board. As the bodies sank, he stood to attention and saluted. "Abschied von guten Freunden. Möge Gott euch beide in seine Obhut nehmen. Ruhe in Frieden."

After a silent pause, the captain said, "Mark, helm please. Same course and speed."

As Mark made his way to the bridge, it occurred to him that poor Tommy's funeral had probably already been held. He felt sad, wishing he could have been there. 'I wouldn't have been welcome, anyway' thought Mark. Even less at Peter's.

Through that Sunday and through the night into Monday they went watch and watch about. It was tiring but Mark found that being busy helped him. His pain receded and his voice felt better, Pip insisted though he kept taking the tablets.

# Chapter 56 Cradled

On the afternoon of Monday 15th February they arrived at the port of Davao on Mindanao, the large island at the southern end of the Philippines.

"Is this country named after you, then?" smiled Mark at Pip.

"Hardly," said Pip, happy to see Mark smile. "After a King of Spain I think."

"Oh yes, they were once Spanish," said Mark.

"My clever Mark," said Pip, hugging him. He often wondered if Mark inside was as stable as he seemed. The past six weeks had seen his life completely upended with a fair amount of trauma, from the deaths of Peter and Tommy, to those of Mike and Giorgio and nearly his own, the loss of his home life, not to mention being shot at. He half expected Mark to collapse, but he seemed strong. If anything, stronger than before. More grown up, Pip thought. But then, Mark had had to grow up quickly or go under, and Pip knew now that Mark had some inner strength so going under was not an option for him.

As they crossed the wide bay towards the town, Mark was asked to take the helm.

"We are going to a boatyard where I have arranged for work to be done on the hull," said the captain. "You must use your skill to place the boat exactly on the cradle so the boat can be pulled out of the water."

"I thought it would be in a dry dock," said Mark.

"The dry dock here is too expensive and is booked. I have been here before and they can clean the boat with this method."

"Are you sure you want me to do this, sir?" asked Mark, wary of the responsibility. "Wouldn't you rather do it?"

"I will be here but you have the skill," replied Meissner.

Mark steered north slowly as the waters narrowed approaching the city which he could see on his port side.

There were several ships at anchor in the roads and a large cargo ship was leaving the city, and coming towards DFH. Mark sounded the whistle with one short blast before steering to starboard and passing the large ship port to port. Meissner nodded approval.

The waters narrowed more to just about a kilometre between the city to port and the opposite shore of Samal Island.

"Is here," said the captain, pointing to the shore. Mark could see a beach and some buildings among trees but beyond that there appeared to be a large shed close to the water, wooden but with the ubiquitous corrugated roof. Meissner sounded the whistle, a longer blast.

"Stop engine," the captain ordered. Mark complied and the boat's forward way slowed. On shore, a dilapidated looking red tractor appeared and was hooked up to what Mark thought was a big cradle with wheels and fat tyres. The transverse sloping bars that would support the boat had what looked like hessian padding. The tractor started to reverse down a low concrete slipway from the shed.

"You want me to aim for that?", asked Mark, incredulous.

"Yes. It's your job," said Meissner.

Mark eyed the angle and position of the cradle, now disappearing under the water except for vertical bars on either side.

"Permission to use three engines, Sir."

"Granted."

Using the engines both to steady the boat and make course corrections Mark tentatively steered DFH between the vertical bars. He stopped the engines as the boat continued to drift slowly forward, suddenly encountering resistance and stopped. They were on the cradle but not quite centrally. The tractor then slowly pulled the cradle and schnellboot out of the water. It was a peculiar sensation as the boat rose higher from the water and then on to the slipway. He felt the boat settle on to the cradle as it left the water, leaning slightly as it did. Mark knew this was because the boat was not quite centrally positioned.

"Excellent, Mark," said the captain. "I knew you would be able to do it. Even though we have a five degree list to port."

"I'm sorry, Is that bad?" asked Mark.

"No, it is ok. You have done very well."

Mark heard clapping from behind him and Pip was on the companionway with a big grin on his face.

A ladder was placed against the boat and a middle aged Filipino man came on board.

"Welcome, Captain Meissner," he said, as he and the captain shook hands. "I can see your boat is overdue for a clean."

"I have not seen it yet, Castaneda," Meissner pointed out.

"You skill is still good, captain. Almost central," said Castaneda.

"My young helmsman here did it. Very good for his first time, He knows this boat well now," the captain told him.

Mark felt a rush of pleasure at this validation. Pip nudged Mark and smiled.

Castaneda turned to Mark. "Well done. We'll soon have the boat cleaned and smooth. Should be all done by Thursday," he added to the captain, who said, "Wednesday would be better."

Castaneda smiled. "Captain, you are a hard man. We will work hard for you."

"Get your things, Mark," said Pip. "We have two or three nights ashore. Time to look around Davao."

"Who will look after the boat?" asked Mark.

"Lothar I expect. I've no doubt he will use the time to service the diesels. Maybe Wilhelm and Jules."

As they climbed down the ladder onto the slipway, Mark wandered round the boat. It was strange looking up at it. The reason for it not making full speed was obvious. There was weed growing on the hull and various kinds of little limpet-like things all over the hull. Mark looked with fascination at the three propellers and rudders. He was surprised that the centre rudder was larger than the outer ones but otherwise they were as he had imagined and had felt them to be, but seeing them confirmed what his instincts had told him.

Mark found it hard to tear himself away from the boat. He found himself feeling an attachment to it. 'Or him' mused Mark to himself. Apart from being his home with Pip for the foreseeable future, he had there learned so many new things and had achieved success.

"Come on, Mark," urged Pip. "You've done well but I think you need a couple of days good rest after what you went through at Kepyat."

"I feel a lot better now," said Mark. Then he reflected for a moment. "Actually, I am pretty tired. Sort of deep down."

"Did you remember your tablets?" asked Pip. Mark nodded.

A Filipino youth came up to them. "I am Joriz. I will drive you to your hotel in the city. It is a good one, very nice."

He went over to a battered Toyota Stout pickup. There were barrels of some kind of paint in the back but Joriz indicated they should put their bags there. "With three people, not so much room in the front."

Soon they were driving along a straight road toward the city centre. Mark, sitting between Pip and Joriz, could see some more modern buildings ahead.

"You like it here?" Joriz asked Mark.

"I don't know yet," said Mark. "It's too hot, I know that."

"Always nice and warm here, and not so much rain as some places," said Joriz.

"You speak good English," said Mark.

Joriz smiled. "Many people in Philippines speak English, We had Americans here for a long time."

"I'd forgotten that," said Mark, wondering what to do about Joriz's hand on his thigh. But then he had to use two on the wheel as a truck pulled out in front of them.

"Here is your hotel I think," said Joriz. "I will come back when the boat is ready."

As they retrieved their bags from the back of the pickup, Joriz drove off before Pip could give him some money for a tip.

"This is the place," said Pip. They went into the lobby which with its high ceiling was cool.

"Middleton," said Pip. "You should have a reservation for me."

"Yes, Mr Middleton," confirmed the receptionist after a pause rifling through a box of index cards and consulting a big diary. They were shown up to their room by a porter who insisted on carrying both bags. There were two beds.

"I can make these together for you," the porter said with a smile.

Before Pip could decline, Mark said, "Yes please."

"I will do this while you have your evening meal later."

They were tired so ate in the hotel restaurant rather than explore around. True to his word, when they returned to their room, the beds were locked together with double bedding and a thick mattress cover to disguise the join. Mark smiled at Pip.

Mark found their love making relaxing and slept soundly.

On Tuesday morning Mark woke late. Pip wasn't in the bed, but Mark heard sounds that sounded like pain noises from the bathroom. He slipped out of bed and tiptoed to the door, tapping gently. "Pip? Pip, are you ok?"

The groans stopped. "Yes, Mark," said Pip, opening the door. "Just my neck giving me some problems."

"You've not been wearing that neck brace," observed Mark. "Maybe you should have been."

"It's such a hindrance, Mark. I was needed on the boat as without Mike and Giorgio it's hard. You know that

354

especially, but being Mark Martin, you stepped up like a man. I am so proud of you. I love you so much, Mark." With that Pip reached out and brought Mark close to him and both naked, they embraced and kissed.

Mark felt his arousal coming again. "Why don't you lie down on the bed and rest that neck. I need a pee and then I'll join you."

Pip smiled, "It's a deal, Mark Martin."

"You haven't used my full name for ages," said Mark. "Why now?"

"Because it's who you are. The clever, resourceful boy who tackled a fire, charmed the customers, became Head Prefect, drove that Cortina through the night, has learned navigation and boat handling to such a high level so quickly. I admire you, Mark Martin."

"You forgot I murdered Peter," said Mark. "Hardly an achievement."

"You believed your own life was in danger and his fall was an accident, Mark. It was not murder. Come back to bed."

Once more while Pip made love to him, Mark was taken to a place where all that mattered was the feel of Pip inside, his own powerful sexual arousal and that feeling of fulfilment and peace.

# Chapter 57 Unexpected Elevation

It was late morning when he woke again. He turned to find Pip looking at him. Mark could see the love in his eyes. "Are we going to be together for life?" he asked, sleepily.

"I hope so, Mark. If that's what you would like. I love you so very much. I'm not asking that you love me although that would be nice."

Mark snuggled up to Pip. "I do love you. Pip. You're a good, kind man. Sexy too. I love it when you fuck me. I know that's weird and supposed to be wrong, but it just feels right for me."

"Don't let others judge you, Mark. If it doesn't hurt anybody else, then don't worry about it."

"I soon got to like you best at The Vault. The others were nice enough, except Fred maybe, but you were so kind and protective, especially when I caught that clap, gonorrhoea."

"We heard Fred could be a bit rough."

"Rough? My arse was stinging like mad and he was rough inside as well."

"I remember slapping you," admitted Pip. "You seemed to like it."

"I did in a way, it was like giving myself to you but Fred went too far. But you've not slapped me since, I think."

"I just want to care for you, look after you, Mark, for as long as I can."

"And then when you get old, I'll look after you," said Mark, kissing Pip's neck, who responded by reaching round and giving Mark's arse a light slap. But as he did so, Pip cried in pain and his hands went to his neck.

"You should put that neck brace on," said Mark.

"It's uncomfortable, but I will when we get up," said Pip.

"When will that be?"

"After I've made love to you again," said Pip, fondling Mark's already erect cock.

They ended up by staying in bed most of the day, ordering a light lunch by room service, making love several more times and Pip otherwise trying to rest his neck.

. . .

There was a knock on their room door at about six in the evening. "Philip? Are you there?" It was Meissner's voice.

"Yes, Wilhelm, we are both here." Pip and Mark hurriedly pulled shorts on and Pip got up to open the door.

"Oh God!" he said, rubbing his neck.

"Put the neck brace on. I keep telling you," said Mark.

Pip opened the door. "Come in, Willy."

"I will not ask what you have been doing today," said Wilhelm with a smile.

"His neck's bad from the accident but he won't wear that neck brace," said Mark.

"Rest in the bed is good then," said Wilhelm. "I hope you let him rest some of the time, Mark."

Mark flushed red, but the captain continued. "Please come to this hotel restaurant in one hour. Jules and Lothar will be there also, and there are two people to meet. Perhaps to get dressed first?" he ended, smiling. He winked at Philip and then left.

"I wonder who the two people are," said Mark.

"Either contacts for more business or more likely new crew members," suggested Pip. "We'd better get ready."

"No time for more sex?" asked Mark.

"God! You're horny, Mark. You've worn me out today. I'm not seventeen any more." Pip gave Mark a hug and a kiss. "I'm first in the shower."

"I'll do your back," said Mark, slipping off his shorts and following him into the small bathroom. Mark sponged Pip down, his back and what Mark thought was his nice bum. He noticed Pip kept wincing each time he turned his head. 'This is not good' thought Mark. 'I'm going to make him wear that neck brace.'

As Pip stepped out of the shower, Mark stepped in. Often Pip would wash Mark's body but this time he didn't.

357

Once dressed, Mark said, "Put the neck brace on, Pip."

"I will, but later, After the meal. It makes eating more awkward."

"I'll keep you to that," warned Mark, seriously.

"I can just see you as Head Prefect, telling people what to do," smiled Pip. "What happened to feelings of surrender?"

"That's only in bed," said Mark. "Otherwise I'm as good as anybody."

"Indeed you are, Mark Martin, No wonder I love and admire you so much."

They went to the restaurant. The captain was there along with Jules and Lothar. Two other young men were there, both not as tall as Mark, Filipinos he guessed. They looked to be in their mid twenties, although Mark knew he was not good at judging ages. He thought they weren't dressed like business contacts.

"Philip, Mark, this is Frasco and Timoteo Baldonado. They are brothers and will be joining the crew of Der Fliegender Holländer. They both have seagoing experience as you would expect in a big port like Davao."

They shook hands and all sat down at the round table.

The captain introduced Pip and Mark to the Baldonado brothers. Mark assumed Jules and Lothar Steiger had already been introduced. "Philip is my cousin although he is English and he is my business partner. He part owns the business and the schnellboot. He is not a sailor though. Mark is his nephew and they are very close. Mark is young and when he joined us he knew nothing about the sea. But he is a clever boy and now is a first class sailor, navigator and helmsman. One day he will be captain of his own boat I think."

Mark felt embarrassed at this unexpected fulsome praise from the captain, despite the description of him as a boy. But then he still had some time before his twenty-first birthday.

They ate a good meal and the Baldonado brothers seemed reasonable to Mark. It seemed that Timoteo, who was the older, had some experience of being a helmsman which Meissner said was why he had recruited him. Timoteo had insisted his brother come as well as a general deckhand.

As they relaxed over a good wine after the meal, all seemed well. Then the captain made an announcement.

"I have decided to designate Mark as my new First Officer. He has learned so much in the last few weeks, and I need a First officer. I was going to wait for his eighteenth birthday on Saturday and have a special meal but we will be at sea on a job then but we will do this afterwards. Lothar remains second most senior, not counting Philip, but for matters concerning command and seagoing, Mark is now second in command. His share of the profits will increase therefore. It is an unusual system but I think it will work."

Mark was completely stunned by this, He sat open mouthed until his brain kicked in and he said, "Thank you, sir. I'll do my best." The others smiled. Steiger just shrugged. The Baldonado brothers looked curiously at this teenager who was now their superior officer. Mark thought back to Mr Harris telling him he was to be Head Prefect and the shock that had given him. He started to feel upset so left the room. Pip followed him into the lobby.

"What's the matter, Mark? It means that you are now officially second in command of DFH. And not yet eighteen, until Saturday."

"I know. It made me think of how I was made Head Prefect and how that surprised me. It was sort of the same, but remembering it made me upset."

"I'm sorry, Mark, but you are doing so well here. You have a bright future in this world."

"Maybe captain of my own boat sometime. Who would have thought that a couple of months ago?"

"Come back in, Mark. You have responsibilities now. Also, on board, you outrank me now," he added, trying to make Mark feel better.

Mark smiled. "Yes, and my first order to you is to wear that neck brace."

"Aye, aye, sir," said Pip, with a loving smile.

359

They went back in and Pip explained that Mark had been a bit overcome by the captain's announcement.

The captain then made a further announcement. "I have been informed by Castaneda that the boat is ready, fully cleaned, caulked where necessary and a new anti-foul paint applied. We have a mail job again from Port Moresby to Rabaul on Friday so we must put to sea early tomorrow to arrive in Port Moresby by Thursday evening. Mark, I will need the course and speed calculations in the morning. Now I suggest everybody gets a good sleep tonight. There will be a call at six o'clock when we will go to the boat. It should be light then. Jules will make his excellent porridge while we are in the calm waters of Davao Gulf."

Back in their room, Mark sat on the bed. "Wow!", he said. "I still can't get over it. I know it's because Mike and Giorgio were killed, but even so, it's one hell of a promotion."

"Wilhelm doesn't worry about age, just what people can do. Remember, he was only twenty-three himself when he was given command of his first boat and that was in wartime. So the fact that you're not quite eighteen won't matter to him. He's seen what you can do, and how resilient you are."

"I don't feel resilient," said Mark. "I wish Mam could know about this," he added sadly.

"She will, one day, I'm sure," said Pip. "Maybe when we get to Port Moresby there will be something from Marcel."

Mark looked at Pip with hope in his eyes. "That would be good. He can tell us that he posted my letter and the post office savings book to her. I'd like to know she got it."

"Yes, but let's hope that she keeps it to herself and doesn't set off more of a hunt. I'm pretty sure Marcel will have made that point in his accompanying letter."

Mark nodded. Then he smiled and said with as much authority as he could muster, "Middleton, put on the neck brace **now**!"

Pip smiled. "Aye, aye, sir". He reached for the neck brace and clipped it on.

# Chapter 58 More Speed

As predicted, at six o'clock on Wednesday morning they were woken by a knock on the door. By six-thirty they were showered and dressed and on their way to the boatyard north of the city, two taxis to carry all seven of them. By seven o'clock the captain was inspecting the hull.

"It looks new," commented Mark, running his hand over the fresh paintwork.

"Castaneda does a good job," said Meissner.

"How did they do the parts where the cradle was?" asked Mark.

"They put him back in the water and out again in a different position," explained the captain.

"He should be good for a few extra knots," said Mark. He had got used to thinking of the boat as masculine following the captain's example.

"And less fuel also," replied the captain, with cost in mind. "But now we must get him into the water."

"The boat has diesel as you asked, Captain," said Castaneda. "Also while the boat was still we have managed the gyrocompass. All perfect now and battery full."

They climbed up the ladder and dropped their bags in the cabin. Mark noticed the captain emerging from his cabin carrying a small heavy bag.

"Mark, I will see the boat into the water, Prepare the course." With that the captain and Pip climbed down and were talking to Castaneda. But Mark got on with his job, spreading the charts on the crew cabin table. Pip returned and sat opposite, watching with pride. Mark looked up. "Where's the neck brace?" he asked.

Pip smiled and went to their cabin next door and returned with the brace.

"It seems like I am replacing both Mike and Giorgio. First Officer, navigator and leading helmsman," said Mark. "The captain said my share would increase but he didn't say how much."

"How much depends on the profits, Mark, But you now get the most after the captain and myself, level with Lothar."

As Mark did his calculations, he heard the tractor engine and then the boat was moving. As it entered the water it floated free of the cradle. Mark thought it felt like a boat again. Mark heard the engines start up and DFH was moving under his own power. Steiger stood in the entrance to the crew cabin, looking at Mark and smiled before going up to the bridge. 'He actually smiled at me' thought Mark. The Baldonado brothers came in and were unpacking their things into their lockers. Timoteo then sat watching Mark, seemingly fascinated by this teenager. Mark rolled up the charts and went up to the bridge with Pip. The captain was at the helm, Steiger had already returned to the engines.

"Here are the course headings for Port Moresby, sir. I've plotted a course to take us north of New Guinea rather than go through Indonesian waters. We will need to make thirty-five knots to arrive by sunset tomorrow. But it's over two thousand nautical miles. It might mean putting in somewhere for fuel."

"You think well, Mark. But the hold is full of einheitskanister of diesel. We will have enough. Thirty-five knots is good. He can do that now with less fuel. Jules is making his porridge so eat your breakfast then come back. You will take the forenoon watch. By then we will be in open sea. Timoteo will take the helm for the afternoon watch but I wish you to stay with him for some time so he can learn."

"Yes, sir," said Mark, then descending to the crew cabin.

In the cabin, Jules produced some maple syrup. "Stir in, is very nice," he advised.

"You mean it hides the taste of the porridge," said Lothar Steiger, but his expression showed he was teasing Jules.

Mark added the syrup and stirred the porridge. "It's lovely, Jules," he said. Jules beamed with pleasure.

"It is rather nice," said Pip.

They ate the breakfast and drank coffee.

"Timoteo, you will be at the helm in the afternoon watch, but I will stay with you while you learn the instruments and get the feel of the boat," said Mark. Giving instruction in that way suddenly took Mark to his first day as Head Prefect, putting Ethan on the chair outside Mr Harris's office and giving out jobs in the prefect common room. He felt the rush of emotion. He quickly left the crew cabin and went into his own. He collapsed on Pip's bunk, sobbing uncontrollably, trying not to make a noise. He knew the captain was waiting for him. He felt Pip's hand on his shoulder.

"Mark, my dear Mark, what is the matter? What brought this on?"

"Talking to Timoteo like that, it was like being Head Prefect again. I just couldn't help it."

"Mark, as soon as we can, we'll get a break. You've been under so much stress lately and you've not really recovered from the ambush, even though you say you're fine now."

"I'd better go," said Mark. "I'm supposed to be on watch, and the captain will want his porridge. And maple syrup," he added, wiping his face.

"When we get to Port Moresby, if there's time, I'd like to look at some new apartments they're building on the promontory. A proper home for us."

"Us? For you and me?"

"Of course, Mark. I love you and want to spend my life with you. I've never felt this way about anybody before. I want to make you happy."

Mark kissed Pip. "I love you too, Pip. But I must go. Now put the bloody neck brace on."

"Yes, sir," grinned Pip.

Mark went onto the bridge. He could see they were leaving the Davao Gulf and the boat was starting to respond to the ocean rollers. The captain stood back to let Mark at the helm.

"What is your heading now?" Meissner asked.

"East-South-East, one-one-five degrees, sir," said Mark. "Until we get to the Umboi channel at twelve hundred hours tomorrow."

The captain smiled. "You are very precise, Mark. I like that. Three engines, increase speed to thirty-five knots. You have the boat."

"I have the boat, sir." Mark opened the three throttles until the desired speed was reached. He knew that to keep the mail contract, they must be back in Port Moresby on time.

The captain went below, no doubt to enjoy his porridge with maple syrup. Mark settled into a routine. As they made progress Mark was able to relax a bit. The boat was going well. At Davao, Steiger had spent much of his time working on the diesels, ensuring they were in first class condition. Like the boat, they were over twenty years old so needed more regular care. The radar screen was now blank, having left the shipping lanes around Davao behind.

"How is he going?" It was the captain. For a second Mark wondered what he meant, before he remembered the captain's way of regarding ships as masculine.

"Very well, sir. The slight swell is not a problem."

"I have the boat. Stay on helm."

"You have the boat, sir."

The captain smiled, a broad grin Mark had not seen before. "Full speed all engines. Now we see now how he flies."

Mark pushed all the throttles fully forward. He heard the engines roar even more as the boat seemed to leap forward. So responsive! DFH gathered speed and was going at over forty knots and still accelerating. The bow was lifting as the boat started to plane over the water.

Mark looked at the speed readings, both the Pitot and impeller. "Wow! Forty-seven knots sir. Both readings."

Meissner just nodded, and stood on the bridge of his beloved boat, smiling.

365

After a few minutes, he said, "Castaneda cleaned out the Pitot tubes and the impeller. Thirty-five knots now. You have the boat."

"Ich habe das Boot," said Mark.

The captain smiled and gently punched Mark's arm as he left the bridge.

"Permission to enter the bridge, sir," came Pip's voice from the companionway.

"Of course," said Mark.

"What was the rush back then?" asked Pip, looking around at the ocean in all directions.

"Nothing. The captain just wanted to put his foot down to see what she - sorry, he - would do after being cleaned. We made forty-seven knots."

Pip stayed on the bridge to keep Mark company. They chatted away, discussing the idea of buying their own place at Port Moresby. The only home they had now was the small cabin on the boat. It rained which cooled things slightly but the weather soon passed and it was sunny again. The ventilation provided by their speed made conditions aboard bearable.

At midday, the captain came to the bridge with Timoteo.

"Mark, you still have the boat. Now you must teach Timoteo how to steer the boat. He will be your deputy on the helm."

Mark stood back so Timoteo could take the wheel. "You have the boat, Timoteo."

"I have the boat," said Timoteo. Mark remembered he had some experience as a helmsman.

But then the captain surprised Mark. "Timoteo, Mark is First Officer. You address him as 'sir' on the bridge. In the cabin, maybe not so formal."

"I have the boat, sir," repeated Timoteo.

Mark explained all the instruments and controls. Timoteo was familiar with most but had not seen a depth sounder before.

After an hour or so talking to and getting to know Timoteo, Mark was tired. With instructions to call if there was any problem or a radar echo, Mark went below to the cabin for a lie down. Pip was there reading a battered paperback.

Mark peered at it, and laughed. "*Lady Chatterley's Lover?*"

"Well, it's not banned now. At least, not at home. I think it still is in Australia though."

"I'm told page a hundred-and-twenty is juicy," said Mark.

"If you're a good boy, I'll let you read it when you're twenty-one," said Pip jokingly.

"Good boy? May I remind you, Middleton, that I am First Officer?"

"And Head Prefect," smiled Pip, but instantly regretted it as Mark's face became one of pain, lips trembling. "I'm sorry, Mark. Silly of me."

"I'm tired," said Mark, climbing up to his bunk. Before long he was asleep. Pip quietly turned to page a hundred-and-twenty.

# Chapter 59 Change of Plan

Mark and the captain steered the boat through the night as they made rapid progress across this part of the Pacific Ocean. They took advantage of the calm weather early on Thursday to heave to so that the fuel tanks could be topped up from the jerrycans in the hold. Everybody was involved, lifting them from the hold, emptying them into the fuel tanks and returning the empty ones. It took about two hours, which Mark had not allowed for in his navigation.

He approached the captain. "I'm sorry, sir, but I had not allowed for a two hour stop. It will be hard to make Port Moresby by dusk tonight."

"What do you suggest, Mark?" asked Meissner.

"Increase speed to forty knots, sir. It will use more fuel but we have enough to get us there."

"Very well. Forty knots it is. No extra drag now."

So Mark gave Timoteo the order and then went to wash the smell of diesel from his hands. He found Pip in the cabin, grimacing in obvious pain.

"What's the matter? Your neck?"

"Yes, it's really painful. Heaving those cans about probably didn't help."

"You need to rest it, Pip. I think you should go to the hospital in Port Moresby this evening."

"I fear you're right, Mark. Thank you, I love you."

"I love you, too."

"Are you on watch?"

"Not until later," said Mark.

"Lie with me, let me hold you."

"Very well, but nothing more. I don't want you doing permanent damage to your neck for the sake of one fuck."

"You're right as usual, Mark. God, how you've grown up in two months."

"Had to, I suppose," said Mark, as he gently cuddled up to Pip.

By mid afternoon they had crossed the Bismarck Sea and were at Umboi. Mark went to the bridge, tasked by the captain of taking DFH into Port Moresby. Mark was slightly concerned by the low fuel state; he would ideally have liked to put on even more speed but decided to maintain the forty knots as long as he could. He took the shorter route past Loani before eventually turning west-north-west towards Port Moresby. It was with some relief that he rounded the promontory to their usual quay as dusk fell and with fuel still to spare.

The captain was on the bridge. "You still have the boat, Mark."

"I have the boat, sir," repeated Mark, partly automatically but also as an example to Timoteo who had come to observe. Mark already had three engines running so that gave him maximum control. Fenders were dropped and the spring attached as Mark brought the boat alongside with barely a bump.

The captain nodded approvingly. "Timoteo, that's how it is done."

"Yes, sir," said Timoteo. Mark wondered what the Filipino was really thinking but he was tired and put it out of his mind. He was also worried about Pip.

But first there was the boat to see to. The many now empty jerrycans had to be offloaded; fifty of them belonged to someone here. Mark wanted to speak to Meissner about taking Pip to the hospital but the captain left the boat into the town almost immediately to sort out refuelling and arrangements for the mail run to Rabaul.

Mark took matters into his own hands. "Lothar, I am concerned about the injury to Philip's neck. I am going with him to the hospital so they can check him over. I didn't catch the captain before he went ashore, so please tell him if he's back before we are."

Steiger simply nodded. So Mark and Pip, wearing the neck brace, found a taxi to take them to the hospital. They had to sit and wait but at last they saw a doctor.

"I'm Doctor Mason," he said in a noticeable Australian accent. "It's about the neck?"

369

"It's been very painful and sometimes I feel a click when I turn my head."

"Why are you turning your head? Don't you wear the neck brace?" said Dr Mason in a slightly annoyed tone.

"Yes, but I confess I haven't been wearing it all the time," admitted Pip. Mark gave Pip a surreptitious dig to say 'I told you so'.

The doctor felt Pip's neck. "I think we need to have an X-ray." He wrote on a card which he gave to Pip. "Take this along to the X-Ray department."

To Mark's surprise, Pip then said, "Doctor, can you have a look at this young man?" He says he's OK but a few days ago he was hanging from a tree with a rope round his neck."

"He was what?" exclaimed Doctor Mason. "Where was this?"

"West Irian," said Pip, while Mark gave Pip an annoyed look.

"It was sore at first but it's much better now," protested Mark.

"Perhaps I'd better not ask for more details," muttered the doctor. He felt Mark's neck and asked a series of questions such as how long the suspension had lasted, which neither could answer accurately.

"I think an X-ray in this case as well, just to be sure, although from a physical examination it would appear you've been very lucky, young man," said the doctor, writing out another card for Mark.

They waited in the X-ray department.

"I wish you'd worn the neck brace properly," said Mark.

"I know, Mark, but it's such a restriction, especially on the boat. You don't realize how much you duck and turn your head when moving around."

Mark thought about that and could see his point. "Let's wait and see what the X-ray says," said Mark.

Pip was called in and Mark sat waiting fidgeting. There were some magazines lying around. Mark half

370

expected to see *People's Friend* but they were old *Time* and *National Geographic* and the like. That took Mark back to waiting at the hospital at home when he had caught gonorrhoea. His downcast mood was interrupted by Pip returning.

"I have to come back in the morning," said Pip. "The X-rays won't be developed until then. Your turn now."

Mark too was asked to return in the morning for the result.

"We're supposed to be doing a mail run to Rabaul tomorrow," said Mark, frowning.

"I know," answered Pip. "Meantime, let's hope there's room at the hotel for us. If not, we'll have to try others."

At the hotel reception, Pip asked if there was a room available. "I'm sorry," he said, "I usually book ahead but events got in the way."

"Mr Philip, I will do my best." The receptionist consulted the big booking diary. "I have a room. It has double bed," he added, looking doubtfully at Pip and Mark.

"We'll take it," said Pip, doing his best to feign reluctance.

In the room, they were aware that their things were still on the boat. They had what they stood up in. "I'm tired," said Pip. "Let's get a bite to eat downstairs and then come back here. I don't want to go back to the boat now."

Mark agreed. Not only was he tired, he was hungry.

"I wish we had our own place here already," mused Pip. Mark could only agree.

After a meal in the hotel restaurant, they went to the room, showered and got ready for bed. Pip was taking off the neck brace.

"Don't take that off," said Mark. "You're supposed to keep it on."

"Even in bed? Mark, it's not comfortable. I doubt I'll get much sleep."

"A bad night's sleep is better than permanent damage to your neck."

371

"As usual, Mark Martin, you're right," said Pip, doing up the clips again.

Mark was laughing.

"What's so funny?" asked Pip.

"You. Stark naked except for the brace. It looks funny."

In bed, Pip held Mark. "I love you, Mark."

"I love you, but sex with your neck the way it is too dangerous."

Lying on their sides, Pip reached and caressed Mark's already half erect cock, and stroked his balls. Mark could feel Pip's hardness against his back. "We've no Vaseline or anything," said Mark, but now filled with desire for Pip. As always he just wanted to give himself to Pip. Pip was using saliva. Tommy! Mark was transported back to the first time Tommy had fucked him. Then in the spooning position, Pip's entry was gentle and slow and Mark was lost in that strange place where he made no decisions, had no thoughts except the feeling of Pip within him, wishing the time could last for eternity. I didn't but Pip had hold of Mark and timed their climaxes together. They lay panting, still locked in unity. Pip kissed Mark's neck.

"How's your neck?" asked Mark eventually. "That one was really intense. Thank you, Pip."

"It was good for me too. I think I needed that after all the stress."

"Sex is good for stress, they say," said Mark. "After that I need another quick shower."

They both showered and fell asleep in each other's arms.

. . .

Mark was woken on Friday morning by Pip gently shaking him. "Mark, breakfast and then see if we can get to the hospital and then back to the boat."

Blearily, Mark rubbed his eyes. "No time for sex then?" he said.

"Mark, you must be the horniest person I've ever met. Even when I was your age, I don't think my libido was as fierce as yours."

"You seem pretty horny to me," said Mark, getting out of bed on his way to the bathroom. "Maybe tonight."

They were half way through breakfast when Meissner appeared. "I got your message, Mark. I thought that you might be here. I need you back on the boat."

"Good morning to you, Willy," said Pip.

"P - Uncle Philip has to go back to the hospital this morning to get X-Ray results," said Mark.

"We do not have the time," said the captain, sitting down at their table and pouring himself some coffee. "We have the mail run to Rabaul and I am sorry but first we must go back to Kepyat where there gives some trouble."

"What kind of trouble?" asked Pip.

"I am not certain, but I think Sukarno's men are closing in and they want us to pick them up from Kepyat along with the gold. It seems very urgent."

"Is that the Indonesian army?" asked Mark, shuddering at the memory of his last encounter with them.

"Yes, and they have no mercy, as you know, Mark," said Pip.

"What about the hospital?" asked Mark.

"You must go, Philip," said the captain, "but I need Mark with me on the boat. Also I do not know how many Menschen we will be picking up. There may be many so all space might be needed."

"Our very own Dunkirk," said Mark; and then bit his lip. There was a moment's silence while Meissner looked at Mark.

"I understand," said Pip. "It's OK, Mark, you'll be back in a couple of days. We'll celebrate your birthday then."

"When do we leave?" asked Mark.

"Now," said the captain.

Mark nodded. He was suddenly aware that he was leaving Pip. He would be on his own. 'Don't be silly' he told himself. 'Be back in a couple of days'. He stood up. "I'll see you soon, Pip. I hope all is well at the hospital." He wanted to hug Pip but not here, in the hotel restaurant.

At the door, he turned and waved to Pip who waved back.

In the taxi back to the quay, the captain said, "Do not worry over Philip. He will go to the hospital and all will be well. I believe that the mail for Rabaul is being loaded now. As soon as we are on board I will take us out of the harbour while you plan the course for Kepyat."

"What about fuel?" asked Mark. "We were very low last night."

"That was done last night while you were at the hospital."

It was as the captain had said. They were under way immediately while Mark plotted the course for Kepyat. He was careful to make notes separately and not make notes on the chart remembering the inspection they had.

Soon they put on speed heading across the Coral Sea.

# Chapter 60 Correspondence

Pip watched Mark leave with a heavy heart. He hated being apart from him now. He felt so protective of him, although he recognized that Mark was not the boy he had first met. But Mark's maturity only led his feelings of love for him to increase.

He went to reception and asked to keep the room for the next two nights and then took a taxi to the hospital. It was a different doctor, Chinese, Pip thought.

"I am Doctor Feng," he introduced himself. "Mr Middleton, I have the X-ray photographs." He pinned up two X-rays on a lit back screen. "See, this vertebrae seems displaced. This is what makes the click for you sometimes feel. The danger is that if it moves too far it might break the spinal cord."

"That does not sound good," commented Pip.

"It is not good," said Doctor Feng. "The good news then would be you are paralysed from the neck down."

"Jesus!" exclaimed Pip. "What's the bad news?"

"You are dead, Mr Middleton," said the doctor, bluntly.

"What can be done? Will it go back?" asked Pip.

"We will give you a different neck brace. This will slightly extend your neck, lifting the pressure from the spine which may pull the vertebrae back into line."

"How long will that take?"

"Weeks, maybe months. And you must wear it all the time. You can take it off for the bath or shower, but otherwise wear it all day and all night."

Pip was stunned by this news.

"Mr Middleton, you have been very lucky so far. But you must not take risks any more."

"I understand, doctor," said Pip, thinking about Mark nagging him to wear the brace.

"Is Mr Martin with you?" asked Dr Feng. "I have his X-ray here."

"No, doctor," said Pip. "He has had to go away for a few days. Is his neck damaged?"

"I need to talk to Mr Martin," said the doctor. "Medical information is confidential."

"I am his uncle and he is still a minor in my care," argued Pip.

"Very well, Mr Middleton, I am happy to say that while the physical examination showed some bruising to soft tissue, the X-ray shows no apparent damage to the spinal cord. He's been a very lucky young man. This was due to a brief hanging, I believe."

"Yes, the rope they used for him was much thicker than the others," said Pip, unthinkingly.

"The others?" said the doctor, shocked.

Pip was annoyed at himself. "Yes, this was in West Irian and two of our group didn't survive an encounter with Sukarno's men."

"Indonesia, so out of this jurisdiction. Undoubtedly a thicker rope would spread the load, no doubt much being taken by the jawbone and back of the skull rather than the neck." He looked again at the X-ray of Mark. "No damage in either place. But ask him to come in himself when he returns."

"Yes, doctor. Thank you very much. I will," said Pip.

Having been there two hours, Pip left the hospital somewhat poorer and unable to turn his head. He decided to call at the post office to collect the business's mail. At least he could catch up with paperwork while waiting for Mark to return.

There was a small packet from Marcel among the usual post. He decided against opening it in the taxi so he returned to the hotel room. All his possessions, such as they were since his flight from England, were on the boat, no doubt by now in the Solomon Sea heading for Kepyat and then Rabaul.

He bought a toothbrush and some underwear before going to the hotel room. He put the business mail to one side and opened the packet. He was surprised when two objects dropped out onto the desk. Puzzled, he picked them up. One was a gold badge about an inch in diameter with a pin. On the front was some kind of crest. Surrounding it were the words *Laudatum* at the top and round the lower half, *Laudatur a Schola*. On the back it said,

*Mark Martin*

*1961*

*For courage*

The other pin badge was in the shape of a shield, blue enamel with gold coloured lettering inset, HEAD PREFECT.

Pip sat back, confused and emotional by this. Somehow Mark's mother had sent these things to Marcel. He wondered what Mark would make of them. He pulled out some papers from the packet.

One was a letter from Marcel.

My dear Philippe

I got your letter with the request. By chance I was travelling to England two days later. So having the address of the mother of Mark I decided to journey north to Bilthaven to see myself. The lady was suspicious in the beginning. I saw she was looking for more visiters with me and she was also looking for a neighbour who might be watching. I made a whisper that I had news about Mark so I went in.

She made the insistence that I have a cup of tea. I gave her the letter from Mark. I had to comfort her because she was crying when she read it. I gave her the little savings book. She was greatly shocked by this. We had a long talk. She wanted to know where Mark is but I said I was unable to tell her but that he was safe. She also asked if he was with you. She knew about you. She said the police had asked her about Philip Middleton. They told her that they thought you were homosexual lovers. She also talked about a public house where the police had arrested some men. But the only witnesses against them were Mark and the boy he killed so they had to let them go.

She showed me Mark's bedroom. Left as it was when he ran away. She took the two badges I have sent from his school jacket and asked me to send them to him because he loved them.

377

She asked if I had time to wait while she wrote a letter. I am sending that letter as well. When I left she was crying again. I think she loves and misses Mark but I told her he is well.

I took all this back home with me but it was some days before I was in Paris to post them less traceable.

Wilhelm has been in contact also about obtaining some more goods. That you are not in Europe now makes buying the goods more difficult but we will find a way.

Jusqu'à la prochaine fois

Marcel

Pip sat and looked at the badges, and re-read the letter. He felt profoundly sorry for Mark's mother. Mark had spoken about her so in many ways he felt he knew her. He wasn't surprised by the cup of tea, 'cuppa' as Mark said. Her letter to Mark was there. There was no envelope, just a piece of folded lined paper obviously torn from a pad. Should he read it? It was there so he decided to.

He unfolded the paper. The handwriting was that of someone who didn't write a lot.

Dear Mark

I have this frenchie here who gave me your letter. I don't know who he is and I cant remember the name he said. I made him a cuppa tho. But he said he had met you and the man from your garage. I know about him now because the coppers were here a few weeks back asking about him and you. I had to say I didn't know cos I didn't. They said you call him Pip. Im thinking when you said you was with Pippa you was really with Pip. I wish I knew. I know you was hiding from me that you are a homo. I think that was you and Tommy as well. I should have known and been there for you. Mark that does not matter your a homo. I still love you and miss you just as much. I will try to find a way of letting that Ethan know your alright. If I can find him without giving out away. I had a visit from that Mr Harris about you. He was very nice tho and said he hopes you are OK. He said he had had to give your job to Debbie someone.

I want you to come home. You wont be caught or hung. The coppers said they know that boy was after you with a gun so it was self defence. Dont matter it wasnt a real gun. It sounded like one people said. The hole of calvert house was terrified. You thort it was real. Nothing will happen to you. They said you are the victim. Please come home my darling boy. I will keep your money safe so you can go to university like what you wanted. I hope this gets to you before your birthday. Happy birthday my lovely son.

I love you Mark, for ever and ever.

Your loving Mam

Mam

Pip had to wipe a tear from his eye reading that. The love this woman had for her son oozed from every line, every word. He tried to imagine Mark's reaction when he got back and he read that letter. He might decide to go back home! Pip's gut went solid at that thought. He would lose Mark. Pip sat and thought. Suppose he didn't show Mark the letter and the badges? Suppose there was no contact from England at all? Suppose he told Mark there had been no letter from Marcel yet again?

Pip knew he couldn't do that to Mark. He loved him so much he knew he would never be able to live with the lie. Every day he would see Mark, thinking his letter hadn't got through and all the time knowing his mother, his 'Mam', whom he loved with all her intellectual failings, had in fact written to him and he had concealed that from him. What a betrayal that would be! He wouldn't be able to look Mark in the face, their relationship would sour anyway.

Suppose Mark did go home? What if we both went? Peter's dead. Mark wouldn't give evidence against him, or the group. The police would be left with nothing.

So Pip steeled himself and resolved to show Mark everything. He deserved that. He tried to visualize Mark handling the Laudatum and Prefect badges. What would his reaction be? Upset? Nostalgic? Happy?

Pip carefully put everything back in the packet and put it in a desk drawer. His neck was now hurting him so he lay on the bed. His thoughts and then dreams were of him and Mark, in their own home, happy and laughing together, sleeping together, a couple in love. It was evening when he woke so he went down to the restaurant.

"Is Mr Mark not dining with you tonight?" asked the waiter.

"No, he's away," said Pip. He'll be back on Monday or maybe Tuesday," replied Pip, thinking of Kepyat and then Rabaul.

Back to his room, Mark on his mind, he tried to think through the possibilities. The letter said the police had no evidence and had released everybody. Peter was dead. Mark would deny everything. He could go back to his West Farm house and to the garage, explain there had been some malicious allegations that came to nothing. He had needed to visit his other business and Mark had gone with him because of all the fuss. Now Mark had come back to explain everything. It would all settle down. Of course The Vault group was finished. Mark could finish his A levels, probably not at school but at college, and then go to university. After that would be up to him, but hopefully they would be together still. He could not let Wilhelm down but as soon as a new First Officer, maybe Timoteo, was in place, they would return. He felt he owed this to Mark. If after that he wanted to return to New Guinea and captain his own boat, that would be his choice. Pip smiled to himself thinking of Mark's happiness when told he could go home, go to university and have the chance of the life he had wanted.

He went to sleep, neck brace secured. After a fitful night, he slept in on Saturday.

"Happy birthday, Mark," he said to himself in the mirror, thinking of his decision as the best birthday present he could give him.

# Chapter 61 Eighteenth Birthday

More than six hundred miles away from Pip as the crow flies, longer by sea, Saturday morning dawned dull and cloudy as DFH cautiously approached the north coast of West Irian, Indonesian territory, DFH's grey shape hard to see against the grey waters on the overcast day. Mark dressed and went to the head. As he went into the crew cabin, Jules was serving up bread, cheese and coffee, and cake for breakfast. Everybody was there except for Timoteo.

Unanimously they started to sing, grinning at Mark.

*Happy birthday to you,*
*Happy birthday to you,*
*Happy birthday dear Mark,*
*Happy birthday to you!*

"Thank you," said Mark, smiling at the recognition.

"After the mail run, we will have a special meal for a special eighteen year old, with Philip there of course," said the captain.

"Thank you, sir. I can go into a pub legally now," said Mark.

After the meal, the captain sent Mark to the bridge to relieve Timoteo.

"I have the boat, Timoteo," said Mark.

"You have the boat, sir," said Timoteo. "Is it your birthday today? I heard the singing."

"It is Timoteo," affirmed Mark. "When we get back to Port Moresby the captain has promised a special meal for everyone. Go and get what Jules had prepared for breakfast. There's birthday cake, too."

Timoteo said, "Happy birthday." He left the bridge. Mark thought he was getting to like Timoteo.

Mark knew they were close to Kepyat. The radar was off, the radio listening on a frequency usually used by the Indonesian Navy, ALRI. He remembered that on his previous visit to Kepyat he had been in bed when they arrived and again when they left, sleeping off the pain and trauma of that day. So he had no memory of the coastline to work from but the captain came to the bridge.

"I have the boat, Mark."

"You have the boat, sir," responded Mark.

"Depth sounder on," ordered the captain. "Do you need the paper feed?"

"I'll turn it on if I'm unsure," said Mark. He listened to the ping and echo and decided there was still at least ten metres of water under the keel. As they approached the coastline it seemed a continuous line of forest with the hills behind. Mark gave an involuntary tremble as he thought about what had happened in those hills. He thought how Tommy had loved his forest, but how he hated this one.

The captain was looking at the coastline through binoculars. "Look out to seaward, Mark. Your good eyes have saved us before."

Mark quickly scanned the horizon but visibility was not good. The ping echo quickened. "Depth about five metres, sir," he reported.

"Port thirty," ordered the captain. Mark steered the boat to port, thinking that Meissner must have seen some landmark. In the mist hanging over the forest, Mark thought he saw something a bit darker.

"Captain, is that smoke?" he said, pointing.

The captain turned his gaze in the direction indicated. "I think so," he said. "Probably cooking fires at Kepyat."

As he said that, Mark saw the entrance to the small inlet. It matched his memory of the chart. "Three metres, sir," he called.

"Stay dead centre," said Meissner. Mark complied as he steered DFH into the narrow creek, listening to the echoes from the depth sounder. They came round a bend and the boat was hidden from the sea, 'A well chosen place' thought Mark.

"Mein Gott!" said Meissner. Mark looked. The smoke was rising from the ashes of what had been Kepyat. Every

382

house had been burnt, the fishing boats also and the little jetty badly damaged.

"Stop the boat," said the captain. "Keep position against the current. Anchor party ready."

Mark turned the boat directly into the slow current of the creek. He estimated the depth was about two metres in this central channel. Just enough. He used all three engines to hold the boat stationary relative to the shore. The anchor party, everybody else, was on the foredeck.

Meissner was scanning the sides of the creek carefully, the side opposite as well. Mark concentrated on keeping the boat still.

Some fifty yards upstream of the village and the jetty, a figure appeared out of the trees. Mark instantly remembered the Manchester United top. This person was holding with both hands a briefcase bag which appeared heavy.

"The gold, I think," said the captain. "Drop anchor!"

The anchor went down and Mark felt it bite into the bed of the creek. He put the engines to neutral but out of caution did not stop them.

It was obvious none of the fishing boats could come out for them, so one of the rubber dinghies was unlashed. Dropped over the side and held by a rope attached to its bow, called a painter, it lay alongside in the current. The rope ladder was used for the shore party to climb down; the captain, Mark and the two Baldonado brothers. All now armed.

The current wasn't too strong and they paddled across to the shore, keeping a careful watch. The Papuan in his red top, moved along the shoreline to meet them. They pulled the rubber dinghy up on some shingle next to the jetty. They could see some bodies lying among the houses.

"What happened?" asked the captain.

"Army come, they said you had brought gold. They wanted gold and guns. They were shooting. Some of us manage to escape from camp and in jeep came down to Kepyat. You had gone."

383

"When was this?"

"Soon after you left," said Redtop. "But on way down we saw blood on the road and thought maybe you all killed. Then here at Kepyat the army come, shooting and burning. I hid with gold."

"Two of us were killed," said the captain curtly. "But you have the gold?"

Redtop nodded. "We go now?"

"We will check the village first," said the captain. "You put the case in the dinghy now."

Redtop put the briefcase on the dinghy. Mark wondered how much gold was in there and what it was worth. They drew their weapons. The captain took Mark's and slipped the safety off. "Now you just aim and pull the trigger."

"Kill people?" asked Mark. He felt very unsure about shooting someone.

"Of course. Before they kill you," said the captain, "You have killed a person before I think."

"Yes, but that was an accident," said Mark.

But the captain was no longer listening. "Frasco and you, come with me," he ordered, indicating Redtop. "We will take the left side. Mark and Timoteo, take the right side. See if there is anybody still alive."

They entered the small village. The destruction seemed complete. There were bodies, some burnt inside their homes. Others lying bloodied where they had been shot. The slaughter of a defenceless coastal community. Men, women and even children lying in their own blood. None showed any sign of life.

As Mark, along with Timoteo, edged through the shattered and burnt out houses of the village, once happy family homes, Mark never saw the sniper who, with an accurate headshot, killed him instantly.

The End

I hope you found "Dancing with Panthers" interesting and a good read. Please leave a review on Amazon and also maybe Goodreads.com  It doesn't need to be lengthy, a few words will be appreciated just as much.

# Table of Watches (work shifts) at Sea

| Name | Time |
|------|------|
| First watch | 2000–0000 |
| Middle watch | 0000–0400 |
| Morning watch | 0400–0800 |
| Forenoon watch | 0800–1200 |
| Afternoon watch | 1200–1600 |
| First dog watch | 1600–1800 |
| Second dog watch | 1800–2000 |

The Dog watch is split so that the same team doesn't keep getting the same watch. By splitting the four hour Dog Watch in to two parts, any given team would be on a different watch in the next rotation. In this way the Middle and Morning watches through the night are shared out evenly.

The origin of the name is unknown. One likely possibility is that because Sirius, the Dog Star in the constellation Canis Major, is usually the first to be seen as night falls, these watches take their name from that.

Another idea stems from the belief that at night, only dogs are awake. Many dog owners might dispute that though.

# Acknowledgements

Peter Lehmpfuhl of Munich

Karl Scheuch for information about S-boats and the excellent website at http://www.s-boot.net/index.html

Picture of Austin Healey 3000 (Credit the late Eddaido on Wikipedia. Red car made greyscale for use. (https://commons.wikimedia.org/wiki/File:1960_Austin_Healey_3000_Mark_I_BT-7_(4586385575)_(cropped).jpg)

Picture of Ford Cortina Mk1 By Charles01 - Own work, CC BY-SA4.0, https://commons.wikimedia.org/w/index.php?curid=60379603 (Figures removed for privacy, made greyscale.)

Picture of a Riga class frigate By Rabbesandelin - Own work, CC BY 3.0, https://commons.wikimedia.org/w/index.php?curid=7295893

Dr Stephen Bushby, Sunderland Royal Hospital.
Historic medical treatment.

Clive Graham (wherever you are now, Clive.)

Cover: 100covers.com

Advance readers

Beryl Giles, Isle of Man

John, from Proud Pages LGBTQIA book club: facebook.com/groups/proudpages

Stan C. Kimer, North Carolina, USA

Members of the Gay Authors' Workshop https://gayauthorsworkshop.uk/

## Books by Patrick C. Notchtree

Other books by Patrick C. Notchtree. Details at http://www.notchtree.com/ All are available worldwide in print and for Kindle, from Amazon. Audiobooks also.

**Maxym: He looks like an angel but kills like a devil.**
Growing up in a Russia plagued by homophobia, Maxym wrestles with his conflicting emotions towards Muslims and his own suppressed homosexuality. Alongside his innate psychopathic tendencies and an unsettling fascination with killing, his exceptional marksmanship skills make him a coveted asset. Trained to be an unrelenting assassin, he walks a precarious tightrope, embodying a paradoxical blend of tender affections and unwavering loyalty to the nation that nurtured him—an enigmatic figure in the tapestry of contemporary Russia.
Maxym's insatiable thirst for revenge propels him into perilous missions across Syria, Africa, Iraq, Libya, and Afghanistan, amassing immense wealth at a young age. However, the year 2022 brings with it a reckoning in Ukraine, demanding an exorbitant price for his actions. Amidst the tangled web of Maxym's journey lies a poignant exploration of the intricate bond between Ukraine and Russia. The stifling atmosphere of Putin's Russia forces him to conceal his true sexual identity, facing mounting danger as time progresses.
Inspired by true events, this gripping tale unravels the extraordinary life of a young Russian, set against the backdrop of a 21st-century ordinary Russian family. This biographical novel delves deep into the human psyche, exploring themes of love, loyalty, and the relentless pursuit of justice. Available for Kindle, audio and in Paperback.
**Not suitable for under 18s or the faint-hearted.**
For more information and any updates to "Maxym" go to http://www.maxym.net/

## The Clouds Still Hang

A complete trilogy which is a candid, true memoir of a gay man's life, telling a story of love and loyalty, betrothal and betrayal, triumph and tragedy; charting one gay man's attempts to rise above the legacy of a traumatic childhood. A true life story of three great loves with 5 star reviews on Amazon and Good reads.

It is the author's true life story, told through his avatar Simon. The first book deals with Simon's childhood friendship and eventually love affair with an older boy and early sexualisation, the second the trauma of his teenage years and early adulthood, the third his struggle to maintain equilibrium and the disastrous consequences of his failure at one point to achieve that and his fight back to self acceptance.

It will strike a chord with many who have been through similar things, as well as those with an interest in such matters, either personal or professional, such as police and probation officers, those involved with the gay / LGBT community etc.

It's a varied, exciting, demanding, sometimes terrifying life story. Of adult nature in places, it contains some explicit sexual narrative, including sexual violence and is recommended for over 18s. Available as an audiobook.
http://www.thecloudsstillhang.com/

## Hunting Harry

A city financier dies leaving millions locked away in secret accounts. His son looks forward to a fortune but there's a catch, the will. It falls to a jobbing actor to play the role of his life to unlock the key to great wealth. Follow the twists and turns of the plot in this novella.

# A Little Book of Islam: A Guide for Curious Westerners

Islam is scary. Muslims are scary. Or so many westerners think, and after the recent history of terrorism carried out by Muslims in the name of Islam, one can understand it if that is all they know about approximately 1.25 billion people on the planet, or about one in six people on Earth. Islam is more than just a religion as the term is usually seen in the west by most people. It is a whole way of life and is central to a Muslim's existence. But is this scary? Fear can often be explained by ignorance of the other and I hope that this little book will help in a small way to spread a little more knowledge of Islam and its followers and help to bridge a widening gap between Muslims and the societies in the west where they live.

## Apostrophe Catastrophe

The apostrophe must be the most misunderstood and misused piece of punctuation in the language. This is made worse by the fact that most people simply fail to understand what it does, and make it unnecessarily complicated. The result is that many people, in an effort to appear correct, use a scatter-gun approach, dropping in apostrophes every time the letter "s" ends a word, for plurals, possessives and contractions alike.

In fact, using the apostrophe correctly is easy - once you know the rule!

Notice I say, "the rule". Despite the confusion about this and many variations, there is in fact just one place where an apostrophe is used. Just one. It really is easy to remember. Buy the book and never get it wrong again!

390

Printed in Great Britain
by Amazon

51309913R00220